<u>Destiny in the Pacific</u>

By

John F. Schork

A Jupiter Pixel Publishing Book

Destiny In The Pacific is a work of fiction. Any resemblance to actual persons, living or dead, business establishments, events or locales are entirely coincidental.

Copyright 2008 by John F. Schork

ISBN-13: 978-0-9843344-9-0

First edition: November 2009

This book is an original publication of The Jupiter PIXEL Company

Jupiter PIXEL Company
18380 SE Lakeside Drive
Jupiter, FL 33469

For enquiries:
john@johnschork.com

In remembrance of

Captain Terry J. Toms U.S. Navy (Ret.)
1950-2008

A warrior and a friend

Preface

As the "greatest generation" passes on, our country is losing a mindset and attitude that was critical to America during the dark days of the Second World War. Most Americans today can remember Viet Nam or Desert Storm as something our country was involved in but not a conflict that might determine the survival of the republic. Even the Cold War and mutual assured destruction by nuclear weapons is a concept that has dissolved into vague worries about weapons of mass destruction.

But in the days after the attack on Pearl Harbor, as Japanese forces surged across the Pacific and Southeast Asia, the ultimate outcome was far from clear. With England already in a life and death struggle with Nazi Germany and much of Europe under occupation, the future of the civilized world was very much in question. Knowing what was at stake, these young Americans responded with courage and true patriotism. By 1945 the industrial might of the United States had asserted itself and the arsenal of democracy dominated every front with men and machines. However in that first year, particularly in the Pacific area of operations, the first line of defense was thin and underequipped. But with determination, ingenuity and unparalleled bravery they turned back the Japanese onslaught. Their story will always be one of sacrifice and courage.

May we never forget them.

Part One

"A gigantic fleet... has massed in Pearl Harbor. This fleet will be utterly crushed with one blow at the very beginning of hostilities...Heaven will bear witness to the righteousness of our struggle."
Rear-Admiral Ito - Chief of Staff of the Combined Fleet - November 1941

"Before we're through with them, the Japanese language will be spoken only in hell!
Admiral Halsey - December 1941

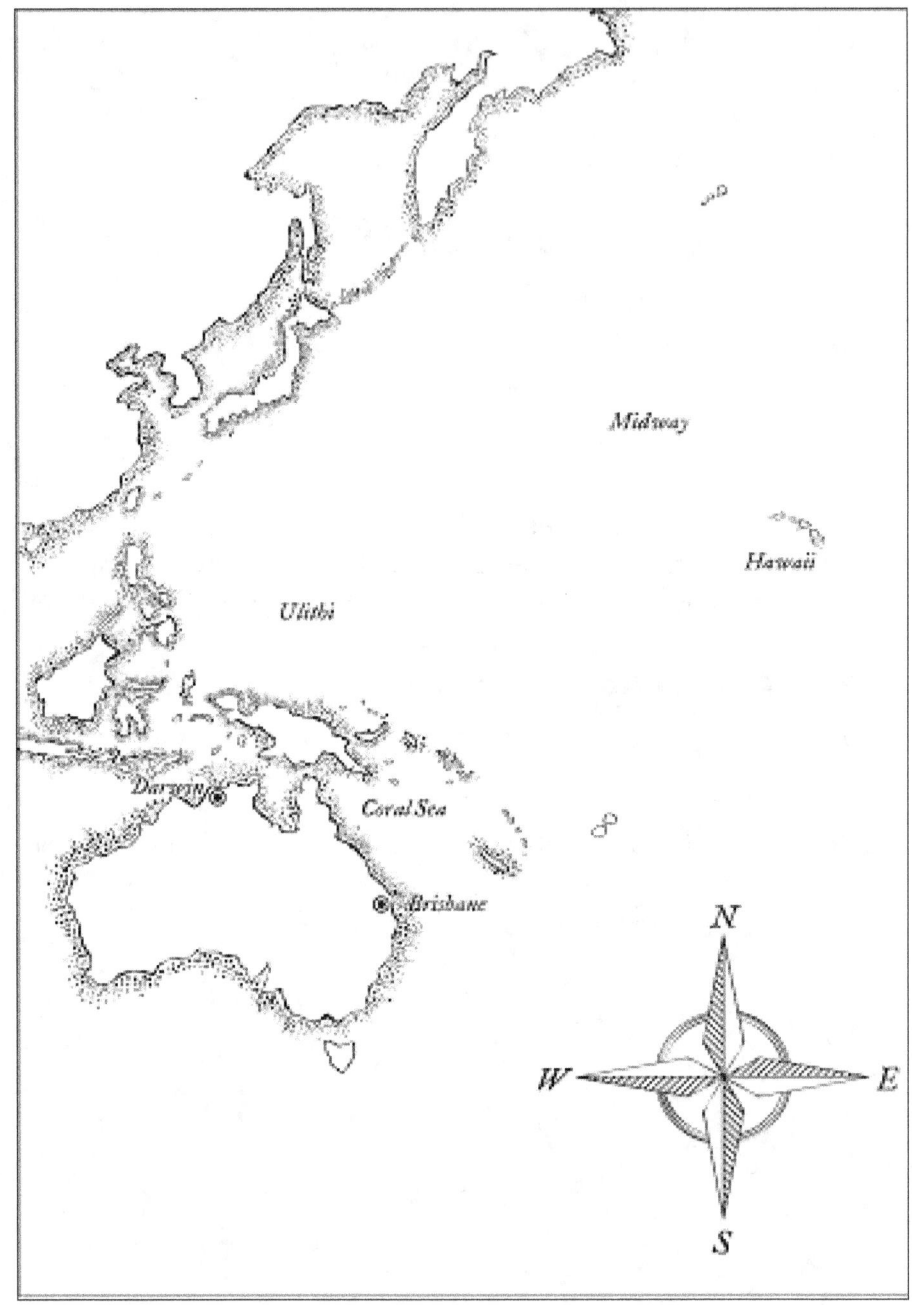

Chapter One

The End of a Career

Lying facedown on a soiled mattress, Bryan Michaels slowly began to move, his face contorted in reaction to the sour smell. The odor of dried vomit and urine enveloped him. He opened his eyes to see a dirty brick wall less than a foot from his face. A sheen of moisture covered the wall, the dampness hung over the cell like a blanket.

Rolling over, Bryan fought his nausea and tried not to be sick. Small beads of sweat shone on his forehead and upper lip. Raising a hand he attempted to rub some of the pain out of his head. A dull throb behind his eyes added to the misery of a queasy stomach. Bryan began to remember last night. He'd been in Barney's, a smoky back street tavern where he drank by himself for most of the night. Most nights Bryan could be found at the Pastime but the manager told the young officer they didn't want to see him back after a fight the previous weekend.

Last night two shipyard workers in Barney's had started needling him. It would have been smart to leave but he never did the smart thing anymore. Touching his jaw he felt soreness from one of several solid punches thrown by the two men. Running his fingers over the left side of his face he felt broken skin and crusted blood.

Bryan took a deep breath and sat up. Swinging his feet to

the floor he felt a sharp pain shoot up his leg. Putting a slight amount of weight on it confirmed a sprained ankle or worse. *Damn it.*

Still wearing his white uniform shirt and dark trousers, Bryan's jacket and tie were nowhere to be seen. A cold sweat began to soak his shirt as he fought to hold down the bile in his stomach, his skin clammy and white.

At the far end of the corridor a door opened, the metallic hinges making a sound that pierced Bryan's throbbing head. A Bremerton policeman stepped into the cellblock. Bryan watched the tall, heavyset man walk the length of the corridor and stop at his cell.

"Your name Michaels?" the man asked.

It took all of his energy to say, "Yeah."

"The base JAG wanted us to confirm we had an officer in lock up. You're an officer, right?"

Bryan paused a moment then said, "Yeah."

The man turned and walked away. Bryan lay back on the filthy mattress and closed his eyes. *Shit, that's all I need.*

Lieutenant (junior grade) Bryan Michaels belonged to the Deck Department of the *Utah*, a battleship currently in the Bremerton Naval Shipyard. After five long months the repairs were complete and the ship was scheduled to depart for Pearl Harbor in two days.

Bryan looked forward to getting underway and out of the misery of the shipyard. In charge of maintaining the exterior of the ship, his men had worked in filthy, cold conditions trying to stay ahead of the salt corrosion in the wet climate. The long tedious hours had begun to wear on everyone. Many men ended up on report after getting into fights or drinking too much on liberty. Bryan couldn't blame them, he felt the same way. The noise, the rain, and the dirt made everyone miserable. Throughout the day and night the staccato sound of rivet guns kept the crew irritable and on edge. Mud from the shipyard found its way into every compartment and passageway making cleanup a non-stop task. The sun appeared only occasionally to remind the crew how much they missed sunny Hawaii.

When Michaels stood his quarterdeck watches on the cold fall nights, time seemed to stretch on forever. He would stay huddled in the deckhouse trying to find some protection from the frigid wind coming off Puget Sound. After the watch, he would often go back to his stateroom and find no heat or fresh water. Because of electrical work, the reduced ventilation left noxious paint fumes below decks. Bryan counted the days until his obligated service would end and he could walk off the *Utah*.

The young officer hadn't always hated the Navy. Less than a year earlier he'd been assigned to Bombing Squadron Six aboard the *Enterprise* flying the Dauntless dive bomber. A graduate of the Naval Academy Class of 1937, a bright future awaited him after receiving his wings at Pensacola in the spring of '39. But today his career was on the road to nowhere, a disaster before it really began.

Waking with a start, he heard the cellblock door swing open. Standing in the doorway, his department head, Lieutenant Commander Rosey Rosenberg didn't look happy. In his hand he carried Bryan's coat, tie and hat.

His cell door swung open and Rosenberg threw the clothes to Bryan

"You're being released to my custody. Get dressed," Rosenberg said, his voice reflecting his disgust.

Bryan unsteadily stood up next to the bunk and their eyes met.

"Hurry up. I don't like spending my mornings in a jail, Michaels."

Pausing for a moment to regain his balance Bryan slowly pulled on his coat.

"Let's go," Rosenberg said impatiently.

Rosenberg stepped aside for Michaels to pass. The two officers followed a uniformed patrolman outside into the holding area, Bryan limping on his right ankle.

"Here's your wallet, Lieutenant, you'll have to sign for it."

Another wave of nausea swept over Bryan as he scrawled his name on the form and picked up his wallet. "Thanks for a wonderful evening," he said, tossing the pencil on the counter.

Walking down the steps into the overcast morning, Bryan filled his lungs with fresh air, the queasiness slowly subsiding. But he'd been here before. The big challenge now was to make it back to the ship without being sick. From the low gray clouds over the jail, a mist began to fall, the wind blowing it into Bryan's face. I hate this place, he thought.

The two men walked over to the grey Ford sedan parked in the lower lot. Bryan got in the passenger seat and Rosenberg slid behind the wheel. The older man put the car in gear and pulled out of the parking lot as the rain began to fall harder.

"I have a copy of the police report and it doesn't look good. The bar owner is pressing civil charges. He has an axe to grind with the Navy and you made yourself a perfect target."

"What does that mean?"

Rosenberg turned onto the main road. "We don't know. But he's said he won't settle out of court. He wants money for damages and a conviction for disorderly conduct. The local judge advocate will handle the case."

Bryan cracked the window open, he still needed the fresh air. Small rivulets of water trickled inside the car. "Why doesn't Larry Hitchcock handle it?" Bryan knew the ship's lawyer and trusted him.

"We're getting underway in 48 hours or did you forget?" Rosenberg's voice had an edge to it. "You screwed up magnificently on this one. Not only a civilian incident but you'll miss ship's movement. When you get back to the ship, assuming you're convicted in civil court, you'll be taken to mast or court martial for missing ship's movement."

Another wave of nausea flooded over Bryan. "If I can't sail with the ship because I have court, how can they charge me with being absent?"

Rosenberg slowed as they approached the main gate to the

shipyard. "I'm not a lawyer but that's the rule. If you're guilty, there's no defense. Now try to clean yourself up."

Bryan said nothing in response. Rosey Rosenberg was one of the few officers on *Utah* he actually respected.

Walking down Pier Twelve Michaels tried to make his uniform look as presentable as possible. He tucked the lining back into a torn seam but a large red ketchup stain on his chest couldn't be hidden.

A cold wind blew off the harbor as the rain increased. *I hate this weather.* His ankle hurt like hell, the pain increasing as he made his way up the accommodation ladder to the quarterdeck. Arriving at the platform he faced aft and saluted the national ensign. He turned to the Officer of the Deck, Lieutenant Ted Small, and saluted.

"Reporting my return aboard."

Bryan considered Small a first class prick and the two had never gotten along. "Very well," the OOD said, returning the salute with a smirk. To his Quartermaster of the Watch Small said in a very smug tone, "Petty Officer Barnwell, please note in the log: Lieutenant (jg) Michaels returned to military authority at 0915.....from the Bremerton Jail."

Rosenberg put his hand on Bryan's back. "Come on."

Bryan walked aft, his face flushed with embarrassment and humiliation. In thirty minutes it would be all over the ship. One more screw up by the "aviator." Once proud to be identified as a Naval Aviator, the term was now used derisively by many of the junior officers aboard the *Utah* who took pleasure in his situation. He descended one ladder to the second deck on the way to his stateroom. He couldn't wait to get out of his filthy uniform and take a shower. A large wooden sign blocked the main second deck passageway. *Shit!* Doubling back he crossed over to the port side and then forward to his room, his ankle throbbing steadily. When he opened the door he found Tim Hutchins at the fold down desk working on stores requests.

"You look like hell," he said, looking up from the small pile of official papers.

Trying to put on a good face Bryan grinned. "It feels worse than it looks." Throwing his coat on the bunk, he sat down at his desk taking the weight off his ankle.

"The duty officer told me you were in the Bremerton Jail."

"Yeah."

"What happened?" Tim asked.

"Not really sure," Bryan said. He pulled off his shoes. "Got in a fight with a couple of locals."

"Your fault?"

Bryan sighed. "Probably."

"Don't worry. It'll work out," Tim said, turning back to his paperwork.

They both knew better. Bryan Michaels had alienated most of the ship's officers and there would be little motivation by the Executive Officer or Commanding Officer to intercede on his behalf. In fact this might be their opportunity to get him off the ship forever.

Thirty minutes later Bryan heard a knock at the stateroom door. Bryan opened the door to find a Marine Corporal in dress uniform.

The young man's face was expressionless. "Sir, are you Mr. Michaels?"

"Yup."

"Sir, you are ordered to report to the Executive Officer at 1030 hours."

"Wonderful."

Standing at attention in the Executive Officer's cabin Bryan stared straight ahead, his eyes fixed on the wall behind the seated Commander Harris. He tried hard to ignore the pain in his leg but it had been ten minutes since Harris had started reading the local police report. Lieutenant Commander Rosenberg sat in a chair behind and to the right of Bryan. Behind them a small fan made the only noise in the cramped stateroom. A faint smell of fresh paint permeated this part of the ship.

Commander Neil Harris looked up at Bryan and tossed the report on his desk. "Lieutenant Michaels, you're a disgrace to this ship, that uniform and the Navy. I've signed temporary additional duty orders transferring you to the Naval Shipyard. You'll remain here until your civil case is settled by the authorities. If you receive time in jail you'll be transferred permanently while you serve your sentence. If there's no incarceration involved you will return to the ship for either Captain's Mast or a court martial. Do you understand these orders?"

Bryan continued to stare straight ahead but answered, "Yes, sir."

"Your father and I were shipmates in the Tennessee. He's one of the finest naval officers I've ever known. This will devastate him. So you've destroyed two lives, Mr. Michaels. I hope you're proud of yourself. Now get out of here."

Bryan Michaels turned and walked out of the cabin.

"Can I do anything to help?" Tim Hutchins asked from the stateroom doorway.

Throwing a sweater into the suitcase, Bryan closed the cover and fastened the latches. "If you happen to have a .45 handy you might put me out of my misery." He swung the case down and reached for his overcoat. "Better get going. I don't want to run into the XO any time soon."

"Pretty bad?" His friend closed the door and sat down on the bunk.

"I think the term is verbal flogging….the son of a bitch. I just don't give a shit anymore." He picked up his hat and threw it against the metal locker.

Tim stood up and grabbed his friend by the shoulders. "Hey,

there's a war coming. The Navy needs officers like you."

Michaels looked him in the eye. "Yeah? Well they sure didn't need me last year."

"Come on, I'll help you carry your stuff to the quarterdeck."

Lieutenant Commander Rosenberg waited on the main deck when the two young officers came out of the hatch.

Bryan saluted Rosenberg.

Tim carried Bryan's suitcase to the quarterdeck leaving the two men alone.

Shorter than Bryan, Rosenberg looked up at him with a hard stare. "Michaels, you can't stop feeling sorry for yourself. I know what happened last year was a tough deal. But it's over. Now get your life back in order and start earning your paycheck." Rosey extended his hand. "Now get going."

Tim carried the suitcase down to the pier. The two friends looked back at the *Utah*.

"Thanks, Tim."

"Hey, it's gonna be okay."

The two shook hands. Bryan picked up his bag and began to walk down the rough wooden planks of the pier. A few sailors loading supplies into a truck looked up as he limped past. A loud chorus of cries came from the gulls gliding effortlessly over the pier. Bryan turned and looked at the ship then continued up the street.

After checking into the Bachelor Officer's Quarters, Bryan walked down the street to the Bremerton Naval Shipyard Administration Building. His ankle still hurt and it took him twenty minutes to reach the two story brick building. The transient personnel office looked like one of a hundred Navy offices he'd been through in his short career. A bored Second Class Yeoman looked up as Bryan leaned over the counter.

"Can I help you, sir?"

Laying the manila envelope on the counter Bryan said, "Checking in for temporary duty."

The man got up and began to go through the contents of the envelope. He closed the folder. "Just a moment, sir." The sailor walked away toward a glass enclosed office at the rear of the room.

Resigned to the always tedious process of checking in at a new command, Bryan put all of his weight on his good ankle to wait. The Petty Officer returned and opened the wooden swinging door to the office area. "Chief Warrant Officer Leonard would like to see you, sir."

Following the man, trying not to limp, he made his way back to the small enclosed office. On the frosted glass door painted white letters said: "CWO T.N.Leonard, USN." *I wonder what this paper pushing asshole wants?*

The Petty Officer opened the door and announced, "Lieutenant Michaels, sir."

A huge man rose to his feet behind the desk. Easily six foot four and 220 pounds, the nameplate said "Transient Personnel Officer."

"Come in, Lieutenant. Take a seat," he said pointing to a worn wooden chair by a locker. A tanned and weathered face showed the effects of many years at sea.

Checking the man's collar insignia he cautiously answered, "Thanks, Boats."

The Petty Officer closed the door.

"We heard you were coming. You caused quite a stir with the heavies this morning." Leonard laughed. "Our XO is just about as pissed at you as he is with Barney."

Interesting, Bryan thought, here's a member of the establishment who isn't acting like last night was the end of the world. "Why's that?"

Leonard pulled out a pack of Chesterfields and offered one to Bryan. "Barney O'Conner, the owner of the bar you tried to destroy, is a gold plated son of a bitch. He hates the Navy and is constantly fucking with our sailors."

15

"That doesn't make sense. He runs a bar three blocks from the main gate. You think he'd want all the sailors in there." Bryan waved off the cigarettes.

Striking a match on the side of the desk Leonard lit the Chesterfield. "There was a time when that was true. But a few years back one of our sailors screwed up. This little piss-ant off the *Lexington* takes his one daughter for a roll in the hay, gets her pregnant and then ships out. The daughter goes off the deep end. Now he's got an unwanted kid and a daughter who spends more time drinking than sleeping. He blames the Navy."

"And now he has an officer to take to court."

The big man smiled ruefully. "It wouldn't surprise me if he didn't set you up with those yard birds. Course that might be hard to prove."

"Well, it looks like I'm here until things get sorted out. I'm screwed with my ship getting underway for Pearl. How long will this take?" Bryan crossed his leg and began to massage the throbbing ankle.

"Hard to tell. The lawyers have to go through all the regular procedures. This is in the municipal court so it should be quicker than the county. I don't think you'll go to trial for at least a month." He stubbed out his cigarette in the wide glass ashtray. "You looked like you were limping. You all right?"

Standing up gingerly he tried to put weight on the ankle. "I did something to my ankle last night. It's not getting any better. Suppose I better hit afternoon sick call. Any chance the duty driver could run me up to the hospital, Mister Leonard?"

"No problem. And my friends call me Tiny."

"Thanks, Tiny."

"I'm sorry, sir. You missed the normal sick call hours." A short hospital corpsman sat at the reception desk of the hospital filing a stack of forms. "Is it an emergency?" A tinge of sarcasm in the man's voice.

"No, it's not an emergency," Bryan said. "But it hurts like hell and I'm staying here until someone damned well takes a look at it. You read me?"

"What's the problem, Petty Officer Gibbons?"

Turning toward the female voice, Bryan saw a Navy nurse in a crisp white uniform her dark auburn hair and deep green eyes perfectly matched. Her nametag said "Sommers."

"Ma'am, the Lieutenant missed afternoon sick call. He doesn't want to wait."

"I think we can take care of the Lieutenant. Remember our job is to minister to all sick and wounded." The slightly sarcastic tone in her voice did not escape Bryan. "Follow me, Lieutenant"

She must think I'm an asshole, he thought, following her down the hallway.

Bryan sat on the examining table while she filled out information for the doctor. Watching her write, he was taken with her grace.

"So you don't really know how you hurt your ankle?" Looking up she had a doubting look in her eyes. "Does that happen often, Lieutenant?" she asked coldly.

"No." He looked down at the floor, feeling his face getting flushed. "Not normally," he muttered to himself.

She rose and turned to go out the door. "It will take me a few minutes to find a doctor. Just sit there and try not to jump on anymore of my corpsmen." She was gone.

The treatment took two hours, complete with several x-rays, two exams and a trip to the cast room. A small bone in his ankle turned out to be cracked. According to the doctor the pain would subside in a day or so and the bone would heal in short order. After getting a small walking cast and cane he returned to the reception desk.

"Is Miss Summers still here?" he asked a new corpsman manning the desk.

"Just a minute, sir. I'll check." Picking up the phone, he dialed and spoke briefly. "Sorry, Lieutenant. She's off shift"

Bryan felt disappointed. He wanted to apologize to her. "Thanks for checking." He paused for a moment. "Do you know her first name?"

The corpsman smiled. "Yes, sir. It's Elisabeth but everyone calls her Liz."

Bryan repeated the name, "Liz."

The next morning Bryan had an appointment with Commander Steve Smith, the senior JAG officer. Arriving ten minutes early for his 0900 appointment he noticed he was the only officer in the waiting room with four sailors.

"Lieutenant, Commander Smith will see you now."

Bryan followed a Third Class Yeoman down the short hallway and into the office. A short, squat man, with thinning hair and a ruddy face, Commander Smith sat at a very large wooden desk reading a folder.

Glancing up, Smith said, "Have a seat, Lieutenant. Jenkins, please close the door behind you." Smith read for another five minutes then looked up. "You certainly stepped in it, didn't you?"

"Apparently someone thinks so," Bryan said, his voice hostile.

"Relax, Lieutenant. I'm on your side. Whether you know it or not you're in deep shit. Now let's go over your side of the story from beginning to end and don't leave anything out."

Bryan's foggy recollection of the evening's events took only five minutes to relate. After telling his story he realized how bad it looked.

"So you don't actually remember who threw the first punch?"

Shaking his head he said, "There was some pushing…it might have been me. I was pretty hot."

"And pretty drunk I daresay?"

"That's probably true."

"Don't get smart with me, Lieutenant. I'm trying to keep your ass out of jail. So take that damn chip off your shoulder and let's figure out some kind of defense. Do I make myself clear?"

"Yes, sir."

When Bryan left Smith's office an hour later, he felt better knowing exactly what the legal process would entail. But Smith had made it clear Bryan's days in the Navy were coming to an end. With luck, he wouldn't go into the civilian world with jail time on his record. Limping down the sidewalk he knew what this would do to his father.

Rear Admiral Chuck Michaels had recently retired in San Diego after 32 years of service. A battleship sailor, he had commanded the *Arizona* and finally Battleship Division Two before retiring last summer. Now he lived in a small house on "C" Street in Coronado, playing golf and sailing his sailboat. Bryan had last seen him after the court-martial last year.

During the two weeks it took Commander Smith to gather information and file the appropriate papers with the City of Bremerton, Bryan spent his time assigned to the Transient Personnel Office working with Tiny Leonard. The routine administrative work helped pass the time. Tiny had Bryan doing barracks inspections, personal effects inventories and a host of other things that needed to be completed for the stream of sailors passing to and from ships in the yard.

At night the two men would stop by the Officer's Club for several beers and then grab dinner at one of the local cafes. They were an odd couple, the young smart ass Lieutenant and the imposing Warrant Boatswain. But the two hit if off well and they enjoyed each other's company.

Tiny Leonard had come up through the ranks. Enlisting in 1914, he'd served in some of the first U.S. destroyers to participate in World War One. His natural talent as a sailor resulted in rapid promotion and selection as one of the youngest Chief Petty Officers in the Navy's history. One failed marriage confirmed him as a sea-going sailor and he'd been a bachelor ever since. Now as the end of his career approached, this job was probably his last assignment.

Two more years of pushing papers and then he'd receive his own set of retirement orders. Leonard dreaded the prospect of retirement. The Navy was all he'd ever known.

On Wednesday the Legal Office passed word that Bryan's trial would begin December 10th in the Municipal Court of Bremerton. Tiny dropped the letter on Bryan's desk.

"At least you'll get out of limbo."

Bryan read the letter. "Perfect timing, I can spend Christmas in the Bremerton jail. Think they have eggnog for the inmates?"

"Hey, don't convict yourself before the judge does. I've got someone working on this."

"What does that mean?" Bryan threw the letter on the desk.

"I have a former shipmate from the *Nevada*, an ex Machinist Mate named Tony Mazzeo. He got out and now works in the shipyard, Shop 43."

"I don't get it."

"Those two yard birds that worked you over? I saw they worked in the shop next to Mazzeo. I asked him to see if he could find out anything about them or what happened. It turns out he knows one of the mugs. I told him to be quiet about it but do some snooping. He's a smart kid. If there's something going on that we should know about, he'll find out. Now let's go get a beer."

Bryan bought the first round and the two sat in the Officer's Club Lounge in companionable silence.

Tiny finished his beer and ordered another round from the bartender. "I had to send your service record over to the Legal Office. Guess they need it to get ready for court."

"Yeah, probably." Bryan took a drink and reached for the peanut dish in front of his friend.

"I saw your page 9. Wasn't prying but I had to sign the custody sheet. You were in an aircraft squadron before the *Utah*?"

Normally, Bryan would have ignored the question. But he felt Tiny Leonard deserved to know the whole story. "Yeah, Bombing Six on the *Enterprise*."

"Dumb question. What were you doing there?"

"Flying Dauntless dive bombers for almost two years." He took a long drink. "But there was an accident. They blamed me, convened a court martial and threw me out of aviation. So here I sit about to be thrown out of the Navy. Not too impressive is it?"

The big man turned to look at Bryan. "Two sides to every story. What happened?"

Bryan's thoughts returned to that morning off San Diego leading a section of aircraft assigned to conduct practice high altitude dive bombing on a towed sled. The big wooden target was under tow by a Navy tug south of San Clemente Island. Bryan had flown these bombing missions many times so the squadron Commanding Officer, Dick Best, assigned Bryan as the section leader. The wingman, Ensign Andy Holland, needed to fly six of the high altitude missions to become fully qualified in the Dauntless. As the newest squadron pilot Andy had only completed one high dive mission since reporting.

Fresh out of flight training in Pensacola, Andy Holland had worked hard to master the skills needed as a fleet aviator. With a fleet exercise approaching, the squadron needed every pilot ready for operational missions. Andy had impressed everyone with his positive attitude and flying ability.

Bryan meticulously briefed the flight. He would be flying with his normal gunner, Bill Nance. Holland still didn't have an assigned crewman so Bryan's original gunner, Terry Matthews, volunteered to go on the flight.

The start and takeoff had gone well, the two aircraft climbing into a high overcast at 14,000 feet. Six miles south of the island they spotted the tug making a white wake with the target sled trailing 1000 feet astern. The overcast and haze made the dive bombing runs a challenge but each pilot made six runs and the hits were respectable.

For Bryan there were few experiences as exhilarating as dive bombing from high altitude. Hanging in the straps, seventy degrees nose down with the target growing larger in the telescopic sight as the plane hurtled toward the earth. Making small corrections as you watched the altimeter spin down to the release altitude. Then squeezing the bomb release button, retracting the dive brakes and pulling up with a 5 'g' round out, the g forces slamming you into the seat. A dozen bombing runs and you felt like you had just gone 10 rounds with Gene Tunney.

Bryan had felt great as he led his section back to the *Enterprise* after a successful mission. Slowly he worked his altitude lower, thundering over the ocean with the waves only fifty feet below him. A white mainsail from one of the many sailboats that cruised off the coast of California appeared on the horizon. There were strict rules against 'flat-hatting,' and Bryan knew that very well. In a moment of supreme bad judgment he gave into the temptation to show off.

Passing Andy a hand signal that told him to loosen up the formation, Bryan pointed the Dauntless directly for the bow of the now rapidly approaching sailboat. The forty foot yawl's white hull cut through the deep blue water on a northerly course. Two people sat in the center deck cockpit. They must have heard the engines because they were looking up at him and waving as he roared past at full power. Rolling to 60 degrees angle of bank, he turned left and pulled the aircraft around to set up for another run. He had always enjoyed flying low and fast, a real test of your ability to handle the Dauntless. One more run and they would head back for the ship.

For the next pass he came up from astern flying parallel to the sailboat's wake. Estimating his altitude at 25 feet the bomber was well below the top of their mast. Abeam the sailboat, he pulled hard left and crossed their bow rolling to almost 70 degrees angle of bank. He wanted to impress these strangers. Reversing his turn he saw a tremendous amount of water thrown up directly in front of the sailboat. In a split second he saw Holland's Dauntless cartwheel into the waves taking Andy and Terry Matthews to their deaths.

He had relived that moment a thousand times since then, the horror never leaving him.

The sailboat turned out to be owned by a retired Navy

Captain who provided a complete statement to the board of inquiry. Brought up on charges of dereliction of duty, Bryan faced a special courts martial which found the young officer guilty. He had been responsible for the death of two men, the loss of a naval aircraft and a public relations disaster for the Navy.

Bryan told Tiny about the accident and the trial. He didn't mention the effect it had on his father. Although the Admiral stood by Bryan, he'd lost faith in his son and Bryan knew it.

After Bryan's mother passed away from cancer in 1930, the two men had developed a very strong bond. Chuck Michaels, despite the demands of his increasing responsibilities, had never failed to be there for his son. But his pride had turned to shame after the accident and now that shame would only increase.

"Let's see what Mazzeo can come up with. He's a pretty savvy fella and he owes me for a couple of times I got him out of trouble."

Bryan stood up. "I'm going to hit the head. Order another round." He put a five dollar bill on the bar. Exiting the lounge he turned left toward the men's room. As he walked across the foyer he glanced at the main entrance to the club. Two nurses entered and turned right toward the dining room. Liz Summers laughed at something the other woman had said. Without thinking, Bryan stepped across the hallway and said, "Excuse me, Miss Sommers?"

Liz turned, her expression one of curiosity. When she recognized him she smiled warily. "Mr. Michaels, right?"

"Bryan Michaels. Bad ankle, remember?" He could see a look of caution in her eyes.

"Of course. How's the ankle?" She said without much enthusiasm.

"It's fine. I wanted to thank you for taking care of me. I'm afraid I was pretty short with your corpsman." He watched her face for any reaction.

A slight smile. "He'll get over it. Besides taking care of

injuries is what we're supposed to do."

She isn't too angry, he thought. He looked at her companion and extended his hand. "Hi, I'm Bryan Michaels."

"Nancy Hostetter. Nice to meet you, Bryan."

He wanted to continue the conversation. "Can I buy you ladies a drink?"

The two of them looked at each other. Liz hesitated then nodded. "Thanks, we've got time for one drink."

At least a start, he thought.

The four of them moved to a table and Tiny ordered drinks. In the next few minutes Bryan found that Nancy and Liz shared an apartment in one of the residential neighborhoods that surrounded the shipyard perimeter. They had trained at the Oak Knoll Naval Hospital in San Francisco prior to their assignment to Bremerton. As they finished their drinks Nancy remembered she had to pick up her tailoring before a local shop closed. Quickly excusing herself, she was followed by Tiny who claimed he needed to check on the recent arrivals at the transient barracks. Bryan couldn't remember any new arrivals.

"It seems we've been deserted, Lieutenant."

"Would you please call me Bryan?"

"All right, Bryan," she said, her mouth breaking into a slight smile.

They sat in silence for a moment then Bryan asked, "Can I get you another drink?"

Liz looked at him, her deep green eyes sparkling. For a moment he thought she would make her excuses and he didn't want her to leave.

She smiled again. "All right."

As he waited for the bartender to mix their drinks, Bryan looked back at their table. Liz Summers sat very straight, her hands in her lap. He watched her for a moment thinking she was truly lovely. Her deep auburn hair was cut in just above her collar, framing a classically sculpted face. I don't think I've ever seen a woman that beautiful, he thought.

He carried their drinks back to the table and sat down directly across from her.

"You're moving farther away, Bryan. Was it something I said?"

"No not at all. I just didn't want you to think I was making a pass at you."

"Is that what you normally do with women?"

"No, of course not....I just didn't want to do anything wrong."

She took a drink and set her glass down.

"Bryan, I'll let you know when you do something wrong."

Their eyes met, both taking a moment to appraise the other.

Bryan moved back to the chair next to Liz and said, "Tell me everything there is to know about you.....I have all night."

Liz had grown up in Seattle and attended the University of Washington Nursing School. Always wanting to travel and see the world, the Navy Nurse Corps had appealed to her. Never did she imagine being assigned to the city across Puget Sound from Seattle.

"I know what you mean. After flight training I got orders back to San Diego. My Dad had been stationed there four times while I grew up and it was like coming home."

She looked across the table at Bryan. "Flight training? I thought you were assigned to the *Utah*?"

"I am. I used to fly."

"In any case, the *Utah's* gone and you're still here. I'm confused." She took a sip of her cocktail.

"The City of Bremerton and I had a disagreement. I'm on legal hold."

Liz looked shocked. "Legal hold. What for?"

"I managed to get into a fight with some of the locals in a bar. The owner's pressing charges."

"What's going to happen?"

He finished his drink, putting it down on the wet napkin. "Court date is next Wednesday. After that, who knows?" Is she having second thoughts about me, he wondered?

Liz reached across the table and put her hand on his. "I know everything will work out."

Very softly Bryan put his other hand on top of hers. "Liz, for the first time in a long time I feel the same way."

Friday afternoon Tiny and Bryan met Tony Mazzeo at a dingy bar near the West Gate. The three of them found a booth in the back. Cigarette smoke hung thick in the air. The bar was rapidly filling up with shipyard workers as they came in to have their first drink of the night. In a short time noisy conversations filled the bar, punctuated by the occasional laugh.

Mazzeo worked as a ship fitter in the yard on the day shift. He and Tiny reminisced about their days together on the *Nevada* while they waited for the waitress to bring mugs of cold beer.

With the mugs in front of them, Mazzeo turned serious. He leaned across the table. "You were right, Boats. O'Connor paid those two guys to pick a fight with the Lieutenant. Guess they thought he was too drunk to figure out what was goin' on."

"Can we prove it?" Bryan asked.

Tiny shook his head. "One man's word against another. But maybe it's enough to get O'Connor to drop the charges if we let on we know about the deal."

"That guy's a real shithead if you ask me," Mazzeo offered.

Bryan didn't say anything. Maybe they could confront the man and call his bluff but the two yard birds would only deny it. They were back where they started. It had been a good try and he told Tiny and Mazzeo he appreciated their efforts.

"Don't throw in the towel yet. We've still got four days to see if we can back up that story." Tiny finished his beer. Raising his hand to get the waitress's attention, he indicated another round for the table.

Bryan stood up. "Not me, Tiny. I thought I'd swing by the hospital, the day shift is getting off shortly."

"It seems that you've been taken with a pretty young nurse?" Tiny grinned at his friend.

"That is correct, Mr. Leonard. And she smells better than you two mugs, so I'll be off. Don't wait up for me." Bryan headed for the door.

He hoped to catch Liz when she came off duty. He hadn't seen her since their dinner two nights before and he was eager to be with her. When he had asked her about the weekend she wasn't sure of her schedule. What had she really meant? He tried to call her but had to leave a message with the duty desk.

Standing against the low concrete wall opposite the main entrance, Bryan spent thirty minutes watching every person departing the hospital. He pushed away from the wall and began to walk back toward the BOQ. Out of the corner of his eye he caught a lone figure wearing a nurse's cape walking toward the parking lot.

The woman didn't see Bryan as she worked the key in the driver's side door lock.

"Liz."

Turning, Liz Summers looked surprised then embarrassed. "Bryan. Hi. Sorry I didn't call back, I've been busy." She opened the door and slid into the driver's seat.

This isn't going well, he thought. "I knew your schedule was crazy, so I thought I'd try to catch you here."

Liz didn't respond, she closed the door and rolled the window down.

"I thought you might like to have dinner tonight," he asked.

She hesitated. "I'm tied up tonight, sorry."

He smiled quickly. "No problem, maybe some other time."

"Sure," she said noncommittally. She started the car. "I better get going. Can I drop you somewhere?"

Bryan shook his head. "No I'm fine. The ankle needs more walking. I'm just going back to the BOQ."

Liz put the car in gear and it began to move. "Good night,

Bryan."

It took twenty minutes to walk back across base to the BOQ. What the hell, he thought. The last time I saw her I thought there was something between us. He remembered her upturned face as he kissed her at her door. She had responded warmly and his heart was flying when he returned to his BOQ room. Maybe I misread everything.

When he passed the main desk, the desk clerk handed him a note. "Phone message for you, Lieutenant."

"Bryan, I am free tomorrow night if you would like to get together. Liz. OR5-5271."

He grinned and headed for the phone booth at the end of the lobby.

"So what made you change your mind?"

Liz had been looking out the large window at the lights on the anchored boats in the bay. "About what?"

"About dinner tonight?"

She looked at him for a long moment. "I don't know."

Bryan felt confused. Their kiss had told him there was some interest, but last night she'd acted like an icicle.

"That's not true. I told myself you had too many problems and I shouldn't get involved."

An honest answer, I'll be damned, he thought. "Well I can't deny the problems."

Liz looked at him, her eyes questioning. "So what happens to you?"

"I don't know. Maybe I go to jail. Will you come visit?"

"Stop that. I don't think it's funny."

"No kidding. I don't either. But what am I supposed to do?"

She said nothing.

"Would you care to order now?" the waiter asked.

Bryan looked at Liz and said, "Let's just enjoy dinner, okay?"

"Okay, Bryan."

"Then how about the prime rib for two, I hear it's great."

Liz nodded.

"And a bottle of your best burgundy."

"That was wonderful. I didn't realize I was so hungry."

"I'm glad you changed your mind," he said lightly.

Her tone turned serious. "I am too."

What's happening here, he asked himself.

"Would you like dessert or coffee?"

Bryan looked to Liz who replied, "Coffee, please."

"So why nursing?"

"My mother was a nurse and I guess I wanted to be like her."

Two cups of steaming coffee sat on the table. The dining room was nearly deserted.

Bryan finished his wine. "I guess that's why I went to Annapolis, that's what Dad did."

"So you'll make the Navy a career?"

He laughed. "Not anymore. I think I'm going to become persona non grata in short order."

They drank their coffee and watched the twinkling lights on the black water.

"So why'd you really change your mind about tonight," he asked.

Liz carefully put down her coffee cup. "Because I find you very interesting, Bryan."

Bryan and Tiny had several nightcaps on Bryan's return to the BOQ later that night. Bryan wanted someone to talk to about the future and Tiny was more than happy to listen. The two finally called it a night in the early hours of morning.

Bryan heard a loud pounding on his door. A slight hangover made him pause as he sat up on the edge of the bed. Checking his alarm clock he saw it was one thirty. "I'm coming, hold your horses." Stepping quickly across the cold linoleum he flipped the lock and swung the door open.

"The Japs attacked Pearl Harbor," Tiny said, his expression telling Bryan this was no joke. "It just came over the circuit on an All Navy broadcast. It sounds pretty bad. There's a radio down in the lounge. Let's go down and listen."

"Gimme a second to get some clothes on."

A dozen junior officers were sitting in the lounge around a large table radio. There were glances from the group as Bryan and Tiny sat down.

"Hello, NBC. Hello, NBC. This is KTU in Honolulu, Hawaii. I am speaking from the roof of the Advertiser Publishing Company Building. We have witnessed this morning the distant view a brief full battle of Pearl Harbor and the severe bombing of Pearl Harbor by enemy planes, undoubtedly Japanese. The city of Honolulu has also been attacked and considerable damage done. This battle has been going on for nearly three hours. One of the bombs dropped within fifty feet of KTU tower. It is no joke. It is a real war. The public of Honolulu has been advised to keep in their homes and away from the Army and Navy. There has been serious fighting going on in the air and in the sea. The heavy shooting seems to be . . . . We cannot estimate just how much damage has been done, but it has been a very severe attack. The Navy and Army appear now to have the air and the sea under control."

Every face showed a look of either concern or anger as the announcer continued to pass on details as they became available. Cigarette smoke curled above the small group, each man alone with his thoughts.

"We are receiving reports of explosions and massive clouds of smoke rising from the Naval Base and Hickam Field.......

"Those slant-eyed bastards," a Marine captain growled.

"A state of martial law has been declared for the entire Territory of Hawaii.....a curfew will be in effect for all civilians until further notice."

Bryan stared out the window, listening as the tragedy continued to be described by the NBC radio announcer.

"The attack was conducted by hundreds of Japanese aircraft that appeared over the island at just before 8:00 o'clock this morning. We have just received reports that there has been major damage to the fleet in the harbor and terrible casualties."

There was no mention of the *Utah*. He thought about Tim Hutchins. What had happened to his friend? What about the men in his division?

"In a joint communiqué, the Army and Navy commanders on the Island of Oahu are preparing for landings by the Japanese. Both Army and Marine units have been deployed to meet the invading forces."

This was a nightmare, it couldn't be happening. Japanese soldiers invading Hawaii? He remembered the newsreels of Japanese attacks in China. It all was so far away, nothing to do with them. Now it was here and he knew his world would never be the same.

"I've got to leave for a meeting with the CO," Tiny said, breaking into Bryan's thoughts.

"I want to see Liz. Let's meet back here later." Bryan had to move, do something, he couldn't just sit and listen to the disaster unfold.

After a quick shower Bryan put on his uniform. Normally he wouldn't wear a uniform on the weekend but today it was the right thing to do. Bryan walked over to the Naval Hospital, an eerie quiet now enveloped the base. It was if the entire base had retreated within itself to try and cope with the attack in Hawaii. At the hospital, small groups of people stood quietly talking in the main reception area. It was ten minutes before Liz met him in the waiting room. She looked serious when she entered and walked over to him. Sitting down, Liz put her hand on his arm.

"I'm glad you came over. I feel alone even though we've all been talking about it this afternoon."

"We've been trying to get any info we can but there's not much on the radio. I'm sure more news will come out soon."

She put her hand on top of his. "Your ship, the *Utah*. Was she there?" Her eyes showed her concern.

Bryan nodded. "That was the schedule. We used to spend a few weekends anchored at Lahina Roads, off the island of Maui. Maybe they were there." But not this close to Christmas, he thought and especially after a long period away from homeport. The *Utah* would be in Pearl Harbor tied up to her berth on the east side of Ford Island opposite "Battleship Row."

"What are you going to do now?"

The frustration of his own situation increased his anger. "Sit here and play their stupid games I guess. I wouldn't want a war to interfere with the wheels of justice," he said bitterly.

A corpsman walked up and told her it was time for the Doctor's rounds. "Bryan, I've got to go. See me tomorrow after work. Something will work out, I know it."

By evening they knew a little more of the situation and the news only grew worse. They received sporadic news on the radio and message traffic from Washington, D.C. Although one of the battleships, the *Nevada*, had been able to get under way, most were sunk at their moorings. The Japs had used torpedo and high altitude bombers. Bryan realized how easy it would have been for the attackers. The ships would all have been manned by the weekend watch sections with most key personnel ashore on liberty or with their families. Stationary targets, the ships would not have had any of their defensive guns manned. There would be no ammunition in any of the ready service lockers. *The bastards.*

At 2000, they received an official message listing the *Utah* as "sunk." The word stunned Bryan. The *Utah*, a battleship in a protected harbor, how could she sink? CBS radio reported the dead numbered in the hundreds. He hoped Tim was safe.

32

"And here I sit on my ass in Bremerton."

Tiny put his hand on Bryan's shoulder as he stood up to go. "I've got some business to take care of. I'll be late. Don't wait for me."

Bryan stared out his window as the door shut.

Tiny wasn't at breakfast or the Transient Personnel Office next morning. Bryan had a barracks inspection at 0900. A message to see his lawyer was attached to the inspector's clipboard. He left the office still wondering about his friend.

At 1100 he stopped by the Legal Office to see Commander Smith. They had gone over the entire case several times. Bryan wanted to get it over with and quit wondering about his fate.

"Come in. We've had some good news this morning."

There had been so much bad news in the last twenty four hours those words sounded odd. "What's that, sir?"

"Mr. O'Connor has decided to drop all charges. The Bremerton Police Department had no other complaint against you in this incident. So we're done. You're off legal hold and released for full duty."

Bryan sat quietly knowing what he'd heard but letting it sink in while looking at Smith for confirmation.

"That's right, this incident is over. Nothing on your record, civil or military. Because the charges were dropped, there will be no issue of missing movement. By the way, I was sorry to hear about the *Utah*."

Slowly it dawned on him. "What happened to make him change his mind?"

Smith shook his head. "Not sure. Maybe he got a dose of patriotism. Didn't want to prosecute a serviceman the week after the attack in Hawaii. But it is what it is, you're a free man."

Walking back to Transient Personnel, Bryan's emotions ranged from relief over the charges to anger at being in Bremerton and not with his ship. He had to find a way back to Pearl.

Tiny Leonard sat at his desk talking on the telephone. He motioned Bryan inside and pointed at the chair. "Yes, sir. I'll take care of it right away." The big man hung up and said, "So, how was your morning?"

"They dropped the charges. Can you believe that? No explanation, just 'you're free to go.' I'm glad that's behind me but I've gotta find a way back to Hawaii. Any ideas?"

Tiny Leonard grinned. "The *Peregrine's* underway this afternoon for Pearl. One of their officers is in the hospital with appendicitis. Just so happens the skipper and I are old shipmates from the *Houston*. He's willing to take you along, but you'll be standing a three watch rotation on the bridge."

It sounded too good to be true. Bryan's Officer of the Deck designation from the *Utah* more than qualified him to stand underway watches on a tug. "I better get my tail in gear and get packed." He stood up to leave but stopped. "Wait a minute. You have this already set up? How'd you know I was off the hook on the charges?"

Leonard's grin deepened. "You know us old bos'n mates, we have a knack for finding stuff out."

"Is that where you went last night?"

"Let's just say I had a conversation with the bar owner in question. Laid out a few facts we knew about the incident and told him the Navy would be happy to put his establishment off limits to all sailors permanently." Tiny put his hands behind his neck, interlocking his fingers and stretching slowly.

"Can you do that?"

"Probably not. But he's too stupid to know that and I figured he wouldn't take the time to check."

"Tiny, I owe you." Bryan extended his hand to the big man.

"Now get your ass in gear and get down to Pier Six as fast as you can. They're getting underway at 1400."

Opening the door he stopped and turned back to face his friend. "Damn, Liz has today off after the weekend duty and took the ferry into Seattle to see her mom. By the time she's back, I'll be gone."

"Leave her a note."

Bryan sat down again. "A note?"

Leonard sat back in his chair, crossing his arms on his chest.

"You're both Naval Officers and we're now officially at war. Who knows where either of you'll end up. You might not see her for years. You don't need the complication and she doesn't either. Write her a nice letter and I'll deliver it for you."

"Yeah, I guess you're right."

Chapter Two

A New Beginning

Standing the 0400-0800 watch, Bryan watched as the sky in the east lightened. The seascape slowly became more defined as the day broke, the horizon finally appearing beyond the waves. Each day at sea always dawned differently to him, the wave patterns and colors constantly changing, a new beginning.

Two hundred miles from Pearl Harbor, the *Peregrine* rode smoothly in a choppy sea. Bryan knew this part of the Pacific could be rough in December but they'd been lucky and their transit had been uneventful. Their navigation track placed them at the entrance to the Pearl Harbor channel at daylight the next day. Other than the limited fleet radio broadcasts, they didn't know what to expect. The last time any of them had been in Pearl Harbor the Navy had been at peace.

During the last week Bryan had enjoyed working with Lieutenant Commander Mike Stanton, the *Peregrine*'s Commanding Officer. A Navy diver, Mike had come up through the ranks, which had kept him in the salvage community for most of his career. Bryan now understood why Stanton and Tiny Leonard were friends. The former shipmates were both outgoing and lived for the Navy. During several conversations on the bridge, Bryan learned a great deal about Tiny and his career from Stanton. Tiny Leonard never mentioned any his exploits which had become legend in the salvage world. His appreciation for the big boatswain only grew.

When the *Peregrine* cleared the Straits of Juan de Fuca and entered the Pacific, Stanton had instituted darken ship procedures and radio silence. A message from Commander Western Sea Frontier warned of possible Japanese submarine activity in the area between the west coast and the Hawaiian Islands. Remarkably the *Peregrine* had not sighted another vessel during the trip. Although not following a normal shipping route, it was still unusual not to spot at least the random tramp steamer or fishing boat. In a week the Pacific had changed from ocean to battlefield.

"Captain's on the bridge," the Quartermaster announced as Mike Stanton entered.

Bryan turned and walked over to where the Captain studied the navigation chart. "Morning, Skipper."

"Morning, Bryan. All quiet?" Stanton continued to look at the chart, marking distance with a set of dividers.

"Engineering took number one lube oil pump down for maintenance, nothing critical. We're on track and still no contacts sighted overnight."

Stanton laid the dividers down on the chart. "I wonder what we're going to find tomorrow?"

"Not the Pearl Harbor you and I remember." Bryan thought about the *Utah*. The word 'sunk' was still hard to grasp. Ships the size of the *Utah* and *Arizona* don't sink, not inside protected harbors. Even after listening to the radio reports he found it difficult to picture.

"I appreciate your help on the transit. As soon as we get in, I'll try to find out where they've got the *Utah* crew mustering. I'm sure they have all of the ships set up ashore somewhere."

The Quartermaster switched the general announcing system on and keyed the microphone, "Now reveille, reveille, all hands heave to and trice up. Now reveille."

Bryan looked at the calendar on the wall, it had only been one week since the Japanese attack.

In the distance the rising sun highlighted the dark shape of Diamondhead. *Peregrine* steamed slowly in the outer defensive area waiting for clearance to enter the channel. The signs of a Navy now at war were evident as the ship neared the island of Oahu. *Peregrine* had been challenged during the early morning by a destroyer escort patrolling the southern approaches. To the north, two military aircraft were flying a racetrack pattern over the southern shore of the island. The bridge radio, now tuned to Pearl Harbor Common, broadcast non stop directions for harbor movement and support functions. At 0628 they were cleared to enter the channel. The radio controller directed *Peregrine* to proceed to the Ten Ten pier and tie up south of the cruiser *Helena*.

The green of the shore contrasted starkly with the muddy brown water of the channel. *Peregrine* moved slowly through large oily patches floating on the dirty water. Pieces of wood, cloth and garbage bobbed on the surface, the bow pushing the flotsam aside as they progressed up the channel.

On the east side of the channel the damaged hangars of Hickam Air Base stood in testament to the accuracy of the Japanese airmen. Aircraft wreckage lay across the ramp, a few men picking through the debris. Ahead Bryan saw the superstructure of the battleship *Nevada*. As they rounded a turn the huge warship came fully in view, aground on Hospital Point. Several barges were moored along side the stricken ship as men scrambled to offload weight to lighten the ship. Streams of water were being pumped over the side, the first steps to re-float her. Men stood quietly on her deck watching the *Peregrine* pass.

Bryan felt like they were intruding, visitors to a horrific accident who were arriving late and didn't really belong. Past the *Nevada* the small ship began a right turn toward the pier. He walked to the port bridge wing mesmerized, the devastation along battleship row hard to comprehend. The *Oklahoma* had rolled over ninety degrees, her keel visible above the dirty water. Ahead of her the *California*, sunk at her moorings, the smoking superstructure still vertical. Next he saw the *West Virginia*, resting on the bottom with massive damage to her upper works. At the end of the row the twisted and broken steel of the *Arizona* showed the violence of an exploding magazine. Looking past the damaged hangars of Ford Island, he searched in vain for the familiar superstructure of the *Utah*. The wire lifeline cut into his hands as he squeezed with all his strength, the anger taking control of him. He felt his eyes tearing up and looked down so the lookouts wouldn't see him. In the water slowly passing down the port side, a sailor's white hat floated in the oily water.

Thank God every Pacific Fleet aircraft carrier had been at sea, he thought. They'll have a chance to fight back. These broken and burned ships will never strike back at the Japanese. Thousands of tons of twisted steel, the Pacific Fleet battle line – gone. Bryan took a deep breath, quickly wiped his eyes and returned to the bridge.

Within thirty minutes of mooring *Peregrine* divers were in the water working temporary repairs to *Helena*'s hull to expedite the dewatering process.

Bryan stood on the stern watching the line tenders for the *Peregrine* divers. In the distance the *Helena* crewmembers were removing damaged equipment from below decks. The divers were working on the starboard side trying to access a torpedo hit located well beneath the water line.

"Bryan, can you stick around and lend a hand?"

He turned to see Mike Stanton next to him.

"I'll stay. Maybe I can do some good here."

Two days later Bryan took off his set of sweaty oil stained khakis. He had slept in small snatches as he expedited the work of *Peregrine*'s salvage crews. The *Helena* was severely damaged from a massive hole in her starboard side. Each day he had led work crews down into the filthy darkness. As he peeled off his grimy clothes Bryan couldn't shake the moment that morning when they opened a buckled hatch on the fourth deck. As water surged out of the hatch, Bryan swung it open to let the rest of the water escape. Dirty brown water flooded onto the deck where they stood, bringing with it an arm connected to only the upper torso of a sailor. In the artificial light the remains at his feet looked totally white. Fighting the horror of what lay on the cold steel deck, Bryan had turned to the sailor behind him and said, "Give me a hand with this, please."

A roughly lettered sign, "USS *UTAH*", was nailed over the double wooden door. Bryan took a deep breath and went inside. Several desks covered the wooden floor of the room on the southern end of the large supply warehouse. Chief Yeoman Purcell, the ship's writer, sat at the first desk. Glancing around, Bryan noticed most of the men were yeomen.

"Chief, I just got back. I need to check in."

Purcell looked up, the man looked tired. "Yes, sir. Do you have your orders?"

Bryan handed him the manila envelope with his orders from Bremerton. "Where is everyone?"

Purcell opened the envelope and started sorting the papers. "Some of the men are over with the engineer working on the hull. The rest have been sent around to lend a hand where needed. The XO's in the back. You better check in with him."

"Chief, I haven't heard anything except the ship sank. Have you seen my room mate, Mr. Hutchins?"

The Chief's demeanor changed. "Sorry, sir. He was killed in the attack. They think he was trying to get some of the men out from forward berthing when the second torpedo hit. They're trying to get into the hull right now to recover bodies." The chief stood up. "I'll see if the XO can see you."

Bryan felt empty. Tim been a good friend during a time when he needed support. He remembered the remains he had found that morning on the *Helena*. Now Tim was floating somewhere in the same awful world of twisted steel and oily water.

Purcell walked back from the small office. "You can go in, Mr. Michaels."

Commander Harris looked up from a pile of letters as Bryan walked in and stood at attention in front of the desk. "Sit down. Let me finish this last letter." The man's appearance shocked Bryan. More than tired, he looked like an old man.

"Yes, sir."

Throwing his pen on the desk, Harris leaned back in his chair. "So what happened in Bremerton and how did you get back here as fast as you did?" The man's voice hollow, his spirit gone.

"Charges were dropped, sir. The bar owner had set up the incident and we found out. I was able to get on a salvage tug, the *Peregrine*, which left Bremerton the day after the attack." The triviality of events in Bremerton struck Bryan as he watched the XO.

Harris looked past Bryan, focusing in the distance. "The ship didn't have a chance. Hit by two, maybe three torpedoes. As soon as she started listing, the topside weight pulled her over. We have eighty two men dead or missing. Tim Hutchins is one of them."

"Yes, sir. The Chief told me." The feeling of emptiness returned.

"Everything's up in the air. They'll reassign people at some point. Right now everyone's pitching in where they can. That's all I can tell you."

"Sir, the *Peregrine* is working salvage in the harbor. I know I can be useful there. Would it be okay to hook up with them?"

Harris nodded, his eyes returning to his desk. "Check in with the Chief so we can keep track of you if we get any orders."

When Bryan thought back on the three weeks he spent working for Mike Stanton on the *Peregrine* he would remember the odors of burned paint, fuel oil, sewage and death. Bodies had floated to the surface as they decomposed, the sea giving up the dead. Bryan steeled himself to the horror but never got used to it.

A week after Bryan checked back into the *Utah* a message

arrived from the Beach detachment that they had found Tim's body. Checking out with Mike Stanton Bryan made his way over to the *Utah*. When he arrived seven bodies lay on the quay wall covered by tarps. The Engineering Officer, Commander Sol Isquith, stood at the pier edge directing several men who were cutting into the hull with torches. Bryan approached him and saluted.

"Good afternoon, sir."

Oil and sweat stained the older man's uniform. Exhaustion showed in the eyes of the sailors holding the cutting torch lines. Isquith turned to look at Bryan. His bloodshot eyes narrowed slightly as he shaded his eyes from the glare of the sun. The two had never really worked together and with a wardroom of over forty officers there was no reason why he should remember Bryan. "You're, Michaels. Deck Department."

"Yes, sir. I'm over on the *Peregrine* lending a hand. I heard they found my roommate, Tim Hutchins."

Isquith turned to face him fully. The expression on his face softened. "We found him down in lower divisional berthing. He must have headed down there after the first torpedo struck." The Engineer stopped for a moment, composing himself. "It looks like the second torpedo jammed the hatch and trapped them down there. He was a good officer, I'm sorry we lost him."

Bryan turned to look at the seven tarps on the concrete pier. "Sir, where is he?"

"Lieutenant, remember him like he was."

He shook his head. "No, sir. I need to see him."

Commander Isquith looked at Bryan, his eyes showing he understood. "Come on."

The two men walked down the dirty pier. Large cardboard identity tags flapped in the light breeze. The first tag said: 'LT Hutchins.'

Sol Isquith leaned down and pulled the tarp back.

By mid-January, sixteen hour days followed by falling asleep in grimy khakis became Bryan's regular routine. There wasn't time for anything except completing one job and moving on to the next.

Late one afternoon a letter arrived from Liz via the *Utah* Beach Detachment. Perhaps it had been the relief of his legal situation or the unknown of what he would be facing, but in that letter he had told Liz he considered her someone very special. He had never done that before and now he hesitated to open her letter. Taking a deep breath he slit the envelop open.

Her words jumped from the page—she felt the same way. He read it again afraid he hadn't read it correctly the first time. "....I am glad we met. I don't want to let this slip away and will do everything I can to see you again very soon. Liz." He sat down on one of the large towing bollards and looked across the blue water of the harbor.

"Hey Mr. Michaels, isn't that your old ship?"

Bryan looked up as the *Enterprise* moved slowly out the channel.

"You're right, Stevens," he said to the young sailor next to him. "That's my old squadron, Bombing Six."

"Gee, sir, how come you're not with them?"

Bryan didn't reply for a moment. "It's a long story," he said and turned to walk toward the bow, remembering Tim dead on the pier. His friend had tried to do his duty when the Japs attacked. Now his old squadron mates were going out to do the same thing.

He found Mike Stanton and asked if he could knock off early. Bryan had every intention of getting commode-hugging drunk.

As he sat in the Officer's Club, Bryan spent more time thinking than drinking. He slowly rotated the wet glass on the coaster watching the lines of water spread on the table. On his left ring finger he still wore his Naval Academy ring. Despite the problems he'd had with the Navy, Bryan never stopped wearing the ring. Now most of his class would be fighting this war. He'd probably be stuck in some shitty backwater job counting ball bearings.

There were no familiar faces in the bar and the noise and cigarette smoke finally drove him out on the veranda which wrapped around the harbor side of the club. Looking out over the dark water he thought it looked peaceful, darkness covering the pain and destruction. Only scattered lights on some of the ships showed salvage activity still underway.

"Almost looks like before the war, doesn't it?" A voice came from behind him.

Bryan continued to look at the harbor. "I was just thinking the same thing myself. If only we could turn back time."

In response to the black out regulations, all lights were extinguished on the veranda. He could only tell the fellow beside him was tall with light hair.

"A luxury we don't have, I'm afraid. We can only look ahead," the man said in a slow and measured tone.

Finishing his drink, Bryan laughed and said, "I'd like to look ahead but the damn Navy has other ideas." Turning, he brushed past the man still lost in his thoughts. "I just want a fucking chance."

Twenty minutes later, a tall Lieutenant walked up to Bryan who sat at the bar nursing his fifth drink of the night.

"Excuse me, Lieutenant," the man said.

Bryan turned to see a Lieutenant with the aiguillette of an aide around his left shoulder. "Yeah."

"My name is Fisher. I'm Admiral Nimitz's Flag Lieutenant. The Admiral wanted me to get your name and unit." The man took out a small pocket notebook and a pencil, waiting for Bryan's answer.

"Admiral Nimitz? You're kidding, right?" Bryan asked. But something in the Lieutenant's tone and demeanor told him otherwise.

"No, Lieutenant, I'm not. You might not have realized it but you were speaking with the Admiral on the veranda a few minutes ago. He wants to know who you are."

Bryan sighed, shook his head and then took a long drink. Taking his time to swallow the liquor he then turned and said "Lieutenant (jg) Bryan Michaels, late of the U.S.S. *Utah*."

Fisher wrote in his notebook, closed it and said crisply, "Thank you, Mr. Michaels."

I wasn't even trying to get into trouble, Bryan thought. The Commander in Chief of the entire Pacific Fleet and I'm talking to him like he's a drinking buddy. *Shit.*

Two days later while Bryan supervised loading acetylene bottles on the fantail, the duty driver from *Utah* drove up to *Peregrine* in a Ford pickup truck. The driver had been sent to bring Bryan back to the detachment. Checking out with Mike Stanton, he wondered if this might be about his encounter with Nimitz.

Commander Harris had regained some of his old fire. "Lieutenant Michaels, can you explain why we received a message to have you report to CINCPACFLT Headquarters at 1400 today to see the Chief of Staff?"

"I guess it has something to do with my conversation with Admiral Nimitz at the club two days ago."

"Your conversation with Admiral Nimitz? What in the hell did you say to him?" Harris said, clearly upset.

"XO, I don't know. I didn't realize it was the Admiral and I'd had a couple of drinks. But I don't think it was anything out of order, honestly."

Harris sat back in his chair. "Someday I am going to write a book, Michaels. And you're gonna be one of the chapters. Get yourself cleaned up and in your best uniform. The duty driver will run you up to Makalapa."

"Yes, sir." Bryan walked out

Ten minutes after the duty driver dropped him at the entrance to the Headquarter, U.S. Pacific Fleet, Bryan stood outside the door on the second floor marked "Chief of Staff

CINCPACFLT." He checked his uniform one more time and opened the door. Inside there were two desks, a Chief Petty Officer sat at one, a First Class Yeoman at the other. Bryan walked over to the chief.

"I'm Lieutenant Michaels. I was told to report to the Chief of Staff at 1400."

The chief's uniform was spotless and his manner efficient. "Please have a seat, sir. I'll let Admiral Draemel know you're here." Rear Admiral Milo Draemel served as Nimitz's Chief of Staff. After the attack, most of the senior officers in Pearl Harbor assumed they would be sacked and shipped off to oblivion. But Chester Nimitz believed in men and their desire to do a good job. Across the board he had retained all of the staff personnel and told them they had his trust and confidence. Still in shock over the attack, these men were already looking ahead toward victory.

The Chief of Staff stood looking out over the harbor. He turned as Bryan walked in behind the chief but said nothing.

"Admiral, Lieutenant Michaels," the chief said and left the room.

"Lieutenant, have a seat." Draemel indicated one of the two straight backed chairs facing his desk.

"Aye aye, sir." Bryan quickly sat down.

"I'm going to tell you a story that I hope you learn something from. Two days ago Admiral Nimitz called me in and told me we needed to find out more about a Lieutenant off the *Utah*. He'd talked with this young man at the club the night before and something about the man struck a chord. As the Chief of Staff, I try to set priorities on this staff. We have an enormous job ahead of us and time is precious. The Admiral has the weight of the world on his shoulders as you might imagine. I told him that we couldn't afford to worry about one man. That's when he told me something I should have already known. He said to me, 'We can't afford not to.'"

Draemel got up from his chair and walked back to the window. "We found out about your court-martial last year and reviewed the accident report. I had several of our senior aviators take a look at all of the facts. Based on that review the Admiral sent a personal message to the Chief of Naval Personnel and Commander Naval Air Forces Pacific recommending you be returned to flight status and assigned to sea duty as soon as possible. Chester Nimitz has a lot of credibility in the Navy and he put that on the line for you. His recommendation came back approved. You'll be receiving orders to report to Bombing Squadron Five aboard the *Yorktown*."

Bryan's thoughts were a jumble. "I don't know what to say, sir."

"I'll only ask one thing from you, Lieutenant. Don't let the Admiral down.

Still trying to understand what had just happened, Bryan said, "Sir, would it be possible to thank the Admiral?"

"Wait here." Draemel got up and went to another side door out of the office. In a moment he returned. "Come this way."

Bryan followed the Admiral through a short hallway into the Fleet Commander's office. Sitting at his desk, Chester Nimitz leaned over, reading a folder.

Nimitz looked up and smiled slightly. "Lieutenant Michaels, come in and have a seat. I've got a few minutes before the afternoon briefing. Chief of Staff, thank you." Draemel closed the door as he left.

"Admiral, thank you for looking into my case."

The Admiral sat back and looked at Bryan. "Lieutenant, everyone makes mistakes. But I'll be honest with you. I think you used bad judgment and it resulted in an accident. But I also think that a professional officer learns from mistakes and it makes him better."

Bryan listened and kept his mouth shut.

"I was court-martialed in my first command. I ran my ship aground because I wasn't paying enough attention to what should have been important at the moment. A hard lesson for sure but nothing compared to losing two men."

"No, sir," Bryan answered.

"Our Navy learned a terrible lesson on December 7th. But it will make us better and stronger in the future. I'm betting you'll be a better officer and aviator on your second go around."

Bryan looked at the Admiral, not saying anything but trying to show by his expression that he understood loud and clear.

"We were able to get you back into a cockpit. What you do when you get there is up to you. We need carrier pilots to take this war to the Japs. I don't doubt the outcome of the war if we can hold the enemy off long enough for this country to mobilize. The world doesn't understand the potential of the United States but they'll soon find out. Your job is to give us time to build up our forces. I'm counting on you and every sailor and Marine that's in the battle now to fight like there's no tomorrow. When it's all over, come back and let me know if you still want to thank me for throwing you into the fight." The Admiral stood up and came around the desk. He extended his hand. "Good luck, son."

Bryan stood as straight as he could and took the Admiral's hand. "Thank you, sir."

Five minutes later Bryan Michaels stood on the front steps of CINCPACFLT Headquarters. Below, the whole harbor watched as the *Enterprise* made her way into the turning basin, returning from the first offensive strikes of the war against the Gilbert and Marshall Islands. Led by Vice Admiral William F. "Bull" Halsey, the Big "E" and her aircrews had drawn their first blood.

Bryan remembered what Admiral Nimitz had said. The aircrews on the Pacific Fleet carriers had to buy the Navy time.

"Admiral, it's time for the afternoon briefing."

Chester Nimitz looked up from a file he was reading to see the Chief of Staff standing at the door. He closed the file and stood up. "I'm ready."

"What did you think of Lieutenant Michaels?" Draemel asked as they walked down the hall to the staff conference room.

"He reminds me of a classmate of mine from Annapolis who never fit in the peacetime Navy," Nimitz replied. "When the first war came along it was if he had found his calling. If our young Lieutenant stays alive, he may do the same thing."

Chapter Three

Airborne Again

Later that afternoon Bryan found the *Yorktown* Beach Detachment offices. Each carrier maintained a small administrative group at homeport to handle support of the ship at sea. In the time honored ritual a yeoman took his orders and he reported to the Detachment Officer in Charge, Lieutenant Commander Nichols.

"Bombing Five, right?" Nichols scanned over the papers Bryan had been given by Chief of Staff's Yeoman when he left the headquarters.

"Yes, sir. Any idea when I'll be able to join the squadron?" Bryan knew *Yorktown* was at sea and he expected to be routed via a tanker or supply ship. He hoped to find some way to log a few hours in something with wings before he left.

"How 'bout tomorrow, Lieutenant?" Nichols signed the reporting endorsement and looked up at Bryan.

"Tomorrow?"

"Ship's pulling in at 1000, but that's not for publication. I expect you can walk aboard by noon. Until then you're on your own. If you need to take care of anything, better do it now. We don't know how long she'll be in port. Things are very much up in the air."

Tomorrow?. Events were going at full speed. "I've been out of touch for a while. Who's the skipper of Five?"

"Lieutenant Wally Short."

Bryan knew of Short but had never met him. Wally Short had a good reputation around the fleet and that encouraged Bryan.

After packing his two bags Bryan decided to stop by the officer's club to celebrate his return to the world of carrier aviation. He knew that aviators from the *Enterprise* might be there and he might connect with some of his old squadron mates.

As he approached the main lounge doors he heard the noise of the traditional "first night in port" happy hour. The cigarette smoke filled the darkened bar, crowded with officers in blue and khaki uniforms. Adjusting his eyes to the light he quickly scanned the room for any familiar faces. On the far wall, under one of the simulated nautical lanterns he spotted Terry McGinnis, one of the pilots from his old squadron. McGinnis had always been a good friend and supported him during the accident board.

"Terry!" Bryan worked his way between the tables. They were all full of loud and boisterous young men with the occasional young lady. Bryan felt a difference in the atmosphere. Many of these officers had already flown in combat against the Japs. The animated conversations were still there, just like before Pearl Harbor, but something was different....they were at war.

McGinnis looked across the room and smiled when he recognized Bryan.

"Michaels, you old son of a bitch. How're you doing?"

The two men shook hands. "Good to see you. You just get in?" Bryan asked as they both sat down.

"Yeah, this afternoon. This is Bruce Linton, one of our new guys. Bruce, Bryan Michaels, he used to be in the squadron."

Linton shook hands and didn't indicate if he knew of Bryan or his past. Terry reached over to the next table and grabbed an empty glass. He filled it from a half empty pitcher of beer in front of him.

"I wondered about you after we saw the *Utah*." Terry sounded tentative, perhaps not wanting to open any wounds.

"I was still in Bremerton on the 7th. I didn't even get here until a week later." He paused. "Tim Hutchins didn't make it. You met him at that party on Maui."

"That's tough," Terry said. "So what are you gonna do now?"

Bryan took a long drink of beer. He put the glass on the table and looked at his friend. "Hard to believe but I've got orders to Bombing Five on the *Yorktown*."

McGinnis's face lit up. "You're kidding me? Bryan, that's great. How'd you ever swing that?"

"Long story and I'm not drunk enough yet to tell it." Bryan had decided not to tell anyone except his new CO what had actually happened.

"Did you know Abbott is the XO?"

Lieutenant Tony Abbott had been the senior member of his board of inquiry. Bryan always felt Abbott, the squadron operations officer at the time, had railroaded the board's verdict past the other two members to protect himself for scheduling two junior pilots together. "Shit, what a way to start."

McGinnis put down his glass. "He transferred about six months ago when he screened for command."

Bryan remembered Tony Abbott. If ever a man didn't deserve to command a squadron, it was him. The true politician, Abbot was a complete asshole who didn't care about his men or officers junior to him. The euphoria of the afternoon began to fade with the realization he would be serving under Tony Abbott again.

The next morning Bryan walked over to the turning basin opposite Battleship Row to watch the *Yorktown* pull in the harbor. He waited an hour until he saw the distinctive outline in the channel. The ship showed evidence of long months at sea. There were streaks of rust running down her side from the hull discharge ports. A light ring of sea grass waved slowly just under the water line.

On the flight deck, sailors worked on aircraft or watched the tugs maneuver the ship pier side. To the sound of shrill whistles the mooring lines were passed to working parties on the pier and they began mooring the big carrier. Bryan knew it would take at least thirty minutes for the accommodation ladders to be rigged in place. He made his way to the pier canteen for a cup of coffee.

An hour later he opened the door to Ready Room Five. Inside, several rows of high backed chairs faced two large blackboards at the front of the room. To one side an Ensign manned the squadron duty desk. He had his head down, writing in a green logbook.

"I'm Bryan Michaels, reporting in." He laid his manila package on the desk.

The Ensign looked up from his writing. "Sorry, didn't see you come in. I'm Tim Fallon." Standing, he offered Bryan his hand. "Nice to meet you. Put your stuff over there and I'll call Admin."

Bryan looked around at the space. Not much different from his old ready room on the *Enterprise*. Mailboxes in the back, a magazine rack, and on a table by the mailbox, an acey-deucy board. It was good to be back, he thought, very good.

While he waited for the Admin Yeoman the door opened and a Lieutenant walked up to the desk.

"I heard we had a new pilot aboard. I'm John Powers, the Ops O. Everybody calls me JJ." Powers had an infectious grin. The two men shook hands and Bryan knew he would like Powers.

"Nice to meet you. Bryan Michaels." He remembered Powers from Annapolis, Class of 1935.

"We just got the word you were reporting. Glad to have you aboard. I understand you have plenty of time in the Dauntless but you're not current?"

Bryan nodded. "Is that gonna be a problem?"

Powers grinned again. "You're in luck. We flew two aircraft off yesterday to Ford Island. All we need to do is get you up to speed on squadron instructions and the BUAIR changes that have come out since you last flew." The Operations Officer didn't make any reference to the accident but he must have known. There were few secrets in the tight knit fraternity. "We have one more new guy checking in fresh out of Pensacola, Ensign Taylor. Over the next week we'll be able to get both of you squared away."

Bryan felt excited at the thought of getting back into the cockpit. "Any idea when we pull out?"

Powers shook his head. "Not for sure. I suspect about a week."

"Know where we're headed?" Bryan asked.

"You can bet it won't be San Francisco." Powers grinned and walked away.

In one day Bryan completed all of his paperwork which would return him to flight status. These included a cursory flight physical with the *Yorktown*'s Senior Medical Officer and a review of his logbook and training jacket. His squadron check included a meeting with the Commanding Officer, Lieutenant Wally Short.

Bryan knocked on Short's stateroom door.

"Come in,"

"Skipper, it's Bryan Michaels." He stuck his head in the room. Short sat at his fold down desk writing a letter.

The Skipper stood up and walked two steps toward Bryan, extending his hand. "Welcome aboard. Sorry I've been a bit scarce. Too many meetings and not enough free time. Have a seat on the bunk."

Bryan handed the Skipper his typed check in sheet.

Short read it over and said, "So you've seen everyone but the XO?"

"Yes, sir. They told me he was up at Ewa talking to the Marines."

"Yeah, he'll be back tomorrow. We're finding out that Navy and Marine Air better be on the same page or it's not gonna be pretty."

"Yes, sir."

"I took a look at your logbook. You have lots of time in the Dauntless, but we've got the new dash three. Think you'll find the improvements are good ones. More range and firepower. Speeds still slower than I'd like but we fly what the taxpayers give us."

Bryan knew the Skipper must want to talk about the accident.

"You know this community is small and everyone knows everyone else's business."

"Yes, sir." *Here it comes.*

"We all knew about the accident last year. There's not much good that ever comes out of those things. Hopefully we learn from our mistakes and don't repeat them."

The same thing Admiral Nimitz said, Bryan thought.

"One of my meetings when we pulled in was with the CINCPAC Chief of Staff. He filled me in on what happened. As far as I'm concerned no one else needs to know about it. I'll tell the XO but that's it. You're assigned to Bombing Five to fly combat and that's what you're gonna do. I expect your experience will be positive for the squadron. What I'm telling you is that your slate is clean with me. Get yourself refreshed in the aircraft as quickly as you can. We'll be doing quick carrier qualifications when we pull out. I expect you to be ready."

"I'll be ready, Skipper. And thanks."

A clear blue sky set the stage next morning as the duty driver drove Bryan and Ensign Bud Taylor to the Ford Island flight line. Wrecked aircraft from the Japanese attack had been dragged to the southern end of the field. The twisted and burned airframes reminded Bryan of the urgency of getting current in the Dauntless. The Mae West and flying cap on his lap smelled new, a reminder of the world he was about to reenter.

Powers had asked Bryan to take Taylor under his wing during this inport period. Fresh out of flight school, Taylor was a former college football player from Wisconsin who had always wanted to fly. He arrived in Hawaii two days ago, the farthest he'd ever traveled from home.

Bryan walked out to the two squadron aircraft parked side by side on the concrete. He couldn't take his eyes off the Dauntless and it only seemed real when he put his hand on the leading edge of the wing. Bud Taylor trailed him but had said nothing. Bryan turned back to the young pilot. "I'll do a preflight and you walk behind me. Once I finish we'll go over to your aircraft and you demonstrate a preflight for me."

"Yes, sir."

"And don't call me sir. The only two guys in an aircraft squadron who rate 'sir' are the Skipper and XO."

"Okay."

The smell of the aircraft and ritual of doing a preflight made him feel at home. Taylor proved to be pretty sharp, asking good questions and catching on quickly. On completion of the preflight Bryan sat down on the concrete under one wing and talked procedures and techniques for over an hour. Pulling out an aviation chart of the local area he briefed a quick familiarization flight to the west end of Oahu.

Bryan looked at his watch. "Our gunners should be showing up shortly. We'll fly with whoever they assign us right now but you normally are crewed with the same guy during ops. Remember, on the deck you are officer and enlisted. In the air you're two guys trying to stay alive. These guys are damned good. A lot of the aircrew are radiomen and they're pretty good with navigation. My advice? As a new guy rely on your crewman to share his experience. You're the pilot in command, don't forget that. But listen to what they say."

Taylor nodded, "Yes, sir."

A grey Navy pickup truck pulled up to the flight line with two men in the back. Both wore dungarees and Mae West life preservers. They jumped down from the truck carrying their parachutes. Bryan waved his hand get their attention. He looked hard at the second man walking toward the parked Dauntless. *Son of a bitch! Bill Nance.*

The two men met and grinned at each other as they shook hands. "I can't believe it. You're in Bombing Five. What happened?" Bryan asked.

"After you left the squadron, I didn't like the atmosphere. So when they were looking for volunteers to cross deck to the *Yorktown*, I made my move. Little did I know Abbott would end up as the XO." Nance said in his Texas drawl.

"Son of a gun. So who are ya crewed with?" Bryan asked.

"You. Whaddya think? I talked to LT Powers and explained things and he made the swap. I flew with him for the last six months."

Bryan didn't know what to say. Bill had traded the Squadron Ops Officer, one of the best pilots in the squadron, for a rusty aviator who hadn't been in a cockpit in over a year. "Thanks, Bill. I'm glad we're back together." He paused then said, "Let's go flying." He turned to Bud Taylor who had been watching them from under the wing of the SBD. "Petty Officer Nance and I flew together on the *Enterprise*."

The second crewman stepped up. "Lieutenant Michaels, this is Petty Officer Antrim," Nance said with a tone of proper military decorum. "He's gonna fly with Ensign Taylor today."

Bryan extended his hand. "Glad to meet you. This is Ensign Taylor."

The four men stood in a circle, two parachutes lying in the middle of them.

"We've been briefing for a while on general procedures. Let's go over the navigation plan, a few coordination items and then you guys can brief your crew procedures. We'll plan on taxiing in about forty five minutes." The other three nodded.

The year since Bryan had sat in a Dauntless cockpit disappeared as he went through his cockpit check and pre-start routine. His hands moved to the various switches almost without thinking. The refresher yesterday with the flight manual helped as he reviewed critical temperatures and pressures for the different gauges on the instrument panel. Looking down at the plane captain standing next to a large fire extinguisher, Bryan signaled ready to start by moving his upturned finger in a circular motion. Magnetos: on, engine: primed, push the starter button and move the mixture forward. The Cyclone engine caught the first time and he watched the engine RPM stabilize. Scanning the instruments, all readings were within limits. Bryan exhaled and realized he'd been holding his breath. For a moment he closed his eyes and put his head back against the headrest. It had been a long journey back.

Keying his radio, Bryan called Ford Island Tower for taxi for both aircraft.

"You ready to taxi, Bill?"

"All set back here."

As the Dauntless taxied to the duty runway Bryan felt a light breeze coming off Pearl Harbor. He could feel the reassuring rumble of the engine and knew he was where he should be. Looking to his right, he saw the bottom of the *Utah*, her superstructure dug into the mud of Pearl Harbor. *Okay, pay attention to what you're doing. You haven't done this for awhile.*

Pulling on the runway he locked his tail wheel and rechecked the flaps down. Bryan had briefed Taylor to follow him with a twenty second interval on takeoff. He looked over to Taylor's cockpit, gave him a quick salute and turned to look down the runway. Trying to maintain a detached manner he keyed the intercom, "Throttle full, pitch full, manifold pressure – 45 inches, okay, we're rolling." The bomber accelerated quickly. After 1200 feet of roll, Bryan pulled back slightly and they were airborne. The runway flashed away below them and the bomber roared across the waters of Pearl Harbor.

Departing down the channel, Bryan climbed to 4000 feet and turned toward Barber's Point. He had briefed Taylor to rendezvous over Pilla Point thirty minutes after takeoff at 5000 feet, left hand turns. For the next twenty five minutes he turned, dove, climbed, and slow flighted the aircraft, absorbing the wonder of flight again.

"Not bad for being on the ground for a year." Nance's drawl came over the intercom as they headed to Pilla Point.

"Hope my formation and landings go as well."

In the distance another Dauntless circled over Pilla Point. It had to be Taylor. Good, Bryan thought, it gives me a chance to join on him and see how I do. Coming into the rendezvous circle Bryan maneuvered to a line of bearing forty five degrees back from Taylor's wing line. Rolling into a bank he pulled on the stick until their fuselages were aligned. Slowly he watched as the distance between the two closed. One hundred feet away he pulled a little power and increased his angle of bank to stop closure. Two quick adjustments put the aircraft in the correct position of a wingman on Taylor's left wing. Following standard Naval Aviation procedures Taylor assumed the formation lead, directed Bryan to cross over to his right wing, indicated that Bryan should move his aircraft forward, and then gave him the lead.

For the next thirty minutes they practiced rendezvous' and formation flying. Checking his watch, he looked back at Taylor and pointed toward Pearl Harbor. Forty feet away the young Ensign nodded vigorously. "Okay, Bill. Let's go see if I can still land this beast."

"I'll be pullin' for ya all the way." The good natured banter made it feel like the old days.

Climbing out after his first approach Bryan heard the intercom come alive.

"You don't intend to try landing on a real ship like you just did back there do you?"

"Why, you afraid to die?" Bryan shot back at Bill.

"Hell, I don't mind dying, I just don't want to look bad."

At the 180, Bryan pulled power and began his turn to final. "Well let's see if I can do any better this time."

"Hard to do much worse," came the drawl back over the intercom.

Bryan laughed and told himself to relax.

Ten solid landings followed and he felt good taxiing back to the ramp.

"I think you finally got the hang of it," Bill said, "Oh shit, look who's here."

Standing on the concrete ramp, Lieutenant Tony Abbott was watching the flight taxi in to park.

Bryan quickly shut down the engine and checked all switches off.

"Bill, you better stay out here and talk to the plane captain."

"Good luck."

Bryan walked over to Abbott. Tony hadn't changed at all since he last saw him in San Diego. Black hair slicked back with a small mustache, the Bombing Five Executive Officer looked the part. His khaki uniform still had knife like creases in the pants. Bryan pulled off his cloth flying helmet and felt the breeze on his wet and surely messed up hair. He stopped in front of Abbott. "Hello, XO."

Abbott stared at Bryan for a moment. "The duty officer told me you were here when I got back this morning. You still remember how to fly a Dauntless?"

"Seemed to go okay this morning." Bryan said cautiously, not able to read Abbott's mood.

Tony Abbott took off his Navy issue sunglasses. "The Skipper told me how you whined your way back into a cockpit."

The anger welled up inside Bryan but he didn't say anything.

"You may be back but it doesn't change the fact that you are a screw up. Smart ass admiral's son with your Annapolis ring doesn't cut any weight with me. You've already killed two people through your own negligence and I don't want to see anyone else die because of you. I'll be watching you. If you mess up once, I'll have your ass. You read me?"

"Loud and clear, sir." Bryan knew he had to control his fury. He remembered Admiral Nimitz. *I'll show this asshole.*

"Now get out there and post flight that aircraft. Or have you forgotten that's what we do in the fleet." The sarcasm in Abbott's tone almost pushed Bryan past his limit.

"Yes, sir." He turned and began to walk back to the aircraft. Nance knelt down looking at the port tire. Bryan walked to the nose of the aircraft and checked the propeller for any nicks or dings on the big three bladed Hamilton Standard propeller. Of all the aviators in the Pacific Fleet, he asked himself, how did I end up with Abbott?

During the next week, Bryan logged twenty six hours in the Dauntless, including over two hundred practice carrier landings. He began to feel very comfortable in the cockpit. Bud Taylor caught on quickly and proved to be a solid young aviator. His final test included a simulated bombing mission with Bryan as the flight lead to "the Rock."

Located off the island of Niihau, Kaula Rock rose almost two hundred feet above of the water. Navy and Marine Corps squadrons frequently used the volcanic island for bombing and strafing practice. Aircraft assigned to the flight were Five-Bravo-Eight and Five-Bravo-Eleven. The identification "Five-Bravo" referred to Bombing Five and "Eight" indicated the number within the squadron. The system was standard throughout the Pacific Fleet.

Officially a crew again, Bryan and Bill Nance had flown together on every flight during the week. The two young men had become good friends during their time on the *Enterprise*. Bryan always found it strange that two people with such different backgrounds could connect so well. Bryan was fourth generation Navy, Nance the first of his family to be in the military since the Civil War, or as Bill would say, "The War of Northern Aggression." Bryan traveled and lived around the world while Bill had never left his home county in Texas until he joined the Navy. But they both loved to fly.

During the flight briefing Bryan told Bud they would make three practice runs on the rock followed by three hot runs. He spent extra time on safety issues including mandatory pull out altitudes, use of dive brakes, making sure their goggles were down and to watch out for flocks of sea gulls during pull out.

The flight reached Kaula Rock at noon and found a thin cloud layer at 14,000 feet. Bryan had wanted to start his bombing runs at 17,000 feet, but he wasn't going to let the new guy take any chances.

"Dash two, we'll commence our runs from thirteen five. I'll go down and clear the target," Bryan transmitted.

"Roger, lead."

Rolling to ninety degrees angle of bank, Bryan let the nose fall through toward the ocean. Airspeed built up to 240 knots as he descended toward the bare black rock rising out of the bluish green sea. There were waves breaking on the west side and sea birds circling around the southern point, their target. Clearing the target ensured there were no small fishing boats hiding in the shadows of the rock. The sides of the rock were too steep for anyone to actually climb onto the island but sometimes fishing boats would shelter under the east side.

Pulling up, he added full power and began his climb to the 'roll-in' altitude. The other Dauntless orbited at altitude and Bryan cut across the circle to put himself exactly opposite Bud Taylor.

"As briefed, make your roll in to the north." He transmitted to the other aircraft. "You all set?" he asked Nance.

"Ready."

The old habits came back easily, propeller pitch to full, mixture to full rich, carburetor heat-on. Putting Kaula rock thirty degrees forward of his left wing, Bryan rolled the aircraft toward the target until the black rock was centered on his windscreen. He pulled the power back stabilizing the Dauntless in a 65 degree dive toward the sea. Checking to ensure the wings were level, he extended the dive brakes. Leaning forward he picked up the target in the telescopic site.

Bill called off altitudes from the back seat, "Twelve thousand....eleven thousand.....ten thousand..."

Bryan compensated for the wind by putting in a little left aileron. Checking for a centered trim ball, he watched the cross hairs touch the target as Nance called two thousand feet. Pushing the bomb release button, he pulled the stick back with both hands, the four "G" recovery bottoming them out at 1200 feet above the white flecked ocean. Dive brakes in, full power and Bryan started the climb back up to pattern altitude. He heard Bud Taylor call 'rolling in' on the target and looked left to pick up the other Dauntless. The aircraft looked under control in the dive and Bryan felt confident Taylor had a good run going. He kept his eye on the younger aviator, not turning away until he saw the other bomber pull off the target safely.

Two more practice dives Bryan rolled in and dropped a bomb which impacted 50 feet short of the rock. The telltale splash was lightly tinged with the red marker color. Taylor made two good runs after a terrible first drop. All of Bryan's hits were within 100 feet of the target.

On the return trip to Ford Island, Bryan felt confident about the return of his aviation skills. He did not feel good about his future with Lieutenant Tony Abbott. Descending into the Ford Island traffic pattern he wondered if his second chance was doomed to fail.

A frenzy of activity gripped the ship and squadrons as each person worked hard to get the *Yorktown* ready to sail. Last minute working parties loaded food and ammunition throughout the day and late into the night. Last minute intelligence briefings tried to get the aircrews ready for expected combat operations.

Bryan focused on preparing for his carrier qualifications the next day. Scheduled to pull out at 0700, by 1100 the *Yorktown* would be conducting flight operations south of Oahu. After one day of carrier landings for the air wing, the remainder of Task Force 17 would join the *Yorktown* and proceed west. No one knew exactly where they were headed but there were plenty of rumors flying around. Bryan had heard Australia, the Marshall Islands and the Indian Ocean.

At 1600 Bryan returned to his stateroom on the 02 level, right under the flight deck. Although he'd gone over his procedures hundreds of times in the last week he wanted to review emergencies one more time. As soon as he sat down with his handbook, he heard a knock on the door.

"Come in, it's not locked," Bryan yelled.

The door swung open. He heard a booming and familiar voice. "What the hell's going on in here? Attention on deck."

Reacting more out of habit than concern for naval etiquette, Bryan jumped to his feet and looked toward the door. Tiny Leonard grinned at him from the passageway.

"Tiny! What the hell are you doing here?" He extended his hand.

Grabbing Bryan's hand the big man shook it vigorously. "Never underestimate a Warrant Boatswain. I'm on my way to Motor Torpedo Squadron Nine."

"How in the hell did you swing that?"

Tiny sat down on the bunk. "The Senior Detailer was a shipmate from the *Tennessee*. Once the shooting started, all bets for retirement are off for the duration. So I reminded him of the extensive knowledge I had of his activities in Hong Kong and Singapore when he was a young Second Class but still married to his wife of today. I told him the price for my silence was an assignment to whatever unit that was going to get into it right now. He's scared to death of his wife so here I am, shipmate."

"It's good to see you."

"And what about you, flying again? How'd you pull that off?"

"I'd be happy to tell you but my story will wait for a cold beer at the club. How about it? It could be a long time before we see another beer."

"You're on. I'll meet you on the pier at 1800. Oh, I almost forgot. I have a letter for you." Tiny grinned at Bryan.

The door had barely closed when he opened the letter and began to read. She wanted him to know as soon as possible. Her new orders were to transfer in March, reporting for duty at the Aiea Heights Naval Hospital, Pearl Harbor, Hawaiian Islands. Bryan sat back in his chair, his eyes closed, the letter held lightly between his fingers.

Chapter Four

The Clash of Battle

Four Hundred miles southwest of Pearl Harbor, Task Force 17 received orders from the Flag staff to change course for the Solomon Islands. Their mission: attack the Japanese stronghold of Rabaul and support Allied landings on New Caledonia. On the 6th of March, 1942 the *Yorktown* rendezvoused with Task Force 11 and the U.S.S. *Lexington*. Sailing southwest across the wide expanse of the Pacific the men of the task force understood their mission. For the first time since the war began, U.S. carrier forces steamed in search of battle with the main Japanese Battle Fleet. To save Australia the Americans must blunt the enemy thrust southward. The fate of an entire continent might rest on the outcome of this mission.

Bryan found the attitude around the ship different from any of his previous cruises. Everyone knew this time they couldn't afford to lose. There weren't enough carriers. The loss of even one flattop might turn the tide of the Pacific war. A victorious Japanese Fleet might be able to gain a foothold in Australia. The American aviators realized this war could be lost.

The air wing flew very little during the transit south. At

dawn the combat air patrol launched to take up protective stations over the task force. SBD's from Scouting Three took off later each morning for their sector searches. Bombing Five polished their bombing skills by attacking a wooden sled towed behind one of the destroyers. Intelligence briefings to the aircrews covered subjects from Japanese capabilities to the dangers of the tropics.

One afternoon Bryan entered the ready room to check the plan of the day.

"Mr. Michaels," Abbott said in a voice louder than necessary.

"Yes, sir." Bryan saw there were a dozen squadron officers in the ready room.

"Why is it that your plane captains can't keep the oil wiped off the underside of our aircraft?" he said

"I'll brief them again, sir." Bryan knew the aircraft were clean. He had personally checked them all within the last hour.

"You mean you already briefed them and that's the best they can do?" Abbott glared at Bryan, looking for an answer.

"XO, I just checked the aircraft and they looked okay to me," Bryan said slowly.

"Then your standards need to improve, Mister Michaels. Do you read me?"

Bryan flushed and the other officers looked away, pretending to be occupied with other things. "Yes, sir," Bryan said quietly.

The door opened and Wally Short walked down the aisle between the high backed chairs.

"Afternoon, Skipper." Abbott's tone was cheerful and he grinned at the Commanding Officer.

"Hello, XO. Anything new from intel?"

"I was just going to call them but had to discuss a problem of aircraft cleanliness." Abbott glared at Bryan again.

"I heard the Japs landed on the north coast of New Guinea. The Admiral's staff is putting together a strike with *Lexington* going after the naval units protecting the beach head." Short sat down in his designated chair and began to read from a clipboard of naval messages.

"I'll go see what I can find out." Abbott turned and walked toward the door. He stopped next to Bryan.

"Don't you have something to do, Michaels?"

"Yes, sir."

Wally Short stood in the front of the Ready Room. On the bulkhead behind him a chalk board listed aircraft assignments. A chart of New Guinea covered an adjacent cork board.

"The Japs have landed here at Lae and also here, Salamanua. There are naval units off shore at each location supporting the landing force. Our job is to get in there and sink as many of the ships as possible. The problem is the Jap airbase at Rabaul here on the tip of New Britain. Intelligence thinks there may be over one hundred combat aircraft on the island, about half fighters. That means we come in the back door." Short pointed to the chart. "We're gonna launch from here in the Gulf of Papua. That puts the Owen Stanley Mountain Range between Rabaul and us. It also means we have to fly over the mountains to get there. Some of those peaks go up to 10,000 feet and the weather is normally shitty. But that's the breaks of Naval Air." He proceeded to brief every aspect of the flight. He organized the squadron into three sections of five aircraft. Each aircraft carried a one thousand pound armor piercing bomb and full machine gun ammunition. Escort by *Yorktown*'s Wildcats from VF-42 would provide the needed fighter protection.

"Any word on Jap carriers, Skipper?" John Powers asked.

"Unlocated according to intel. So heads up. There're enough land based Zeros at Rabaul to make things interesting in any case. Also the Aussies are operating in the area, as well as the Air Corps. You might see anything from a P-40 to a B-17, so pay attention to your recognition rules. Okay, get your section briefings completed and be ready to man aircraft at 0715.

JJ Powers led the third section with Bryan in the number three position. During the short section brief, JJ made a specific point that they must press low for the most accurate hits. "If you're going to go to all the trouble of dropping your bomb at least make sure you hit something."

At 0710 the general announcing system came to life, "All pilots, man your aircraft." The Bombing Five aircrews headed for the ready room door, cloth helmets and navigation bags in their hands.

Climbing up the steel ladder to the flight deck seemed different to Bryan from the hundreds of times he'd made the same journey before. He tried to act relaxed and joined in the casual banter among the crews but this time they were launching to kill men and sink ships. *Don't screw this up, Michaels.*

Coming out of the hatch into the catwalk Bryan looked out across the water at *Lexington* and several destroyers. All ships were on the same course, steaming downwind with the relative wind almost zero. The tropical sun beat down on the flight deck as he walked aft, seeing his aircraft, 5-B-12, parked on the port side by the landing signal officer platform. Bill stood on the wing, checking his twin .30 caliber machine guns in the aft cockpit.

As Bryan climbed onto the wing he felt the *Yorktown* heel over to port. Task Force 17 slowly began to turn into the wind to launch combat sorties against the Imperial Japanese Navy. The sight of all the ships maneuvering in unison stirred Bryan. He looked up at the flags, now whipping in the strong wind. Stretched taut, the American flag vibrated with 30 knots of wind. Bryan remembered Admiral Nimitz and Tim Hutchins. *This is what it's all about.* Bryan knew then that he wouldn't want to be anywhere else in the world right now, regardless of what might happen. For a brief instant he thought about Liz but pushed the thought out of his head. He walked back to Bill Nance who had already strapped in the aft cockpit. He extended his hand.

"We're gonna do this, Bill. I'm glad you're with me."

"I wouldn't let ya go with anybody else."

The big Cyclone engine ran smoothly as Bryan completed his post start checks. Bryan hated waiting to launch. After finishing all checklists he looked up at the many spectators in "Vulture's Row." Officers and men, all anxious to watch the show, filled the catwalk on the side of the carrier's island.

The taxi director ran up to Bryan's plane captain signaling him to pull the wheel chocks. Simultaneously the director signaled Bryan to hold brakes. The young man leaned against the thirty knot wind coming directly down the flight deck. He looked at Bryan and directed "off brakes" by opening his clenched fists several times in succession. Leaning over, he checked Bryan's tail clearance then gave the taxi forward signal. Bryan came up slightly on the power until the aircraft began to move. He tapped the brakes but allowed the forward motion to continue. Following the director he moved to the center of the deck lining up on the painted guide line. As number two for launch he put his flaps down and rechecked the flight controls free.

The taxi director turned control over to the launch director who gave the full power signal. Bryan smoothly pushed the throttle up to 46 inches of manifold pressure, checking for 2600 rpm. The big radial was now roaring at full power, vibrating the entire airframe. Bryan checked oil pressure and cylinder head temperature, seeing both were within limits. He saluted the director, who touched the deck with his flag and 'Bravo-One -Two' began to roll down the deck.

Bryan watched the airspeed move off the zero indicator and noted 70 knots airspeed as they left the end of the flight deck, the Dauntless clawing for the sky. Only fifty feet above the waves, the bomber began to slowly climb. Wheels up, check instruments and climb straight ahead, Bryan told himself in a practiced routine. Now they had to locate the formation circling somewhere over the ship.

Ten minutes later they rendezvoused with their section. Two minutes after that JJ maneuvered the section in position behind Wally Short.

The dark blue of the Dauntless fuselages stood out against

70

the brilliance of the morning sky and the white clouds. Bryan checked his compass noting the course agreed with his pre-flighted heading to Lanla Point, the first point of land on their track to Salamanua. What waited for them at the target? Would they have to fight off Jap zeroes or would they catch the enemy by surprise?

At 15,000 feet the formation cruised toward New Guinea the Wildcats at 17,000 feet on both sides of the bombers. By direction the group maintained radio silence. For a moment Bryan wondered what thoughts were going on behind those other canopies? Were they scared or just anxious? Was he scared or anxious? All he knew was that he had never felt quite like this in an airplane.

Checking his navigation card Bryan estimated thirty five minutes until landfall. Looking ahead he glimpsed the first images of the large island, far in the distance.

"How're you doin' back there?"

"Wishin' I had a cup of coffee and a smoke," Bill answered.

"Looks like thirty minutes or so to the coast. Keep your eyes open, no telling where the Japs might come from."

Scattered cumulus clouds covered the southern slopes of the Owen Stanley Range. The mountains rose rapidly from the coastline and the dark green vegetation contrasted sharply with the brilliant blue of the sea. The bombers climbed slowly to 17,000 feet as they approached the crest of the mountains. Checking his navigation chart Bryan estimated fifty miles to Salamanua, fifteen minutes flying time. He felt his heart beat quicken. Bryan knew the importance of stopping the Japanese in New Guinea. If the Japs occupied the southern coast, including Port Moresby, they would have an operating base 200 miles from the Australian mainland. Isolate Australia and the balance in the Pacific could change quickly for the worse.

"Target area on the nose at ten miles, section leaders detach." Wally Short's transmission jolted Bryan out of his strategic thoughts. This was it! Individual sections would maneuver to roll in on targets at the leader's discretion. In the distance, twenty transports and warships floated at anchor off the shallow beach.

Bryan's section lined up on JJ's right wing. The other sections headed toward the anchored ships. Bryan felt the aircraft begin to descend. Quickly he checked his carb heat, bomb selector switch, gun charging switch and arming circuit for the bomb fuse. *What am I forgetting?* Distracted, Bryan had let the distance close on his lead. He hastily pulled the throttle back. Everything was happening very fast.

"Third section, we're going for the transports on the southern end of the beach," Powers transmitted.

Bryan tried to see what JJ was describing as he heard the other sections calling in on their targets. *What's happening now? We should be at the roll in.* Suddenly JJ rolled hard left, exposing a 1000 pound bomb shackled to the centerline rack of Power's Dauntless. At three second intervals the section followed their leader. *Don't screw up, Michaels.* He slammed the stick over and the big Dauntless rolled inverted.

"Here we go!" he yelled as he pulled the stick hard to complete his roll-in.

Dive brakes! I forgot the dive brakes! Shit. Bryan grabbed the lever and pulled hard feeling the aircraft slow as Nance's cadence began.

"16 thousand.......15 thousand......"

Bright muzzle flashes from the ships were followed by tracers floating past the bombers. *Level your wings!* A huge explosion rocked the northern most transport, debris flying out in a large circle around the doomed ship. Bryan fought the wind blowing them off target.

"8 thousand.....7 thousand...."

Come on damn it, come on. The pipper was now moving toward the target. *Too fast, too much correction. There that's it.*

"5 thousand.....4 thousand...."

Two more explosions erupted in the water near the transports but both missed the ships. Suddenly bright tracers arced across Bryan's line of vision from left to right. *Six seconds to release, I've gotta ignore the AAA.*

"Three thousand...."

The transport filled the telescopic scope. Bryan aimed for the center of the Jap transport. He checked the trim to make sure his wings were still level.

"Two thousand."

Bryan pushed the bomb release and pulled back hard on the stick with both hands. Slowly the nose rose toward the horizon, the G forces driving him into the seat. Struggling to hold his head up he saw three Jap ships directly in front of him. He slammed the throttle to full power and stopped his climb.

Gun flashes twinkled from the anchored ships and he watched the lazy red arcs of tracers come directly at them.

"Those sons of bitches," he yelled as he banked slightly left lining the fuselage up on the center transport. He fired the two .50 caliber machine guns in the wings, adjusting his aim using the tracer rounds spaced every five bullets. Bryan let the stream of tracers walk over the deck and superstructure of the transport, seeing pieces of debris fly off the ship.

The Dauntless raced past the ship and Bryan pulled hard to the right then reversed as tracers arced over their canopy. Still at full power he took the bomber down to 25 feet, tracking north across the blue green choppy water. Two minutes later he began a climb away from the water. Taking deep breaths he felt his pulse begin to slow. *We made it.*

During the pullout he'd heard the twin .30's open up from behind him. "Whaddya see?" he asked on the intercom.

"Hosing down Japs."

"Did you see our hit?"

"You nailed it. It's still burning back there."

"I've lost sight of the section, keep your eyes peeled."

"Rog."

He kept full power on the aircraft, taking a second to check oil pressure, engine temp and fuel. Everything looked good but there were no friendly aircraft in sight. Turning south he began climbing to 16,000 feet. Bill's words came back to him, "You nailed it."

"So you can confirm Lieutenant Powers hit the transport farthest from the beach?" The debriefing officer had sketched a diagram of the landing area and ships as pilots remembered them.

Bryan nodded. "Dead center. It must have been ammunition, the ship just came apart."

The return to the ship had been uneventful. Never able to find his squadron, Bryan joined on a flight from the *Lexington*. Once back near the Task Force they found *Yorktown* and made a safe recovery. They were the last aircraft to return.

The debriefing officers asked several more questions, and then allowed him to leave. Heading directly for the squadron maintenance office Bryan filled out his flight record and wrote a maintenance required chit on his starboard main landing gear. A severe cut required replacing the tire. Finally he arrived at the ready room.

"It's about time you got back," Tony Abbott said as Bryan walked into the room.

Bryan decided to say nothing and walked over to JJ Powers. "Great hit, JJ."

"Thanks. Just gotta get low enough that you can't miss." Powers grinned at him. "It looked like you got a hit but I lost sight during the rendezvous."

"I think I got the one closest to the beach," Bryan said.

Tim Fallon walked over and said quietly, "Better knock it off. The ordnancemen found the XO's arming wire gone when he landed. He dropped his bomb on safe and he is *pissed*."

The three officers moved over to the coffee pot and poured cups from the thermos jug.

The after action report noted of the fifteen attack runs by Bombing Five, there were five hits on naval vessels in the Salamanua area. It went on to note that of the fifteen aircraft only one dropped its bomb safe.

According to U.S. Fleet Intelligence, the Imperial Japanese Fleet had retired north to rearm and refit. The *Yorktown*, constantly underway since Pearl Harbor, took the opportunity to drop anchor in a sheltered bay in the Tonga Islands. *Yorktown* and her air group had been pushed hard for the last three months. This brief respite would allow for critical maintenance on the ship and squadron aircraft.

Training lectures and tactics discussion filled the days at anchor. During meetings JJ continued to stress the need to press the target for accuracy. His direct hit on the last mission drove his point home to every one of the pilots.

As the days passed, the intelligence picture began to indicate the Japanese intended to land on the southern coast of New Guinea and seize Port Moresby. A successful landing would consolidate Japan's strategic position from the Solomons to the Dutch East Indies cutting Australia off from the east and the west.

American commanders predicted this campaign would bring out the Jap carriers. During recent battle the Japanese used land based aircraft to cover their thrusts south. This tactic allowed them the luxury of not risking their most important capital ships. Now they had no choice. In response, the *Yorktown* prepared to get underway.

Bombing Five and Torpedo Five pilots went over ship recognition every day. The tactical plan involved using the SBD's from Scouting Five to locate the main battle fleet, then launch a combined strike with bombs and torpedoes. Fighting Forty Two would provide protection from the Japanese Zeros but no one had any illusions about the capability of their Wildcats against the Jap Zeros. The rugged Wildcat could take a lot of damage but couldn't climb or turn against the Zero.

Everyone on *Yorktown* sensed the impending battle when she weighed anchor from Tongatabu at the end of April.

Bryan stood in the hangar bay of *Yorktown* looking out toward the bright blue sea. Small white crests topped the swells as a wind blew from the southwest. The crisp sea air provided a welcome change from the humidity of the anchorage.

He needed some fresh air, having just heard in the ready room that the Japs had landed on two islands in the Solomons: Tulagi and Gavutu. The strike against the landing force was scheduled for tomorrow morning. A steady vibration from the engines gave the ship a feeling of life as she surged north at almost 28 knots.

"What's the word?"

Bryan turned to see Bill Nance beside him. "Strike in the morning against some Jap ships that just landed on a couple of islands up north."

Nance stood there looking out at the rapidly passing ocean. "Any word on Jap carriers?"

"Nothing specific. But you gotta think they wouldn't be trying something this far south of Rabaul without some kind of air cover."

"You're probably right. But I'll let the Admiral worry about that. I'm gonna head down below before the chow line backs up to the foc'sle." Nance turned to leave.

"Hey, Bill. Get some sleep tonight. Tomorrow's gonna be a big one."

The tall Texan grinned. "You do the same."

Early next morning the Air Group attacked ships off the landing beach and enemy forces on the islands. On the first strike Scouting Five's aircraft dropped on several warships in the harbor at Tulagi. All of the bombers had problems with their windscreens and telescopic sights fogging up during the dives from cooler upper air to the humid heat at release altitude. The second strike, led by Wally Short, attacked a Jap destroyer with undetermined results. Later in the day three smaller patrol craft were sunk along with some troop barges. Three *Yorktown* aircraft did not return. Bryan and Bill flew on the last strike, attacking ground targets on Tulagi. Everyone on the ship continued to wonder where the Japs were?

Chapter Five

A Piece of History

After a night of fitful sleep, pilots began trickling into the ready room at 0400. Despite the practiced nonchalance of the young aviators, a level of tension ran through the room. Bryan walked down to the ready room at 0415. Cigarette smoke hung over the compartment when he opened the door to see six pilots already in their chairs. Pouring a cup of coffee he walked over and sat down next to JJ Powers.

"Couldn't sleep?" the senior pilot asked.

"Not much," Bryan replied. "Anything going on?"

Powers shook his head. "They're gonna launch the scouts and CAP when the sun comes up. That's about it for now."

The two men sat in silence. In the background quiet conversations between the other pilots added to an atmosphere of camaraderie.

"How's Taylor holding up?" Powers asked.

Bryan thought about his roommate. The pressure of combat and flying off the ship had transformed the former football player.

"He's doing okay." That said a lot in the demanding world of carrier flying.

By 0445, men in flight suits, smoking cigarettes and drinking coffee filled the ready room seats.

At dawn the early combat air patrol launched along with a

group of aircraft from Scouting Five. Across the empty ocean, aircraft searched for the enemy they knew sailed against them.

Two hours later crews remained on alert in the Ready Room, the long wait beginning to take a toll on their energy.

"All right, listen up." Wally Short finished reading a note from the duty officer and stood up at the front of the ready room. "One of the guys from Scouting Five radioed that he spotted two carriers and several other warships about 180 miles north of us. That must be the Jap main body moving down with the Port Moresby landing force. We'll go with the lineup from last night. *Lexington* is launching first and we'll be right behind her. Keep your heads on a swivel. There'll be Zeros out there today so be ready. Good luck and good bombing."

Grabbing helmets and life vests, the crews stood up, stretched and headed toward the door. The lack of normal preflight banter told the story, everyone knew this could be the big action they had been waiting for since December 7th.

The launch and rendezvous were completed without incident. Over the last two months the ship and air wing had become a well trained team and now they were ready to face the ultimate test.

Bryan maneuvered 5-B-12 to their assigned position in the last section. Lieutenant Commander Bill Burch, skipper of Scouting Five, led the formation. The Bombing Five aircraft were strung out behind him. As the large group leveled at 15,000 feet, Bryan checked his instruments. He noted oil pressure at the bottom of the acceptable limit.

"Bill, oil pressure's hanging right at 20 psi."

"Hell, I checked all the maintenance records this morning. Nothing in there about an oil problem." Nance sounded genuinely angry.

During a peacetime mission, they would immediately head back to the *Yorktown* for a precautionary landing. "I'll keep an eye on it." If they lost their engine a hundred miles from the ship, particularly during combat, no one was going to come looking for them. But all other engine instruments look good, at least for now.

Bryan scanned the eight day clock in the instrument panel. His dead reckoning navigation put them fifteen minutes from where the Japs were supposed to be when they launched. At flank speed the enemy ships might have traveled twenty or thirty miles from their last reported position. Here the experience and talent of the squadron commanders made the difference. Intelligence could only do so much. Finding the enemy and attacking their ships depended on the men in the cockpits. Jap carriers, Bryan thought, this is really it. Those are the same ships that attacked Pearl, who killed Tim and now we've got a chance to hit back. He thought back to his first mission against the ships off New Guinea, he was scared then but wouldn't admit it to himself. This time he was angry.

The common frequency for the U.S. attack began to come alive indicating *Lexington*'s air group had started their attack. Some of the calls were routine, while occasionally there would be a call for someone to break left or right. Bryan could make out a dark smudge on the horizon which might be smoke. Fifteen miles on the nose the Jap Fleet waited for them.

The radio crackled with calls from the *Lexington*'s aircraft. A desperate call for one of the aircraft to 'break left' told everyone the Jap fighters were involved.

"Heads up, Bill. I can see a ship smoking up ahead." He pushed the throttle up as the formation accelerated toward the melee. Bryan put his goggles down and completed his pre-attack checklist and checked the arming circuit closed. That bomb will kill Japs he thought grimly.

Short began to maneuver his aircraft and the other sections followed suit. Beneath them a Japanese aircraft carrier steamed at high speed, black smoke rising from flames on the flight deck. Black puffs of anti-aircraft fire burst overhead the carrier, fired by destroyers trying to protect the wounded ship. It was time to pay back for Pearl.

"Bombing Five's rolling in......" Wally Short's radio call alerted the following sections to be ready. Less than a minute later

Bryan watched JJ's wing come up as he rolled over into his dive. In smooth succession the next four aircraft followed. Bryan took a deep breath and pulled the stick back slightly then pushed it hard to the left.

"Here we go…." As the world rolled around him he caught a full view of the blazing carrier against the blue water, its curving wake evidence of its desperate attempt to avoid the bombs raining down from the Americans.

As they rolled wings level in the dive, the aircraft was buffeted by a AAA burst, slewing them to the right. *Shit. Overcorrect hard left, have to track the carrier.* Red tracers floated up from the inferno below and he could see two bombers to his left, both trying to compensate for the high speed of the enemy ship.

Suddenly Bill's .30 caliber machine guns opened up in short bursts. *Altitude, shit what's my altitude.* 11 thousand….*are my wings level?…track left you son of a bitch….* Flaming red tracers flew over their left wing and canopy. *Christ someone's behind us….*"BILL…..BILL…you got em?"……..*Keep tracking….*6 thousand…..A huge explosion on the forward part of the flight deck….*aim for the center….aim for the center.*

"Got 'em!" Nance yelled on the intercom.

The crosshairs were directly in the flames of the Jap carrier's flight deck when Bryan depressed the bomb release. One thousand pounds of high explosive plummeted toward the target. Pulling with all his might he fought the g forces during pullout, sweat streaming into his eyes, he blinked the burning away looking left and right for his section. Two SBD's were climbing off to his left. *Must be JJ.* Scanning the sky for enemy aircraft he pulled hard and put his nose on Power's aircraft.

"What happened back there?" he asked Bill, trying to catch his breath.

"The son of a bitch must have figured he could get tail end Charlie. He was fast and started to over shoot. As soon as he pulled his nose up I cut loose in his belly. Must have hit a fuel tank, he just blew up."

"I owe you one, buddy. Keep your eyes open. I'm sure there're more of 'em out here."

Small groups of aircraft rendezvoused and began the return trip to the *Yorktown* and *Lexington*.

Following a debrief with the ship's intelligence office, Bryan returned to the ready room to find that the *Neosho*, a tanker, and the *Sims*, her destroyer escort, had been sunk that morning by aircraft from another Jap carrier group. The elation from today's battle rapidly changed to concern about the other Jap carrier.

"Skipper, any idea what the plan is?" JJ Powers asked as Wally Short came in the ready room door.

The pilots looked toward Short who walked over to the large chart of the surrounding area.

"We think there're two more carriers in this general area." He circled an area on the chart with his finger over two hundred miles north of *Yorktown*'s current position. "Looks like a repeat of today. The scouts and CAP will launch at dawn, everyone else will be in ready alert. We'll plan on the same lineup as today. Why don't we get together for a brief at 2100. Ops, get the word out to all aircrews. Duty officer, have the Maintenance Officer come see me in my stateroom."

Bryan sat in the third row of seats. He watched the reaction across the room. Most of the pilots went back to what they were doing. Abbott, looking agitated, got up and walked to the door. Something is bothering him, Bryan thought.

The 2100 brief mirrored Short's brief from that morning. With little hard intelligence, everyone understood they had to be flexible and react to unfolding intelligence.

As the brief finished JJ Powers called his division together.

"Like I said earlier, good job by everyone today. Let's do it again tomorrow. If there are two carriers, count on more air opposition. Keep your gunners on their toes. Nance knocked down a Zero today who attacked during the bomb run. Watch out for that. The crazy bastards are willing to fly into their own triple A to get a shot at us. And remember the lower you pickle the fewer chances for release errors. I'm gonna put my bomb right in a Jap flight deck tomorrow, whatever it takes. There are folks counting on us and I'm not letting them down."

Bryan remembered Nimitz's words. They had to hold the Japs to give the country and Navy time to build up. Tomorrow this small group of men had to do the job. In some ways it made it easier to look at it that way. Don't worry about next week or next month. Your job is to sink those Jap carriers, nothing else matters. He looked over at Bud Taylor watching JJ go over his roll-in technique. The young officer looked much older than he did when they first met. But as he looked around the ready room, he realized everyone did. *I wonder if I do?*

Bryan walked under the red lights of the *Yorktown*'s hangar bay. Mechanics climbed on the aircraft, getting them ready for tomorrow's strike. The occasional white light from a flashlight flashed as an inspector checked the work for completeness. On several of the Wildcats ordnance men overhauled the .50 caliber Browning machine guns. 5-B-12 sat on the starboard side aft. Several mechanics stood by the nose. He recognized Petty Officer Gardner, the leading mechanic on the night shift.

"How's she looking?" he asked Gardner.

"Hi, Mr. Michaels. We're checking out that low oil pressure reading."

"Just as soon not have to think about that tomorrow," Bill Nance called from the pilot's seat.

Bryan watched as they worked a small rotary pump attached to an extra length of pressure tubing.

"What's it read now?" Gardner called up to Nance.

"About 28 psi, nah make that 29."

Garner turned to Bryan. "Looks like it's just a bad indicator. We'll put in a new gauge and run an op test. You'll be okay for tomorrow."

Bryan thanked him and stood back while Nance climbed out

of the cockpit and made his way down to the deck.

"Better get some sleep. Looks like a 0430 brief for tomorrow's strike."

Bill Nance stuck his hands into his dungaree pockets. "Hell, I never sleep much anyway, it's too damn hot in berthing. I oughta get a pillow and go sleep in the catwalk."

The two men stood watching the mechanics work on their aircraft. Over the main announcing system they heard the tinny voice call, "Taps, Taps, now lights out. The smoking lamp is out. All hands turn in to your bunks, now taps." Bryan always thought it unusual to hear the traditional "taps" call on an aircraft carrier where men worked around the clock. But naval traditions went back for hundreds of years and a war or advances in technology wouldn't change that. He wasn't sure why but that made him feel good, to be part of something bigger than the individual. Remembering the old phrase "...Men who go down to the sea in ships...," Bryan knew that someday these battles would be part of history.

"Guess I'll try to get some sleep," Bryan said.

"Think I'll go down to the mess deck and write a letter. Know my folks would like to hear from me. But hell, I don't know what to say. The censors will cut out anything about what we're doing and I can't think of much else to tell em."

Bryan smiled at Nance. "Bill, tell them what you had for dinner. Parents don't care what you say. They just want to get a letter."

The young gunner walked away. "Think my mom would understand "shit on a shingle?""

Bryan laughed and headed for his stateroom. He'd sent a letter to his father after the encounter with Admiral Nimitz and transfer to Bombing Five. The reply sat in the small safe above his desk. He would never forget the short but powerful words from his dad: "....no father has ever been more proud of a son. No matter what this war brings, never forget that."

Bryan opened the door to find Bud Taylor at his desk. The

young pilot hunched over a pad of paper, his fountain pen scratching furiously down the page.

"You're a good man. I wish I was as good about writing."

"Amy didn't want me to join the Navy. She really didn't want me to go to flight school and she doesn't want me over here. Guess I'm just trying to keep our marriage on track until I can get home." The big man grinned at Bryan. "It wouldn't hurt you to write your nurse either."

The letter from Liz sat next to the one from his father. She'd written it just prior to her departure on an Army transport for Pearl Harbor. In those two thin pages she told Bryan that she couldn't wait to see him again. He felt the same way about her, but so much had happened since those days with her in Bremerton. He realized the chances of surviving a long drawn out war as a carrier aviator were not good. The possibility of having a future with Liz clashed with the reality of flying combat. Suddenly it became very important to him to write her a letter in case something happened to him tomorrow. Even if they never saw each other again he wanted her to know how he felt, what could have been. Too dramatic, he asked himself? That may be all we ever have, he thought. He reached for his stationary box and pulled out a sheet of paper. "7 May, 1942. My Dearest Liz....."

The launch had been a hurried affair. A radio transmission from a *Lexington* scout pinpointed the Jap task force at 0815. Two larger carriers and their escorts were 200 miles north of Task Force 17. Immediately the Admiral ordered a combined strike launched from both *Yorktown* and *Lexington*. Racing to their aircraft, the aircrews knew the Japs would be launching their own strike also. The first aircraft left the two American flight decks at 0831.

Today, Bryan's oil pressure gauge worked perfectly. Flying in the number two slot behind JJ Powers, the clear blue skies and a calm ocean reminded Bryan of flying off San Diego. Flying combat would never be routine but today it felt like they'd been doing this for a long time. Bill Nance had been in a good mood, wise-cracking during the rendezvous and outbound leg to the target.

Scouting Five again led the *Yorktown* air group. Bombing Five cruised a mile in trail, flying 500 feet above the lead squadron. Proceeding north, Bryan began to see cloud buildups and isolated rain squalls. He realized they would be fighting the weather looking for the Japs while the *Lexington* and *Yorktown* were in the clear.

At 1030 Bryan heard the first excited radio calls. Through the clouds Scouting Five had spotted one of the Jap carriers. They were commencing their attack. Within a minute the radio transmissions from the fighters told everyone there were Zeros in the air.

"You heard that last call. Watch out for the bastards." Bryan knew he didn't have to warn Bill Nance but it helped him focus on the job at hand. Quickly he went through the cockpit making sure all switches were set correctly. He felt his pulse quicken as they closed with the enemy. Flying formation on Powers he could only look away for an instant but a quick glance revealed multiple layers of clouds peppered with rain squalls surrounding the squadron. Bad bombing weather but it could keep the Zeros off them.

As they flew into an open area the flight was immediately taken under fire by ships in a formation below them. Black bursts of fire began to appear around the flight. Bryan heard the radio call "Zeros!" as Bill Nance opened up with his machine guns. He pushed the throttle to full power to stay with Powers who was maneuvering left and right looking for a spot in the sky to commence the attack. Tracers crisscrossed the sky in front of Bryan as Japanese fighters began their attacks on the first flights.

Looking left, Bryan saw two Zeros attacking their division, the red meatball on their wings and fuselages bright against the clouds. "Bill, check left wing, now."

Their aircraft shuddered as Nance poured fire at the two fighters. Bryan saw pieces of metal flying off Power's aircraft as JJ began the attack . *Oh shit!* He heard a muffled radio transmission from JJ, "Bravo Four, we're hit...in......" The damaged Dauntless rolled and pointed its nose at the ocean.

After a two second delay, Bryan pushed the stick hard left, matching Powers dive. As the horizon spun across his windscreen, he searched for JJ below him. Tracers flew past the canopy and he slammed the control stick to the right, bringing the bomber upright, it's nose now 70 degrees down, pointing directly at the Jap carrier.

He felt the sickening impact of bullets hitting the fuselage as the scarlet red patterns of anti-aircraft tracers rose to meet them. He saw the Jap carrier was steaming at high speed in formation with her escorts. The flight deck remained unmarred by fires or damage. He saw several planes parked next to the island. Anti-aircraft fire from the ships increased as they dove toward their target. *You bastards....11* thousand...*there's JJ in front and slightly left...dive angle....75degrees...9* thousand....behind him Bill's machine guns were firing almost constantly... *aim for the center....7* thousand................*there's JJ........he's too damn low.....pull....5* thousand....*track.........you.........bastard...............track..3* thousand ....*pickle.....pickle....now pull.*

A huge explosion from the forward part of the flight deck filled Bryan's windscreen and in a brief instant he saw JJ's Dauntless crash into the water alongside the Jap carrier, a giant plume of water marking the impact. The carrier filled his field of vision and Bryan knew he'd waited too long.

With every bit of his strength he pulled back on the stick. The g forces crushed him into the seat as he waited for the impact, his mind knowing they were about to die. Miraculously the aircraft bottomed out 200 feet above the water. Instinctively Bryan pulled hard right then left as tracers flew around the aircraft. Sweat streamed down his face and he felt his heart pounding in his chest. Staying low to avoid Zeros he made sure the dive brakes were in and pushed the throttle as far forward as it would go.

"Bill. Bill........you okay?"

"Yeah."

"Let's get out of here......you see anybody?"

"Other than Japs? No......"

Bryan saw a rain squall two miles ahead and pointed the

Dauntless directly for the grey mass of water and clouds where the Zeros couldn't find them.

Five minutes later they were enclosed in the clouds, rain drumming off the windscreen. His heart had slowed its pounding and he took time to assess their situation. Despite the bullet hits, the big radial engine purred smoothly, oil and hydraulic pressure were good. He didn't like the fuel total but he would use the most economical throttle setting on the return flight. The vision of Power's final dive came back to him. His friend did just what he said he would, he put one right into the Jap flight deck.

The aircraft broke into the clear and Bryan quickly scanned the sky. He saw one aircraft ahead and well below him but it looked like a Dauntless not a Zero. Pushing the throttle forward, he dove rapidly on the stranger. The side number read 5-B-2, Abbott's aircraft. The XO had been leading the second division but there were no other aircraft in sight. Whether he liked the son of a bitch or not, procedure called for Bryan to join on Abbott and make the return flight to *Yorktown* together.

300 yards out, still descending through thin clouds, Bryan saw a flash and a lone Zero slide in behind Abbott. The enemy pilot didn't see Bryan.

"Break left, XO. Break left." Abbott's aircraft slewed left in response to Bryan's warning. The Zero pulled hard, bleeding off airspeed in an attempt to maintain a firing position on Abbott. The lead Dauntless's gunner opened up and Bryan saw his opportunity. As the Zero pulled left after Abbott, Bryan viciously rolled the bomber to 90 degrees angle of bank and pulled back as hard as he could. Fighting to hold his head up he saw the Jap firing at a violently twisting Abbott. Bryan closed to 100 yards behind the Zero who still didn't see him....I'll ram the son of a bitch if I have to, he thought as he pushed the firing button. The airframe shuddered he watched his tracers converge on the Zero. Pieces began to break away from the fuselage and the left wing erupted in flames. Bryan kept the button depressed watching the bullets tear into the cockpit. Suddenly the port wing snapped off and the Zero cart-wheeled into the ocean. His guns empty, Bryan pulled up, looking for the other Dauntless.

Abbott was turning left toward a cloud bank. Bryan turned to set up a rendezvous. "Bring it right, XO. I'll join."

"Roger.......thanks."

Straining to see Abbott in the light rain, Bryan knew he could join up before they went into the clouds. He pulled the power back slightly, not wanting to overshoot as he joined up. Suddenly the cockpit began to disintegrate around him. A roar from the wind stream told him the canopy had been shattered. For a moment he froze in panic and confusion. Nance's voice sounded far away saying something he couldn't understand. He felt his hand on the stick and looked down at the instrument panel. Panic grabbed him again, he couldn't see the panel.... frantically Bryan put his hand to his face. His goggles were gone and his helmet torn.

"Bill, can you hear me.....I can't see.....Where are my wings?" He screamed in the intercom as panic overcame him, the world now blurred. He sensed light and dark areas but no detail. Wind whipped through the broken Plexiglas canopy.

"Bryan, pull the nose up....pull your nose up...there...that's it.....you're left wing down...okay that's good...hold that....can you HOLD that?"

"Yeah....yeah....hold on...just a minute....."

"Bryan, I'll rig the stick back here...do you hear me? I'll rig the stick back here."

The Dauntless could be flown from the back cockpit and many pilots spent hours teaching their gunners to fly.

"Where's the Jap that got us?" he asked, trying to keep from panicking – he still couldn't see the instrument panel.

"Hold on a second. We're in and out of the layers, I don't see anyone. XO either. okay, I got the stick set back here."

"Just hold the wings level. What's our altitude?"

"Thirty eight hundred feet."

"Just give me a minute...watch the altitude....don't go any lower....and watch for the Jap."

"Okay….okay."

The Dauntless flew on for several minutes, neither man saying a word.

"How about the compass heading?" Bryan asked, his panic now under control. He had formed a navigation plot in his mind and had a plan. They would head back to the area of the task force and bail out. He couldn't ditch with his eyes injured and although Bill could fly the Dauntless, trying to ditch one in the open ocean from the back seat was impossible.

"Looks like 167 degrees."

"All right, that's okay for now. Let's check out everything else and see where we stand." Bryan told himself to calm down. He had to keep fighting the panic trying to wrest control of the aircraft away from them. *Take your time, think things through, you can do this.* Removing his flying gloves, he gingerly felt around his eyes. His face was sticky with blood. A dull ache came from his thigh but he ignored it.

"I've got a big problem back here." Bill said. "A round missed me but tore the hell out of my chute. Don't think I'll be using that today."

"Let's get back to the ship and we can get someone to join on us." Bryan wasn't sure what help that would be but at least they'd have company. Emergencies airborne were always easier to handle with a wingman, if only for the moral support. "You're okay, right?"

"Yep, not a scratch. How about you?"

"My vision's still fucked up. I can see, but not enough to land. Think I took some shrapnel in the leg but it's not a problem."

"How was the bomb run? I was too busy to look." The tone in Nance's voice sounding very calm.

"It looked good. I saw Powers go in right next to the Jap carrier but he nailed her with his bomb, dead center on the flight deck." The loss of his friend started to sink in. Never any guarantees. "We should be far enough away from the Japs in ten minutes. I'll broadcast and see if we can pick up a wingman. Keep looking for the XO."

"Wilco."

"Shit," Bryan said in frustration. Keying the radio didn't produce a side tone. The radio was dead, probably a victim of the Jap attack.

Bill understood what the bad radio meant to them. "No lock on the beacon either." Nothing else to say, they had no way to home in on comrades or the ship. Now it was up to luck and flying a good search pattern.

"What time is it?" he asked Nance.

"1126."

"We've been on a rough course for the ship for about 45 minutes. That means the ship should be anywhere from 11 to 1 o'clock at 75 to 100 miles. We'll go for 40 minutes and then start an expanding search for the ship. What's the fuel right now?"

"Looks like 185 gallons between all tanks."

"That will give us about 45 minutes of searching once we hit the start point. We'll be fine. Just keep us on course." He kept blinking and his eyes continued to water but the vision did not improve. Putting his head back on the seat rest he closed his eyes and tried to relax, glad to have Bill Nance with him. The unknown was always easier to face with a friend by your side. Bryan had been in tough spots before. He knew about fear in a cockpit but in the past he'd been dealing with problems that he'd trained to face. It had been a matter of following procedures and staying focused. This situation had no answer. He wouldn't bail out and leave Nance. His vision wouldn't allow him to ditch the aircraft and Bill couldn't see enough from the backseat. Hell, even with perfect vision, ditching a Dauntless in the open ocean was difficult. Hitting the waves wrong and you might flip the aircraft over leaving both of you trapped underneath. Dig in a wing and you cartwheel, tearing the aircraft apart. Too steep an angle of descent and you dig the nose in stopping instantly and guaranteeing injury. Once back near the ship they must find another aircraft and join up. For now Bill could keep them on course and level but if they found anyone, he'd never done an airborne rendezvous. *Shit.*

"Bryan, it's 1212."

"Let's start a turn 90 degrees to port and we'll hold that for ten minutes."

Nance replied, "All right, coming port 90."

Bryan felt the aircraft begin a slow bank to the left and saw the shadows from the sun shifting.

"Aw crap. We got another problem," Nance said.

"What's that?"

"The compass card isn't turning. It still says 167."

The terrible reality of their situation came to Bryan. For the last hour, they had covered 200 miles and now didn't know what direction they'd been flying. Directly overhead, the sun gave them no indication of direction. Where were they and where were their ships? "Start a slow left turn and let's think about this." What in the hell was there to think about? They were running out of gas, couldn't bail out or ditch and didn't know where they were.

The two didn't say anything for five minutes.

"Tell ya what. Let's get you out of here using your chute. I think I can put this down all right. Just talk me through it a couple of times like you did at San Clemente when we practiced landings."

Bryan knew he would never abandon his friend. Everyone had to die sometime. Why not now, he couldn't be in better company.

"We're about out of options, Bill. But I ain't gonna leave you here and that's that. We either make it together or not at all."

"Got any ideas?"

"Take a look at the sea state. What's it look like?" Bryan knew they had to go for broke.

"Pretty damn flat. Looks like Lake George in August."

"I think we try to make Dauntless history. You're gonna ditch this baby from the back seat."

"You tell me what to do and I'll give it a try."

92

"Okay, let me tell you everything I know about ditching. Then we'll go over the procedures as many times as we need. When you're ready, we go."

The Dauntless indicated 35 gallons of fuel when the two men decided to go for broke. Canopies were locked open and Bill jettisoned the .30 calibers over the side. Bryan checked his life vest over for any tears. Both men tightened their straps as much as possible.

"Bill, thanks for sticking with me. It means a lot."

"Ya know, I think the two of us always were a pretty good team."

"You ready?"

"Yeah."

Slowly the Dauntless descended toward the brilliant blue sea.

"What's your rate of descent?"

"300 feet per minute."

"Okay good. Check the pitch full forward."

"We're good."

The wheels were remaining up in accordance with the Bureau of Aeronautics procedures for the SBD-3.

"Can you make out the direction of the swells?" he asked Nance.

"Yeah. Ain't big, and they're pretty uniform."

"Remember we want to land parallel to the swells."

Bill sounded terse. "I gotta turn about 30 degrees to starboard"

"Go slow and don't let that rate of descent increase while you turn." Bryan felt helpless but the aircraft continued to fly smoothly, a good indicator Bill had all of the parameters under control."

"What's our altitude?"

"Passing 400 hundred feet."

"Airspeed?" Bryan asked.

"85 knots."

"Put in a little nose up trim and pull a little power. We're looking for 75 knots."

"Okay, speed's coming down, passing 200 feet."

Bryan's heart pounded in his chest. "Remember to hold the nose up. Add a little power if you have to. Don't let the nose fall through."

The last thing Bryan remembered was Nance yelling, "Hold on!"

Chapter Six

The Long Road Back

The Battle of the Coral Sea proved significant for several reasons. For the first time in warships fought a major naval engagement without sighting each other. In addition, the Japanese abandoned their attempt to attack further south toward Australia. The United States lost the *Lexington* and the *Yorktown* received damage serious enough to require a return to Pearl Harbor for repairs. The Japanese lost a light carrier, the *Soho*, but no other capital ships. Carrier aviators from both navies paid a high price and the carriers returned with many missing aircraft and empty staterooms.

Lieutenant (junior grade) Bryan Michaels and Petty Officer William Nance were listed as "Missing in action, presumed dead." Navy units, including long range PBY's, searched the Coral Sea after the battle looking for survivors. While a number of aviators, both American and Japanese, were found, Michaels and Nance were not among them.

Lieutenant Lee Cordner, Royal Australian Naval Reserve leaned back on the after bridge railing of ML 828, a fast patrol boat of the Fairmile class. Outbound from Cairns on a deep penetration mission, the 80 foot boat cruised at 18 knots across the gently rolling sea. Below decks a four man team from the Army prepared for their landing in a small bay on the southeastern tip of New Guinea. The team would serve a dual function as both air and sea surveillance of the northeastern coast of New Guinea. Combined headquarters wanted as much advance warning of any Japanese air or naval activity which might threaten the flank of their ground forces opposing the Japanese on the northern coast of the island.

If the sea state remained calm, Cordner estimated they would be able to drop the team under cover of darkness about 0300 the next morning. Although there hadn't been much Jap air activity lately, you could never dismiss the possibility of a long range air patrol coming out of Rabaul. A Fairmile could give a good account of herself against the bombers, but fighters provided the greatest threat. In the previous year ML 828 had survived three air attacks. Two months ago they had been jumped by two Zeros south of Woodlark Island. Japanese cannon fire killed two of Lee's gunners manning the Oerlikon.

The sun neared its zenith as the crew prepared to take over the 12-1600 watch. Sub-lieutenant Harry Owen, Lee's Number One, would relieve as the Officer of the Deck. Although underway meals on a Fairmile were never anything to write home about, today the cook was making one of his better entrees, lamb stew.

"Object in the water, fine off the port bow," Petty Officer Lorton called from the small raised platform used by the lookouts.

Grabbing his glasses, Lee walked to the port side of the bridge and scanned with his naked eye. He picked up a small yellow object perhaps 2000 yards out. "Slow ahead, both engines. Port 15, steer 340," he yelled down the brass voice pipe.

The commands were echoed back from the wheel house. Simultaneously the hull slowed in the water and began to come left. Harry Owen climbed up the ladder to the bridge.

"Morning, Skipper."

"Morning, Number One. We've got something on the bow at 1000 yards. It looks like a raft. Grab a couple of the lads and be prepared to recover survivors. And Harry, could be Nips, don't take any chances."

"Aye, sir."

The two men sat opposite each other in the raft, their bodies swaying together in response to the swells. Neither had slept during the night but both now dozed as the sun climbed high overhead them.

Bryan's thoughts, conscious and unconscious kept returning to the ditching. Bill's frantic warning followed by the jolting crash, web straps cutting into his body as he slammed forward in the seat. The smell of burning oil from the big radial engine as it stopped instantly, tearing itself apart. Bryan remembered the panic he felt as he desperately struggled to free himself from the seat and the parachute that would drag him into the depths. His blurred vision, water pouring into the cockpit and feeling Bill's hands on his shoulders pulling him out of the cockpit and inflating his mae west. The dreams continued as the ocean rocked them back into a drowsy sleep.

Bryan woke first, the sound of engines coming across the waves.

"Bill......listen." Both men lifted their heads from the rubberized fabric. "Those are engines."

Nance looked over Bryan toward the direction of the noise. "It's a patrol boat."

Whose patrol boat, Bryan wondered? Although it didn't matter at this point. In an open raft, without food or water, if they weren't picked up soon......

"Bill, if it's Japs..."

"I can see 'em. Looks like Aussies," Nance almost shouted.

"Stop both engines." Lee Cordner stood at the starboard side of the bridge, looking down alongside the hull. A sailor tossed a line which uncoiled as it flew through the air and dropped across the center of the rubber raft between the two survivors. The dungarees on one man and the life vests told Lee he had two Americans, probably off an aircraft carrier. "Lend a hand there. Let's get them aboard, Number One. Pick up the raft too."

His men leaned down, two sailors each grabbing a survivor.

"Aye, sir," Owen called back.

Cordner watched the two men hauled aboard. Both stood on the deck with water dripping off their soaked clothes. Two sailors pulled the two man raft aboard and carried it aft.

"Get them below," he called down to the deck. "All engines half ahead, set 18 knots. Starboard 15, steer course 025."

The rumble of the engines increased as the Fairmile smoothly accelerated in the turn.

Thirty minutes later Cordner went down to the small wardroom. Harry Owen had relieved him with the news they had an American Dauntless crew that had been in the water since yesterday. Although Cordner hadn't received any news, the Yanks had told them there had been a two day carrier battle in the Coral Sea. It sounded like the Americans had sunk at least one, maybe two Jap carriers. Lee knew the Japs were moving south and this must have been part of that campaign.

The two men sat at the small table, cups of water in their hands. Both were wearing skivvy shorts and undershirts, with blankets thrown over their shoulders. Their faces were sunburned and the officer had multiple scratches on his face. Petty Officer Hawthorne, who doubled as the boat's medical petty officer was applying antiseptic to the cuts.

Bryan's elation at being picked up by an Australian patrol boat was tempered by the pain in his left eye. Once in the raft he had kept his eyes closed most of the time. By sunrise he could make out Nance across the raft, despite the blurriness. Whenever he tried to look to his left a searing pain pierced his left eye. The Australian medic told him he would do his best to clean out the wounds but anything to do with the eyes was beyond his capability. Bryan heard a voice and turned toward the hatch.

"I'm Lee Cordner, the Skipper. My number one gave me some basic info but I'd like to hear it from you."

"Thanks for pulling us out. I'm not sure how long we would've lasted in that raft," Bryan said.

"Too right, I'm afraid. This is not the place to be in an open raft. If the sun doesn't get you, the sharks will."

"We're off the carrier *Yorktown*." Bryan continued to sip water as he covered the events, as he knew them, of the last two days."

Cordner interrupted, "So this Jap task force was 150 miles southeast of New Guinea?"

"That's where they were at noon yesterday," Bryan answered. "Why?"

"We're headed toward the southern tip of the island to drop off some army chaps. I'd prefer not to run into the bloody Jap fleet." Cordner looked at Bill Nance, sitting quietly on the bench. "You look none the worse for wear. Are you all right?"

"Yes, sir. Happy to be dry and I may not stop drinking water til we get to port."

"We should be back in Cairns within three to four days unless we get another mission. No worry for you, just relax and enjoy the trip." Cordner grinned at Bill.

"Yes, sir."

"We're going close inshore early tomorrow morning to drop off the diggers. After that we head for home. If you're up to it, I'll have one of my lads give you the grand tour, you might find it interesting. Let us know if you need anything."

Bryan and Bill Nance accompanied Harry Owen to the bridge as the sun began to set. Lee Cordner scanned the horizon through a set of glasses as they climbed up the ladder.

"Skipper, I've got a couple of Yank volunteers," Owen said.

Cordner turned. "Welcome, we've got a beautiful sunset for you to enjoy. Did you get the full tour?"

Bryan answered. "Quite a boat."

"The Brits have been in the motor torpedo business since the first war. We've been building our patrol forces for the last several years using their designs. The Fairmile is quite capable and perfect for working in the islands." Cordner hung his glasses on a hook under the forward bulkhead.

"I know our Navy's starting to build out the PT squadrons. Haven't seen them in person, most are still on our east coast," Bryan said.

Cordner leaned on the after rail. "Your chaps certainly tangled with the Nips in the Philippines. General MacArthur came part of the way south on one of your PT's. Sounded like all the boats finally bought it."

The stories of the last stand by the American forces in the Philippines in the face of overwhelming Japanese forces still bred anger in every Pacific Fleet sailor and Marine. Stories had been filtering out of the islands via the guerilla forces. The brutality of the Japanese Army made this war very personal for those who had friends left behind.

"That was a tough time for everyone. But we're starting to get even for the Philippines and Pearl Harbor."

The men stood on the deck watching the sun slowly move toward the horizon.

"Permission to come on the bridge?"

Bryan turned to see an Australian Army Lieutenant at the top of the ladder.

"Andy, come on up. Gentlemen, let me introduce Lieutenant Andy Harkins of the Queensland Rangers. Andy this is Lieutenant Bryan Michaels and Petty Officer Nance, late of the aircraft carrier *Yorktown*."

The tanned young man smiled and shook hands all around. "Pleasure to meet you."

"Andy's team will be going ashore tonight at a small bay near Papago Point. Bit of a nature trip if you know what I mean."

Bryan realized he meant they were going behind enemy

lines. "How long will you be out there?" he asked.

"Hard to say. We watch the Japs and try not to get snatched. A month or two I should expect."

"They'll stay as long as the cold beer holds out and the native women stay friendly," Lee joked.

"Most of the natives where we're going would just as soon eat you as look at you. But if you keep bringing us cold beer I'm sure we'd stay there for the duration."

The casual banter on such a deadly subject reminded Bryan of the ready room before a mission. Better to joke about the grim reality of war than let it get everyone down. He liked these two Aussies. With allies like this, he thought, it was just a matter of time before we beat the Japs.

Bryan stayed behind when the others left the bridge. He enjoyed talking with Cordner and wanted to learn more about the boat. The two men continued their conversation as the darkness enveloped them. Two sailors brought coats and mugs of tea. Lee talked about the 828 and his career in the Navy. After university in Sydney, Lee began working for a large Australian shipping company. With the war clouds over Europe he volunteered for the Naval Reserve and was assigned to a reserve unit. In 1939 he was activated and assigned to the new patrol squadrons that were being put together on the east coast. A year later he took command of 828 operating out of Cairns. Since the Japanese attack in 1941 the 828 had been operating in the Coral Sea. Most of their recent work had been in preparation to repel the possible invasion of the mainland.

"In a patrol boat I suppose it's a bit like an airplane. You're on your own. I couldn't stand the life on a big ship with the wardroom and formality. Here I know every member of my crew. We count on each other and do what has to be done. Nothing better, by my book."

"I know what you mean. An aircraft carrier is like a small city. You don't even know most of the people you see. The chain of command tells you a little piece of the puzzle and you function as part of a big machine."

"Tell you what, Bryan. Why don't you get some supper, take a rest and I'll have Harry bring you up when we drop Andy's people at Papago. It'll give you a chance to see what patrol boats can do."

"I'd like that very much, thanks."

When Bryan came on deck at 0200 a partial moon sat above the horizon. The Fairmile continued north at ten knots across a gentle swell. Looking ahead he could see a dark shoreline several miles away. The 40 millimeter Bofors and 20 millimeter Oerlikon guns were now manned by their gunners.

"Hello, Bryan. Just in time. That far point is Papago." He pointed at the land that jutted out off the port bow. "Just this side of the point is a small sheltered bay where we intend to drop Andy."

"So the bay's big enough to take the boat into?" Bryan asked.

"According to the chart we should have plenty of water under the keel. Small boat landings on open beaches are more difficult with the surf. The army chaps will be carrying a radio and there's less chance for a dunking."

The muffled engines were barely audible from the bridge. Bryan noticed that all lights were out and even conversations were quiet. A slight offshore breeze created a slight chop on the water's surface.

Harkins came up the starboard ladder, dressed in khaki shorts and shirt, devoid of insignia.

"Lee, all my gear is laid out on the fantail. How much longer?"

"Thirty to forty minutes, no more. Anything you need?" Lee asked.

"No Japs within thirty miles would be nice," Harkins replied.

Lee and Bryan laughed.

Land rose on both sides as the patrol boat crept into the dark

102

bay. Several hundred yards on the right, Bryan could make out a narrow beach. On the bow a sailor stood with a lead line taking soundings as 828 moved farther into the bay. Slowly the bow began to swing toward a small sandy strip where Bryan guessed the commandos would land.

"Stop both engines," Lee said quietly down the voice tube.

A minute later Bryan saw the working party on the fantail lower two black rubber rafts over the side. Several men began to hand containers down to two men who were now in the boats. Two more figures went over the side. In a moment the two rafts emerged into the open headed for the northern side of the bay. Lee and Bryan watched until the rafts disappeared into the night.

"Mission accomplished. Let's get out of here. Slow ahead both engines, port 30."

The moonlight's shadows shifted across the deck as Royal Australian Patrol Boat 828 steadied up and moved back toward open water.

A mile offshore Lee leaned down and said, "Half ahead both engines, set 15 knots. Steer 160." He turned to Bryan. "There you have it, patrol work at its finest." The Skipper raised his glasses and began to scan the horizon as they cleared the land on both sides.

"Contact off the starboard bow," the lookout behind said urgently.

Bryan looked to the right but saw nothing.

Cordner leaned over the voice tube, "Full ahead both engines. Close up action stations. Starboard 15 steer 170. Prepare to engage surface contact."

The Fairmile surged ahead and Bryan saw the gun crew on the foc'sle train the Oerlikon to the right.

"Target is a Jap patrol boat, open fire," Lee yelled at the crew on the bow. "Engage target as she bears," he yelled down the voice tube.

Harry Owen raced up the starboard ladder.

"Get back to the Bofors, Number One."

Owen disappeared. From the bow the rapid crack of the 20

103

millimeter pierced the night.

"Keep your head down, Bryan. If the Japper doesn't see us we may be all right.

Spray flew back toward the bridge as the Fairmile closed the Japanese vessel at full speed, the target now outlined by the moonlight.

The 20 millimeter continued to fire, tracers arcing through the night toward the target. Five seconds later the Japanese boat turned hard away from the 828. From the fantail the 40 millimeter Bofors began to fire. Bryan guessed the distance between the two boats had closed to 300 yards as a line of tracer fire looped lazily from the rear of the target. The red balls floated toward the fantail and then accelerated to a blur as they went over the 828.

"Target that machine gun," Cordner yelled at the Oerlikon crew who continued a steady fire at the stern of the target.

There were multiple flashes on the enemy patrol boat and flames began to flicker from the starboard side.

"Starboard 15, set 10 knots." Lee kept his distance as the gun crews poured fire into the Japanese boat. A muffled explosion erupted from inside the target and pieces of flaming wreckage flew into the air. Now fully engulfed in fire, the hull began to settle into the water.

"Cease fire. Cease fire."

Bryan heard the flames crackling from the other boat. The 828 slowly closed to 100 yards. He turned to see Cordner looking across the water. As the range decreased they watched the hull sink further into the water.

"Men in the water off the starboard side," the lookout said from behind them.

Cordner didn't move but continued to watch the burning ship.

"One less Nip to deal with," he said, his voice without emotion. He stood watching the hull burn then said, "Half ahead both engines, starboard 15, steer 160" The Australian turned and reached for his binoculars.

The 828 came around smartly, leaving the burning hulk rocking slowly on the dark water.

The next afternoon Bryan sat on the ready ammunition box for the Bofors gun watching a wide wake streaming out behind the Fairmile. The bright midday sun cut through a thin high cloud cover and he had unbuttoned his shirt to enjoy the sun.

"Hell, you look like you're goin' native."

Bryan turned to see Bill Nance grinning at him.

"I borrowed a set of sunglasses from Lee Cordner and a little sun never hurt anybody."

"Cept if you're floating in a raft a million miles from anywhere."

Bryan laughed.

"How's the eye doing?" Nance asked, his voice now serious.

"Still hurts like the devil when I look left. At least the blurriness is going away."

"How soon before we get in?"

"Should be tomorrow morning."

Bill sat down next to him. "Not a bad way to spend a war. Any idea what happens to us now?"

"I talked to Cordner. There's a Navy office there. They'll set up transportation for us somewhere."

"Damn, we're a long way from anywhere down here." Nance stretched his legs out on the gray deck.

"Getting back to the ship would be my first choice. But I'm sure it will take several different ships to finally link up with the *Yorktown*."

Nance said, "How about getting' your eye fixed first?"

"I don't know. I'll try to see a doc as soon as we get in port. But I bet it's going to take some time before I can pass my flight physical."

"Yeah, you're probably right."

"Finished with engines," Lee Cordner called down the voice

tube then turned to Bryan. "Welcome to Australia, mate."

"We owe our lives to you and your crew, Lee." Bryan realized how different thing might have turned out.

"Buy us a beer and we'll call it even," Cordner laughed. "Looks like your chaps got our message."

Bryan turned to see a U.S. Navy Lieutenant Commander standing on the pier. He extended his hand to Lee. "Thanks for everything."

"It was truly our pleasure. If you're stuck here for too long, the crew can generally be found in the lounge at the Majestic Hotel in the evenings. You can buy us that beer."

On the pier, he and Bill walked over to the American.

"You must be Michaels and Nance," the officer said with a smile.

"Yes, sir."

"Glad to see you. My name's Harrold. I'm the Admin Officer for the detachment here in Cairns. I've got a car and we have you set up to see a doctor, an intelligence officer and then we're buying you the biggest steaks in Queensland.

Bryan answered for both of them. "Sir, that sounds okay with us."

The car pulled away from the pier parking area toward the main part of town. Bryan sat in the left front seat, Lieutenant Commander Harrold drove.

"Never will get used to driving on the wrong side of the road. We have an Australian Navy doctor who takes care of us. We'll stop by the clinic. Then down to our building to talk with the spooks. Lots of radio traffic flying around about the big carrier battle. Is that where you went down?"

"Yes, sir. On the second day."

"What ship?"

"*Yorktown*, Bombing Five," Bryan answered.

"It sounds like she took some hits toward the end of the battle. The operations folks have her on the way back to Pearl for repairs." Harrold turned down a wide boulevard.

"Pearl Harbor? We may never get back. How 'bout *Lexington*? At least we'd have a ride."

Harrold turned to look at Bryan. "I guess you wouldn't know. The *Lexington* went down."

"She what?"

"Yeah, just came in on the wire. That info is classified right now so don't talk about it."

"Shit."

They drove in silence for another two miles, stopping in front of a large two story building.

"Let's go in and have the docs take a look at you two."

Bill Nance came away with a clean bill of health, fully fit for duty. Bryan spent almost an hour with Commander Les Sim, the Australian Naval Surgeon. The doctor did not like the look of Bryan's leg which had remained tender and swollen. He was concerned there might be shreds of his uniform that were carried in with the metal fragments.

"We'll get you scheduled for surgery this afternoon. With a possible infection, there's no time to waste."

Sim finished writing in a medical folder. "We need to get every one of the shell fragments out and make sure there's no foreign matter imbedded. Shouldn't take more than an hour and we can use a local anesthetic. Now let's have a look at your eyes."

Thirty minutes with the intelligence officer completed their official return to force procedure. The Lieutenant shared the information he copied from the classified radio traffic and after action reports. While they knew the Japanese carriers were hit, there was no confirmation that either had sunk. The *Yorktown* had taken at least one bomb hit which caused a great deal of damage below decks. She was returning at best possible speed to the shipyard at Pearl Harbor. It sounded like the *Lexington* bore the brunt of the Jap attack, including torpedo hits. Despite a valiant effort to save the ship, internal explosions finished her off. The *Yorktown* recovered all task force aircraft and the surface ships saved most of the crew of the *Lexington*. The battle had already been given a name, Coral Sea.

The two survivors had a quiet lunch in the cafeteria at the Navy building. Bryan didn't have much of an appetite thinking about his surgery scheduled for 1400.

Dr. Sim found and removed a shard of metal on the left side of Bryan's eye socket which was causing the intense pain whenever he attempted to look to the left. The Doctor told him that the muscles controlling lateral movement of the eye were susceptible to palsy and even after removal of the foreign body the pain might not go away. The injury could also precipitate a host of other problems in the future from severe headaches to eventual paralysis of the eye. While Les Sim was not a flight surgeon, he told Bryan an injury like his would disqualify him from flying in the Australian Air Force. The leg wounds were thoroughly cleaned and other than a slow recovery Sim expected no complications.

Four days after his surgery Bryan finally felt well enough to leave the hotel where he and Bill were billeted. His leg felt better each day despite the tenderness. A cane helped him walk and exercise the stiffness from the injury. The pain in his eye remained severe anytime Bryan tried to look to the left. Doctor Sim told him to keep the eye irrigated and protected until a specialist could examine it.

Bryan and Bill Nance finally made it to the gentleman's lounge at the Majestic. Despite a full wallet, courtesy of the Southwest Pacific detachment disbursing clerk, neither Bryan nor Bill were able to purchase a drink. By the end of the party both of the Yanks were made honorary members of ML 828's crew.

The next morning he received a call from Lieutenant Commander Harrold. He had been directed to secure air transportation for the two survivors to Pearl Harbor. Bryan set the phone down and realized he'd be able to see Liz. A lot had happened since they had seen each other. How would she feel when they met in person?

Chapter Seven

The Reunion

"Five A" designated the travel priority reserved for "combat critical personnel." When Lieutenant Commander Harrold notified Sydney that Lieutenant Michaels and Petty Officer Nance were ready to travel, their priority assignment came back from the travel office in three hours. Within twenty four hours they were manifested on a Mariner flying boat from Sydney to Pearl Harbor. The Australian Air Force provided a flight to Sydney and they were on the huge flying boat sixteen hours after leaving their hotel in Cairns. The trip across the Pacific took two and a half days, culminating with landing in Honolulu.

Stepping stiffly into motor launch holding by the aft hatch, Bryan felt numb from the hours of droning across the Pacific. His thoughts on the flight had been mostly about Liz and what would happen when they met. How many times had he wondered if they would ever see each other again? Now he was almost there. The Navy coxswain threw the grey utility boat into gear and turned toward the quay wall.

The pier hummed with activity, vehicles and men moving supplies to staging points. At one end cranes loaded pallets onto a medium sized transport. In the distance he saw Diamond Head, the enduring symbol of Oahu. They were home.

"All military personnel check in with the transportation office at the head of the pier." A tall Chief Petty Officer repeated his announcement as people stepped off the launch.

Lieutenant Michaels and Petty Officer Nance. We're trying to get to the *Yorktown* beach det."

The First Class Petty Officer looked through several sheets of typed paper. "Yes, sir. Says here they're in Building 14. We have a bus that runs right by there. Leaves in ten minutes."

Bryan sat on the hard bus seats and reflected this was not the way he expected to come home from war, bouncing down the Kam Highway with all the local traffic.

"You know at one point I didn't think we'd ever get home. And now we're beating the boat back." Nance grinned from the seat next to him.

How ironic, Bryan thought. We get shot down and end up back in Pearl Harbor before the *Yorktown*. We may be the first Navy crew that actually fought in the battle to make it back to Pearl.

"I'm Michaels and he's Nance, Bombing Five." Bryan addressed a Chief who sat writing on a muster sheet.

Without looking up, the man said, "We don't know when she'll be in. Should be within a week. Until then we've been told all replacements are going to be assigned to the transient personnel unit pending reassignment." The Chief continued to check the lists on the typed sheet.

"Chief," he said, louder than intended. "For your information we are not 'replacements.' Petty Officer Nance and I are attached to Bombing Five and just flew in from Australia. We're tired, dirty and not ready for a bunch of bureaucratic bullshit."

The Chief looked up and saw the cuts and scratches that covered Bryan's face and the cane in his hand. He stood up as a Lieutenant Commander came out from a small office.

"Did I hear you just flew in from Australia?" the officer asked.

"Yes, sir," Bryan said. He didn't recognize the officer.

"You were at the Coral Sea?"

110

"We were shot down on the second day. Got picked up by an Australian patrol boat. They took us to Cairns. We just flew in on a Mariner."

"Come on back," he said. "Chief Talbot, please arrange billeting for them. I need to make a phone call." As they walked into his office, he said, "I'm Lieutenant Commander Henley, the new Intel Officer. Have a seat. I'll get them to bring in some coffee. Sit down and relax." Henley picked up a phone and dialed. "This is Lieutenant Commander Henley. Is Commander Austin there? Fine, I'll wait."

The Chief brought in two mugs of steaming coffee. He put them on the table in front of Bryan and Bill.

"Yes, sir, it's Van Henley. I think I have someone here you want to talk to. I've got a crew from the *Yorktown* that was at the Coral Sea. They just flew in from Australia. Yes, sir, right away." He replaced the receiver. "Finish your coffee. I'm going to drive you up to Pac Fleet Intel, my old unit. They want to talk to you real bad."

The two aviators spent the next three hours talking to a series of debriefing officers, culminating with the Commander Ed Layton, the Fleet Intelligence Officer. They were in his office when the phone rang.

"Yes, sir. I'll bring them up right away." Layton hung up the phone. "Admiral Nimitz would like to see both of you."

As they walked across the compound toward the main headquarters building Nance whispered to Bryan, "What am I supposed to do? I've never met an admiral."

Bryan smiled at his friend. "Just be polite, say 'yes sir' and 'no sir' and answer his questions. I've met him, he's a good man."

Commander Layton smiled as he pushed the door open.

After a five minute wait in the Admiral's outer office, they were shown inside by the admin chief.

"Admiral, this is Lieutenant Michaels and Petty Officer

Nance off the *Yorktown*," Layton said.

Admiral Nimitz stood up from his chair and came around the desk. Extending his hand to Bryan, he said, "I've met the Lieutenant. Petty Officer Nance, it's nice to meet you. Please sit down."

They all sat around a small round conference table at the side of the office. Nimitz sat back looking at them, his four silver stars bright on the pressed khaki shirt, a twinkle in his blue eyes.

Commander Layton spoke first. "Admiral, we're sure that these men are the first combatants to get back to Hawaii from the Coral Sea. My people have thoroughly debriefed them and we'll have the report on your desk by tomorrow morning."

"Thanks, Ed. That'll be fine." He turned to Bryan and Bill. "Now what I'd like to hear from you is what's not in the report. If you were in my shoes, what do you think I need to know?" The Admiral sat back, clearly waiting for Bryan to speak.

"Sir, I'm not sure where to begin but I'll try. We found out the Japs aren't invincible. But they are tenacious. On both days of the battle we were attacked by Zeros during our dive runs. They were ignoring their own AAA. And those cannons on the Zeros are tough. Even one hit can do a bunch of damage. I think our aircrews are good. We may be pretty green but it didn't take too long to catch on. No one was afraid to press the attack. I watched Lieutenant JJ Powers do one of the bravest things I've ever seen. He was hit prior to roll in but pressed his attack and pickled so low he couldn't miss. It was a direct hit on the Jap carrier. He crashed next to the ship during his pull out. Admiral, this Navy knows how to fight."

Nimitz didn't say anything but leaned back in his chair. After a moment he said, "I'm sorry Lieutenant Powers didn't make it. There's nothing anyone can say or do to lessen the pain of losing shipmates. All we can do is remember them and their sacrifices. How about you two? What happened?"

Bryan covered their activities during the two day of Coral Sea, culminating with Bill Nance ditching their Dauntless from the back seat and their adventure with ML 828.

"That's quite a story. You're lucky the Australians happened by when they did. I know we kept up searches for a week after the battle but it's a large area to search."

Layton shifted in his chair. "Admiral, we've taken enough of your time."

"I do have a meeting I need to attend." He stood up and shook hands with Bill Nance. "Commander, why don't you take Petty Officer Nance back to your office? I'd like a word with Lieutenant Michaels."

"Yes, sir. Let's go, Nance." Layton led them out of the office.

Bryan remained standing next to the table, not sure what to do. Nimitz walked back to his desk.

"Are you all right?"

"Yes, sir. Took some shrapnel in my leg. That's healing fine. I got some fragments in my eye. That's what's bothering me now. In Australia they said wait until I got back to Pearl and have it looked at by a specialist. It'll be fine, I'm sure."

The older man remained standing. "Are you still glad you're back in a cockpit?"

"Yes, sir. I'm doing what I know how to do. You were right, we have to stop them."

"As important as the Coral Sea battle was, it was just the beginning. There are going to be many more battles before we're done. And unfortunately a lot of men are going to die. But that's the way it is." The Admiral walked over to Bryan. "I'm proud of you, Bryan."

"Thank you, sir."

The Admiral sat down at his desk and stared at the painting on the wall of the U.S.S. Constitution. He keyed his intercom and asked his writer to step inside the office. "Chief, have the Fleet Surgeon give me a call."

The *Yorktown* detachment duty driver turned into the wide

parking lot at Aiea Naval Hospital.

"Thanks for the ride," Bryan said as he exited the jeep. Taking a deep breath, he walked to the main entrance. Inside the door a directory listed the different clinics next to an information desk manned by a young corpsman.

Bryan checked the large directory sign over the reception desk noting the Ophthalmology Clinic was on the second floor. His appointment with Dr. Ames at 1500 had been arranged by Captain Hollandsworth, the Pacific Fleet Surgeon.

"Excuse me." Bryan leaned against the desk counter.

A Second Class Corpsman looked up. "Yes, sir."

"I just got in to Pearl and I'm looking for a nurse who's stationed here." Bryan still wore the khaki pants he borrowed from Lee Cordner and the shirt he wore during the ditching.

The Petty Officer looked warily at Bryan. "I'll be glad to help you, sir. What's her name?"

"Sommers, Liz Sommers."

The man opened a loose leaf notebook and paged through the tabs. "Here she is, Lieutenant. She's working on Ward Two, day shift."

"Can I go down there?"

Putting the book back on the shelf, the Corpsman stood up. He pointed down the breezeway on Bryan's right. "Yes, sir. Go down the hall and take a right. The next door on the left is Ward Two."

Bryan shifted his weight from the counter to his cane. "Thanks."

"Good luck, sir."

As Bryan walked slowly down the passage his nervousness grew. They'd known each other for such a short time. Was he building up his hopes falsely? Her letter had said how she felt about him but things change. Maybe she didn't feel the same way now. Reaching the Ward Two entrance he turned into the entryway.

"Can I help you?" A nurse in her white uniform sat looking at a patient chart.

"I'm looking for Liz Sommers," Bryan said.

"Bryan....you don't recognize me do you?" The nurse laid the chart down and stood up.

Confused he said, "I'm sorry."

She smiled. "I'm Nancy Hostetter. Liz and I were stationed at Bremerton. I met you one night in the O Club."

"Nancy, sure. I'm sorry, I wasn't thinking."

"We only met once and Liz had your full attention." Nancy laughed.

"Is she here?"

"She's on break right now. But if I know her she'll be outside in the courtyard. Let me get Sally to watch the desk and I'll walk you down there."

Nancy and Bryan moved slowly down the shiny linoleum hallway.

"How are you?"

"Okay."

Nancy looked at Bryan with the eyes of an experienced nurse. "Just a little rough around the edges?"

"Yeah."

"She's been worried about you," Nancy said.

"Is she all right?"

Nancy nodded. "I think seeing all of the wounded gets us all down once in a while. She likes spending her breaks in the courtyard. It gives her a little break from the ward."

The courtyard consisted of benches, trees and flowerbeds nestled between the two largest hospital buildings. Nancy escorted Bryan to a screen door that led to the side walk.

"There she is, over on the bench by that large palm tree."

"Thank you," he said quietly as he pushed the door open.

"Mind if I sit down?"

Liz turned slowly, opening her eyes. "Certain..." She looked at Bryan for a moment, a confused look on her face. Slowly standing up she reached out and touched the cuts on his face with her hand. Their eyes met and he knew she felt the same way he did.

The cane clattered to the sidewalk as he put both arms around her. They held each other but said nothing.

"Watch your eyes, I'm turning on the overheads."

Bryan shaded his eyes as the bright ceiling lamps came on.

Ames walked back over and sat down in the chair next to Bryan.

"What do you think, Doc?" Bryan asked.

"The Australians did a nice job cleaning you up. You're very lucky as I'm sure you realize. If that splinter had been in almost any other area of the eye you would have lost vision totally or lost the ability to move your left eye laterally."

"So what's gonna happen?"

Ames shook his head. "It's too early to tell. Over time the pain might go away. Or you may suffer some of the possible side effects such as migraines. It's hard to tell."

"What about flight status?"

"I'm not a flight surgeon. But I've been around aviation commands for most of my career. This type of problem is always disqualifying for fight duty. I'm sorry."

Bryan walked slowly down the hall from Ames office. He looked down the stairs to the first floor and saw Liz and Nancy standing near the reception desk. Put on good show, he thought, as he walked up to them.

"Hello, ladies."

Both of the nurses smiled at him. They looked crisp in their white skirts and blouses.

"You two get out of here before Commander Standish tracks us down," Nancy said. "I'll see you later." She smiled and walked away, her heels clicking on the highly polished tile.

"What was that all about?" he asked Liz.

"I've got duty today and would normally be here overnight. Nancy offered to take my duty." Liz reached down lightly and took his hand. "Let's get out of here."

She walked him out to a dark green 1934 Chevy convertible.

"Nice car," he said carefully sliding into the front seat.

"We bought it from one of the doctors. His family was going back to the states and he was headed for a ship."

Liz put the car in gear and pulled out of the parking lot.

Bryan had always enjoyed convertibles and the wind felt good as they drove down the highway toward Pearl City.

"Where are you taking me?"

She turned and flashed a beautiful smile. "There's a little café near Pearl City. I think you'll like it."

The Blue Grotto Restaurant had a small open air dining area overlooking the water and they were almost alone. The waiter brought them both gin and tonics.

Following an awkward moment, Bryan took a drink and looked at her. "I knew I missed you but I didn't realize how much," he said.

She smiled at him then looked down at the table as if trying to control her emotions. "I thought I might never see you again."

"I had some of those same feelings myself." He reached over and took her hand. "I guess this war has rewritten the rules."

"Bryan, I don't know why we were able to find each other. Maybe it's what they call fate. I'm just glad it happened."

"So am I."

She smiled at him as he raised her hand and lightly kissed it.

After a dinner of fresh mahi mahi, they sat finishing their wine. Despite hours of talking, neither of them had mentioned the future.

"What did Dr. Ames say about your eye? She asked.

"He said I was a lucky guy." The sarcasm in his voice

obvious to Liz.

"What does that mean?" she asked.

"Lucky to be able to see with both eyes. Of course I won't be able to fly again." He stared into his wine glass.

"He said you can't fly anymore?"

"It's not his decision. But he expected a medical board would give me a down check."

"Bryan, I'm sorry."

He shrugged. "I'm not gonna feel sorry for myself. That would have been easy to do before the Coral Sea. But too many guys will never come back for me to feel sorry for little old Bryan. What pisses me off is that I'm a good aviator and I want to be able to do my part."

"You did your part," she said. "More than many men will ever do."

"But the war's not over. I don't want to spend the rest of the war sitting at a desk. This is my Navy and my fight. It took being out there to realize that."

"Bryan, give it time. Things will work out, I know they will."

He saw the look in her eyes and knew she was right. He would have to take it one day at a time. "I better get back to the beach detachment They were going to set up billeting and I never found out where."

Liz reached for his hand. "Bryan, Nancy and I share a room at the BOQ. Because she has the duty, she'll stay at the hospital tonight."

Three days later Lieutenant Commander Henley called Bryan into his office.

"This is classified but the ship will be in on the 27th. They're going to take her directly into dry dock and begin repairs."

Bryan had seen some of the damage reports submitted by *Yorktown* after the battle. "It's going to take some time to patch her up this time. Wonder what they're going to do with the air wing?"

Henley shook his head. "Doesn't mention that. I'm sure they have a plan but we'll be the last to know."

"Then with your permission I will secure for the remainder of the day."

"Get out of here.....and take Nance with you."

"Are you sure they don't make rum in Texas?" Bill Nance was watching Bryan pour his second rum punch from the pitcher he had pulled from the picnic basket.

Liz laughed. "Bill, they make fine beef but leave the rum making to the Cubans."

"Fair enough.....fair enough."

Bryan sat back on his towel watching the light surf roll in on Waikiki Beach.

"This week has been wonderful," Liz said, reaching over to hold Bryan's hand.

"Yeah," he said, his voice flat.

"You heard something?" she asked.

He nodded and reached for his glass. "The ship's just about back."

Liz put her arms around his neck and leaned close to him.

They sat quietly for a moment.

"I'll be right back."

They looked over to see Bill Nance walking down the beach, apparently following two young women who were walking barefoot in the sand.

"Love, it's in the air." Bryan laughed.

"You're right, Mr. Michaels," Liz said and gently kissed him.

A raucous chorus of whistles and sirens met the *Yorktown* as she pulled into Pearl Harbor's turning basin. Tugs moved the battered warrior slowly into dry dock number one. A small army of shipyard workers swarmed over the ship and repairs were underway before the dock completed dewatering.

Bryan and Bill were able to get aboard thirty minutes after the final mooring lines were secured. On their way to the Ready Room they saw the heavy damage from the Japanese attack. Yard workers were busy setting up equipment on the hangar bay. *Lexington* aircraft were scattered among the *Yorktown*'s own, another stark reminder of the outcome of the battle.

He opened the door to the ready room and went inside.

"Bryan, welcome back." Larry White, one of the squadron pilots stood next to the duty desk.

The Skipper turned in his chair and saw Bryan. Short grinned. "The prodigal son returns." He got up and shook hands with Bryan. "Good to have you back, Bryan. We got a message three days after the battle that you and Nance had been picked up. How are you?" Short asked as he glanced down at the cane.

"A little banged up, Skipper. I may have a problem with my eye, took a splinter when the canopy came apart."

"We need you back as soon as you feel ready. I think we'll be underway in a couple of days."

"I can't believe they can get all the repairs done by then"

Short shook his head. "All they're doing is enough to get us back to sea. Everything else will have to wait."

"Skipper, when you have a minute I'd like to talk to you about Bill Nance. He's the reason I'm still alive."

"Stop by my stateroom later," Short said.

More pilots came into the ready room when word got out that Bryan had returned. He enjoyed seeing familiar faces and comparing notes about the last day of the battle.

Thirty minutes later, he stood talking with several of the pilots when Tony Abbott opened the door. The XO stopped with his hand still on the knob and looked directly at Bryan.

"Michaels, I didn't know you were back aboard." Abbott regained his composure and walked over to the group of junior officers.

"Just came aboard, sir. I brought Petty Officer Nance with

me."

Larry White and Bud Taylor moved to open a path for Abbott.

"Welcome back." Abbott had his hand extended.

Out of reflex Bryan shook hands. "Thanks, XO."

Abbott turned to White and Taylor. "Gentlemen, would you excuse us? Bryan, have a seat."

"Yes, sir," he said and sat down in the chair next to Abbott's.

"I wanted to thank you for saving my ass on the way back to the ship. If you hadn't seen that Zero and taken him out I doubt if I'd be here today." Abbott paused for a moment. "The two of us have never gotten along. I thought that you didn't take this business seriously. The accident sealed it for me. But I was wrong. I may be a son of a bitch but I'll admit when I've made a mistake. And it wasn't just what you did for me. You've been a leader in the squadron in addition to being a good stick. By the way, I submitted you for the Distinguished Flying Cross for getting that Zero. You deserve it. You have a real future in this business and I'm glad you're in the squadron."

Abbott's change of attitude surprised Bryan. "Thanks, XO. I'm glad to be here." He hesitated then said, "I haven't told anyone except the Skipper, but I took some shrapnel and may have a problem with one of my eyes."

"What kind of problem?" Abbott slid back in his chair.

"There was a metal splinter that lodged on the side of my left eye. They got the splinter out but I can't move my left eye laterally without a red hot poker going off in my head."

"Did you see the flight surgeon?"

"Not yet. He's my best hope. The eye doctor at Aiea gave me a thumbs down based on what he knew of aviation rules. I'm hoping our Doc can figure something out."

"Let's hope so. Until then, get settled in and check on your men."

Bryan started to stand but then sat down. "XO, I want to put Bill Nance in for the DFC."

"What happened?"

"When we were hit, I couldn't see anything. Bill took over from the back seat and managed to ditch the aircraft successfully. He pulled me out of the cockpit and got me into the raft. Without him I wouldn't be here either."

"Why didn't you both bailout? You knew no one had ever ditched a Dauntless from the back seat didn't you?"

"Bill took a round in his parachute so he couldn't bail out," Bryan said.

Abbott leaned forward. "And you wouldn't leave him, would you?"

"No, sir."

"Bryan, give me the facts. I'll personally write Nance up for the DFC."

Chapter Eight

An Unknown Future

It is customary for the arrival or departure of senior officers on board U.S. Navy ships to be announced on the internal communications system. The rank or title of the visitor will be followed by the appropriate number of bells commensurate with the seniority of the officer or official being recognized. The steady flow of senior officers aboard the *Yorktown* since arrival in port made those announcements so routine that most crewmen paid no attention.

"Rear Admiral, United States Navy, arriving...."

Repairing battle damage and corrosion prevention had taken most of Bryan's plane captain's efforts since the return to Pearl. Now he stood in the forward hangar bay watching his men using rags and solvent to wipe down the nine Dauntless aircraft of Bombing Five. The effect of salt water could quickly damage critical components on the landing gear, bomb racks and in the cockpit. The other major effort by the squadron involved replacing the spare parts used during the last battle, including new aircraft. The first three of six replacement bombers were scheduled to be hoisted aboard at 1500. Despite working around the clock the ship and air wing were running out of time. The rumors still circulated around the ship that *Yorktown* would put to sea tomorrow to join

Hornet and *Enterprise*. Bryan couldn't see how that could possibly happen.

The general announcing system came on: "Lieutenant Michaels, Bombing Five, lay to the quarterdeck.....I say again, Lieutenant Michaels, Bombing Five, lay to the quarterdeck."

That's unusual, Bryan thought, as he walked forward to the quarterdeck. Junior officers on carriers were seldom ever mentioned on the announcing system. Stepping through the hatch to the reception area Bryan looked for the Officer of the Deck. The young Lieutenant stood talking to a taller officer wearing the solid gold shoulder boards of an Admiral. Looking again, Bryan recognized the visitor. He walked up and saluted.

"Good morning, sir."

The older man turned and smiled. "Bryan!"

"Hi, Dad."

The two men shook hands.

"It's good to see you, son."

They moved over to a far side of the quarterdeck.

"What are you doing here, and in uniform?"

Chuck Michaels laughed. "I was recalled to active duty. Just got into Pearl this morning on the Mariner. I've got a meeting at Fleet Headquarters this afternoon but I wanted to try and see you first."

"Where're you headed?"

"I'll tell you all about it over lunch. Come on, I've got a driver and we can go to the club."

Changed into a fresh white uniform, Bryan checked out with the duty officer and met his father on the pier. The Admiral watched silently as they drove past the salvage operations underway on the battleships. His old ship, the *Arizona*, was now beyond salvage and would rest on the bottom of the harbor until resources could be directed to clear the wreckage.

"It's hard to believe, Bryan. Reading the reports, even watching the news reel footage doesn't bring home the devastation until you can see it and smell it."

"It's something I'll never forget." He paused then said, "Do you think they can get those ships back in action?"

Chuck Michaels nodded. "Some of them. It will take time and a lot of work but we'll still need firepower to beat the Japs."

"We're lucky Halsey was at sea during the attack." Bryan said.

"I'm sure the Japanese planned on having the carriers in port. I think a smart sailor always expects the worst and plans that way. I know Bill Halsey. He's a tough old bird and if anyone can beat the Japs at their own game, he's the man."

The car pulled up to the Makalapa Officer's Club.

"Pick us up at 1300," the Admiral said to his driver as they got out of the sedan.

Father and son enjoyed a quiet lunch on the veranda. Bryan surprised himself when he realized how much it meant to be sitting here with his father. So much had changed in both their lives and they were fortunate to be able to see each other. Bryan told him about the encounter with Admiral Nimitz and the subsequent chain of events.

"As a flag officer you never really retire. There's a network that connects active and retired flags. I was pleased and surprised when I got a phone call from the Chief of Staff after you met Nimitz."

"Dad, it was really something to meet him. He stuck his neck out for me. I got to see him when we flew in from Australia. I guess we were the first guys who'd been in the battle to make it back to Pearl."

"How was it out there?" Chuck asked his son.

"It's hard to describe. People are scared but everyone knows what has to be done. I was pretty scared on my first mission. But once I started by attack run I was too busy. I guess the biggest thing is not letting your buddies down." Bryan felt good telling his father things he might not share with anyone else.

"I'm proud of you, Bryan. You've come back from a tough situation."

Bryan took a long drink of iced tea. "I may have another problem."

"What's that?"

"I got a metal splinter in my eye when we went down. The Aussies were able to remove it but there's still some damage. It might keep me out of the cockpit."

His father didn't say anything.

"I'm not going to let it wreck my career. If I can't fly then I'll find out what I can do. I want to stay in this thing until the end."

"When will they decide?"

"I'm supposed to hear something this afternoon." Bryan knew the flight surgeon hoped to get a medical board scheduled quickly.

"How about I pick you up at 1800. We can get some dinner and talk about it?"

"Dad, there's something else I need to tell you about."

Liz Sommers sat in the driver's seat of the Chevy parked at the exit from the carrier pier area. She and Bryan had a date for dinner. There had been just enough time for her to stop at the BOQ and put on her favorite green dress.

She watched the steady stream of sailors and shipyard workers coming out of the security gate at the pier. Rumors were rampant about the *Yorktown*. The most prevalent story sent the damaged carrier to Hunter's Point Naval Shipyard in San Francisco for complete repair. A few rumors had her staying in Pearl at the shipyard for a month then sending her back at the Japanese. No one knew for sure. Tonight Liz decided to enjoy the evening and not worry about tomorrow.

Bryan walked from behind the security fence and waved at her, his white uniform contrasted sharply with the dungarees of the sailors walking alongside him. She watched him approach, happy to be with him again.

He walked up to the car and bent down to kiss her. "Hi. Been waiting long?"

"Maybe ten minutes." She turned the ignition as he got in the passenger seat and slammed the door.

"I've got a change in plans for tonight." He took off his hat and put it in the back seat.

Liz turned and looked at him with a smile on her face. "Why am I thinking dinner is off and you have some critical mission to perform?"

Bryan laughed. "Oh no, we're still on for dinner. Just a slight change in location. Instead of the Blue Grotto, how about we go to the Royal Hawaiian?"

"That's pretty fancy for a couple of junior officers." The Royal Hawaiian's reputation as one of the nicest hotels on Waikiki Beach came with a corresponding cost. She'd been there once before but only for a drink.

"We're meeting someone." Bryan waited for her question.

Liz turned right and headed for the highway into Honolulu.

"Are you going to tell me or is it a surprise." She had her eyes on the road.

"My Dad."

"Your Dad? I thought you said he was in San Diego?"

"He arrived today. They recalled him to active duty and he's here to get ready for his assignment." His father had not been specific on his new job. He told Bryan he wanted to wait until after his meeting with the staff.

"Bryan that's wonderful. But you're not supposed to surprise girls like that."

"Don't worry, he's a great guy. You're gonna like him, I promise."

Rear Admiral Chuck Michaels arrived in the dining room early. Due to tight billeting for senior officers he'd been assigned to the Royal Hawaiian for the duration of his stay in Pearl Harbor. Still thinking about his briefing with the Chief of Staff, he ordered a martini and sat back to wait for Bryan.

He remembered his surprise when Bryan mentioned that he was seeing a Navy nurse. The younger Michaels had never spent much time chasing the opposite sex and his father wondered if he would ever find a wife. After Bryan's court martial and loss of flying status, Chuck Michaels wondered if his son would ever even get his life back on track. But things have a way of working out, he told himself. Now Bryan had a solid record in combat and a girlfriend. And if that wasn't enough, he'd said that he loved the young lady. Never one to share his feelings with anyone, a proclamation of love by Bryan meant this girl must be something very special. Finishing his drink, he saw Bryan enter the Royal Hawaiian dining room and stood up at the table. Walking next to his son strode a stunning young lady. *I'll be damned.*

"Dad, this is Liz."

Chuck Michaels extended his hand to the young lady. "Liz, it's a real pleasure to meet you."

"Thank you, Admiral." Liz immediately liked Chuck Michaels. Perhaps it was the smile or the eyes but she saw a strong family resemblance.

Pulling out her chair the Admiral said, "I hope this didn't catch you off guard."

"No, sir. The Navy Nurse Corps is very flexible. And I've always wanted to have dinner here."

Bryan would look back at the evening with his father and Liz at the Royal Hawaiian as one of his favorite memories. The three of them talked and laughed through the night. Several bottles of good wine complimented the fresh swordfish and no one had room for desert. The Admiral and the nurse were talking like long lost friends when the salad arrived. A final round of after dinner drinks provided the perfect ending to a wonderful night.

"There's something about good brandy at the end of a meal. We've got to win this war and get back to France. No one else should even try to make it." Chuck Michaels held his snifter up to the candle.

"Then I propose a toast. To the brandy of France and an early victory." Bryan raised his glass.

"Hear, hear," his father echoed.

Liz raised her glass last and quietly said, "To an early victory."

Both men saw the tears in her eyes.

"I'm sorry." She sipped at her brandy.

Chuck Michaels put his hand on her shoulder. "Don't apologize. What you do every day gives you the right to wish for whatever you want."

Bryan watched Liz put down her glass and quickly wiped the tears from her eyes. He reached over and put his hand on hers. She looked at him and smiled.

"If you two will excuse me. I have an early meeting with the staff," the Admiral said and slid his chair back.

"No word yet?" Bryan asked.

"Not officially. But I should hear tomorrow. Whatever they want me to do is fine with me. I know how to follow orders and I'm lucky to be here in any capacity." He stood up. "Liz, I can't remember when I had a better time, thank you. Bryan, if you need to get hold of me try the Chief of Staff's office. He'll know where I am most of the time. Now it's time for old men to go to bed. Good night, you two."

Liz pulled the Chevy into a vacant parking place near the pier's security gate. Bryan still wore his whites while she had changed into her working uniform. Checking her watch she saw there was still plenty of time for her to make the morning shift turnover at 0600. She turned to look at him.

"Hey, we're here. Time to wake up."

Bryan opened his eyes and smiled. "I guess I dropped off. Didn't get much sleep last night." He smiled at her.

"Can you get off tonight?" she asked.

Bryan remembered the rumor about sailing today. He didn't know what to tell her.

"I'm not sure what's happening. I don't think anybody really does. Why don't you plan on picking me up here at 1700. If I hear anything different I'll try to get a phone call to you."

The realization that he might be going back to sea so soon struck her like a blow.

Bryan walked slowly toward the head of the pier then stopped and came back to the car. He reached down and took her hand. "Remember I love you." Leaning down he kissed her gently on the lips.

Liz looked up at him, her eyes were misty. "I will."

He reluctantly let go of her hand and turned to walk back to the ship.

At 0815, Bryan stood on the flight deck waiting for the replacement aircraft to be hoisted aboard. His men sat on the deck with toolboxes ready to begin checking out the new bombers. Standing on the number three elevator, he watched Bud Taylor emerge from a hatch and walk over.

"Skipper wants to see you in the ready room."

Bryan handed his clipboard to Taylor. "There's our aircraft, down the pier by the dumpster. If you don't see them hooking her up within fifteen minutes, go up to flight deck control and find out why. Got it?"

"Got it. Now go."

Making his way to the ready room, Bryan passed a lot of civilian yard workers still aboard for final repairs. Activity everywhere told the story of a warship desperately getting ready to sail.

Closing the ready room door he saw the CO and XO sitting in their chairs.

"You wanted to see me, Skipper?"

"Sit down, Bryan. How's the load aboard going?" Wally Short asked.

"Behind schedule, sir. It'll be alright, I can see the aircraft on the pier. It's just a matter of time."

"Bryan, I got a message from the Naval Hospital. They want you to go TAD for treatment and evaluation of your eye." The Skipper held an unfolded message form.

"You mean leave the ship before she gets underway?"

Short nodded. "That's about the size of it. Word just came down that we're sailing this morning, so you're going to have to get busy. Admin will get your orders."

"Skipper, suppose I'd rather not miss this at sea period?"

Short and Abbott looked at each other.

"You had a tough time at the Coral Sea. No one would fault you for missing this time out," Tony Abbott said.

"That's not it, XO. I'm part of this squadron. If I can't fly I'll stand the duty and work operations. Let me do my part."

Short looked at Bryan and turned to his XO. Abbott nodded.

"Okay, Bryan. We didn't get this message before sailing. But when we get back, you go in for treatment."

"Aye aye, sir."

Walking back to the flight deck Bryan knew he'd made the right decision. It would be hard to justify what he'd done to Liz but he refused to remain ashore while his squadron went into battle.

"What's the story?" he asked Bud Taylor, now standing in the starboard catwalk looking down at the Dauntless on the pier.

"They delayed the hoist aboard until they finish loading ammunition back aft. Should only be half an hour. After that we're the number one priority." Taylor started to hand the clipboard to Bryan.

"Keep an eye on things for a few minutes. I need to write a letter to Liz."

"Sure thing," Taylor said. "They announced the last mail run would leave the ship in an hour."

When the postal officer escorted the sealed mailbags to the fleet post office annex, it contained a letter addressed to LT(jg) Liz Sommers at the Naval Hospital, Aeia.

131

The deck crew rapidly moved their last aircraft to the starboard side and Bryan's men attached the tie downs in preparation for sailing. Bryan inspected each bomber to ensure they were secured correctly for sea. Kneeling down under the last aircraft, he heard the shrill burst of a whistle.

"Now shift colors. The ship is underway," the ship's general announcing system blared.

Walking over to the starboard catwalk he looked down. The line handlers on the pier, their job over, stared up at the massive warship as she slowly began to move. The tugs began pulling *Yorktown* into the turning basin off pier 16. Bryan looked up and saw the national ensign flying from the mast. Below the colored signal flags fluttered the small blue flag with two white stars which flew for Rear Admiral Jack Fletcher. The crusty Fletcher commanded Task Force 17 and *Yorktown* served as his flagship. Already at sea, Task Force 16 consisting of *Hornet* and *Enterprise* were under the command of Rear Admiral Raymond Spruance. The combined forces would be the largest group of United States warships to sail together since the war began.

Looking up at the green hills surrounding Pearl Harbor Bryan wondered when he would see them again. He could just see the Naval Hospital and thought of Liz. She would be working on the ward by now. There had been no way to get a phone call off the ship when he knew of the sailing order. At least he got a letter off in time, he hoped she would understand.

Two destroyers moved in column down the channel toward open sea. The *Yorktown* would have several destroyers and a cruiser as escorts during this operation to protect the big ship from Japanese submarines and aircraft. Bryan slowly walked aft as the carrier moved into the channel and headed seaward.

On the eastern side of the channel people stopped to watch the *Yorktown* pass. What were they thinking, Bryan wondered? Did they think we could beat the Japs? Were they wondering if we'd ever make it back?

Trees lining the channel wall passed slowly as the carrier

cleared the point where the *Nevada* had run aground on December 7th. Lost in thought he noticed there was another group of civilians standing under a group of banyan trees. They must have used the road that ran parallel to the channel and stopped just prior to the end of the breakwater. He saw several cars parked at the end of the road. Next to a Ford truck sat a green '34 Chevy.

Bryan walked to the extreme aft end of the flight deck and searched the group of people standing near the cars. To one side of the group a lone figure stood in a white uniform. He waved his arm in a wide arc and she immediately waved back. Liz continued to wave as she walked to the edge of the rocks that lined the channel entrance.

Standing on the end of the flight deck, Bryan watched Liz until he could no longer make out the splash of white against the rocks. He walked slowly up the flight deck. As the *Yorktown* cleared the channel, he felt the increasing vibration as her engines increased revolutions and the wind began to increase across the flight deck.

Rear Admiral Chuck Michaels walked into the office of the Chief of Staff, U.S. Pacific Fleet.

"Chuck, good to see you. It's been a long time," Milo Draemel said.

"I think San Diego, '39 at the Fleet Exercise debrief."

"You're right," the Chief of Staff said. "I'm glad you're here. We're putting together one hell of a plan to whip the Japs and your experience will be important."

"Bob, I signed on for whatever the Navy wants me to do. Let me know and I'll give you a cheery aye aye." Michaels expected to be made part of the CINCPACFLT staff, probably working logistics or schedules.

Draemel smiled. "That's the way I figured it. I hope you haven't unpacked your bags, I need you in Australia."

"That's something I didn't expect to hear but it's fine with me. What do you want me to do?"

"Work for Douglas MacArthur. Actually you'd be working for Tom Kincaid, who's working for MacArthur. Tom is being assigned as the commander of the new Seventh Fleet. We're currently in the process of building it up to support the drive to the Philippines. Kincaid needs experience to put together a force almost from scratch. The ships and men will flow over time but for now most of the activity will be destroyer, submarine and PT boat operations. We're leaving it up to Tom but I suspect he'll make you his operational commander in the islands to support the offensive action as it heads north. We'll keep you here for ten days or so getting fully briefed on every aspect of the new operating area."

"Milo, I don't know what to say, except I'm ready to go. I knew Kincaid in D.C. years ago, he's a superb officer. I've never crossed paths with MacArthur but that should be interesting." Not only was he not going to be riding a desk, he would be forward deployed and fighting the Japanese.

"That would be an understatement. But I'll tell you, the PT boats under John Buckley, did a hell of a job for MacArthur in the Philippines, including getting him out of there. I think he has a warm spot for sailors right now."

"Let's hope we can keep it that way." Michaels paused and his tone changed. "I wanted to thank you for helping my son get back in a cockpit. I know it wasn't easy but it means a lot to me and I think he will do well."

"Chuck, I'll tell you. I was against getting involved at first. I decided the Admiral had better things to do than take up the cause of one junior officer. As always, Chester Nimitz demonstrated why he's where he is. He saw something in your son and was willing to take it all the way to the top. By the way, I saw a recommendation for the Distinguished Flying Cross come across my desk for his attack on the Jap carrier at the Coral Sea. I think Admiral Nimitz will enjoy endorsing that citation."

"I'm not sure what did it but he's changed since I last saw him. Maybe grown up a bit. Perhaps it's the war, I don't know. But he's a good officer and I'm proud to be his father."

A battered *Yorktown* headed north at 20 knots. Throughout the ship a sense of purpose gripped everyone. Bloodied by one battle, the men expected another fight in the next several days. Temporary repairs barely made up for the extensive damage suffered at the Coral Sea. There were rumors the water tight integrity could not be ensured. The Captain had come on the announcing system just after leaving Pearl Harbor and summed up their situation. The fleet commander needed the *Yorktown* at sea.

New aircraft and pilots quickly integrated into the air wing to make up for the losses from the Coral Sea. The bombing and torpedo squadrons from the *Saratoga*, VB-3 and VT-3 had come aboard. Their old fighter squadron, VF-42, had been blended into the new VF-3 under Jimmy Thach. Bombing Five had temporarily assumed the designation Scouting Five and would perform most of the search operations. But it takes time for a carrier and air wing to come together as a smooth working team. The old *Yorktown* team was gone.

Initial briefings confirmed they were steaming for the area around Midway Island. If intelligence estimates were correct the Japanese were mounting an operation to capture the small atoll now in the hands of the U.S. Navy and Marine Corps. Strategically important, Midway served as a logistics and refueling base for long range patrols by ships and aircraft of the Pacific Fleet. If the Japanese captured the island and used it as a base for the same purpose, the ability of the U.S. Navy to operate in the Pacific would be severely impacted. Recent intelligence reports put the Japanese strength at three carriers and escorts. Against the Jap carriers the U.S. Navy sortied three carriers that had been in constant action since the war began. Normally the American force would have been under the command of Vice Admiral Bill Halsey, the most experienced carrier admiral in the fleet. However Halsey was in the hospital in Pearl Harbor with severe skin problems brought on by the constant stress of command. In his place Admiral Nimitz selected Rear Admiral Spruance to command the three U.S. carriers.

Ray Spruance, a well respected naval officer and tactician, had never commanded an aircraft carrier or carrier task force. The Japanese were estimated to be using their most experienced forces which had executed the attack on Pearl Harbor. One report placed the Japanese Fleet Commander, Admiral Yamamoto at sea with the force. The odds were certainly in favor of the Imperial Japanese Fleet.

The first four days at sea for *Yorktown* were typical: practice landings, gunnery practice, damage control drills and intelligence briefings. One tragic accident occurred the first day when a Wildcat landed long, missed the barricade and crashed into an aircraft parked on the bow. The Wildcat's propeller tore into the cockpit area of the parked aircraft, killing the other pilot. An ominous beginning for the cruise.

Bryan coordinated aircraft preparation, attending briefings and working on operational details for the squadron. Bill Nance had been assigned as the "floater" gunner who would step in for any of the regular crewmembers unable to fly. Nance would have preferred to be on the schedule but accepted his situation. Bryan drafted him as an unofficial assistant to help stay on top of the aircraft location and status.

Bill Nance leaned back against the grey steel of the starboard catwalk watching the plane captains wipe down the squadron aircraft. The *Yorktown*, now in company with the *Hornet* and *Enterprise*, continued steaming north. The two task forces had rendezvoused on the 2nd of June and were now one hundred miles east of Midway.

"Our aircraft are looking pretty good."

Nance turned to see Bryan standing in the catwalk looking across the flight deck.

"Wish one of them was ours," Nance said.

"Yeah, I know. But we'll do what we can."

The lanky Texan spit over the rail into the deep blue water. "You heard any scuttlebutt?"

"They think the Jap carriers are coming in from the northwest. First thing tomorrow we'll launch searches in that direction. I know the PBY's from Midway are searching too. If we find 'em, we launch."

"This time it feels different. I'm not sure why," Bill said.

Bryan jammed his hands into his pockets. "I know. I guess everyone has it figured out that if we lose our carriers we're screwed in the Pacific. There's only the *Saratoga* left on the west coast."

"Shit."

"The Skipper asked me to be up on deck tomorrow as a turn pilot. Why don't you plan on sticking with me? You can help with the pre-flights and anything else that comes up."

"Can do. It beats the hell out of waiting down below."

Bryan nodded. "I thought the same thing."

Liz Sommers looked up from reviewing the medication record for a patient when an orderly dropped the afternoon mail delivery in the wooden box by the nurse's station. Something made her walk over and look through the small pile of mail. She laid the chart down on the desk and picked up a single letter.

After shift turnover Liz walked into the courtyard and sat by herself on one of the benches. Carefully she opened the envelope and withdrew the two folded pages. Putting the empty envelope on her lap, she began to read the first page slowly. Holding the papers very steady, she finished reading the first page then the next. Liz placed the letter in her lap and looked across the courtyard.

"Please come back."

Chapter Nine

A Test of Wills

Ten Dauntless dive bombers of Bombing Five, now designated Scouting Five, launched at dawn to search north of the *Yorktown*. Their orders were to cover the area out to a distance of 100 nautical miles. At 0830 the aircraft recovered aboard, unsuccessful in their attempt to locate the Japanese fleet.

Bryan walked into flight deck control to check the respotting plan for the aircraft that just returned when the squawk box came alive.

"Japanese carriers reported 200 miles west southwest. Begin refueling and rearming for an immediate launch."

Bryan ran down to the ready room. Wally Short stood briefing the newest location data to the squadron aircrews. *Enterprise* and *Hornet* were also preparing for launches and would be airborne at least an hour before *Yorktown*'s aircraft.

"Skipper Leslie of Bombing Three will be the overall lead of the first strike. We'll be held on deck to launch until we get locating data on the other two carriers. When the word comes down, man your aircraft on the double. We want to push for the target as soon as possible. The Japs are probably gonna be coming the other way so stay heads up. I want good thorough pre-flights of the aircraft and the weapons as soon as this first strike gets airborne. No mistakes today, gentlemen. There's a lot riding on what we do out there."

Tony Abbott saw Bryan and walked over. "Skipper's taking our first strike. We're setting up a second wave to go after what the first strike misses. I'll take that one. The flight deck agreed to let us have a turning spare for both strikes in case any of the primary bombers have a problem. We need you to pre-flight and turn the spare both times. If anyone's aircraft can't make it, they'll shut down, hop out and run over to your aircraft. If they don't need your aircraft, you can taxi forward and it'll be used for the next strike. Got it?"

"Yes, sir. I'll take Nance with me and we'll have everything set and ready to go."

"Bryan, I know how much you want to get into this. It's gotta be tough."

Bryan grinned. "Wouldn't want to be anywhere else, XO." He sat down in the back of the ready room and listened as Short covered all the briefing items. It felt strange not being able to be part of the attack. Still he knew if he was on the beach at Pearl he couldn't live with himself. As the brief concluded he picked up his helmet and went to find Bill Nance.

Less than an hour later word came down to man aircraft on the run.

"The Jap strike is inbound, ETA 1130. The Captain wants the deck clear ASAP," the duty officer yelled as aircrews bolted from their seats.

Bryan and Bill ran to their assigned aircraft which was parked on the port side of the flight deck.

"Let's get this thing started ASAP," he yelled over the noise of engines already turning over.

"You got it," Nance yelled as he jumped onto the wing.

All around them the engines coughed to life. White clouds of exhaust fumes drifted over the parked aircraft.

Checking the engine instruments and radio indications,

Bryan liked what he saw. He gave the plane captain a thumbs up. Twisting in his seat, he saw the light cruiser *Astoria* off the port beam. Three destroyers ringed the big carrier at a distance of one to two nautical miles. Signal flags began to flutter on the halyards as the entire formation began to turn to port.

Bryan watched Wally Short taxi his Dauntless into position. A quick engine run up and the Skipper began to roll down the deck. One by one the bombers climbed into the sky carrying their 1000 pound bombs. Looking down at a director, Bryan saw a director indicating they were going to launch.

"Bill, looks like someone had a problem. Get ready to swap out with whoever shows up."

A yellow shirted taxi director gave him the signal to taxi forward. Bryan followed out of habit.

"What the hell's going on?" Nance called from the backseat.

"Damned if I know, I'm just gonna follow the directors." This didn't make sense, he thought. Should he come up on the radio and ask the tower? But they were under radio silence.

"Bill, I think they're gonna launch us." He maneuvered to the center line and watched as the launch officer indicated full power to him. "They sure as hell are, get ready!" Running the throttle forward, he frantically checked instruments. "Here we go." Bryan saluted and the launch director's flag touched the deck.

"Never a dull day," Bryan called to Bill, irrationally happy.

"Skipper's never gonna believe this."

"Rendezvous was at 12,000, keep your eyes open."

"Rog."

"Maybe there were Japs inbound and the Captain wanted the deck clear."

"Yeah, makes sense."

"Well, we've got a thousand pound bomb strapped on this baby and we're not takin' it back."

To his right, Bryan saw several bombers angling toward him

in a left hand turn.

"Bill, I'm gonna join on this section." He hadn't realized he'd been moving his head anytime he needed to look left. Now his old habits came back and he tried to look left without turning his head, the pains sharply reminding him every time he tried. Thank God he could rendezvous looking to the right.

"That's just fine with me. I'd rather be here than down there waiting for the Japs to attack," Bill replied.

Joining on the Skipper's aircraft, Bryan saw the surprise look from Wally Short and raised one hand indicating he didn't know what was going happening. Short tapped his shoulder indicating they should join on his wing. Bryan acknowledged with an exaggerated nod.

Once in position, Bryan leaned the fuel mixture, setting the power for the most economical long range cruise. He knew the Jap carriers were at least 200 miles away and fuel would be critical.

Finding a moving ship across hundreds of miles of open ocean is never easy. When that ship is an enemy ship intent on not being found, the challenge is greater.

The effort by *Yorktown*'s search paid off at 1430. Lieutenant Sam Adams spotted the carrier Hiryu steaming north at high speed in company with one battleship and several escorts. Short's section heard the position report and Bryan turned with the Skipper as he set course for the enemy carrier. Over the primary strike frequency the chatter indicated more of *Yorktown*'s morning strike was heading for the Jap carrier.

"Keep your head on a swivel. The Zeros could be anywhere."

"You put the bomb into the flight deck and I'll keep 'em off our back."

Bryan was glad he had Bill with him.

It took almost twenty minutes until they were in the area where the target should be. Radio calls crackled from the receiver as the first group attacked the Jap fleet. Desperate transmissions

141

told the story of a fanatic defense by the enemy's fighters. Suddenly their flight broke through a thin layer of clouds. Bryan saw a carrier ten miles ahead already burning fiercely. Short raised his hand and made a toy gun symbol with his hand reminding everyone to arm their weapons.

"Carrier on the nose, burning like a son of a bitch! Heads up."

"Right."

Bryan pushed the throttle forward to stay with up with Short, the aircraft accelerating in a shallow dive. Looking down he saw sheets of flames rolling across the carrier's flight deck. Still steaming at a high speed, her wake curving in desperate attempt to avoid more hits, the stricken warship fought for her life.

Bryan heard clipped radio calls from the first attackers, now fighting off Jap Zeros as they headed home.

Short leveled his wings then rolled rapidly to the left. One quick glance around and Bryan slammed his stick hard left.

"We're in."

Wings level….through the windscreen he could see flames covering the aft part of the flight deck….70 degrees…get the dive brakes out…check tracking….watch out for the Skipper…11 thousand…..10 thousand……from behind him the twin .30s hammered as Bill fought to keep their tail clear….the carrier was turning…correct left….8 thousand….below he saw a Dauntless pulling up….pickle at two…pickle at two…a bright explosion on the bow…he got him….3 thousand, now the flames filled the windscreen…pickle…pickle…the Dauntless dipped as the bomb left the rack.

"Bomb," he said and pulled with all his might on the stick. There was a sharp crack and he felt the aircraft slew to the right as he leveled off at 1,800 feet. Bryan shoved the stick hard right to level the wings as the plane wallowed to a wings level attitude.

"What's that?" Bill yelled from the back cockpit.

Turning his head Bryan looked down and saw a four foot tear at the port wing root. Part of the flap was missing and torn metal stuck up in the wind stream.

"Port wing. Shit. You okay"

"Yeah, but look at that hole."

Bryan was descending down to wave top level and turning southeast toward the U.S. fleet.

"It's okay…..it's okay, keep your eyes open."

"Shit, we've got company. Zero closing at six o'clock."

Bryan knew there was nothing he could do. There were no clouds near enough to hide. He couldn't outrun or turn with the Jap.

"I'm goin' for the deck."

Bill's twin machine guns begin to fire. No match for the Zero's cannon, they would at least distract the pilot. Bryan pushed the Dauntless down violently, leveling five feet off the tops of the waves. Bursts of fire arced over the right wing ripping the water in front of them. The aircraft shuddered as the Zero scored hits with his 7.7mm machine gun.

It was only a matter of time, Bryan thought as another burst from Nance's guns echoed behind him. More tracers flew by the canopy and he felt the impact of shells.

"Fighter….one of ours…" Nance's voice was strained over the intercom.

"What fighter?" Bryan yelled.

The Zero realized too late that there was a Wildcat fighter behind him. Browning .50 cal machine gun bullets tore into the Japanese aircraft cockpit. In a moment the Zero careened into a wave top and cart wheeled into the sea.

"He….got…" Bill Nance fought to get the words out.

"Bill, you okay?"

Silence from the intercom. Bryan looked right and saw the blue gray fuselage of an F4F, side number 5-F-4 moving forward of his wing line. *I owe that guy a drink.*

"Thanks, Fox Four," Bryan transmitted on the common frequency.

"You okay?" the radio crackled back.

"You have a steer back to mother?" Bryan knew the general

direction home to *Yorktown* but welcomed any help.

"Stick with me, we're diverting to Blue base."

Bryan recognized the code word for the *Enterprise*. Did that mean the *Yorktown* had been hit? He banked right to join on the fighter.

"Bill, how're you doing back there?"

The tone of Nance's voice confirmed Bryan's fear.

"Been better….."

"What's wrong?" Bryan pressed.

"Got hit in the side." Bill said slowly, the pain obvious in his voice.

"We're heading for *Enterprise*, they're closer. Get the first aid kit and try to get a bandage on it."

No response from the rear cockpit.

"Bill, get a bandage on it," he shouted into the intercom.

"Right….."

Bryan felt helpless. He had to get the aircraft back as quickly as possible. There was about one hour of fuel left if he didn't have to use too much power. He looked over at the little fighter then down to their damaged wing. Sometimes you need a friend.

Thirty minutes later Bryan saw two carriers steaming east, the familiar outline of *Enterprise* several miles closer than the *Hornet*.

"Bill, there's the *Enterprise*. She's waiting for us. Just like old times, eh?"

"Hey…..that's good…..it's gonna be okay……"

"Stay with me, Bill. We'll have the docs on you in ten minutes."

He wondered if the damage had affected the landing gear. Hydraulic pressure was good and they should come down normally. If they didn't, he knew his orders would be to ditch next to the ship. If that happened, Bill was out of luck.

Bryan checked the canopy locked open, mixture rich, pitch

full forward. In case there might be damage to the flaps he'd leave them up and accept the increased landing speed. Abeam the ship, just before he started his turn to final, Bryan selected the wheels down. His heart pounded as he saw both main mounts indicate down and locked. He picked up the Landing Signal Officer at the end of the flight deck. The paddles told him he was a little high and Bryan pulled off power. Lowering the left wing he stopped a drift to the right. Lined up on the centerline, the Dauntless crossed the end of the flight deck just after the LSO gave Bryan the "cut" signal.

Shutting down the engine as soon as the aircraft was tied down, Bryan climbed out of his cockpit. Bill lay slouched to the left, his head hanging down on his chest. Torn metal was evident where the Jap machine gun bullets had found their target. Reaching down Bryan gently lifted Bill's face.

"Bill, we're here. You're gonna be all right."

"Sir, get out of the way, we'll take him."

Looking down he saw corpsmen in their white jerseys. Stepping out on the wing he watched them climb up on the Dauntless. The two men reached into the cockpit and released Nance's safety belt. They had him by each arm and lifted him out to several men on deck. They gently placed him in a wire stretcher aft of the port wing. Bryan saw the blood smeared on the yellow of Bill's life vest as four men carefully lifted Bill.

"Report to Flight Deck Control," a plane director yelled up at him.

"In a minute," Bryan yelled back and jumped to the flight deck and ran after the stretcher.

"Gangway, make a hole," the lead stretcher bearer yelled at a group of men standing outside a hatch. Above the hatch a red cross indicated the flight deck battle dressing station.

Bryan followed the men into the small space. He saw a doctor kneeling over the stretcher. Bill's helmet had been removed and the doctor watched the corpsmen cutting off his clothes with surgical scissors.

"Get the stretcher up on the table," the doctor ordered.

145

Four men lifted Bill, still lying in the stretcher, to a metal table anchored to the floor. Nance lay on his back with only skivvy shorts on. The doctor wiped blood off Bill's chest with a large white towel. An ugly two inch gash, four inches under his right nipple oozed a steady stream of blood.

"Start an IV with saline. He's in shock. Russell check his airway and start ventilating him."

The corpsmen went to work. One inserted a needle in Bill's arm and attached an inverted glass bottle. Another man pulled a black rubber device from a cabinet, placed it over Bill's mouth and began to squeeze it, forcing air into his lungs.

The doctor noticed Bryan standing near the door of the small space. "Who're you?"

"He's my gunner, we're off the *Yorktown*."

"What's his name?" the doctor asked.

"Nance, Bill Nance."

Turning back to the corpsmen the doctor said, "We're gonna insert a chest tube, get me a surgical pack." He leaned down to Nance's ear and said, "Bill, I'm Doctor Hanson. We're going to take good care of you. Just relax, son." He turned to Bryan, his eyes showing the deep concern over Nance's condition.

A corpsman focused a large light with a metal reflector on Bill's chest. Doctor Hanson picked up a thin scalpel from the canvas medical pack now open on a tray next to the stretcher.

Bryan watched as the doctor made an incision about two inches below the wound.

"Chest tube," he commanded.

One of the men already had a red rubber tube and metal pan ready to pass to the doctor. He inserted the tube and placed the outer end in the pan. A gush of blood filled the pan.

Bryan stepped closer, he felt helpless, and there was nothing he could do. He saw Hanson shake his head.

"Damn," the doctor said quietly.

The man working the respirator removed it as Doctor Hanson took a small flashlight and checked Nance's eyes.

"Am……am……" Nance tried to speak.

"Relax, son. We're going to take you down to sick bay. We need to repair the damage. Do you understand?"

Bill moved his lips, "Bry…..Bryan?"

Bryan moved to his side.

"Bill, I'm here. You're gonna be fine, they need to operate." Bryan grasped Bill's left forearm and squeezed. "I'm with you all the way. I'll be right here."

Bill looked up at Bryan, his eyes focused for a moment on him. The young sailor smiled. "Thanks…."

Hanson turned to one of the corpsmen. "All right, let's get him ready to move. Russell, call down and see if Commander Allison is available for surgery."

Bryan followed the stretcher team to the number two elevator. Klaxon horns sounded as the platform descended to the hangar bay. Once in the bay, the transport team moved to a hatch on the port side and took Bill carefully down one ladder to the sick bay. *Enterprise* sick bay included a fully equipped operating room now prepped and waiting for the team as they entered the white tiled medical area.

A Chief Corpsman stopped Bryan at the door to the operating room. "You'll have to wait out here, sir."

Two hours later, Commander Steve Allison found Bryan in a small lounge area. "Roger Hanson told me you were waiting for your gunner. I'm Doctor Allison. I operated on Petty Officer Nance."

Bryan looked at the man, searching for some indication of the results.

"I repaired as much as possible. The bullet must have tumbled after hitting a rib. There was extensive damage to the liver and upper GI tract. He lost a lot of blood. I'll be honest. I don't know how he survived to make it back to the ship."

"Is he going to live?" Bryan asked.

"Lieutenant, the outlook's not good. The next 24 hours will

be critical. I've done everything I can. Now it's up to God."

"Can I see him?"

Allison nodded. "He's heavily sedated but you can see him. He's in the forward ward, right down the passageway."

Bryan stood up. "Doc, thanks. He's a great young man."

Allison smiled wearily. "They all are." He turned and walked aft.

At 1846 Petty Officer Bill Nance succumbed to his wounds. Bryan Michaels was at his side.

"I heard about Petty Officer Nance. Losing a friend is tough.

Bryan turned to see Wally Short standing next to him. "Thanks, Skipper. He saved my life twice and there was nothing I could do to save his."

Short sat down in the ready room chair next to Bryan. The *Yorktown* aircrews were spending their time in Ready Four, the home of the *Enterprise*'s Bombing Six. "There's nothing you or anyone else could have done. Bill Nance was a great gunner. He knew the risks, just like you did. I'm just damned glad we have men like him."

"Yeah, I know." Bryan felt empty.

"Word is that *Yorktown* was hit hard, bombs and torpedoes. I don't know what we're going to do. One thing I do know is that you're done flying. And while we're on that subject, how the hell did you get airborne?"

"I don't know. My guess is the Jap attack was inbound and they wanted the deck cleared."

Short nodded. "You're probably right. We've got eight aircraft aboard. The battle's not over yet so I suspect we'll fill in the holes over here. I can use you as our squadron liaison with the *Enterprise*. Get to know the maintenance folks here and see what they can do for us.

"Yes, sir," Bryan said. "This was my old squadron. I know

most of the key people."

"We can still get our licks in on the Japs and I want to be ready."

"You okay?"

Bryan turned to see Bud Taylor standing next to him on the fantail. "Yeah."

"The Skipper told me about Bill."

"They tried….."

"I'm sorry. I know how close you two were."

"Bud, I'm tired of watching my friends die."

"You never really think this is what war is all about."

"Yeah, good men dying."

"The Skipper just passed that they think three of the Jap carriers went down today."

Bryan looked at his friend. "That's just a beginning."

"I heard there was a big battle off Midway," the young sailor said. "Have you heard anything about the *Yorktown*?"

Liz smiled down at the young man, both hands were completely bandaged, burned during the Battle of the Coral Sea.

"Some of the details are just being released by the PAO, but nothing about the *Yorktown*." She saw the disappointment in the patients eyes. "But I'm sure we'll know something very soon."

"Thanks, Miss."

Liz walked slowly back to the desk, they must know something, why won't they tell us?

Nancy Hostetter walked around the corner from the main corridor. Her face betrayed bad news. Stopping next to the desk she reached down and put her hand on Liz's shoulder.

"I just came down from the front office. Liz, the *Yorktown* went down off Midway."

Liz did not look up but stared straight ahead saying nothing.

"The word just came down from headquarters. They want us to be ready for the arrival of the *Fulton* the day after tomorrow with survivors. Liz, I'm sure he's all right."

"Would you watch the desk for me?" Liz looked up at Nancy, her eyes misted over.

"Sure, kid. Get out of here."

Sitting in the courtyard Liz Sommers looked across the hibiscus flowers at the brilliant blue sky. Soft white clouds floated slowly across the expanse. Taking a deep breath she tried to tell herself that he must be all right. He'd come back from the Coral Sea. Bryan was a survivor. At the same time she'd seen too many injured in the ward to kid herself. This war killed young men and that wasn't going to change. They had been so happy to find each other and now it might all be lost.

She sat on the bench for twenty minutes then stood up, straightened her skirt and walked back to the ward.

Later in the afternoon as Liz dispensed medications at the far end of the ward, Nancy Hostetter walked up.

"Liz, Bryan's father is at the main reception desk."

Although she had only met Chuck Michaels one time, she was glad he came over.

"Cover for me."

She saw him standing at one of the veranda doors that led to the courtyard walkway. Tall as Bryan, the Admiral stood very straight as he looked out at the garden.

"It's a place I go when I need to be alone," she said.

Chuck Michaels turned and smiled. "Liz, hello. Is there someplace we can talk?"

She nodded. "Let's go outside."

They walked to the nearest bench and sat down.

"Have you heard about the *Yorktown*?" Michaels asked.

"Just this morning." She hesitated. "Do you know

anything?"

The Admiral shook his head. "Just that she went down on the 5th. The survivors were picked up by the accompanying ships and transferred to the sub tender *Fulton*. No news on anything specific."

"We've been told to be ready for the *Fulton* the day after tomorrow." She turned to look at him, tears in her eyes.

He put her hand in his. "I know. There's nothing easy about this. We'll know something soon. Until then all we can do is pray and hope for the best."

Liz stared straight ahead. "I love him. I don't think I've told anyone that except Bryan and now you. But I wanted you to know how I felt."

Chuck Michaels smiled. "I know my son pretty well and he feels the same way. He wouldn't want either of us to worry. Let's try to get on with business until the ship docks. We'll know something then."

The submarine tender *Fulton* arrived in Pearl Harbor on the morning of the 8th of June, 1942. Aboard the ship were the survivors of the *Yorktown* that had been transferred from the host of escorts which originally pulled the men from the water. Despite the ferocity of the attack and requirement to abandon ship in a short amount of time, the casualties were lighter than expected. Of a crew of 3800 men, almost 3400 returned to Hawaii after the battle. Chuck Michaels checked the consolidated survivor list four hours after the *Fulton* arrived pier side. Lt (jg) Bryan Michaels was not listed among the *Yorktown* crewmembers returned aboard the tender. The Admiral knew that there are often inaccurate reports immediately following an event. He hoped that Bryan was on one of the other ships. Michaels had lived with the life and death finality of the military life for over 35 years. That didn't make it any easier to deal with the possible loss of his only son. Now as he sat in the back of a staff car heading back to Fleet Headquarters he wondered about the quiet young nurse and how he would tell her the news.

Following his 1300 briefing, the Admiral called for his staff car. If he had learned one thing in the Navy, when you have a tough job then get on with it. He dreaded his meeting with Liz but she of all people deserved to know.

"Chief, I'm going over to Aiea. I should be back by 1500."

The Admin Chief hung up the phone. "Sir, the Chief of Staff would like you to stop by his office."

"Right now?"

"Yes, sir. That's what it sounded like to me."

"All right, I'll leave from there. Should still be back by 1500."

When Chuck Michaels entered Milo Draemel's office he had no idea what the Chief of Staff might want. Michaels realized he was annoyed that Draemel had diverted him from Aeia.

"My Chief told me you had something for me."

Draemel held up a naval message. "Chuck, I wanted you to see this right away."

The message came from the Commanding Officer, USS *Enterprise* to Commander U.S. Pacific Fleet. Subject line "Midway After Action Sitrep #8." The second paragraph was titled "USS *Yorktown* Aircrew currently aboard *Enterprise*." His eyes raced down the names until he saw "Michaels, Bryan Lt(jg) VS-5." The typing on the page blurred for a moment.

The Navy does not condone public displays of affection between naval personnel in uniform. For that reason the visitors in the reception area of the Aeia Naval Hospital were startled when a young Navy nurse in uniform threw her arms around a tall Rear Admiral old enough to be her father.

Chapter Ten

A New Direction

Rear Admiral Chuck Michaels stood with his hands clasped behind him. His gold shoulder boards shone in the morning sun as he watched the U.S.S. *Enterprise* moor starboard side to at Ten Ten pier. The strains of "Anchors Aweigh" echoed along the quay as the Navy Band helped to welcome the victors home from the Battle of Midway. Standing beside the Admiral, Liz Sommers watched expectantly as the lines were made fast and cranes began to move accommodation ladders into place. The two watched but said little, each alone with their thoughts.

From the ships loudspeakers boomed, "Now station the import watch, on deck section two. Make all required reports to the Officer of the Deck at extension 433."

Dock workers made the final connections, securing the ladders in place as a Navy sedan came down the pier. On the front bumper a blue flag with 4 stars waved. Chuck Michaels watched Admiral Nimitz exit the staff car and start up the ladder, a small entourage following him.

"Ding Ding, Ding Ding, Ding Ding, Ding Ding.....Commander in Chief U.S. Pacific Fleet, arriving."

The great gamble was over. Chester Nimitz had put together a remarkable victory and was here to welcome the men who won that battle against the Japanese Imperial Fleet. Chuck Michaels and the rest of the staff watched the after action reports flow in from Ray Spruance and were stunned when the final count showed that young American aviators had sunk four of Japan's first line carriers in two vicious days of combat. The toll had been terrible on the aircrews, almost all of the torpedo squadrons had been annihilated. Torpedo 8 off the *Hornet* lost every aircraft they launched against the enemy. Loss of the *Yorktown* hurt the U.S. deeply but new carriers were already on the ways at shipyards back in the States. Most importantly the Japanese had been repulsed and the majority of their most experienced naval aviators had been killed.

Michaels knew they were watching and living history in the making but today he only cared that his son was coming home alive.

"Is that him?" Liz asked. "At the top of the ladder."

"That's him," the Admiral answered quietly.

Looking down the pier, Bryan wasn't sure what to expect. Did anyone know he was coming in? Would Liz be able to get down here? How about his Dad, was he still in Pearl? Then he saw them both, standing side by side at the back of a small group of sailors.

Liz looked at Chuck Michaels questioningly.

"Go," was all he said.

The two ran toward each other and into each other's arms then kissed. They clung together oblivious of the world around them.

"Sorry, it took me longer to get back than I thought," holding her away from him to see her face. He leaned forward and kissed her.

She pulled him back into her arms. "It was worth the wait," she said, smiling through the tears. "I love you."

He kissed her again and they turned to see his father standing at the edge of the crowd smiling at them. They walked over to him seeing the smile on his face.

The two men shook hands.

"Welcome home."

"Thanks."

Bombing Squadron Five had temporarily set up shop in Hangar Two on Ford Island awaiting replacement aircraft and personnel following return to Hawaii. New aircraft carriers would be coming out of shipyards back in the states and the Navy would need these newly reconstituted squadrons to fill out the air wings.

In the two weeks since the *Enterprise* returned the aircraft and aircrews, the maintenance personnel had also been reunited. The squadron lost six men in the Battle of Midway including Bill Nance. After two major battles and losing a ship from underneath them, the men of Bombing Five finally had a chance to rest and regain their strength.

Bryan had taken advantage of the time to see his father everyday until the Admiral departed via Mariner flying boat for his new assignment.

An examination at Aeia Hospital and consultation at Tripler Army Hospital produced nothing positive or negative that he could discern. Only when he received the report did the harsh reality hit home. He not only would not fly again, he might spend the rest of the war in civilian clothes. The written report from the Naval Hospital, Aiea, Hawaii to the Chief of Naval Personnel recommended that "Lt(jg) Bryan Michaels, U.S. Navy, be removed from flight status due to partial ocular paresis and associated ocular neuralgia resulting from wounds suffered in combat." It further recommended that his "release from active duty would not be inconsistent with the normal resolution of cases of this type."

The afternoon he received the medical report, Bryan found himself on the perimeter road which circled Ford Island standing next to the overturned hull of the *Utah*. Rust had already attacked the exposed metal and oil clung to the hull at the water line. She rested in isolation now. The salvage crews had long since finished

155

their work. Now all of the effort in the harbor was focused on those ships that could be repaired and returned to action. But the *Utah*'s war was over. She and the *Arizona* had been determined to be beyond economical salvage. Now the former pride of the fleet rested on the harbor bottom, forgotten by a Navy now plunging forward at breakneck speed to engage and defeat the Empire of Japan. There were no markers or memorials to her or the men that died that Sunday morning in December. Bryan sat down on a bollard and looked at the forlorn wreck.

"Well, old girl. Looks like we're both done."

He pulled out the copy of the medical board report and crumpled it into a tight ball. With a quick sidearm he hurled the paper into the turbid water.

That night he met Liz in the parking lot of the Bachelor Officer's Quarters. They drove west to Pearl City and the Blue Grotto.

"I got the report from the medical board," he said after their drinks arrived.

Liz didn't say anything but took a drink from her cocktail.

"I'm grounded from flying and potentially on my way out of the Navy."

"Bryan, I'm sorry. I don't know what to say." Her eyes were sympathetic. She put her hand on top of his.

"There's got to be something I can do. I can't believe I'm done just like that."

"Have you talked with Wally Short?" she asked.

"He can't do anything. It's way past his pay grade." Bryan drained his bourbon and water, raising his hand to get the waiter's attention.

"You could go back to Annapolis and teach. They must need instructors."

"Liz, I don't want to teach. I belong in an outfit that's going after the Japs. Not sitting on my ass back in the States."

"Maybe I like the idea of having you in one piece when this war is over." She looked hard at him.

"You know what I mean," he said.

The waiter brought his drink and set it down on the table.

Liz waited until the man moved away.

"You've fought in two major battles. Besides being shot down and wounded, it looks like you've scored hits on two Jap carriers.

"That's not the point. I've seen men like JJ Powers and Bill Nance give their lives to help win this war. I haven't done anything yet."

"Do you have to get killed to do your part?" Her voice tense.

"Liz, you don't understand."

"I understand I love you. And I'm selfish enough to want you to survive and not end up in one of these wards crippled for life."

"Let's just drop it," he said. "It doesn't matter, there's nothing I can do anyway."

It had taken several phone calls to locate Lieutenant Fisher, Admiral Nimitz's flag aide. Once he had Fisher on the line, the aide remembered Bryan.

"When I saw the Admiral he told me to come back and tell him if I was glad he got me back in a cockpit. I'd like to do that. Can you help me?"

There was a pause on the other end of the line. "Are you sure you want to do that?"

Bryan wondered why the aide would ask that question. "Sure, why wouldn't I?"

"It might have been a rhetorical question. Are you sure he asked you to come back and see him?"

"That's sure what it sounded like to me," Bryan said.

"All right, give me your number and I'll see what I can do.

But I have to warn you I need to clear this through the Chief of Staff."

As a matter of courtesy, Bryan told Wally Short that he had asked to see the Fleet Commander.

"You what?"

"Skipper, he asked me to come back and see him."

Short looked hard at him. "You did see him after Coral Sea didn't you?"

"Yes, sir. This is different."

The Skipper put it together. "You want to appeal the medical board, don't you?"

"Skipper, I've got nothing to lose. If I don't do something I'll spend the war counting rolls of toilet paper in Norfolk or out on the street."

Short sat back in his chair. "What the hell, give it a shot. But don't get your hopes up. He may be the Fleet Commander but the Medical Corps call the shots when it comes to this kind of thing."

"Thanks, Skipper. I've got to try."

It had taken borrowing uniform items from several squadron mates and a trip to the barbershop before Bryan felt ready to see Admiral Nimitz. Arriving thirty minutes early, the Chief ushered him into the Admiral's office after only a five minute wait.

Chester Nimitz sat at his large desk reading a file when Bryan entered the room. "Come in and have a seat, I'll be right with you." The Admiral returned to reading the file. In another minute he looked up at Bryan and smiled. "I've been reading one of the intelligence summaries from the battle off Midway. When you asked to see me I had my staff pull the debrief summary from your squadron."

"Yes, sir."

Nimitz closed the manila folder. "I also had a chat with your

158

Commanding Officer, Wally Short."

Bryan wondered where this conversation was going.

The Admiral looked down at some notes on a pad of paper. "It appears you conveniently avoided reporting for your medical screening and instead sailed on *Yorktown*."

In a quiet tone Bryan said, "Yes, sir."

"And apparently while still officially grounded, you launched on a strike against the Japanese carrier Hiryu."

"Yes, sir but......." His voice trailed off.

"I understand there was some confusion on the *Yorktown* flight deck, which is understandable during a sea battle. And it appears that you were launched at the direction of the ship, not through your own efforts." The Admiral looked up from the paper, his blue eyes boring into Bryan.

Maybe this wasn't such a good idea, Bryan thought. "There was a lot of confusion, Admiral."

Nimitz returned to his notes. "So you joined on your Skipper's wing and participated in the attack on the Hiryu, delivering a 1000 pound bomb and scoring a hit."

Bryan sat quietly, not sure what to say.

"It also says that you lost your gunner after being attacked by a Japanese Zero. The young sailor I met after Coral Sea?"

"Yes sir, Bill Nance. During our run on the Jap carrier. He was a long way from Texas."

"Bryan, I'm from Texas. Did you know that?"

The Admiral surprised Bryan by calling him by his first name. "Yes, sir."

"I always found it interesting that so many Texans joined the Navy. Most of us had never seen the ocean. Funny thing." The Admiral opened another manila envelope and said, "I have the report of the medical board here. I suspect that's the reason you wanted to see me?"

"Admiral, I don't know what else to do. This war is personal. I've lost good friends and two ships. All I want is a chance to stay in the fight. There's got to be something I can do to stay out here and get another crack at the Japs. Sir, you helped me once. I hoped you might do the same again. You said we needed to hold the line until the country mobilized. I believe you and I think it's important. I don't want a ticket home."

Nimitz closed the folder and stood up. He turned and walked to the large picture window that overlooked Pearl Harbor. "It seems that your flying days are over. There isn't much anyone can do about that, even a Fleet Commander."

"Yes, sir. I know that. I convinced myself during that last flight that flying with the eye wouldn't work. But I spent four years at Annapolis and understand driving ships. The next best thing to flying an aircraft is driving a PT boat. Admiral, I can do that. There must be a need for officers with combat experience in those units."

Nimitz turned and looked at the young man sitting in front of his desk. Bryan Michaels symbolized why Nimitz knew America would triumph in the end. This young man was willing to go into battle and possibly die. He knew the risk and knew what he could lose, but Michaels still wanted to go back out into the Pacific and take the fight to the enemy.

Two weeks later orders were received for LT(jg) Bryan Michaels to report to the Commander, Motor Torpedo Boat Squadron Six for duty. An amended medical report was received in due course by the Bureau of Naval Personnel suspending LT(jg) Michael's flight status but finding him physically qualified for continued active service.

Part Two

"It now appears that we are unable to control the sea in the Guadalcanal area….the situation is not hopeless, but it is certainly critical"
USCinCPAC Command Summary – October 1942

Most of the men are stricken with dysentery...Starvation is taking many lives and it is weakening our already extended lines. We are doomed. "
Major-General Kensaku Oda (Referring to the state of Japanese troops on Guadalcanal)- 12th January 1943

"Goddam it, you'll never get the Purple Heart hiding in a foxhole! Follow me!"
Captain Henry P. Jim Crowe - 13th January 1943 - (Guadalcanal)

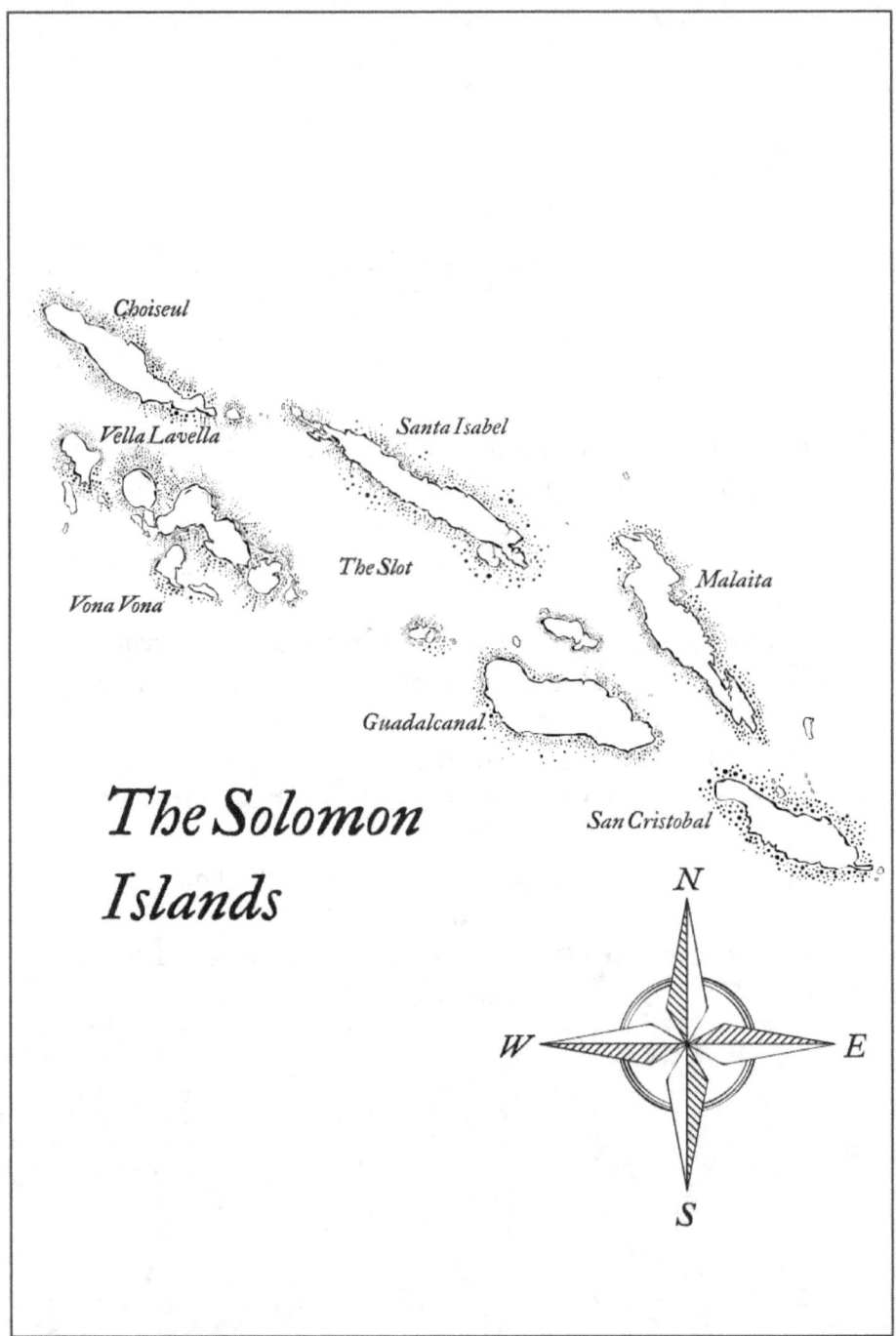

Choiseul

Vella Lavella

Santa Isabel

The Slot

Vona Vona

Malaita

Guadalcanal

The Solomon
Islands

San Cristobal

N

W · · · · · · · E

S

Chapter Eleven

Thundering Engines

"Now station the special sea and anchor detail." The general announcing system echoed across the deck of the U.S.S. *Monaghan*, DD-354. The dark green outline of San Cristobal lay in the distance. After completing a twelve day transit from Pearl Harbor the Farragut class destroyer was reporting for duty with Task Force 73.8. The new Seventh Fleet had begun to build forces in this forward anchorage for the initial push north toward the Japanese strong hold of Rabaul.

Bryan had arranged passage to catch up with his new squadron, now operating out of San Cristobal. A diversion by the *Monaghan* to take part in a search delayed their arrival but gave Bryan a chance to brush up on signals and tactical manuals.

"A long way from Annapolis."

Bryan turned to see Commander Pete Long, CO of the *Monaghan*. "Hello, Skipper," Bryan replied. The two officers both graduated from Annapolis, Long was Class of 1933. The only two regular officers on the ship, they'd found a common ground in their hatred of the Japanese. During the transit, Long invited Bryan to dinner twice and allowed Bryan to visit the bridge at any time.

"You've been here before, haven't you?" Long asked.

"Yes, sir. I was on *Yorktown*." Bryan's thoughts flashed back to Bill Nance and their time in the Coral Sea.

"All I know is that it's a long way from anywhere." Long put his foot on the life line next to Bryan.

"If this is where we have to go to kill the bastards, it's okay with me."

Long looked across the water. "This is where is has to happen. The Japs have pushed their way across the Pacific and now it's time to stop 'em. I suspect they think we'll roll over but they're in for a surprise."

Bryan nodded. "Yes, sir. I think you're right."

Long turned to head for the bridge.

The sleek destroyer backed her engines for one minute prior to the anchor letting go and splashing into the brilliant aqua water of Maniau Harbor. Small boats were already approaching the warship when Bryan came on deck with his gear. A brilliant mid-day sun beat down on the metal deck plates and Bryan felt the sweat trickling down his back. Now he remembered how hot it could get in the Solomons. He carried his sea bag to the quarterdeck and found the Petty Officer of the Watch.

"When you have any room in one of the boats, I need to get ashore."

"Yes, sir. We'll have a run leaving with the mail in ten minutes."

Bryan saw a series of wooden piers on the shoreline. In the harbor several destroyers swung on their anchor chains while smaller cargo lighters were tied up to the piers. At the far end of a long beach another set of piers ran into the water from a clearing filled with Quonset Huts. Alongside the piers the sleek shapes of half a dozen PT boats sat quietly.

A rumble of engines came from the other side of the *Monaghan*. Bryan turned to see three PT boats in formation heading toward the far piers. They left wide wakes behind them and wisps of white exhaust. Small American flags fluttered smartly from the masts of each boat. The boats began to slow down in unison as they neared the beach, remaining in a single line until the first boat peeled off toward the longest pier. In sequence the sound of the engines dimmed and the two other boats pulled into their berths.

Bryan remembered the first time he heard the throaty roar of the big Packard engines. He had spent six weeks at the PT training course in San Diego. It was during his first week of training that he heard those powerful engines echoing across the harbor. The sound always got his attention.

Squadron Six was equipped with the new 80 foot PT boats manufactured by Elco. Powered by three Packard 12 cylinder engines, they would hit over forty knots at top speed. Packing both 20m and 50 caliber guns, the small warship's main armament was the four 21 inch torpedoes mounted in deck launchers.

The first time he went out in the smaller 77 foot boats in San Diego, Bryan knew he'd made the right decision requesting a transfer to PT's. The boats literally flew across the waves. With the ability to turn like an aircraft they could run circles around the destroyers and cruisers that were assigned to play targets for the fledging crews. Bryan had a natural feel for turn rates, closure speeds and the dynamics of planning a torpedo run. When he completed the formal course he felt ready for battle.

Bryan's travel orders put him on the Army Transport Goethals to Pearl Harbor where he would await transportation to Motor Torpedo Squadron Six. The Transient Personnel Office in Pearl confirmed the squadron's ultimate destination would be San Cristobal. When the *Monaghan* opened up for space available transportation he jumped at the chance. His time on the Goethals convinced him that travel across the thousands of miles of the Pacific was best accomplished in a warship, not plodding along at 10 knots.

Arriving in Pearl Harbor, he found Liz enrolled in a special one month training course at Tripler Army Hospital. When he asked her about the class, she would only say that it focused on lessons learned in the war so far. They both also knew his time in Pearl would be short.

Although Liz didn't mention their argument at the Blue

Grotto, Bryan felt a tension between them. When he tried to talk about it she would change the subject. On the last night he walked onto the veranda at her apartment to find her crying.

"What's wrong?" he asked, knowing the answer.

"We're always saying good bye. I guess I'm feeling a little sorry for myself." She turned and smiled as tears rolled down her cheeks.

He put his arms around her. "Lieutenant, feeling sorry is authorized. But only for tonight." He kissed her and she clung to him.

"Before when you left I don't think I thought about how long you would be gone. But this time ..." She moved to the railing as his voice trailed off.

"Liz, I suspect it's going to be for a while."

"That's what I'm having trouble with. You leave tomorrow and I don't know when I'll see you again." The tears continued to stream down her face.

Bryan took her hand. "I guess that means you love me."

She put her hands around his neck. "Of course I love you."

He would always remember her standing by that green car as he turned to walk up the pier to the destroyer.

The utility boat took fifteen minutes to run from the *Monaghan* to the main pier ashore. Bryan traveled light, one sea bag and a battered briefcase with his orders, service, medical, and pay records. He lifted the bag on his shoulder and walked down the pier to the first Quonset hut. The sign said, "Harbor Master." It took only twenty minutes for the Yeoman First Class to get Bryan a ride around the bay to the PT base.

As the jeep bounced down the perimeter road, Bryan saw at least ten boats at the piers. Several Quonset huts sat back from the piers, aligned parallel to the water. Behind the Quonset huts and inside the tree line were a dozen canvas tents. Home sweet home, he thought. Pulling into the pier area, the driver stopped at the second hut.

"Here's the squadron office, sir."

Bryan thanked the sailor and off loaded his gear. Leaning his sea bag against the corrugated hut wall, he opened the screen door and went inside. A high partition divided the building with three single desks lining the wall. One of the men sitting at the desks looked up.

"Yes, sir. Can I help you?" The man remained sitting, his fingers still resting on a portable typewriter.

"If this is Squadron Six, I'm reporting in, name's Michaels," Bryan said and put his brief case on the floor in front of the man's desk.

"You found us, sir. We've been expecting you. Even have some mail for you. I'm Chief Little, Squadron Admin. If you have your records, I can start checking you in."

Opening his case, Bryan handed his records to the Chief and sat down in a chair by the desk.

"How long have you guys been here?"

Little didn't look up as he opened Bryan's service record. "Got here three weeks ago. The Seabees had most of the base already built."

"Is it just Squadron Six at the base?"

The man nodded. "Yes sir, just us. Sometimes we get a boat in here from Rendova but that's just for gas or repairs."

"How many boats in the squadron?"

"Ten right now. We should be getting two more. That's what the messages say anyway." The Chief Yeoman flipped through the pages of Bryan's service record. "Lieutenant, why don't I have Tucker take you over to your tent and you can drop your gear. Give me thirty minutes and I'll have all of the reporting endorsements done. By then the Skipper should be back. He's out checking the 131 boat after they changed an engine."

The skinny sailor at the other desk stood up and grinned at Bryan. "Sir, I'm Yeoman Striker Tucker. I'll take you over to your tent."

"He's in with Mr. Cameron. Here's your mail Lieutenant."

167

Chief Little handed Bryan two letters. The larger envelope's return address simply said, "Michaels, COMSOUWESTPAC Staff." The other letter was from Liz.

"Thanks," Bryan said as he went out the door.

A five minute walk brought them to Bryan's new home, a square 12 by 12 foot canvas tent with two of the four sides tied up for ventilation. Two wooden cots sat on the dirt and sand floor. A large wooden crate sat in the center of the tent.

"You're in here with Mr. Cameron. He's got the 145 boat."

He put his brief case down on the empty bunk and Tucker laid his sea bag at the foot of the bed. "I'll draw a sleeping bag and mosquito netting from supply for you."

"The bugs aren't friendly I gather?"

"Sir, I'm from Georgia. I thought I knew bugs. This place has got more kinds of the nastiest bugs you'd ever want to see. I'll get you some repellent too. They're making us take malaria pills. They say it'll keep ya from getting it. Hope so."

"Tucker, thanks for helping me with my gear. I think I'll walk down to the pier and look around. Will you tell Chief Little I'll be back in twenty minutes?"

"Sure thing, sir."

He stopped at the corner of the dirt street and opened the letter from his father. The short note said hi and congratulated him on his newest assignment. The last line very typical for his father, "….don't mention it to anyone, but you are part of my task group. Good hunting……" He decided to save Liz's letter for later.

Bryan pulled on his cap and headed for the water. Now past mid day, the sun beat down, the heat waves shimmering over the dock area. Men were busy on the boats and along the pier. Most of the sailors were bare chested or only wearing skivvy shirts. The boats had dark green hulls and grey upper decks that contrasted against the blue water and sky.

Walking out on the pier he nodded to several sailors cleaning what looked like .50 caliber parts in half of an old oil drum. They were scrubbing the operating mechanism in solvent. Clean pieces lay on a large rag next to them.

"Could you tell me where the 145 boat is?" he asked one of the men.

"Yes, sir. Second boat down on the outboard side."

"Thanks." Bryan decided he might as well go introduce himself to his tent mate.

A white "145" painted on the forward bridge bulkhead identified Cameron's boat, moored outboard of PT 139. He saw a sailor on the deck of 139 leaning against the forward torpedo tube. Bryan asked him, "Have you seen Lieutenant Cameron?"

The man stood up and said, "Yes, sir. He's aboard his boat. Come on across."

Stepping up and walking around the forward deck of 139, he saw the sailor had already walked over to the 145 boat to see another sailor. He turned to Bryan. "He's coming up, sir."

A tall lean Lieutenant emerged from the deck house hatch of PT 145. Sandy haired, the man wore a New York Yankees baseball cap. He smiled at Bryan. "I'm Doug Cameron. You looking for me?"

Bryan walked to the deck edge and extended his hand. "I'm Bryan Michaels, they tell me I'm your new bunk mate."

Cameron grinned. "Glad to meet you. Just get in?"

"Came in on the *Monaghan* this morning."

"Come aboard. Let me buy you a cup of coffee."

Bryan learned that Doug Cameron had been with the squadron since it commissioned. So far the squadron had not seen any heavy combat. Several of the boats had been attacked by Japanese aircraft but only suffered minor damage. Their arrival had been two weeks after the landings at Guadalcanal and the Skipper expected they would begin heavy patrolling north in support of the Marines soon.

"I see you're wearing wings. You're a long way from any airfield."

"Yeah, I took some fragments in my eye at Coral Sea. My flying days are over."

"You were flying at Coral Sea?"

"Yeah, off the *Yorktown*. In fact we were picked up by an Aussie patrol boat after an encounter with a Zero. I liked what I saw."

Cameron looked at him. "So you weren't there when she went down at Midway?"

Bryan shrugged. "No, I was there. I'd flown off before the Japs hit. Ended up on *Enterprise*."

"You've seen a lot of action. I'd think you were due for a break." Cameron got up and refilled their cups.

"The Japs got my roommate at Pearl Harbor and my gunner at Midway. I haven't evened the score yet."

Cameron looked back at him but didn't say anything.

When Bryan returned to the Admin Office, Chief Little had several forms for him to sign. "The Skipper wants to see you when we're done here."

Bryan knocked on the door.

"Come in."

Walking into the small office, Bryan stopped in surprise.

"Welcome aboard." Lieutenant Commander Jerry Rosenberg stood up and offered his hand.

"I didn't know you were the CO."

"No reason you would have. But I knew you were coming. Sit down."

"And you still wanted me?"

Rosenberg's expression turned serious. "I always knew you were a good officer. You just needed to get squared away and stop feeling sorry for yourself. I've kept tabs on you since Pearl. I know you could have taken a stateside assignment but didn't. That says a lot to me." The older man paused, then continued, "I think this is going to be a dirty back alley fight down here. I need officers who aren't afraid to fight."

"I'm new to PT's, but I've seen the Japs before. I know the bastards can be beaten. Plus I've still got some scores to settle."

"I need you as a boat commander. The 137 boat has a good crew and number two."

"What about their skipper?" Bryan asked.

"Harry Rightmire. He's still here but I'm putting him on the 142 boat. They've had big problems and I want to see if Harry can get them squared away. They've been my problem children since we commissioned. I relieved their skipper and sent him back to Pearl."

"I've got some experience with problem children. Maybe I can help."

"I guess you do. You want the job?"

"I'm willing to give it a shot"

Rosenberg sat back and stared at him. "All right. I may regret this. But let's see what you can do. By the way, I saw you were on the Lieutenant promotion list, congratulations."

"A long way from the Bremerton City Jail," Bryan said.

Rosenberg opened a file on his desk. "Before we're done, you may wish you were still back there."

As he walked back to his tent, Bryan wondered if he had made the right decision. He knew sailors and he knew what it felt like to be the misfit. *Time to put some of that Annapolis leadership to work.* Lost in thought, he heard someone call out his name. Turning around he saw Tiny Leonard walking toward him from the pier area.

"Tiny?"

"None other, Lieutenant Michaels. Damned glad to see you!"

Several sailors looked surprised when the hulking Warrant Boatswain bear-hugged the new Lieutenant.

"You were going to Squadron Nine, weren't you?" He stood back to see his friend, tanned and twenty pounds lighter than Bremerton.

"You know how those things go. There was an opening and

Six was shipping out earlier, so I volunteered."

"Keep me company while I empty my sea bag."

The two friends walked toward the billeting area.

"You've been busy since the last time I saw you in Pearl."

"Yeah," Bryan said.

"Rosenberg gave me the blow by blow. Sounds like some pretty nasty stuff."

"I was lucky. A lot of guys weren't."

The two men walked down the sandy path.

"The Skipper said you could have gone back to the states."

"Hell, the only thing back in the states is booze and women, and I don't need either." Changing the subject, Bryan said, "So what do they have you doing out here?"

Leonard laughed. "Keeping these 90 day wonders from destroying government property. I'm the squadron maintenance officer. Unless the tender's around we have to keep these boats running with almost no support. But I've got some great mechs working for me."

"I didn't know Rosenberg was the Squadron Commander. He was my department head on the *Utah*."

"Hell, sounds like old home week. He's a good man. I think these reserves are hard for him to get used to, but he's trying."

"Not a lot of regulars?"

"Nope. Most everyone in the squadron was wearing civilian clothes a year ago. I guess the good thing is that these are the first wave of guys who volunteered. That shows me they want to fight."

Doug Cameron sat on an ammo box, scribbling on a letter pad. He looked up as Bryan and Tiny walked up to the tent. "I see you've met our head wrench turner."

"We knew each other in Bremerton. Tiny's the only reason I'm not in the brig right now."

Cameron looked curious.

"It's a long story. I'll tell you sometime," Bryan said.

"So what did Rosey tell you?" Cameron asked.

"I'm gonna take the 142 boat." Bryan leaned down and unhooked the sea bag snap.

Leonard and Cameron looked at each other.

Tiny sat down on Bryan's bunk. "So what did he tell you about the boat?"

Bryan pulled his folded clothes out of the bag. "That they were the screw ups of the squadron."

"And he assigned them to you?" Cameron put his pen down.

"Actually I volunteered," Bryan said.

Leonard laughed. "That's my boy, always taking the hard road. You've got your work cut out for you. There are a couple of real foul ups in the crew. Deke Curtis will be your number two. Nice kid but he's still wet behind the ears."

Bryan shrugged. "How's the boat mechanically?"

"Good. We just replaced one of the engines."

"That's all I need," Bryan said enthusiastically. "Hey, where's the head. I need to take a leak."

Cameron pointed toward a low building. "Around in back."

Tiny and Doug watched Bryan walk across the clearing.

"Seems like a good man," Doug commented.

Tiny nodded slowly as if he was considering Doug's comment. "He is." As Cameron turned back to his letter, Tiny repeated softly to himself, "He is."

That night when Doug Cameron left to check on his boat, Bryan opened Liz's letter. It had been postmarked the day after he left Pearl Harbor. Seeing her handwriting made him feel close to her. He knew what they shared was special and every day he realized it more. Reading the second paragraph caught him by surprise and he read the paragraph again very carefully.

"I wasn't able to say anything when you were here because of strict orders. My training was in preparation for a change of duty. A dozen of us are going to be assigned to your area. You know I can't be more specific. My new unit will be Naval Mobile Surgical

Unit 417 and we'll move around where needed. That's all I know for now. Nancy will be going also so I'll have a friend to share the adventure. I hope to see you."

Bryan didn't know if he should be happy or angry. This part of the war wasn't somewhere he wanted Liz to be.

Aboard the light cruiser *St. Louis*, Rear Admiral Chuck Michaels looked over the movement report from the commander at San Cristobal noting the arrival of the *Monaghan*. He knew that Bryan was aboard and about to report to his new command. The Admiral had mixed feelings. Bryan wanted to fight this war, even though he'd already done his share. Vicious battles between Japanese and American surface forces were now a daily occurrence and his son would be right in the middle of it. He remembered a term from literature, "harm's way." That accurately described the desperate battle in the waters around these islands. Bryan was going in harm's way and there was nothing he could do about it.

Chapter Twelve

Into the Breach

After three days with his new crew, Bryan wasn't sure what to make of them. Each day they had gone out for short training missions. The first day Doug Cameron rode with Bryan to give him the lay of the land. The second day he took his boat out for solo operations. Today they had gone in formation with Doug leading in PT 145.

The crew knew their jobs. Communication between crewmembers was timely and professional. During the different drills each man reacted quickly and generally in the correct manner. They acted as though they knew their jobs but didn't have confidence in themselves. Bryan knew from his aviation experience that a lack of confidence is fatal in battle.

His number two, Ensign Deke Curtis, looked seventeen years old. Bryan wasn't sure he shaved every day. Soaking wet he might have tipped the scales at 140 pounds, no more. Just like the crew, he knew his job but had no confidence.

It had been a busy day. They ran every drill in the manual from torpedo attack procedures to air attack defense and even abandoning ship. The crew knew their drills but how would they react in combat? The 142 boat had yet to hear a shot fired in anger but Bryan knew that would change shortly. The Squadron's patrol area now included the Tadasser Straits, one of the most heavily traveled routes for Japanese logistic runs to Guadalcanal.

Japanese lighters, barges, patrol boats and the occasional destroyer cruised the dark waters off the islands in a desperate attempt to re-supply their troops on Guadalcanal. So far the give and take had been about equal with each side inflicting casualties and suffering them also. Intelligence estimated that at least half of the supplies sent from Rabaul did not make it to the Japanese ground forces. Tomorrow the 142 boat would be going on a patrol to the northern end of the Straits with PT 145 in search of the "Tokyo Express."

Bryan adjusted the course slightly starboard, estimating the harbor entrance four miles ahead. They would be pier side by mid day allowing them the afternoon to finish up any maintenance and provision the boat for tomorrow's mission. Bryan turned the conn over to Deke and leaned back against the cockpit bulkhead. He looked around the deck. Seaman Sunny Lopez manned the starboard .50 caliber. A quiet kid from New Mexico, he'd scored good hits during surface battle drills. His counterpart on the port .50 was Gunner's Mate striker Tony Heimbigner, a large powerful man who appeared to be completely comfortable on the twin gun mount. Behind Curtis stood Quartermaster First Class Tim Gravely who helped with charts, navigation and backed up Signalman, Leo Schultz. At the aft 20 mm gun mount, Gunner's Mate Second Don Baurichter stood with his loader John Harris. He didn't see his lead Torpedoman, Harlon Wilskie, who had gone below. The wiry Wilskie had proved to be a talented torpedoman, with a tenacious no-nonsense attitude.

"Why don't you take her in, Deke?" He didn't know if the previous skipper had ever let the young Ensign take the boat alongside the pier. Some commanding officers weren't comfortable with anyone else maneuvering the 35 ton boats in tight situations. The rudders were small and at slow speeds it took using the engines to jockey alongside a pier. Bryan decided Deke had to learn sometime. For a moment he considered going below but realized that would put even more pressure on the young officer.

"Okay, Skipper," he responded, his voice tentative.

Several of the sailors looked at each other. Their reaction told Bryan what he needed to know. This must be Curtis's first time. He hoped Tiny Leonard had some expertise at hull repair.

Doug Cameron waved his hat in the air, the accepted signal for Bryan's boat to "maneuver independently."

Bryan stood behind Curtis. "We'll go alongside them after they tie up."

Curtis quickly turned to look at Bryan for guidance.

"You've got the boat. Do what you need to do."

"Aye aye, sir." Curtis turned to Gravely. "Pass the word to secure all guns, safe torpedoes and line handlers lay topside."

Gravely looked pleasantly surprised. "Yes, sir."

Men started moving on deck and finished securing the weapons. Curtis pulled the power, slowing to ten knots and with a big grin, cranked the wheel to put the boat in a 360 degree turn to allow the 145 boat time to tie up first.

On deck the crew was paying extra attention to Curtis behind the wheel. Bryan decided he would bite his tongue and let the young officer do it by himself. In the distance the 145 boat tied up to the main finger pier. He watched Curtis adjust the course to line up slightly offset from the berth.

Fenders were being lowered over the side as Curtis slowed PT 142 to three knots. Twenty yards from Cameron's boat he signaled the engine room to put the engines to reverse for ten seconds then to neutral. "Lines over," Curtis yelled. Fore and aft, manila lines were tossed to sailors on 145. One minute later he added, "Secure engines."

The gunners began putting canvas covers on the guns.

Bryan walked over to the day hatch on his way to his small stateroom. "Nice job, XO," he said as he ducked below.

Standing behind the wheel, Deke looked surprised, then grinned and said, "Thanks."

The crew of reserves and volunteers did contain one "prewar" sailor. Motor Machinist Mate Second Class Charlie Morrison was the "old man" of the crew at 29. Three tours on destroyers out of San Diego established him as a superb mechanic on duty and liberty risk off duty. He learned to drink hard in the bars near the Naval Station. Multiple run-ins with the Navy resulted in his losing stripes on three different occasions. His temper had always been his downfall and so far his time in Motor Torpedo Squadron Six had been no different. Only the intervention of Tiny Leonard prevented Morrison from being put on report after he got into an argument with the maintenance chief on the tender. Leonard had told Bryan that Morrison knew how to run engines but he didn't trust the rebellious petty officer.

Bryan finished the log and went aft to find Morrison. He climbed out of the day hatch and walked back toward the engine room hatch. Deke and Baurichter stood next to the 20 mm looking at the breech mechanism.

"Mr. Curtis, I'd like to conduct a debrief with you after I talk to Petty Officer Morrison."

Deke looked over and said, "Yes, sir."

Descending the ladder into the engine room the temperature went up twenty degrees. The three engines were still cooling down, the heat building in the space which now lacked the underway airflow from hull vents.

Bryan saw Charlie Morrison kneeling down by the main oil service line to the number two engine.

"Any problems?" Bryan asked.

Morrison looked up but didn't say anything. He slowly got to his feet and wiped his hands with an oily rag.

"No, sir." The tone of his voice indicated irritation with the interruption of his post shutdown routine.

"We're heading north tomorrow on patrol. I need to know if we have any problems with the engines." He looked at the short man who wore dungaree shorts and a skivvy shirt.

"If we had any problems, I'd tell you...sir." He continued to wipe his hands on the rag.

"Where are you from, Morrison?" Bryan wanted to see if he could get him to talk.

"Chicago." The short mechanic looked at Bryan, not taking the bait.

"Why'd you join the Navy?"

Morrison leaned back against the log table. "The judge said either the Navy or jail."

"You ever been shot at, Morrison?" Bryan didn't like his surly attitude.

"No, sir. Why?"

"Because we're going to get shot at. And I need to know you can handle these engines when it gets tough." Bryan stared hard into the man's eyes.

"I can handle these engines. Why'd you ask me that?" His eyes were wary.

"Because in my experience, it's the tough talking guys who let you down when the shit hits the fan."

Morrison glared at Bryan who turned and headed for the ladder.

"These engines will be ready.........sir."

Bryan didn't look back as he climbed the ladder. On deck he saw Deke bent over looking at the torpedo locking mechanism with Petty Officer Gravely.

"It's time for our debrief," he said. "Let's head up to my tent. Petty Officer Gravely, the op schedule has us departing at 1830 tomorrow. Keep the crew busy getting the rest of the maintenance done and the ammo loaded."

"Aye aye, sir," Gravely said as the officers headed down the short gangway. Quartermaster First Class Tim Gravely was the senior enlisted crewman on PT 142. A merchant marine sailor before the war, he provided leadership and a watchful eye on the younger sailors. Feeling responsible for the crew, Gravely had welcomed the departure of the previous commanding officer. He'd seen good and bad officers and put Lieutenant Thomas solidly in the latter category. But Gravely wasn't sure what to make of this former aviator. Lieutenant Michael's first impressions were good and when he turned the conn over to Ensign Curtis, Gravely decided he might just be one of the good ones. Deke followed Bryan as he walked toward the squadron tents. The two officers fell in step.

"Ever bring the boat in before?" Bryan asked.

Deke hesitated a moment then replied, "No, sir."

"Well you obviously had been watching closely. You don't bring a PT alongside a pier that well unless you know what you're doing."

The young man smiled with appreciation.

"Where'd you go to school?"

"SC, class of '41."

"What'd you study?"

"Economics."

"Econ! How'd you end up on a PT boat? I thought the Supply Corps would have snatched you up."

They arrived at Bryan's tent.

Deke shrugged his shoulders. "They tried to get me to sign up but I wanted more action than sitting at a desk counting sheets."

This skinny baby-faced kid might be made of something sterner, Bryan thought.

"Come on in. Let's see if Doug did his job."

Deke followed him inside and stood while Bryan opened the lid to a wooden box at the edge of the tent.

"Bingo!" He reached in and pulled out two cans of Pabst Blue Ribbon beer. Cool water ran off the cans. "There's a can opener on that box."

The two sat down on the bunks.

"I gotta say being able to have a beer at the end of the day beats being on a carrier." He took a long pull on his beer. "Deke, I wanted to talk to you away from the boat."

Taking a drink, Deke looked wary.

Bryan continued, "Our crew has a reputation around the squadron as a bunch of misfits. From what I've seen they don't deserve it."

"No, sir, they don't."

"They can't go into combat thinking they're second best. We've got to build up their confidence. I've watched them perform. They know what they're doing. Hell, look at your approach today."

"Yes, sir," Deke said.

"We need them to realize they're well-trained and ready for combat. You need to believe that too, Deke. No one knows how they'll react when the shooting starts. But when men have confidence in themselves they can handle almost anything."

The young officer nodded.

"And while I'm thinking about it, my name is Bryan. We're in this thing together. How about another beer?"

"Sure thing, Bryan."

"Now tell me about Morrison."

"He's a strange one. There's a chip on his shoulder. It's been there ever since he joined the crew in Panama. I don't know if it's his record from before the war or what. He got busted a couple of times, never made it past second class petty officer. Guess it's hard to take a step back and at the same time see new sailors with the same rank."

"I've seen it before," Bryan replied. "But our lives and the lives of our men depend on those engines. Treat him fair. But if we see any indication he's not getting the job done, he's gone."

"Yes, sir."

The two boat formation departed San Cristobal at 1830 and headed north at twenty knots. Rosenberg wanted them at the northern entrance of the Tadasser Strait by 2100.

The Japanese supply effort for their troops on Guadalcanal had been sporadic. Despite an effective coast watcher establishment, Allied intelligence could not predict Japanese logistic runs on a consistent basis. To date most of the vessels coming south had been small auxiliaries escorted by patrol boats. The intelligence officers felt the supply flow that made it ashore couldn't support the numbers of troops estimated to be on the island.

The scattered to broken cloud layer overhead provided some protection against patrolling Jap aircraft. Maintaining an average of twenty knots, the boats transited a flat sea broken only by the occasional floating log or sea snake.

Bryan had already noticed a different demeanor by Deke Curtis. More relaxed on deck, he always had a good word for the crew as they went about their duties. Only time would tell how the young man would react when the shooting started.

Bryan picked up what looked like Taboa Point, the last good navigation check before they reached the patrol area. He looked at his watch and estimated sunset in forty minutes. A light flashed from Cameron's boat.

"Join up," the signalman Schultz passed to Bryan.

The wake had already died on the lead boat as Bryan slowed the 142 and came up on Cameron's port side. Doug had a megaphone in his hand.

"Any problems?" Cameron yelled across the water.

The boats were now rocking in the swell with 30 feet separating them.

"We're okay", Bryan replied. "How about you?"

"No problems. I plan to head north for twenty minutes then head inshore. I'll set up a racetrack off Taboa Point."

"Understood," Bryan called back.

Cameron yelled, "Good luck." He turned back to his bridge and the PT boat surged ahead.

Back underway, Bryan called to Deke. "Let's have sandwiches passed out to everyone and get some coffee made. It's gonna be a long night."

All hands went to battle stations as the sun went down. Each man wore a kapok life preserver, steel helmet and any extra personal equipment they wanted. Some carried knives, canteens, first aid pouches and .45 caliber pistols. Most tied whistles to their life preservers for signaling at night. Preparation could make the difference between life and death.

There hadn't been any specific intelligence on expected enemy activity tonight. Patrolling the re-supply route used by the Japanese might provide targets of opportunity and would at least gain experience for the new PT crews.

At eight knots, it took an hour and forty five minutes to make one complete track on their search pattern. A partial moon and scattered cloud layer provided some illumination on the water. The winds remained light with wave heights of one to two feet. By midnight the monotony of patrol began to set in despite this being the crew's first real combat patrol. With an hour to go before starting the trip back to San Cristobal everyone was tired.

Bryan hadn't left the bridge since they began the patrol pattern. He wasn't sure what to expect from the Japs. Remembering the Jap patrol boat off New Guinea, he knew how quickly things could happen on the water at night.

"Deke, why don't you check on the gun crews? See if they need some coffee from the galley."

Curtis nodded. "Can do, Skipper."

Bryan turned to see Charlie Morrison, an unusual sight outside the engine room while underway.

"The oil line for number one is leaking badly. I'm worried what will happen if we need full speed."

"What's your recommendation?" Bryan asked.

Morrison wiped his hands with a rag. "Shut down number one and replace the line. Shouldn't take more than fifteen minutes. If we can slow down to five knots, she'll be stable enough to get the job done."

"So we won't have full speed while the engine's shut down and you want just steerage way on the boat."

"Yes, sir."

Bryan didn't like the idea of slowing down but he would need all engines if something happened.

"All right, get busy. Let me know as soon as I can bump the speed back up."

Morrison headed for the engine room hatch. "Yes, sir," he

yelled over his shoulder.

Throttling down, Bryan grabbed the radio handset and keyed the switch. "Razor One, this is Razor Two. Slowing for fifteen to effect repairs."

The radio speaker crackled the response, "Roger. Let me know when complete."

Bryan clicked the radio twice to acknowledge Cameron's order. As the boat slowed and the engines spooled down Bryan felt vulnerable. Speed was the PT boats main advantage and now they might as well be in a dugout canoe.

Ten minutes later the radio came alive. "Razor, Razor, this is Juliet Bravo One One." The transmission came from a patrolling PBY Catalina. Intelligence had briefed them that the aircraft would be in the area.

Bryan listened to the radio traffic between the aircraft commander and Doug Cameron.

"Razor, have located two contacts bearing 345 degrees ten miles from Taboa Point. Will illuminate."

"Roger Bravo One One, Razor standing by."

The Catalina must have picked up the contacts on radar and planned to drop parachute flares to mark the target. They could only be Japs.

"Deke, run down and tell Morrison I need those engines right now."

Suddenly a bright spot of light illuminated off the starboard quarter followed by a second parachute flare. Bryan estimated the distance at ten miles. Cranking the wheel around toward the light he began to inch the throttle ahead. Come on, Deke, what's the hold up?

"Skipper," Deke yelled from behind him. "Morrison said the line's in, they're buttoning up now. Full power available on two and three and he'll start number one in five minutes."

"Thanks, Deke."

As the speed built up to over twenty knots Bryan saw multiple flashes on the water ahead of the bow. Tracers arced across the darkness and a searchlight beam swung across the dark water. The Japs used searchlights on their destroyers for targeting at night, he thought, this could be the Tokyo Express.

PT 142 pounded into the waves, spray flying over the bow. Gripping the wheel with both hands Bryan adjusted course, pointing the bow directly at the tracers. "Man the torpedo tubes," he yelled over the roar of engines. "Deke, we may have a Jap destroyer out there,"

Curtis vaulted over the low combing and ran aft to the torpedo crew.

Bryan watched the engine instruments come up on the number one engine. He had all throttles full ahead, the three engines driving the boat at over thirty knots. Salt spray flew back from the bow as the hull pounded into the dark water, soaking the crew as they hurtled toward the enemy. The gunners were braced at their guns fighting the pounding from the hull. In the black sky two more flares drifted down several miles off the bow.

"Razor One, Razor Two closing your position over," Bryan called over the radio.

The radio remained silent in response.

Slowing the boat, Bryan quickly searched the horizon. At the edge of the pool of light cast by the last flare, he saw the other PT boat. There were no other vessels in sight.

"There may be Japs close. Keep your eyes open."

Gravely ran aft to the 20 millimeter crew.

Seaman Lopez trained his twin .50s in an arc across the bow, the metallic rattle now audible over the slowing engines.

Pulling the throttles to idle, Bryan listened for any sound on the water. The night remained quiet.

The boat continued to close the distance to Cameron's boat as the last flare hit the water and snuffed out.

"Razor One, Razor Two closing on your port beam, over."

"We've been hit, request assistance."

Bryan didn't recognize the voice.

"Get fenders over the side. Everyone stay sharp." He

wanted to get close and find out the extent of the damage. If Cameron had been hit, command of the mission would shift to him.

Lines were passed and the two boats made fast to each other. Bryan left his engines idling as he climbed out of the cockpit, walked to the gunwale and jumped to the other boat. The smell of burned paint and electrical shorts assaulted his nose. Large gashes criss-crossed the upper works.

"Where's Lieutenant Cameron?" Bryan asked.

"Over here, sir."

Bryan recognized Doug's XO, LT(jg) Larry Durbin. Two battle lanterns illuminated the aft area of the cockpit. Doug lay on his back, a blood stained Navy blanket covering his upper body. Bryan knelt down beside him.

"Doug, it's Bryan."

Cameron opened his eyes, turning his head slightly to look at his friend.

"I was setting up a torpedo run on a destroyer....the flare was a good drop. Never saw the second Jap. They hit us before we could launch our fish."

"Here, let me check you out." Bryan lifted the blanket. "Get me a first aid kit," he ordered Durbin. The crew had already removed Cameron's life jacket and khaki shirt. Under the pale light Bryan saw dark red blood oozing from two holes in Doug's side. He knew all they could do was bandage the wounds and hope Doug could hold on until they made it back to base.

Cameron groaned and closed his eyes, "Oh, shit."

"Doug, we'll bandage you up and get you back to San Cristobal. Just hang with us."

"The Jap headed south......he's....down....there, Bryan....I...know...it."

Bryan knew his friend desperately needed medical attention but there were two Jap destroyers within range of his torpedoes.

"Doug, I'm going after them. You just relax." Bryan turned to Durbin seeing the fear in the young man's eyes. "What's your damage?"

"We're taking water, but the pumps should be able to hold it." The dark water slapped against the hull reminding everyone how vulnerable they were.

"All right. Start back for San Cristobal. Make the best speed the hull will take. I'll make a sweep south to look for the Japs. We'll rendezvous later. Have a red flare ready. We'll use that as a rally point."

"Yes, sir."

Bryan climbed back aboard his boat.

"XO, cast off," he yelled.

Bryan knew the chance of locating the two destroyers was slim if the Japs stayed at high speed. Heading south at over 30 knots he searched the dark horizon along with his crew. The intermittent moonlight provided sporadic illumination as the boat crashed into the waves. Spray flew over the deck, the salt stinging the lookout's eyes.

"Skipper, there's something thirty degrees off the port bow," Petty Officer Schultz called.

Bryan put in left rudder and the big flared bow began to move.

"Mark it on the nose," Schultz cried, pointing dead ahead.

"Standby for torpedo attack," Bryan yelled and Wilskie ran forward to the forward starboard tube to remove all locks. Evans pulled himself over to the port tube fighting the violent movement of the deck.

There it was....Bryan saw the threatening outline of a single destroyer on the bow at three miles. "Target on the bow...looks like a Jap tin can...course about 160 degrees." A quick calculation in his mind and he cranked the wheel hard over to set up an attack from the starboard quarter. Suddenly the beam from a large spotlight flashed across the water, catching the boat in its full glare. Night had turned into day.

"Open fire, any gun that will bear....take out that fucking light," Bryan yelled knowing they had to escape the high powered beam.

On the fantail the 20 millimeter cannon began to fire. Almost simultaneously both .50 calibers opened up, the noise deafening. A second search light came on as a round from the destroyer's main gun screamed overhead the boat, exploding behind them.

Caught in the glare of a searchlight the boat was hit with a hail of automatic weapons fire. Splinters and ricocheting bullets flew across the open deck. Another high velocity shell screamed over them, exploding directly in their wake, the whine of shrapnel splitting the air.

"Standby on the torpedoes," Bryan yelled. The torpedomen hung on to their tubes ignoring the destroyer's fire, ready to manually fire the fish if the electric firing circuits failed.

One of the searchlights winked out, victim of the combined fire of the twin 50's. A huge explosion erupted from the water 20 yards off the port bow. Shrapnel thudded into the hull and whizzed overhead. With the gyro setting on the torpedoes set at zero azimuth, Bryan knew he had to take into account the speed and course of the target. He could now make out a large wake boiling up behind the destroyer. Tracers bounced across the water and over the PT boat as they closed the target. Estimating 800 yards to go, Bryan knew they couldn't miss now.

"Fire One!" he yelled at Wilskie and pushed the fire button. He felt the entire boat lurch as the 2000 pound torpedo left the tube. A quick correction with the wheel and Bryan called, "Fire Two." Immediately he turned the wheel hard left and the bow slewed around throwing spray back over the bridge. They were below the minimum depression angle for the Jap's main guns but automatic weapons continued to fire.

"Deke, make smoke," he yelled. Several rounds of machine gun fire hit the forward deck throwing wood splinters in the air.

The XO ran aft and hit the main power switch on the smoke generator. Already warmed up, the pump began to billow gray smoke clouds. The wind stream behind the boat swirled the smoke in deep pinwheel patterns. Bryan knew they were blocked from the view of the Jap. *Where the hell's the second tin can?*

Waiting for the torpedoes to hit, Bryan began to make small turns left and right, spreading the smoke in a wider pattern and trying to make their course unpredictable. At least one of the torpedoes should have hit by now, he thought. If both missed or didn't explode, the Jap would turn the tables on them. The hunter would become the hunted. Better to find the 145 boat and head home rather than waiting to see. Behind them, in the swirling smoke, there was no evidence their torpedoes had hit the Jap. Changing course west, he left Guadalcanal in his wake.

A good radio direction cut and red flare enabled the two boats to rendezvous forty minutes after Bryan's encounter with the Jap destroyer. During the transit they assessed their damage, which turned out to be superficial. Despite the fusillade of fire, none of the crew suffered any wounds.

Closing on Cameron's boat, Bryan could tell the pumps on PT 145 were losing their battle with the Pacific. Larry Durbin stood on the port side with a loud hailer.

"What's your status?" Bryan yelled.

"The Skipper's gone." The finality of those words hit hard. "We're taking on water faster than the pumps can clear it."

Bryan sensed the young officer's fear and ordered Durbin to transfer the crew from 145. "Once everyone's clear, set your scuttling charges," he called across the water.

"What about the Skipper's body?" Durbin asked. The young officer looked tired.

"We're gonna take him home," Bryan said, suddenly feeling very tired.

The transfer of the crew went quickly in the smooth sea state. One other man, their signalman, had also died in the swift exchange of gunfire. The two bodies, now on stretchers, were passed over the small gap between the hulls.

A thirty minute fuse on an explosive charge next to the

189

mainline fuel tank would rupture the tank and also rip the bottom out of the boat, sending her to the bottom. As PT 142 pulled away from the abandoned boat her surviving crew stood on the fantail next to the bodies of their dead shipmates.

Chapter Thirteen

The Fog of Battle

Jerry Rosenberg poured a cup of hot coffee from a stainless steel thermos. The clock on his wall read 0624, three hours since the 142 boat had returned to San Cristobal, barely making it home before fuel exhaustion.

"Tangling with Jap destroyers on your first trip. That's one way to break into the game." Rosenberg pulled open his lower desk drawer removing a bottle of Jim Beam whiskey. He poured a shot into one of the cups and handed it to Bryan. "Don't have any cream or sugar."

"This'll do fine."

"I'm sorry about Doug. He was one of my best skippers and a fine officer."

Bryan remembered his friend, lying on the cold deck of his boat, mortally wounded and still worried about getting the Japs. He took a drink of the whiskey

"How's your boat?" Rosey asked.

"She looks chewed up but nothing important. Engines are good. No other problems except those shitty torpedoes."

"We've heard of problems in other squadrons but those are the first ones we've fired."

Bryan put his cup down on Rosey's desk. "I know we were

close enough. Both of those should have hit. They just didn't go off."

Rosey nodded. "Tiny thinks the problem is that these torpedoes were designed before the war. They weren't made to take the constant pounding they get on PT boats. The reports I've seen talk about erratic runs, premature explosions, failure to detonate and lousy depth control. If you do get a hit there's only a three hundred pound warhead, good enough for a destroyer but not worth a shit on a cruiser."

"So what are they gonna do about it?"

Rosey took a drink of his coffee. "A Chief Torpedoman working for Tiny used to work at the Naval Torpedo Factory in Newport. They've been working on putting some home made fixes in both the guidance section and detonators to beef them up. We'll see what luck we have."

"Hell of a way to fight a war," Bryan snorted.

"The chain of command says that the fix is the new torpedo, the Mark Thirteen. But we won't see it for a while."

"Something else. We were in pretty close to the Jap but the .50s and the 20 millimeter didn't provide the kind of firepower we needed to hold off the Jap guns until we could launch our fish."

Rosenberg grinned. "That's something we might be able to fix. Tiny has a line on two 37millimeter guns that he wants to mount forward of the bridge on two of our boats. The armor piercing rounds will slice through a destroyer like butter."

"Where did those come from?"

"Hard to believe but they're replacement guns for the Army Air Corps P-400's, the old P-39 Aircobra."

"How can we get 'em?"

Rosey grinned. "There weren't a lot of P-400's on Guadalcanal to begin with and most of them have been shot down. So we think we can get our hands on the replacement guns. All we have to do is mount them and re-rig the firing circuit."

"If you're looking for somewhere to mount it, I know just the boat."

"All right, that's a deal."

"How about ammo and training?" Bryan asked.

"No problem on the ammo. It's available and there's plenty in the system. Training is more of an issue. We've been looking for someone who can teach us about the gun and also do minor work on it."

"Let me work on that. There's gotta be someone on this island that knows something about that gun."

"See what you can dig up, but now go get some sleep."

"I've got one more thing to do."

Rosenberg watched Bryan walk out of the office. "I think Michaels found his war," he said to himself.

There were a large number of squadron personnel on the pier looking at the damage to PT 142. Several of his crew were on deck drinking coffee and looking across the harbor. Bryan expected they would have hit their racks after the long night.

The two machine gunners, Lopez and Heimbigner were sitting on the aft lazarette with cups of steaming coffee. They stood up as he walked aft.

"You guys should be getting some sleep," he said.

They both grinned.

"We tried, Skipper, Heimbigner said, grinning.

"You guys did well last night."

Lopez beamed. "Thanks, Skipper." The exact opposite of the beefy Heimbigner, the young sailor didn't have a spare pound on his frame.

Funny thing, Bryan thought, these two are different as night and day but they've showed they know how to fight.

Bryan saw sailors from other boats looking at the damage across the topside of the boat. His two machine gunners were enjoying the recognition of returning from a tough battle. The first signs of pride, he thought.

"Have you seen Petty Officer Morrison?"

"Yes, sir. He's down in the engine room."

Bryan found the stocky Motor Machinist Mate behind the centerline engine.

Morrison stood up. "I'm finishing up some routine maintenance."

Bryan didn't miss the lack of a 'sir' from the man. He stared hard at Morrison for a moment. "You did a fine job on that repair last night."

The young man paused before answering, and then tentatively said, "Thanks."

"Petty Officer Morrison, I don't know what the future holds for this boat and crew. I do know that we'll all learn to depend on each other more than we could ever imagine. This boat is depending on you. I'm depending on you. From what I've seen so far, that trust is well placed. I'm glad you're running this engine room. And I want you to remember that it's your responsibility. I'll rely on you for good advice and you can count on me to tell you what's going on when we're out there. Fair enough?"

"Fair enough, sir."

A small cemetery had been constructed by the Seabees on the north end of the island. Most of the squadron showed up for Doug Cameron's funeral. He and his Signalman, Petty Officer Phillip Masterson, were laid to rest after a Navy Chaplain conducted the traditional service. The similarity to the burial at sea for Bill Nance struck Bryan. Even though one service was at sea in the middle of the huge Pacific and the other on a stinking tropical island, both honored Americans a long way from home who had given their lives in performance of duty. The looks in the eyes of the men at the burial on San Cristobal mirrored what he'd seen on the carrier, sadness and the brutal awareness that they might be next. Bryan felt just as empty when he returned to his tent as he had after the service on *Enterprise*.

Deke Curtis handed a cup of steaming coffee to Bryan, who

took it gratefully.

"You read my mind," Bryan said. "Here take the wheel."

Thirty minutes from base, PT 142 was completing its forty second patrol over the last two months. They were returning alone, the 139 boat having headed back early due to engine trouble. Now the early morning sea was empty. Lopez and Heimbigner manned their machine guns, the threat from air attack always with them.

Bryan took a drink of the hot liquid. "God this is terrible. Can't we steal some good coffee from the base?"

Deke laughed. "We're already getting a reputation as the local pirate crew."

"That's not such a bad thing," Bryan said. He watched as the XO made a small course correction, handling the 80 foot boat like it was second nature.

"You ever think about the odds?" Deke asked, his eyes still on the water.

"What do you mean?"

"Two months, forty patrols and not a scratch on any of our guys."

"Lot of luck I suppose," Brian said.

"Yeah, I guess so. But I'm an econ major. I understand probability and statistics. Luck only goes so far."

Bryan remembered JJ Powers. Best pilot in the squadron but he ended up in the sights of a Jap Zero at the wrong time.

"That's why you can't worry about it. If you do, you can't do your job. We're lucky to have a good crew and a good boat. That's gotta be enough."

"I'll be honest. During the last few scrapes I've been scared more than ever before. I've just got this feeling my time is up."

"Deke, we've all felt like that."

"So what do you do?"

"Same thing you've been doing. Keep fighting the boat and put it out of your mind."

"Yeah, I guess you're right."

Bryan knew Deke was now ready for his own command.

"Skipper?"

Bryan turned to see Petty Officer Morrison. The mechanic's skivvy shirt was stained with grease and he needed a shave.

"Charlie, what's up?"

"Been watching number three all night. She's running a little hot. I'd like to take a couple of the cooling lines off and check them out. We'd be out of business for two maybe three hours."

"If you think it needs to get done, go ahead. I'll let the squadron know when we get in. You need any help?"

"Nah, Wilskie and Baurichter volunteered to help. I know they're gunners, but I can teach 'em."

Deke and Bryan both laughed.

"Hey, Charlie. How about keeping your eyes open for some good coffee for the boat. Never know what might turn up."

"Can do, Skipper. I think I know where there might be what we need."

On the fantail Petty Officer Gravely was talking with Don Baurichter as Morrison headed back to his engine room.

"Hey Gravely, the Skipper said it was okay to take the cooling lines off three when we get in port."

"Thanks, Charlie," he replied as Morrison went down the hatch.

"Old Charlie sure got his shit together," Don Baurichter said.

Gravely smiled. "I think everyone's got their shit together. All it took was getting rid of Thomas and getting a new skipper. Hell, look at Curtis. He was scared of his own shadow when Michaels got here. Now he should probably get his own boat. The whole squadron knows it too. I just hope they leave us together and don't bust us up to help those other sorry sons of bitches."

Baurichter laughed.

As the engines shut down, Chief Little called up to Bryan, "Lieutenant, the boss wanted me to have you stop by and see Mr. Leonard as soon as you got in. He said it was about your new toy."

"Can do, Chief." He turned to Deke. "Maybe some good news."

At the far end of the squadron area, one Quonset hut stood alone from the others. It housed the ordnance section which performed maintenance on torpedoes and guns for the squadron. When Bryan arrived he found Tiny Leonard hunched over a workbench with one of his chiefs.

"Solved all of our problems yet?" Bryan called to his friend.

Leonard looked up, sweat streaming off his face. "This is Chief Torpedoman Schilling. He thinks we have a way to protect the torpedoes from the pounding while they sit in the tube."

A tall skinny man looked up from the bench and nodded.

"How soon will they be ready?"

"The Chief is going to install this one and we'll take it for a test ride. If it stands up, we'll start converting all of the fish tomorrow. But I'm guessing you didn't stop by to talk about torpedoes."

"Rosey said you had a new toy for me."

Leonard stepped away from the bench. "Lemme show you." He walked to the far end of the hut. Pulling the tarp back he revealed two 37 millimeter cannons. "Feast your eyes on these babies."

The guns were still in the wooden packing crates. Bryan knelt down and examined them. Both guns were in good condition. "How soon can you get one mounted on my boat?"

"It you lend me Baurichter and the rest of your gunners we'll be ready to move it down to the pier tomorrow morning and have her bolted on by sundown."

Standing up Bryan walked around the two guns. "Ever fire one of these?"

Leonard shook his head. "Nope, not me. But we've got a manual, that's a start."

"That's all I needed to hear. We'll figure it out."

Two boats were fitted with the new 37millimeter cannon. Bryan's 142 and Roy Lundeen's 135. Bryan found a Marine Gunnery Sergeant who had worked on the gun before the war. After several sessions with his gunner's mates, the cannon became operational in Motor Torpedo Boat Squadron Six. Tiny Leonard rode out for the first test firings off Cape Espiritu. The gunners fired forty rounds without a hitch. Bryan knew the increase in range and firepower gave them a big advantage over the Japs. He didn't intend to wait long to demonstrate their power to the enemy.

Two days later PT 142, along with Lundeen's boat, sortied to investigate a report of landings taking place near Lanna Point. Lanna Point lay on the western side of Guadalcanal and the Japanese were trying to reinforce the two regiments that intelligence estimated were on the island. It would be the first operational test for the new gun and Tiny Leonard used that as leverage for permission to go on the mission.

"I'm surprised Rosey let you go with us. I'd have thought he didn't want to take a chance on losing his maintenance officer." Bryan stood behind the wheel as the two boats headed north toward their target.

"I don't plan on getting lost. You know something I don't?" Tiny yelled over the roar of the Packard engines.

Bryan looked over to see his friend grinning.

The two boats cruised in right echelon with Bryan leading the formation. The transit to Lanna Point would take 40 minutes.

"Maybe we'll get a chance to try both of your new toys tonight," Bryan said to Tiny. He referred to the 37 millimeter and fixes to the torpedoes that were installed in the last week.

"That's why I'm here."

Bryan turned to Petty Officer Gravely. The man stood at the rear of the cockpit leaning against the handrail. "Would you see if there's any hot coffee down below?"

"Yes, sir."

Gravely disappeared down the hatch.

Tiny leaned closer to Bryan. "Good man."

"Damned lucky to have him," Bryan replied.

"How's it going with Morrison?" Tiny asked.

Keeping his eyes straight ahead, Bryan answered, "No complaints. He keeps those engines humming."

"That's good to hear. I had my doubts, but I'm willing to give a man a chance."

Deke Curtis came up from down below. He handed two cups of coffee to Bryan and Tiny. "Estimating ten miles to Lanna Point."

Bryan looked at his watch, it was 2253.

"We've got about two hours before we need to head back home. Lanna Point is one of the spots where the intel guys thought the Japs might try to land supplies." He picked up the radio handset and keyed the transmitter.

"Tiger Two, Tiger One."

Lundeen answered immediately, "Go ahead."

"Tiger One commencing search to the south. Detach as briefed."

The answer told Bryan all he needed to hear.

"Roger, detaching."

Lundeen had been briefed to proceed north of Lanna Point and conduct an independent search, rendezvousing at 0100 five miles west of the point. Bryan felt confident in Lundeen's experience and judgment. The two patrol patterns put the two boats close enough for mutual support if either got into trouble.

Bryan reduced speed to ten knots as he turned toward the land.

"Everyone stay alert and keep your eyes open." Each of the topside crewmembers wore binoculars, the quarter moon providing illumination for their search.

Deke Curtis walked up behind him. "I rechecked, we're fully darkened Skipper."

"Thanks, XO."

One light could make the difference between being the

hunter or the hunted.

Forty five minutes later Bryan strained to make out the beach. The distinctive Lanna Point jutted into the straits providing a good navigation aid. Throttling back to idle, they drifted for twenty minutes, the current moving them south along the beach.

"Deke, takeover," Bryan said stepping back from the wheel. "Let's run north along the beach for three miles and set up another drift."

"Right."

The boat vibrated slightly as the rpm's increased on the engines.

"Nice night."

Bryan turned to see Tiny behind him.

"You disappeared. I figured you went down for chow and a beauty nap."

Leonard crossed his arms across his broad chest. "You must know by now that Warrant Boatswains don't need chow or sleep."

"So you're not interested in the beer locker after we get back?"

Tiny laughed. "I didn't say anything about not needing booze. Actually I was down in your engine room."

Bryan moved over closer to Tiny who had walked to the edge of the cockpit. "Problem?"

"Nah, just wanted to see how Morrison was doing."

He had Bryan's full attention. "Good or bad?"

Tiny lowered his voice slightly. "He's a big fan of yours. In fact he described you as the first PT boat skipper he'd ever met who knew what the hell he was doing."

Bryan's smile was hidden by the darkness.

Schulz stood on the port side of the cockpit holding the binoculars to his eyes. Without removing the glasses he said, "Skipper, it looks like there's something on the beach. Maybe a mile ahead just starboard of the bow."

Immediately every set of glasses focused ahead. Bryan

could make out the dark shape of a hull or maybe two against the lighter sand on the beach. The Japanese used motorized barges for moving troops and supplies ashore. Often they were towed by larger ships then cut lose for the run to the beach.

"Surface targets on the beach. Stand by on the forward gun," Bryan said quietly to the men in the cockpit. Although they were a mile from the enemy everyone knew sound carries well across the water at night. "I'll take it, XO." He moved to the wheel.

The gunners, Don Baurichter and John Harris, stood by the new gun.

"Deke, hold the fifties when we open up. I want the 37 and 20 mm to target the hulls."

"Roger, Skipper." Curtis turned to brief the gun crews.

Estimating the distance to be approaching a half mile Bryan turned the wheel slightly to port to unmask the 20 millimeter on the stern.

He turned to Tiny, "Let's see what she'll do.....OPEN FIRE!"

The crash of the forward gun shattered the stillness. A moment after the first shot from the bow, the 20 millimeter opened up from the stern. Both guns kept up a steady fire at the beach, the rounds impacting the dark hulls. The smell of cordite was sharp from the 37.

"Be ready to use your fifties if we get any fire from the beach," Bryan yelled to his machine gunners. There were now flames flickering on the nearest hull. More shells crashed into the two barges now visible against the white sand. "Tiny, I'm gonna move in closer. Tell the fifties to sweep the jungle around those barges."

Leonard nodded that he understood. The noise from the two deck guns echoed across the dark water. A moment later the starboard .50 caliber opened up, tracers careening into the trees and underbrush behind the beach.

"Cease fire. Cease fire," Bryan yelled after another minute and one by one the guns quit, the silence in stark contrast to the brutal noise of the massed barrage of the last few minutes.

The crackle of flames could be heard across the water, fires growing on the first barge. The reflection from the burning hulls illuminated the water between the PT and the beach. Bryan didn't like being highlighted this close to the beach. He pushed the throttles forward and turned the boat out to sea.

Tiny Leonard stared back at the scene of destruction on the beach. "Son of a bitch."

Chapter Fourteen

Allies Again

The small airstrip on San Cristobal served primarily as logistic support for the base and as an emergency landing strip for the aircraft from Henderson Field on Guadalcanal. Located on the northern end of the island, it took thirty minutes by jeep for Bryan to make his way from the harbor to the field. He rode in the second of two jeeps, the first jeep carrying the local commander, Captain Frank Gossett. Rosey rode with the Captain. They were all meeting their boss, the Commander of Task Group 73, Rear Admiral Chuck Michaels.

Bryan's jeep followed Captain Gossett's to the bottom of the two story control tower. Dust rose from under the vehicles as they pulled to a stop. He joined the two senior officers in front of the tower.

A sailor jogged out to the officers and saluted. "Sir, the R-4 is due in ten minutes. They just called in on the radio."

Gossett, a tall skinny man, saluted the sailor. "Thank you, son."

Rosey turned to Bryan. "How long since you've seen your Dad?"

"Back in Pearl, right after Midway."

Rosey squinted into the morning sunshine. "Quite a change for a battleship sailor. Tin cans and PT boats."

Bryan nodded. "Little different from the *Arizona*. But I'm

sure he'd rather be out here than riding a desk in Pearl."

Rosenberg knew the older Michaels had lost his wife before the war. Not much to stay home for, he thought.

"There she is," Gossett said as they all heard the sound of the R-4D transport's engines.

Rear Admiral Chuck Michaels climbed down the short ladder extending from the aft cabin hatch. He returned the salute of the three officers.

"Welcome to San Cristobal, Admiral," Captain Gossett said.

"Thank you, Captain." Michaels shook hand with Gossett who introduced Rosenberg.

Chuck Michaels stopped and smiled at his son. As Bryan saluted, the Admiral extended his hand. "It's good to see you," he said, his eyes saying much more.

"I've brought along a special team, gentlemen. Bryan I think you know two of them."

Lee Cordner climbed down the ladder and turned to face the group.

"Gentlemen, this is Lieutenant Commander Cordner of the Royal Australian Navy. He's leading a team that I will brief you about shortly."

Cordner shook hands around and grinned at Bryan. "Hello, Yank."

"Lee Cordner, I never thought I'd see you again."

"Gotta be careful with Aussies, we have a habit of showing up when we're least expected."

Another man climbed down the ladder. "You remember Andy Harkins?" Lee asked Bryan.

He nodded. "I can't wait to find out what this is all about."

"Contrary to what I suspect you believed, this is not an inspection trip." Michaels sat at a small table with Gossett and Rosenberg in the headquarters hut. "You might have figured something was up when our Aussie friends climbed off the aircraft."

Gossett shrugged, "Did seem a bit unusual, sir."

Michaels continued, "We have a problem and it's going to take everyone involved to solve it." The Admiral opened a folder and produced a chart of the islands north of Guadalcanal. "I'm sure you saw the message traffic the night before last on the PBY that went down at the northern part of New Georgia Sound."

The two men nodded.

"What the message traffic did not say was the PBY, which was on a transport mission from Brisbane to Espiritu Santo, had been diverted to search for a downed aircraft. Unfortunately there was a passenger on board carrying highly classified information. It's the kind of information that changes the courses of wars. We have to get him back or verify that he's dead. There's another wrinkle. Two Navy nurses apparently were manifested space available just before the PBY left." What Michaels could not tell the two officers was the missing Lieutenant Rogers was a cryptologist and knew of the Navy's breaking the primary Japanese operational code JN-25. If the Japanese realized their code had been compromised the Allies would lose a critical operational advantage.

"Nurses! What the hell were they doing there?" Gossett said.

"Part of a new forward deployed surgical unit."

"Shit," Rosenberg added.

"That's a long way up there, Admiral. Why use PT boats?" Gossett asked.

"We only have a rough idea where they went down. So there's going to be some searching required. A sub can't search and bigger surface units would be too vulnerable to air attack from Rabaul. We need boats that can hide along the shore and also defend themselves while they're searching."

"Why the Aussies?" Rosenberg asked.

"Cordner has experience in those waters. Harkins is one of their most experienced behind the lines operators. We're counting on them linking up with a coast watcher on Vella Lavella. Hopefully we can get some of the local natives involved in the search. The coast watchers have a cadre of natives they use for all sorts of duties. They can also travel by canoe without too much interference from the Japs."

Gossett leaned over and looked at the chart. "Do you have an op plan yet, sir?"

Michaels nodded. "What we came up with in talking with the Australians is a primary search group of two PT's. We would use the rest of the squadron to ferry fuel, ammo, and provide back up if one of the primary boats is knocked out. Initially we would send them north to link up with the coast watcher and land Captain Harkins to start the search on land. Our two boats would conduct their own search in the area the Catalina went down. We search until we find something."

Rosenberg shook his head. "That's gonna be a hot area up there. Between the Tokyo Express coming down the slot to the patrolling Jap aircraft I'm not sure how long a boat can survive."

Michael's voice became hard. "So there's no doubt in anyone's mind, loss of the entire squadron is considered acceptable to accomplish this mission. I expect every man to be aware of that fact. They deserve to know the rules."

The two officers looked at the Admiral with a look of surprise. The Navy always made a maximum effort to recover lost personnel. But there had to be a point where any prudent commander must weigh the cost.

"Gentlemen, I wish I could divulge the reason but you'll have to take my word."

"Yes, sir," Gossett said.

Michaels stood up and stretched his back. "As you might imagine time is critical. We need to start the boats north as soon as possible."

Rosenberg looked at the chart and then at Michaels. "Sir, I have two boats that are ready to go this afternoon. They've got good crews, are the best armed and have the most recent experience."

"Good. Let's get the CO's and XO's of those boats together

as soon as you can. I'll have our Aussies there and we can finalize plans."

"Twenty minutes back here, sir?"

"Fine. I'd like a chance to talk with my son."

Rosenberg looked the Admiral in the eye. "Sir, he's one of the CO's."

Michaels turned and walked out the door. "I'll make sure he's here."

Lee Cordner and Bryan sat talking on a wooden bench outside the headquarters. They both turned as Admiral Michaels walked up.

"Gentlemen, stay seated. Bryan I need to talk with you and we don't have much time. Commander, will you excuse us?"

"Yes, sir. I'll go find Captain Harkins. Those army types tend to get into trouble on naval establishments."

The Admiral sat down next to Bryan.

"Dad, you look tired."

Michaels looked at his son and laughed. "Have you looked in a mirror?"

"I guess this part of the world takes it out of everyone."

The Admiral said, "We both have a meeting in fifteen minutes. You've been selected for a mission I assigned to Squadron Six."

Bryan knew something was bothering his father. "You don't sound like that makes you very happy."

"It's going to be dangerous. But it's important. I wouldn't send people this far north if it wasn't."

"Then it's not a problem. I've got a good crew and we'll take care of whatever needs to get done," Bryan said. "Is that what's bothering you?"

"You know me too well." The Admiral paused for a moment then continued, "I saw Liz last week. Her unit was in transit. They'd been training in Brisbane and were on their way to Tualo as part of the forward support for the next big push north."

"Tualo?" Bryan brightened at the idea of seeing Liz. Their letters had been sporadic and he didn't know for sure where she was.

The Admiral nodded. "The Aussies found out in New Guinea that if you can get the badly wounded to level two treatment, their odds of survival go up 100 percent Level two involves almost full surgical capability. They need the doctors and nurses close to the action to pull it off."

"That island is well within range of Jap bombers from Rabaul to say nothing of naval gunfire from the Tokyo Express…"

"Bryan," the Admiral interrupted. "Liz was on a PBY that went down last night in the northern part of the Slot."

"What?" Bryan answered automatically, realizing the horror of his father's words.

"That's what this mission is about. You'll get the full brief at our meeting…"

"That went down? Liz?"

"We don't know anything else right now. What we do know came from a sketchy radio transmission and a coast watcher's report." Chuck Michaels saw the look of bewilderment on his son's face. "I'm in a tough spot. You've been selected by your Squadron Commander as the best skipper for this mission."

Bryan looked out at the airfield. He felt sick. "Don't take me off this. I can bring her home if anyone can."

"You won't like this but the primary reason you're going up there is to find an intel officer who hitched a ride."

"That's fine. I'll get him back too."

Chuck Michaels looked at his son. "Bryan, I'm going to send you on a mission where you're considered an acceptable loss to get this intelligence Lieutenant back safely. I'm willing to take the risk because I know what it means to you. But you have to be able to keep your head on straight."

"Don't worry about me." He wiped the sweat from his eyes. "It's my fault she's out here."

"In case you've forgotten, she's a Navy nurse. It goes with the territory. She didn't have to do this, she volunteered."

"That doesn't make me feel any better."

"We'd better get going," the Admiral said.

PT 142, in company with Roy Lundeen's 135, cruised at twenty two knots across a choppy sea. The two boats had been underway for three hours from San Cristobal enroute to Vella Lavella.

On arrival they would land Andy Harkins and Sergeant Tully Graves in an attempt to link up with Harry Richardson. The local planter had been in the Solomons since the early 30's. Officially a Lieutenant in the Royal Australian Naval Reserve, Richardson joined the coast watcher organization right after the war started. Now he stood watch on one of the larger islands close to the Japanese base at Rabaul.

After landing the Aussies, both boats would begin a search of the shoreline of the Vella Gulf, south of the island. Based on their last radio transmission and a report from Richardson, it was the most logical place to start.

Numerous small islets dotted the waters between the larger islands, many of which could shelter survivors. The extensive beaches also provided potential cover for anyone from the many Japanese patrols. The steady traffic by barges and patrol boats moving south from Choiseul to re-supply the Japanese Army units would make hiding for a prolonged period of time difficult. Everyone knew the challenge of survival in these islands could be difficult any time, during combat it became almost impossible.

Bryan had been at the wheel since they got underway. He couldn't push the horrible reality of the situation from his mind. He kept seeing the image of Liz in an aircraft crash. His own experience did nothing to quell his fear for her.

"I never understood why they didn't put torpedoes on our Fairmiles," Lee Cordner said.

Bryan turned to see his Australian friend. He liked Cordner and it made him feel good to have an old hand along for the mission.

"For all the good these things are, I'd rather have more gas or guns," Bryan replied. "Hell, if a Jap destroyer is running full out they can run away from these things."

Cordner laughed. "Let's hope we don't run into any destroyers."

"How's your old boat doing?"

"She's in the yard right now, bit of a cruncher on the hull. Hit a submerged log. Should be right as rain when they're done."

Bryan adjusted the course slightly. "So you volunteered for this little trip?"

"Actually I'm attached to a bit of a pick up unit now. My commander knew I'd been up here before the war. He told me it made sense to send me and I couldn't think of any good reason to disagree."

"Lee, this may be the most important thing I've ever done. You think Harkins can find this coast watcher?"

Cordner laughed. "I think Andy is part aboriginal. If anyone can beat the Japs in the jungle, it's Andy."

What if it didn't make any difference? Suppose she lay in some twisted wreckage buried deep in the jungle or at the bottom of New Georgia Sound?

"I had a cup of coffee with your chap Tiny. Good man."

"They don't come any better. We're lucky Rosenberg let him come along. I figured we're so far from home we needed to take our best ship fixer with us."

"Let's just hope the fuel is there in the morning," Lee added.

By sunrise the two PT boats would be down to 20% fuel. The *Monaghan* would rendezvous with the two boats and pump their tanks full. If the destroyer wasn't there they were in deep trouble. Their only course of action would be to hide the boats against one of the islands and radio for assistance. Bryan liked to have more options but that was their only choice. The original idea of using squadron PT's for re-supply was rejected when they looked at the fuel consumption numbers. Also the PT's would have to carry the fuel drums on deck making them even more susceptible to air attack.

210

Deke Curtis came out of the forward cockpit hatch. "Skipper, why don't I relieve you and you can get some chow."

Bryan knew that made sense. Tonight would be a long night transit and he needed to be ready for anything.

"Thanks, Deke. Lee and I will get some chow and I'll try to grab a quick nap. Call me if anything comes up."

"Rog."

Despite his exhaustion Bryan lay on the bunk in his small cabin unable to sleep. What would have happened if this intel Lieutenant hadn't been on the plane? Would they have just written Liz off as 'missing, presumed dead?' If she was alive he would find her. But what would he do if he had to choose between Liz and Rogers?

The boat suddenly slewed hard over to the left as automatic fire echoed in the darkness. Bryan rolled out of bed and threw open the door on his way to the bridge. Emerging into the dark he saw a figure sprawled on the deck. Quartermaster First Class Gravely was at the wheel.

"What happened?" Bryan yelled.

"Jap aircraft," Gravely said shakily.

"I've got it," he said taking the wheel. "Are the guns manned?"

"Yes, sir."

Bryan pulled power on the engines and made a sharp course correction to starboard. Jap float planes liked to follow the phosphorescent wakes of PT boats and make their attacks from behind. With the broken cloud cover he might be able to disappear under the shadow of the clouds. He grabbed the radio handset.

"Devil Two this is Devil One. Attacked by air contact. Speed now five."

Immediately he heard Roy Lundeen reply, "Roger, I have you in sight."

Now they needed to move away without attracting attention. Bryan listened but couldn't hear aircraft engines. Maybe their attacker had gone home.

"Gravely, take the wheel."

Bryan knelt down over Deke who lay on his side.

"Hang on, Deke. We'll get you below."

Tiny Leonard came out of the hatch with Lee Cordner.

"Whaddya need, Bryan?" Tiny asked.

"Can you and Lee get him down to his cabin? That Jap might still be around here and I don't want to take any chances."

"Righto," Cordner said knelt down to help roll Deke onto his back.

The focused beam from the battle lantern added to the light from the small overhead light bulb. Deke Curtis lay on the bunk with Tiny Leonard bending over him. Lee Cordner stood to one side holding the battle lantern. Blood soaked the thin Navy blanket under Curtis. Leonard opened a canvas first aid kit and took out a heavy paper package labeled "Dressing, Gauze, 4 Inch."

"Here, hold this against the wound," Leonard told Petty Officer Schulz, handing him the opened bandage.

Curtis lay on his left side facing the bulkhead. His shirt had been cut off, exposing an ugly round hole just below his shoulder blade. Leonard pulled adhesive tape off a one inch roll and began to tape the dressing against the wound.

"Okay, now help me roll him over on his back."

Sweat covered Curtis's ashen face and a thin trickle of blood flowed from an exit wound on his lower right side.

"That's good, Deke. In and out, nothing left in there." The big Boatswain tried to sound positive but he knew the wound was bad.

Ten minutes later Tiny went up to the cockpit followed by Lee Cordner. He noted the speed had picked up to ten knots.

"Jap gone?" Tiny asked.

Bryan nodded. "I think so. How's Deke?"

"Not good. One round hit him in the back and came out near

his groin. No telling what kind of damage it did on the way through. We did get most of the external bleeding stopped, but I don't know what's going on inside."

"Shit."

"He needs a doctor."

Bryan considered his options. He could turn around and have Deke at the hospital on Tulagi in about three hours. That would blow their rendezvous with the *Monaghan* and set the mission back 24 hours. He knew the mission must take priority, even if it meant the life of his XO. There was no guarantee anyone survived the crash of the PBY. But at the same time he didn't know if Deke would survive long enough to make it to Tulagi.

"Is he awake?"

Leonard said, "Yeah. He's in pain but I didn't want to use morphine in case he might be going into shock."

Bryan turned to Cordner. "Lee take the conn. We're steering three two zero magnetic. Lundeen's boat is off our starboard quarter. Guns are manned."

"I got it, mate."

Making his way down to Deke's small cabin Bryan knew what his decision must be. How do you look a man in the eye and tell him he's expendable?

Curtis lay on his back. Schulz sat in the chair next to the bunk. He stood up as Bryan entered.

"Take a break," he told the Petty Officer.

"Aye, sir," the man said and slipped quietly out the door.

The boat moved rhythmically under his feet as Bryan sat down in the chair. Deke's face turned slightly and he looked at Bryan.

"How ya doing?" Bryan asked quietly.

"God damn, my insides are on fire," Curtis said slowly, the pain etched on his face.

"I wish there was something we could do," Bryan said knowing there wasn't. "We'll get you aboard the *Monaghan* when we rendezvous at first light. They've got a doctor and they can get you back in port and into a hospital."

"Okay." Curtis stared up at the low overhead without looking at Bryan. He knew the score.

"I wish there was some other way."

"Skipper, it's okay," the young man said quietly and closed his eyes.

Bryan went back on deck. He knew it wasn't okay but it was the way it had to be. That didn't make it any easier.

"Tiny, would you go down and stay with Deke? I think it'll be easier for him if you're there."

"Sure," the big man said and went below.

Lieutenant Tom Hallihan sat on the muddy jungle floor with his back against a rough barked palm tree. His bruised and cut face showed the results of the crash and struggle ashore from PBY 41423. Around Hallihan five other survivors listened to the sounds of the jungle coming alive for a new day. The small clearing on the island of Vona Vona had been their first stop after struggling off the nearby beach.

Hallihan had been the co-pilot of the ill fated seaplane. Lieutenant Geneers, the aircraft commander, had been killed in the crash. Ensign Kirkpatrick, the navigator, sat next to Hallihan, his arm supported in a sling made from several pieces of rope. The only enlisted crewman to make it ashore, Radioman Third Class Barry Collins, knelt next to Kirkpatrick. On the opposite side of the small clearing, two women rested side by side, their backs against a large boulder.

Lieutenant Jerry Rogers stood up and looked toward the biggest break in the foliage.

"It's getting light," he said to no one in particular.

Hallihan roused from his half sleep. "When it gets a little lighter we need to look for water."

Liz Sommers got to her feet and walked over to Hallihan. Kneeling down she gently put her hand on his forehead. "How's the eye?"

"Doesn't hurt as much but still can't see out of it."

Her khaki uniform covered with dried mud and sand, she stood up and surveyed the group. Thirty hours ago they were clean and rested, only an hour from landing at Espiritu Santo when they had been attacked by a Jap airplane. She remembered the terrible sounds as one of their engines seized up and the crewmembers yelled to brace for ditching. The violent impact was followed by water pouring into the darkened aircraft as they struggled to get the life raft out the hatch and inflated.

The fear and confusion resulted in a desperate scramble to exit the sinking Catalina. One by one they jumped into the ink black water and struck out toward the life raft. A calm sea allowed them all to swim to the raft and climb aboard. Most took several tries to get into the unstable raft and the last survivors were pulled aboard by their clothes.

It had taken the shocked group thirty minutes of paddling by hand to reach a small strip of beach where they dragged themselves onto the sand, exhausted by their ordeal. Lieutenant Hallihan wasn't sure which island they were on and they didn't have a map. Collins told Hallihan he'd been able to get out a "mayday" call but there had been no response.

In their haste to escape the sinking aircraft no one had remembered to bring the survival packs which contained food, water and medical supplies. Their situation was critical and pushing into the jungle for cover was their only option. The heat and humidity had quickly sapped their strength and the small amount of water they were able to find in large banana-type leaves only provided a few swallows per person.

Hallihan estimated they were one hundred miles from the nearest friendly territory. The only reasonable plan was to try and signal friendly forces as they passed the island. The survivors could use the signal mirror from the raft. On a sunny day a mirror flash could be seen up to twenty miles. He hoped it would be enough.

They began to see more detail around them as the sun continued to illuminate the jungle.

"There's no reason to stay here. Let's make our way inland and try to find higher ground. We might find a stream." Hallihan stood up, ready to move. "I'll go first. Follow in single file. Try to be quiet. We don't know if there are Japs on this island. Kirk you bring up the rear."

"Right."

The group followed Hallihan as he headed away from the beach and farther into the jungle. Thick underbrush hid thorn bushes that pulled at their clothing. They struggled through dense foliage and sensed the terrain rising as they went. Mosquitoes and gnat-like flies covered any exposed skin adding to their misery. The muddy ground contributed to slips and falls as they climbed higher and their uniforms were soon covered in slime.

Bryan pushed the throttles of PT 142 forward, accelerating to a cruise speed of 23 knots. Sunrise found the boat still below a broken layer of clouds. It would be a six hour run to Vella Lavella if they had no problems. Deke had been transferred to the *Monaghan* while they took on fuel. The young officer had survived the night and Bryan hoped that meant Deke would survive.

But right now he had to focus on the mission. Get Harkins to the island and start searching for Liz. Nothing else mattered.

"Stop. I've got to rest." Nancy slid to the ground.

The column stopped and Hallihan made his way back to where Liz knelt down next to her friend.

"People tolerate heat differently," Liz said to Hallihan.

"Yeah," he said.

Liz felt Nancy's forehead and frowned.

"I'm okay. I just need to rest for a while," Nancy whispered.

Sommers knew better. Nancy's skin felt hot and dry despite the humidity.

"All right, let's rest for twenty minutes," Hallihan said quietly.

The survivors spread out and found what shade they could.

Liz said quietly to Hallihan, "She's in the first stage of heat exhaustion. I've got to get her temperature down and she's got to have water."

Tom Hallihan turned to look at the small group. Drips of sweat ran down his bruised face dropping to the jungle floor.

"Okay. You keep her here. I'll go on with Kirkpatrick and we'll see if we can find some water. Collins and Rogers can stay here with you."

"Thanks," Liz said.

"Thank me when I find some water."

Two radio messages from Harry Richardson directed the two Aussies ashore at Palacapang Point on Vella Lavella. According to the coast watcher, there had been very little enemy troop activity in that part of the island. Richardson transmitted he would have some of his native soldiers meet them on the beach at 1300 hours and guide them back to camp.

"Not bloody crazy about landing in daylight. But I guess we have to chance it."

"Andy, we have to trust Richardson. It's his territory isn't it? That was one of the few places we don't have to deal with the reef. We'll also be able to pick out the coral heads near the beach. So buck up, mate. King and country and all that, right?" Lee said.

"Bugger off," Harkins said, grinning.

Bryan studied the chart of landing area with Tiny Leonard looking over his shoulder.

"We'll have the guns manned as we go in. We'll cover Harkins until they clear the beach." The potential threat from the shore did not concern Bryan as much as the appearance of a Jap Zero. Close inshore the PT could not use its speed or maneuverability against the Jap aircraft guns. The boat would be an easy target.

Checking the charts and conferring with Lee, Bryan decided to take the PT boat all the way to the beach and not try to use a raft to row in. Absence of a continuous reef plus the sandy bottom of the point made using the boat the safest and quickest way to put the two men ashore.

Arriving at Palacapang they found clear water on the lee side of the point. There were none of the telltale dark spots under the surface which denoted coral heads waiting to tear the bottom out of any boat that ran over them. Taking no chances the Australian lay on the bow searching the water as they slowly made their way to the beach. When the boat reached the beach line Bryan nosed the bow into the sand long enough for Harkins and Sergeant Graves to jump ashore.

"Good luck you old bastard," Lee called after Harkins.

The two men, wet from the waist down, stood at the water line.

"You just be here when we get back, mate," Andy yelled back.

The two Australians turned and walked up the beach. Lee watched them until they disappeared into the tree line.

The water changed from aquamarine back to deep blue as the boat headed into deeper water. With the personnel drop completed, Bryan signaled Roy Lundeen to detach and begin his search of the coast line of Ranongga Island which lay southwest of Vella Lavella. The last intelligence briefing hadn't placed any Japanese forces on the island.

Turning south Bryan called, "Lee, would you get me a course to Ghizo Island?"

"Right."

Ten minutes later the boat moved east southeast at twenty knots on course for a small island in the area Richardson thought the PBY went down.

Liz Sommers looked at her friend lying on the floor of the jungle. Nancy's eyes were closed, her face flushed with the heat. Trying to get her body temperature down, Liz had opened Nancy's shirt and rolled up her khaki slacks. The shade helped but her real need was water.

Nancy's eyes opened slowly. "It's so hot."

Liz nodded. "I thought I knew hot. It's the humidity. Lie back and rest. They'll be back with water soon." Liz really didn't believe it, but she hoped. She stared around at her companions. Rogers was quietly watching the jungle. Collins showed all of the enthusiasm of a young sailor despite the tough situation. Both were scratched by the brambles from the jungle and covered with insect bites. How quick we've all gone to hell, she thought, but I can't worry about that now, Nancy needs me.

Collins turned to look across the clearing. "Be quiet," he said softly.

A loud voice barked a command from the foliage.

"Oh shit," Collins said. The sailor slowly stood up with both hands extended over his head.

Chapter Fifteen

Thrust of the Sword

In the early morning light Bryan found the *Monaghan* cruising slowly on a westerly heading. A camouflage paint scheme broke up the smooth lines of her hull. As they closed he noticed rust on her hull showing through the shades of gray. The war had taken a toll on both men and ships. He could see all of the destroyer's anti-aircraft guns were manned.

Bryan hoped to see Roy Lundeen's boat at the rendezvous. There had been no radio communications during the night and his faith in Lundeen's ability did not overcome his concern that the 135 boat might have encountered the Tokyo Express. The brief and violent encounters in the "slot" often left floating wreckage as the only record of battle.

Their search of Ghizo Island had turned up nothing except floating wreckage that was Japanese not American. Anxious to get back to continue the search, he knew if the survivors of the PBY were alive, every day increased their chances of capture.

As he prepared to take the PT alongside the *Monaghan* Bryan scanned the skies anxiously. Whether it had been the cloud cover or luck, there had been a lack of enemy flight activity in the area. He never understood why but the appearance of Jap aircraft went in cycles. During some missions enemy fighters were on you constantly, while other times you might go for days without seeing one.

"Skipper, there's Mr. Lundeen's boat," Schulz called, lowering his binoculars.

"Send them a flashing light. Ask them if they had any luck."

Holding a hand signal lamp, the signalman quickly flashed a Morse code message to the approaching boat. In less than thirty seconds a message winked back from PT 135.

"Nothing found, Skipper."

Bryan nodded. The hundreds of miles of coastline of all the small islands would take to search. But they didn't have time. He had to find her.

Stabilized alongside the *Monaghan*, Bryan looked up at the bridge wing to see Pete Long watching the activity. Their eyes met, the message understood – keep at it.

As they completed pumping fuel and started to disconnect, one of the destroyer's crew tossed a canvas message bag down to the deck of 142. Bryan opened the drawstring and removed the message pad. It read: "Will be at point C2 tomorrow at 0530 for refueling. Will monitor 14.454 megacycles in case of emergency. Your XO resting comfortably. Doc says he will be OK. Good luck, Pete Long." Bryan looked up at the bridge wing of the destroyer to see Commander Long. Bryan held up the paper and saluted Long. The CO returned his salute.

Bryan maneuvered his boat beside Lundeen's as Roy finished refueling.

"Did you see anything?" Bryan called through the megaphone.

Roy Lundeen shook his head and raised his own hailer. "Some native boats but no Japs or downed aircraft."

"Did you cover your whole area?"

"The east coast completely and part of the west."

Bryan thought for a moment. "Finish the western side and then check out Baga Island. I'll head down to Vona Vona."

"Can do."

"Any other problems?"

"None here."

Waving to Lundeen he called out, "Good luck."

Roy waved and turned back to his cockpit, his three engines accelerating as he turned east.

Liz saw a short man in a khaki uniform emerge from the brush, a rifle pointed directly at her. In a terrible instant she realized he was a Japanese soldier. Two taller men also carrying rifles followed the short man who she could now see was heavy set and needed a shave. He looked at her with curiosity and anger as he gestured with his weapon.

"Tate!" the man yelled at her as more men began to yell at the Americans.

"Liz?" Nancy asked.

Her friend was disoriented and Liz bent down to help her.

A kick to her ribs knocked her to the ground, the pain lancing through her side and taking her breath away.

"Tate!" he yelled at Liz who lay stunned on the ground.

A bewildered Nancy was being jerked upright by the two taller soldiers as Liz got back on her hands and knees. For a moment she thought she would vomit but a deep breath kept her stomach down. She staggered to her feet as the soldiers kept motioning menacingly with their rifles. She understood they were to raise their hands.

In an unfolding nightmare she watched the other three pushed into a line where at least eight Jap soldiers surrounded them. Each American now held their hands clasped behind their neck and a Japanese in a better quality uniform walked behind them issuing orders. He must be an officer Liz thought.

One of the soldiers put his rifle against a tree and began to pat down Rogers. Some of the soldiers were talking to each other but their rifles remained pointed at the Americans while their officer watched the man who had now moved to Collins.

Liz watched Nancy swaying slightly in the heat as more

insects swarmed around their heads.

Another soldier had produced a length of rope and had tied Roger's hands together, moving on to Collins as the other soldier finished patting him down.

The man moved to Nancy and began to search her. Suddenly the horror hit Liz as the short man she first saw walked up to her and smiled. His breath was rancid and he stank of sweat. The look in his eye scared Liz and he smiled again as he put his hand on her waist and began to work them up her body. She felt his hands move to her breasts and he began to squeeze. In a reflex action she brought her right hand around and slapped him full on the face.

She saw a blur as his hand came up hard slapping her backward into a tree.

The officer barked at the man as his hand came back ready for a second blow. Two of the soldiers laughed and the soldier backed away from Liz. He picked up his rifle and moved to the head of the column.

Her head pounding, Liz again got to her feet. The soldier with the rope quickly tied her hands behind her.

"I ku zo," the officer yelled to his men.

Motioning with their rifles, the men started the prisoners down the trail.

An hour later PT 142 approached the island of Vona Vona from the west. Twenty miles long, the island was typical of the Solomons. Covered with dense jungle and dotted by sandy beaches, there were several small native villages on the west coast.

Lee Cordner walked forward to the bow as they moved closer to the beach. Bryan had decided to conduct today's search by moving close inshore and proceeding slowly along the beach at five knots. The crew would search the jungle and beaches with binoculars for any sign of survivors. Bryan didn't know how the survivors might try to signal. He decided they could use anything from fires to parachute panels, flashing lights, or gunshots. His crew knew to report anything they saw out of the ordinary.

Because of the constant threat of air attack, the fifty caliber mounts were continually manned. In addition to searching the shoreline, crew members were also expected to be watching for small specks that might become a diving aircraft in a matter of seconds. The wooden hull of a PT boat did not stand up well to cannon fire from Jap fighters.

"Skipper, a flash from the tree line," Schulz yelled.

"Where?" Bryan asked. He raised his binoculars.

"About a hundred yards north of that tall tree at two thirty." Schulz's extended arm aligned with a large banyan tree near the shore line.

If they were Japs they wouldn't signal, they'd open up, Bryan thought. He pushed the throttles ahead accelerating to ten knots. Spinning the wheel he started a turn out to sea and then continued around until 142 pointed at the banyan tree. Pulling the throttles to idle the boat rocked gently in the waves two hundred yards off the sandy beach.

"Everyone on your toes," he yelled. Bryan heard the cocking levers cycle on both .50 caliber mounts. He turned to see Lee and Tiny standing next to him.

"Thoughts, gentlemen?"

"Worth checking out," Tiny said.

Lee added, "A bit of caution if you ask me."

Bryan started the boat slowly toward the beach. "Get the smoke generator ready to go."

The only sound was the muffled exhaust rumbling quietly at the stern. No a word was spoken on deck as the boat closed the beach. What was waiting? Jap machine guns or American survivors?

One hundred yards to the beach Gravely yelled, "There're men coming out of the tree line." Instantly Heimbigner and Lopez aimed at two figures just out of the tree line.

Four sets of binoculars were raised simultaneously.

"White skin and khaki trou!" Schulz yelled. "If those aren't Americans I'll eat my hat."

Bryan's heart leaped. Were they the right Americans?

"Break out the raft in case we can't get into the beach," Bryan ordered as he turned the wheel and pointed the boat toward the two figures on the beach. The current began to pull them south and he gunned the engines to put them back on line for the beach. "Tiny, keep your glasses on the jungle. The Japs could be using them as bait. "Lee, keep us clear of coral."

Both men acknowledged Bryan's orders.

As they continued to close the beach they watched one of the men collapse in the sand, the other man kneeling down beside him.

"Everything looks clear," Tiny Leonard called out, the binoculars still focused on the horizon. "But I don't like the feel of this."

"Neither do I," Bryan said quietly. With only the centerline engine providing power the distance closed to twenty yards. He felt the bow nudge the sand and immediately closed the throttle. "Go get 'em," he yelled.

From the starboard side Don Baurichter and John Harris jumped into the waist deep water and started wading furiously toward the beach. The two men broke into a run as they hit dry land. Quickly picking up the down man, the two gunners carried him toward the boat. Behind them, the other man followed. Plunging into the water they pulled the man to the side of the boat where Gravely and Schulz leaned over the boarding net. The two sailors reached down and pulled the American aboard. Turning, Baurichter and Harris waded back to the water's edge and grabbed the other man. They helped him to the side of the boat where he scrambled up the net with an assist from behind.

Putting all engines in reverse Bryan began to back the boat away from the beach. He felt the hull vibrate but remain stuck in the sand. Slowly Bryan advanced the throttles and with a lurch the powerful engines pulled the boat clear.

At the stern, the men were sitting and drinking from canteens. The island turned on the horizon as the bow now pointed to the open ocean and the distance from the beach began to increase.

"Lee, take the wheel," Bryan said to Cordner.

Sitting on the deck, surrounded by the PT crewmen, the two survivors had finished drinking and were leaning back against the cockpit bulkhead.

Bryan knelt down next to the older of the two, a Naval Aviator wearing the double bars of a Lieutenant, his uniform torn and filthy. Insect bites covered his face and one eye remained swollen shut.

"Tiny, bring the medical kit up." Turning to the man Bryan said, "I'm Bryan Michaels."

The man focused with his one good eye. "Hallihan, Tom Hallihan. Thank God you saw us."

"Were you on the PBY that went down the day before yesterday?"

Hallihan said, "Yeah. I was the co-pilot. You were searching for us?"

"Did you have two nurses with you?" Bryan asked, ignoring his question.

"Yeah, part of a medical unit."

"Where are they?" Bryan asked quickly.

Tom Hallihan shook his head. "I don't know. We were together that first night. When we headed inland, one of the nurses wasn't doing well so Kirk and I went looking for water. We were gone for two hours. When we got back, all four of them were gone."

"Gone where?" Bryan felt sick.

"I think a Jap patrol may have found them. We came across a fresh camp with empty Jap ration cans around a fire pit."

Bryan felt his body sag. "You said the four of them."

"Yeah, the two women, my radioman and another passenger, Lieutenant Rogers."

Bryan stood up and looked out to sea for a moment then turned back to the group. "Let's get them cleaned up and fed. We're heading for Vella Lavella."

Putting one foot in front of the other Liz followed Nancy as the small column moved farther into the jungle. Her head and side ached from Japanese blows and thirst cut through her like a knife. How far would they make them march? She knew Nancy was in terrible condition, now staggering more than walking. Ahead of Nancy the two men continued down the trail. Where were they going?

PT 142 transited the Ghizo straits at thirty knots on course for Vella Lavella. Bryan had to find the coast watcher and Harkins to figure out what to do. A radio call on the assigned frequency brought the first encouraging news of the day. The message from the coast watcher Richardson contained the code indicating Harkins had arrived. Using a simple Australian Navy code they transmitted a terse reply to Richardson and the coast watcher network.

"Rogers apparently captured this morning on Vona Vona. Believe he is still on island. PT 142 enroute to rendezvous with Richardson. Will examine options and advise."

Bryan knew the message would be relayed to his father. He wondered if he would receive orders or be allowed to use his own initiative. But first they had to find Andy Harkins.

It took one hour for the decoded message to be delivered to Rear Admiral Michaels at fleet headquarters. He frowned as he read the short text. Capture of the cryptographer would now raise command attention to both the Fleet Commander and MacArthur himself. During his time in theater Chuck Michaels had learned it was better if the General did not get involved in purely naval matters. As the Supreme Commander of Allied Forces in the Southwest Pacific, MacArthur would get his staff into the evaluation and decision process which meant common sense would often be left out of the equation. Michaels hoped that MacArthur's

227

intelligence officer did not start issuing orders in the name of the General.

Suddenly Nancy collapsed in front of Liz. The nearest soldier yelled at the officer as he kicked Nancy's side.

The young officer walked up to the stricken nurse, who remained motionless on her stomach. He said something to a soldier who reached down and rolled her onto her back. Leaning down the officer reached down and gently slapped Nancy's face several times. He looked at her for a moment then made a terse comment to his men.

Nancy's face was bright red and Liz knew her friend was in critical condition from the heat.

"I can help," she said to the man who looked up. "I'm a nurse, she needs water."

The Japanese officer ignored her and pulled a pistol from his holster. He worked the action to put a round in the chamber and aimed at Nancy's head.

Lieutenant Rogers said something quickly in Japanese. The officer stopped and answered him. Rogers replied and then nodded. Rogers turned to Collins.

"Come on, we'll carry her."

The dark green foliage of Palacapang Point stood in stark contrast to the blue green ocean of late afternoon. Bryan retraced his previous course to the beach to meet Andy Harkins as he and Sergeant Graves emerged from the jungle. They were accompanied by two natives, both clad in only khaki trousers with large machete knives hanging from their belts. The two natives climbed aboard and without a word went aft. They sat down on the deck acting as though they rode on PT boats every day. Bryan saw unusual looks from his crew as the sailors went about their business.

Twenty minutes later PT 142 headed south with Roy Lundeen's boat in close formation enroute to a small cove on the western side of the island. There they would meet Richardson and more of his native fighters.

"We're lucky Richardson is working this part of the island right now. Apparently he roams far and wide. We were able to make it back to Palacapang Point from his camp, but just barely. He was leaving for Vunato, Ted and Abner's village. He says he gets along well with the elders."

"Lee, are you familiar with this cove?" Bryan asked.

"Sorry, mate. I checked the chart but there wasn't much in the way of soundings. We'll have to ease our way in. I'll use a lead line when we get in close."

Bryan wondered if they were wasting their time. The Japs had Rogers and Liz. What chance did they have of getting them back?

"Didn't know if you could get a boat that big into this cove." Harry Richardson squatted at the edge of the water as Lee, Bryan and Andy got out of their raft.

The coast watcher must be over 50 Bryan thought, his skin tanned like leather and not an extra ounce of weight on his slender frame. The man wore a faded khaki shirt and trousers with bush boots.

Andy Harkins introduced Lee and Bryan.

"Let's sit down and see what we've got," Harry said and walked off toward a tall banyan tree.

The rest of the men joined him, sitting down on the ground at the base of the tree.

Bryan unfolded a chart of the local waters.

"Here's where we picked up Hallihan and Kirkpatrick," he said. "He thinks the other people were here when he last saw them." Bryan moved his finger north several miles on the chart.

"But this Hallihan chap never saw any Nippers?"

Bryan shook his head. "They found a campsite with empty Jap ration cans but nothing else, no sign of the people they left behind. The senior man didn't think they would have struck out on their own with the sick woman. So who else could have taken

229

them? Other natives?"

Now Richardson shook his head. "Not bloody likely, no reason. The natives hate the Nips as much as we do, probably more. No, it had to be the Nips. One of the lads from this village has spent some time on Vona recently. Let's see what he says."

Richardson introduced the young man as Joseph Tonatogon. Schooled at a missionary school on New Georgia, he spoke very good English with a definite British accent.

The four stood around an island map while Joseph described the Japanese camp.

"My people have watched them since they arrived. There are about twenty five soldiers at any time. They built the camp on a small river that runs into the island's interior. There are tents and small huts here and a small pier right there. That's where they get their supply boat each week."

"Probably comes from Choiseul," Richardson offered.

"Tell me about the boat," Bryan asked Joseph.

"A motor launch, maybe twenty meters in length, diesel engine. It has a deckhouse in the front and they carry cargo on the aft deck."

"Any guns?"

"Not big guns. There are sometimes army troops on the boat. They have guns." The young man looked very earnest.

Lee looked closer at the map. "So it's once a week for the supply run?"

The young man nodded affirmatively.

"Thanks, mate."

Richardson leaned back against the tree and lit a pipe. "There you have it, gentlemen. Not a good situation in my estimation."

Cordner stood up. "I'm guessing the Nips will be moving the Americans north. Maybe to Rabaul. We could try and intercept the boat."

"Except we don't know for sure when the boat will make its run. Joseph, do they come at night or during the day?

"Only during the day I think."

Bryan felt the frustration rising within him. There had to be something to do.

Harkins turned to Richardson. "If we wanted to sneak into camp would your blokes guide us?"

The older man raised his eye brows. "Just slip in and slip out, eh?"

"Something like that. Sergeant Graves and I have a little experience. If we had someone who knew the terrain I think we could give it a go."

"Two men to take on twenty or thirty Jap infantry?" Lee sounded skeptical.

Andy Harkins pulled out a pack of Players cigarettes and lit one. "We're not going to challenge them to a bloody battle. If we can find out where the Yanks are being held we can try to sneak in and get them out. Maybe a diversion with your boats at the same time, Bryan."

"If you can get some of my boys over to Vona they can scout the area." Richardson banged his pipe on the tree trunk.

Bryan knew he had to try.

An hour later, Harry Richardson transmitted a coded message outlining his estimate of the prisoner location and plan to attempt a rescue. Sent "Operational Immediate," the message made its way to the Seventh Fleet Commander and General MacArthur within the hour.

Chapter Sixteen

A Defining Moment

Liz Sommers sat on the hard dirt floor, her back against the wooden wall. Insects buzzed in the still, humid air, providing the only sound in the hut. Stains of sweat soaked through her torn khaki blouse, the temperature already over 80. She looked at the body of Nancy Hostetter on the floor near the door. Numb with grief and fear, Liz felt truly alone. Could she have done anything else to help Nancy? She had cried for help when her friend stopped talking, but there had been no response by the Japs. When the guards finally entered and realized Nancy wasn't moving, it had been too late.

The two nurses had been friends for almost three years. Now Nancy lay dead on a dirt floor in a hut thousands of miles from home. For what, Liz asked herself? As she sat in the growing darkness, Liz realized she would never see home again. What would Bryan do when he knew she was lost forever? So this is fate, she told herself. This is really happening and it's the brutal reality of war. She looked at Nancy, dead because those bastards wouldn't let her take care of her friend. Anger swelled up within her. The Japs started this war, the Japs have killed innocent people all over the Pacific and now they were probably going to kill her. But she made a decision. No more fear. Whatever happens, I won't let them win.

The door swung open and a Japanese soldier entered. Behind him came Rogers and Collins. The American's faces were bruised and battered. Blood spattered their shirts, further evidence of the brutality of the guards. The second guard motioned with his rifle. The men bent down and gently lifted her body. Rogers looked briefly at Liz and nodded.

Although she hardly knew the two men, that look gave her hope. They were Americans and somehow they would help each other.

The guards barked orders in Japanese and motioned the two men out of the door.

Liz stared at the soldier, her eyes riveted on his. I hate you, she thought, you and everyone like you.

In the growing shadows the two American flyers struggled to dig a shallow grave for Nancy Hostetter. The dense underbrush and vines made digging difficult. Flies and mosquitoes attacked the two men unmercifully as they clawed at the jungle floor with two small shovels. Two Japanese guards squatted in the shade of a large tree watching their efforts. None of the burial party, Americans or Japanese, were aware of the observers watching their labors when the sun finally set.

Joseph and his companion, Andrew, had been observing the Japanese camp since early afternoon. PT 135 delivered the two men to a point only a mile offshore during the late morning. A quick row ashore and swift march through the jungle put the two men on a hill above the Japanese camp by early afternoon.

The two American sailors finished shoveling dirt on the small grave.

"What a shit deal, Lieutenant."

Jerry Rogers nodded, wiping the sweat out of his eyes. "Yeah, it's a shit deal alright."

Looking at the two Jap guards still sitting smoking cigarettes, Collins asked, "Should we say some words?"

The young officer stared at the mound of earth hoping it would deter the animals long enough for her body to decompose. "No, just remember what happened to her. Don't let her be

233

forgotten."

The guards finished their cigarettes and motioned to the Americans. Rogers and Collins started back toward the camp.

Joseph gently nudged his companion. The two men crept quietly away through the dark jungle.

Chuck Michaels sat down in front of Vice Admiral Thomas Kincaid's large desk. The two men had known each other for over thirty years. At one time Michaels had been senior to Kincaid but that relationship had not affected their current situation. Now Michaels was responsible to Kincaid for the coordination and operations of the surface units assigned to the fleet. Kincaid walked a tightrope, depending on Chester Nimitz for allocation of resources but at the same time supporting MacArthur's strategy to proceed up the Southwest Pacific island chains enroute to retaking the Philippines. Nimitz and MacArthur had very different views of how to strategically attack the Japanese and the Seventh Fleet often ended up in the middle.

As everyone who worked for MacArthur realized in time, the General would make a considered decision and woe be to the subordinate who fought that course of action.

"The General has taken direct control, Chuck." Kincaid looked decidedly uneasy.

Michaels didn't like the tone of Kincaid's voice. "Why do I think I'm not going to like what you're going to say."

"Because I don't like it. But protecting our code breaking operations takes precedence over all other operational issues."

"What does that mean?" Michaels asked.

"MacArthur ordered General Kinney to conduct a B-17 attack on the Japanese compound on Vona Vona. Rogers must not be interrogated by Japanese intelligence."

"Christ."

"Chuck, I don't like it anymore than you do. But the knowledge Rogers has might possibly mean the loss of hundreds or thousands of Americans. Strategic information like that must be protected."

Michaels shook his head. "With all due respect to General MacArthur, he can kiss my ass."

The look on Kincaid's face hardened. "Admiral, your job is to follow orders. Whether we like them or not, these are operational orders issued by our immediate superior in the chain of command." Kincaid rubbed his eyes and sat back in his chair. "Chuck, this is a cruel, bloody war and it's going to get worse before we're done. If the Japs discover we've broken their main naval code, our counter intelligence efforts will be set back months, if not years. We just can't take the chance."

Michaels looked at his Fleet Commander knowing the decision had already been made. He understood why MacArthur had given the order but he also remembered the young nurse he'd gotten to know in Hawaii. He sighed and said, "So a group of young Americans will die so that others may live."

"Chuck, we have our orders. Issue a recall to those boats."

Chuck Michaels could tell by Kincaid's tone that the subject was closed. The Fleet Commander expected loyal dissent from his subordinates. Provide your objections, but once the order is given press forward with full enthusiasm.

"Do we have a time for the strike?"

Kincaid nodded. "Tentatively dawn tomorrow, if the weather holds."

Michaels stood up. "I'll get the word to the boats." He wondered what this would do to his son. How could anyone expect Bryan to go along with this? The father had never seen the son so happy and clearly in love. Now his country meant to kill that love in the interest of strategic aims.

Joseph Tonatogan sat working on a sketch of the Japanese camp for Andy Harkins and Lee Cordner as Bryan and Roy Lundeen walked up to the fire. Both had just returned from an early morning refueling rendezvous with the *Monaghan*.

Lee looked up. "Joseph is describing the Jap camp for us."

All of them sat quietly as his pencil moved on the chart.

"Andrew and I made our way up from the beach and found a good spot on this ridge to watch the camp. Here are the huts where the Japanese troops sleep. This is the cook shed. Across the way is a hut where they must keep women prisoners." His pencil tip was now on a small square closest to the water.

"What makes you say that?" Harkins asked.

"I saw two American men carrying the body of a woman out of the hut."

"You saw them carrying a woman's body?" Bryan asked.

Joseph nodded. "Yes."

"How did you know it was a body?"

"We watched them dig a grave and bury her." He said quietly.

"What did she look like?" Bryan had to know, but at the same time dreaded what this young man might say.

"Too far away to tell much. She had a khaki uniform so we guessed American. We've never seen any Japanese women on the island."

Bryan stared at the map.

"Andy, what do you think?" Lee asked, breaking the silence. "Can we get the rest of them out of there?"

Harkins took his time looking at the map while he lit a cigarette and took a deep drag. "I think it's worth a go. We'd slip in after dark and use some kind of a diversion to help us get away unnoticed. I'd like some time to observe the set up before we try it."

"How many men do you need?" Bryan asked quietly.

"Well, that's a bit tough. Normally I'd need eight or ten good men to try something like this. All we have is the Sergeant and me. I s'pose Harry might lend us some of his lads. They know how to handle a rifle and no one knows the jungle like they do."

"I'll go get Harry," Joseph said.

"If we go ashore here, "Andy said pointing the chart. "We

236

can be in position in an hour, no more."

"How about timing?" Bryan asked.

"If we want to use one of the boats to support us, I think we try to grab the prisoners just before sunrise. That way the patrol boat could be in place on the river." Harkins looked around the group for signs of disagreement. He continued, "I'll have Ted and Abner, two of Richardson's most experienced men. Joseph offered to go as our scout, but he's never fired a weapon. There's a bloke here named Longol from this village who offered to go. Richardson says he's a good man. Apparently the Japs killed his father and brother about a year ago. He hates the bastards. So there you have it, five for the raid." Harkins looked at the men around the table.

"I'm going," Bryan said.

Cordner looked surprised. "You can't go. We'll need both boats for the raid."

"I want you to take the 142 boat up the river." Bryan said to his friend.

"You're bloody crazy," Lee said.

"I'll second that motion," Lundeen offered, happy his boat would be holding offshore.

"I may be. But I've also got a personal stake in this one."

"What would your father say?" Lee asked, his look hard.

"Guess I'll have to worry about that when the time comes," Bryan responded.

Lee shook his head and turned to Harkins. "So what's our timeline for this little jaunt?"

"We have no idea when they may be sending a boat for the prisoners. I'd hate to sneak in there and find everyone gone." Harkins threw his cigarette on the ground and ground it out with his boot.

"Right then," Lee said as he stood up. "Let's get ready to move. Roy, I'll meet you in a minute, we need to go over a few things."

"Sure thing."

Lee reached out and stopped Bryan. "You're sure about

237

this?"

"Sure as I've ever been about anything, Lee."

Harry Richardson walked across the village's central area and directly to the table where Bryan and Andy Harkins were talking. On the table between them lay the original drawing by Joseph of the Japanese encampment. The coast watcher had a serious look on his face, very much out of character.

"Bryan, bit of a problem here."

Bryan looked up. "Hello, Harry. What's up?"

"A message came in and I just finished decoding it. You better take a look at this."

Bryan read the message.

"What's up, mate?" Harkins asked.

"They've ordered a recall for the boats."

Harkins looked surprised. "Just like that?"

Bryan said, "It doesn't make sense. Get Lieutenant Rogers back regardless of the cost, that's what we were told. Now they just cut and run?"

"Bloody generals and admirals can't make up their minds."

"Too right," Richardson added.

"I'll go tell Cordner," Bryan said.

As he walked across the clearing to the banyan tree where Cordner and Lundeen sat talking, he ran it through his mind. What happened? No one had more current intelligence on the captives or their location than the people right here. We know right where they are and unless a boat took them off last night, they're still there. Lundeen patrolled the area until 0300 and saw nothing. What in the hell is going on, he wondered?

Cordner and Lundeen both were as surprised as Bryan.

"Maybe whatever information Rogers had was perishable and it's not important now," Lee offered.

"Yeah, maybe."

Lundeen said, "Maybe they're sending in some Marines to get them?"

"And not tell us?" Bryan asked.

"Well I can't believe they'll just let them sit there until the Japs send them north. Hell, we know right where they are."

"So does our big brass," Bryan said with a chilling thought in his mind.

"What does that mean?" Cordner looked curious.

"If you don't want the Japs to send Rogers north but you know where he is, you send in a cruiser and lob six inch shells into the compound until everyone is dead."

"You're crazy," Lundeen said incredulously. "We'd never do that."

"Why were they willing to lose an entire squadron to get this guy back and now they give up when we know his location. Hell we told them exactly where he is."

The three men sat in silence.

"So what do we do now?" Roy Lundeen asked.

Bryan paused for a moment. "I'm going ahead with the plan. Assuming Harkins is still game."

"You mean ignore the recall order?" Lundeen looked surprised.

"That's a bit dicey don't you think?" Cordner added.

"Damn it. We stand the best chance to get those people out alive. My orders said getting Rogers back took priority over everything else including our lives. I'm just following orders."

"Bryan, you were ordered to return to base."

"I'm using my own initiative as the commander on scene. If they want to court-martial me later, fine. I've been there before."

Lundeen and Cordner looked at each other.

Bryan continued, "This puts both of you in a tough spot. I don't think we can pull it off without your help. But I hate to take good men to jail with me. It's up to you and I'll understand if you say no."

Cordner grinned. "Aussie's tend to be a bit rebellious by nature, this suits me fine."

"Hell, I'm from Montana. We don't like anyone telling us

what to do."

"Thanks," Bryan said, knowing his two friend were putting their futures on the line for him. "Then I say we make our move tonight. With a one and a half hour run to the island we should be underway no later than 0100. That should put us at the camp by 0500 waiting for it to start getting light. We'll plan on Lee being in position at the mouth of the river at the same time. We'll slip in and be back to the 135 boat by 06 or 0700 at the latest."

"Simple and straight forward. It must be an Australian inspired plan," Lee said.

The three men laughed and walked back toward Andy Harkins.

When Bryan returned to PT 142, Tiny Leonard was waiting for him.

"Lee briefed me on your plan. Bryan, you're out of your mind," Tiny said, anger in his voice. "Ignoring a recall and going on this mission by yourself. What the hell are you thinking?"

"That I have to get Liz back, Tiny, simple as that." Bryan knew he had to be square with his friend.

Leonard put his hand on Bryan's shoulder. "They'll court-martial your ass then kick you out of the Navy. Are you sure you wanna to take that chance?"

"Tiny, I almost got kicked out of the Navy once. It's not the end of the world. She's on that stinking island and I'm gonna get her out or die trying."

"What about the rest of these guys. They didn't sign up to support your damn heroics."

Bryan lowered his voice. "If I thought this mission didn't have a good chance, I'd go by myself. But it's a good plan."

The big Warrant Officer stood in front of Bryan. Slowly he shook his head. "You damned aviators. I pulled your ass out of the fire once before. I didn't do that to let you get yourself killed. I guess I better go with you."

"What in the hell do you know about raiding parties?"

"You forget, Bucko. In the old Navy we had something called 'landing party training.' Who do you think they always used for the ship's landing force?"

"I bet the boatswain mates." Bryan said.

"You got it, my friend. I've loaded more rifles than you've ever seen."

"Now I know the Japs don't have a chance," Bryan laughed.

The two turned and went below decks.

Pulling on his boots, Bryan heard a knock on the door of his stateroom.

"Come on in."

Gunner's Mate Second Class Don Baurichter stood in the door.

"What's up, Guns."

"Sir, I'd like to volunteer to go with you tonight." Baurichter looked uneasy.

"I'd love to have you with us. But we need you on the 37."

"Harris and Wilskie are fully trained on the 37 and the 20. Skipper, I'm qualed with the Thompson and I know you need people."

He couldn't argue with the big gunner and Bryan knew it. "All right, let me talk with Mr. Leonard. I'll let you know."

Baurichter turned and went forward.

The squeak of the door opening jarred Liz out of her doze. Looking up in the semi-darkness she could barely make out the figures of two men entering the hut. With relief she saw they were her two companions, not Jap guards. From behind the men she heard a guard bark something in Japanese and close the door. They heard the metal bolt slide into place.

Jerry Rogers knelt down in front of Liz. "Are you okay?" he asked.

"I'm okay. What's going on?" she asked.

The two men sat down on the dirt floor, moving slowly to allow their eyes to adapt to the minimum light coming from a small vent.

"No idea. The two Japs just moved us over here. Maybe they have more prisoners." Rogers said.

The young radioman Collins said quietly, "Sorry about your friend."

Liz remembered Nancy and her anger returned.

"Goddamned Japs," she said.

"Have they given you anything to eat or drink today?" Lieutenant Rogers asked.

She shook her head, "Not since last night."

Collins stood up and examined the two windows which were shut. "Just like our hut, locked from the outside."

Turning to Rogers, Liz asked, "What are they going to do with us?"

"I don't know. Maybe send us to Bougainville. After that, who knows?"

Rogers knew the dangerous truth of his own situation. He wondered what the chain of command was doing?

In the daily operational schedule for the 20th Air Force, the individual missions were listed by sequence number. At the beginning of the list for tomorrow's flight operations: Mission 0001 was assigned to the 312th Bombardment Wing. B-17D aircraft were scheduled for a 0445 takeoff to be on target at Vona Vona Island at 0530 hours. Each aircraft would carry four 1000 pound and six 500 pound general purpose bombs. All bombs were to be armed with contact fuses for instantaneous detonation on impact. The listed target: "Japanese Army troop concentration."

Chapter Seventeen

The Fog of War

Two dugout canoes were lashed on deck of PT 142 when it cleared the small cove at 0100. Roy Lundeen's boat followed in trail fifty yards behind. The rumble of the Packard engines echoed off the tall trees surrounding the village where only two cooking fires showed

Bryan pushed the throttles forward. Turning to Gravely he said, "Let's get the fifties manned and everyone else on lookout for Jap floatplanes."

"Aye aye, Skipper."

Spray began to fly over the bow as PT 142 accelerated past twenty knots, the hull lunging into the waves as the Packard engines roared.

"You're sure you want to do this, mate?" Lee Cordner stood beside his friend.

"Don't see any other way. The Japs sure as hell won't be expecting anyone to hit their camp. Surprise is on our side."

"Let's hope so." The Australian's eyes kept sweeping the dark sea.

Arriving off the island, both boats throttled back to five knots as the 142 boat closed within a mile of the river mouth. The mufflers of both PT's kept their engine noise low, the sounds of waves breaking on the beach masking their presence.

Sailors and natives lowered the two canoes to the water. The islanders nimbly climbed down and grabbed the long paddles. After lowering equipment down to each, the rest of the landing party carefully descended the nets and gingerly stepped into the narrow canoes.

Bryan stood next to Cordner on the port side. Andy Harkins sat in one of the boats looking up at them.

"We'll try to be back here by 0600," Bryan said. "If we aren't here by 0700 tell Roy to stand off and plan to be back here at sundown. We may need to go to ground for some reason."

"Right."

"Fuel isn't an issue now. But if you need fuel contact *Monaghan*. She's cruising south of here and monitoring 14.454 megacycles."

The Australian offered his hand. "Good luck, Yank."

Bryan looked grim in the moonlight. "Thanks." He climbed down to the waiting boat.

Powerful strokes pulled both canoes away from the hull of the PT boat. Joseph knelt in the lead canoe, guiding them to a landing point on the southern beach. A following sea aided their progress and the transit to the shore took only fifteen minutes.

Both canoes rode the small swell in, the rowers in the rear guiding the bow with their paddles. As the bows ground into the sand the men climbed out of the wooden hulls and pulled them up on the dry sand. Everyone helped to carry the boats above the high tide mark, hiding them in the underbrush at the edge of the jungle.

Swiftly the party gathered together and checked their gear. After several minutes they started northwest in single file. Joseph led the column, followed by Andy Harkins. From the jungle came the sound of an occasional bird cry. In ten minutes the group disappeared in the darkened trees.

The moonlight provided enough light for the men to follow each other single file through the underbrush. Under a high jungle canopy Bryan was able to see the variety of plants growing on the rising slope. He followed Joseph as the young man worked his way through the thick underbrush. No one said a word as they worked their way north paralleling the river. The humidity increased as they penetrated further into the jungle. Insects, roused by their passage, began to attack the men, prompting slaps on exposed skin.

"Quiet," Andy Harkins whispered back toward the men.

Bryan wore a web belt with a holstered .45 pistol and a long sheath knife. A small pack carried a canteen and additional ammunition. Bryan's khaki trousers were tucked into his socks to keep insects out. Sweat now soaked through his shirt, the dark stains spreading to his back. The experience of forging into the darkness unsettled him but he kept telling himself that Liz was up ahead somewhere.

The earthy smell of rotting vegetation rose off the floor of the jungle as they pressed forward. Although still before sunrise, the heat and humidity became oppressive as they moved farther inland. The single file of men made few sounds as they followed Joseph into the darkness.

Their guide stopped and held his hand up. Harkins moved forward to the young man as the rest of the men knelt down to rest.

Bryan turned to check on Tiny directly behind him.

"You okay?" he asked.

"Yeah, fine," came the whispered answer.

Bryan heard something in the distance, a humming sound.

Andy crept back to Bryan. "We're several hundred meters out. You can just hear their generator. I'm going to move in a little closer and take a look. You want to stay here or come along?"

"Let's go," Bryan said quickly.

The three men moved forward carefully. Joseph led with Harkins five yards behind him. As they moved closer the sound of the generator grew louder. Two perimeter lights showed through the foliage. A host of insects buzzed around the lights that hung from bare poles. They worked their way up a small slope to a break in the underbrush. They lay on their stomachs looking down at the camp, now clearly visible in the glare of incandescent lights.

"The second hut on the left is where they went to get the body of the woman," Joseph said quietly. "That far hut by the last light pole was where they took the two men after the burial."

"Where are the guards?" Bryan asked.

"Like most guards this time of day, they probably found a good spot and are taking a snooze." Harkins continued to scan the compound with his glasses. "At least they don't have any perimeter wire that I can see. We should be able to get right up to the huts without much trouble."

Bryan looked at his watch. "We need to get moving. It's going to take time to work our way around to the far hut."

"Right," Andy answered. "I'll take Abner and you go with Ted."

"Okay."

"We'll set up the rest of our people to provide fire if something goes wrong. I'd put Leonard up here with your Gunner's Mate. This chap Longol can get in closer to provide cross fire if needed. I want Sergeant Graves at the perimeter to keep an eye out for the Nippers."

Bryan nodded. "Let's slip back and brief everyone. We should be able to move out at 0500."

The small group gathered around a bright spot of light provided by Harkin's flashlight. A quick sketch on the back of a map laid out the camp and where each man would be.

"Don't shoot unless it's life or death. This is like a bee's nest, we'd prefer the little bastards stay inside their huts. Sergeant Graves will be right here and his job is to watch for Jap movement. Tiny, you and Baurichter will be ready to lay down covering fire if any of the Japs come at us from the huts. Longol, if you are here you can provide cross fire on anyone taking cover from the two Yanks with the Thompsons."

The muscular Longol squatted next to Ted. Wearing only khaki shorts, a long machete hung from a rope around his waist. He nodded.

"Abner and I will work our way around the perimeter to this hut where we think the American men are kept. The Lieutenant and Ted will check the northern most hut for the American woman." He looked at his watch. "Right now it's 0455. It should take us thirty minutes or so to get to the far hut and back. Everyone stay in position until 0540, then return back here. Our alternate rendezvous will be on the beach where we came ashore. Joseph, I want you take these two men to the observation point and then come back here and wait."

Bryan looked at the men kneeling around the small map. A strange collection, he reflected, but I'm glad they're here tonight. "If things get fouled up and you get separated for some reason, make your way to the beach then go three miles south. Lay low until sunset and the boats will come back for you. Everyone got that?"

The men all nodded silently.

Harkins tapped Abner on his arm. "Ready, mate? Bryan, we're off. Give us five minutes then head out. Good luck."

Bryan smiled. "See you back here."

The wiry Australian moved into the underbrush followed by Abner.

"Long way from the Bremerton jail."

Bryan turned. Tiny Leonard sat on the ground with his back against a tree trunk. He knelt down next to the big warrant officer.

"Thanks for coming, Tiny."

"Wouldn't have missed it. At least I'll have company in jail, right?"

Bryan saw Tiny's grin in the faint light.

"I'll make sure we get a cell together," Bryan said.

"You watch your ass out there," Tiny said, his voice now serious. "This ain't the wild blue yonder and they play by different rules in the jungle."

"I'll remember that." Bryan looked at his watch. "I better shove off."

Tiny watched Bryan walk away. "Good luck, flyboy."

Offshore Lee Cordner checked the time and put the three engines into gear.

"Best get this show on the road."

248

"Aye, sir," Petty Officer Gravely said.

"Schulz, send a flashing light to 135 telling them to detach."

The tall signalman grabbed the hand signal and aimed toward the dark hull of their companion PT. A series of dashes and dots from Schulz were answered by a quick dot-dash, dot-dash which acknowledged receipt. Slowly the other boat's bow turned away heading north east to assume picket duty.

"All positions fully manned?" Lee asked Gravely.

"Yes, sir. We've got Harris on the thirty seven and Wilskie back aft on the twenty."

"Let's hope we don't need either of them."

PT 142 accelerated to ten knots and Lee set a course for the mouth of the Vona River.

Tiny Leonard lay on his stomach beside Don Baurichter at the observation point. The two had their Thompson sub-machine guns at their sides as they watched the compound for any sign of Japanese activity. Tiny liked the young sailor. He reminded Leonard of himself twenty years ago, a little full of himself but ready to get any job done.

"Sure is quiet," Don said.

Tiny kept his gaze on the compound. "Let's hope it stays that way."

"That guy Longol is pretty scary. Doesn't say much."

Tiny nodded. "I guess he's hell on wheels when it comes to killing Japs. The Japs killed his father and brother. He swore some kind of blood oath. I'm just glad he's on our side."

Emerging into the area illuminated by one of the perimeter lights, a lone Japanese soldier shuffled across the compound toward one of the huts.

"Shit," Leonard whispered. "Just when I thought this was going to be easy."

The man walked to the northern end of the clearing, stopped and stood his rifle against a low railing. He lit a cigarette and leaned back against the wooden support.

Tiny hoped Bryan had seen the man.

The sentry turned his head and looked toward the jungle. In a moment the man threw his smoke on the ground, reached for his rifle and began walking toward the edge of the jungle.

Bryan moved slowly, the thorns on the bushes snagging his clothes. He couldn't see the compound clearly but knew they must be roughly fifteen yards north of the perimeter still moving in the right direction. For an instant Bryan heard a noise to his right then it was gone. He turned and held up his hand to Ted who immediately stopped and knelt down.

Several branches moved in the bush. Bryan saw a figure standing not more than two feet away, wearing a khaki uniform and holding a rifle.

Without hesitating Bryan lunged forward and tackled the man who pitched backward to the ground. He freed his arm from behind the Jap and swung with all his strength, hitting the soldier's face squarely. Bryan continued to rain blows down on the man's face in a rage. Trying desperately to protect himself, the Jap soldier reached up and raked his fingers across Bryan's face. Bryan responded with a clenched two fisted blow to the man's face with all the strength he could muster. The sentry let out a loud groan and fell back limp on the ground.

Bryan continued to lash out at the man's head but realized the man wasn't moving and Ted now knelt beside him.

"Quiet, quiet," the islander hissed.

His chest heaving, sweat dripping in his eyes, Bryan turned to look at his companion. The young native held a long knife at his side and Bryan realized Ted had stabbed the sentry while they struggled.

Trying to slow his breathing, Bryan listened for any sounds coming from the compound. The steady hum of the generator was the only noise in the darkness. Bryan pulled himself off the dead body of the Japanese soldier and got to his hands and knees, his heart still pounding in his chest. The sickly smell of the Jap's sweat now mixed with an awful smell from the man's bowels. .

"Let's go," he whispered to Ted.

Andy Harkins looked across the compound. Only ten meters from the hut, he tried to see how the door locked. There just wasn't enough light. He could only hope to force it with his knife.

"Abner, you keep watch. I'll check the door."

The wiry islander nodded.

Staying low, Harkins made his way to the door. In the pale light he saw an unlocked metal slide bolt on the door. Slowly he opened the wood door and peered inside. Despite the darkness he could see what looked like a man sleeping under mosquito netting. As quietly as possible he continued to open the door wide enough to slip through. A second mat lay on the wall to his left where another man lay snoring under more netting. The Nips didn't provide sleeping mats and mosquito netting to prisoners, Harkins thought, but he had to be sure. Slowly he crossed to the nearest mat and knelt down. The man lay on his back, his breathing rhythmic. On a low wooden table next to the mat a uniform had been folded. He pulled his flashlight from the back pocket of his trousers and put his fingers over the lens to mute the light. Pushing the switch forward, the pale light illuminated a folded Japanese army blouse. Instantly he shut the light off and waited to see any reaction from the sleeping men. Their steady breathing told Andy it was time to leave as quietly as he came. But where were the Yanks?

Bryan could now see the hut from his concealed position on the perimeter. Ted squatted next to him.

"Looks quiet," Bryan whispered. "I'll move up and check the hut. You stay here and watch out for Japs, right?"

"Right."

Slipping his thumb under the web strap he pulled off his small pack and laid it on the ground next to his companion. He moved toward the hut in a crouch. The building was a fifteen foot square structure made of roughly cut lumber with a roof of corrugated tin. He saw one window with closed wooden shutters. A steel bolt ran through two metal loops to secure the door.

Looking around Bryan saw no activity and began to move the metal bar. The rusty metal made a grinding sound as it slid. Checking the compound one more time he began to open the door. Peering inside he saw only darkness. Taking a breath he slipped through the door and slowly pulled it closed. He pulled out a one cell flashlight and turned it on. Two men sat on the floor with their backs against the wall. One wore khakis, the other dungarees. Both of their faces were bruised and bloody. Their eyes opened, blinking into the pale light.

"I'm an American. We're here to get you out."

The two men began to get to their feet.

"Thank God," one man whispered.

Bryan panned the light to his left and saw a woman's body laying on the floor, her back to him. Relief flooded over him as he realized it was Liz. She raised her head and tried to look over her shoulder. He knelt down next to her.

"Liz, it's Bryan."

She rolled toward him, raising herself up on one elbow. Still only half awake she asked, "What? What did you say?"

Bryan put his hand on her shoulder and shined the light on his own face. "It's Bryan."

She quickly raised herself up to a sitting position and grabbed his shoulders. Her arms went around his body and she pulled him to her. They held each other for a moment.

Bryan released her and turned to the men.

"Are you Lieutenant Rogers?"

"Yeah. Who're you?"

"Bryan Michaels."

They all turned as the door opened several inches.

From the partially opened door came a harsh whisper. "Lieutenant." Ted moved inside. "Two soldiers are coming across the compound." Ted carried a Lee Enfield .303 rifle slung over his shoulder.

Bryan pulled his .45 pistol from the holster and moved to the door. Two Japanese soldiers, wearing uniform trousers and sleeveless undershirts, were slowly walking across the clearing. Each man had a towel over his shoulder and carried a small bag.

Bryan couldn't tell how close they might come to the hut. He knew their chance of success depended on remaining undetected. The sun would be up soon and every minute he delayed their departure from the hut impacted their chances of survival.

From their view overlooking the compound Leonard and Baurichter saw the two Japanese but held their fire. Tiny hoped Bryan and Andy had already found the captives and were gone. His watch said 0533. Seven more minutes and they would head back to meet the others.

Tully Graves held his Fairburn commando knife at the ready when an explosion shattered the early morning. The Australian Sergeant looked south to see more explosions in quick succession, realizing they were impacts from aerial bombs. He also saw the explosions were moving rapidly toward the compound.

The two Japanese ran back toward one of huts. Other doors began to open and soldiers emerged, most in their underclothes.

"Open fire," Tiny Leonard said as he squeezed the trigger of his sub-machine gun. He aimed at several soldiers crouching outside their hut watching the bright explosions which were now less than 200 yards from the camp. Baurichter began firing and the Japanese died in a hail of bullets. More Japanese ran out of the surrounding huts and turned toward the river.

Bryan watched the chaos in the compound and the bright flashes of the bomb explosions. The concussion waves from the bombardment pulsed across the jungle.

"We've got to get out of here!" he yelled. Grabbing Liz by the wrist, he headed for the door. "You two follow us," he said to Rogers and Collins. "Ted, cover us then follow. Let's go."

A large explosion tore apart the jungle less than 100 yards away as Bryan pulled Liz through the door and toward the bushes. The two ran toward a break in the foliage were thrown off their feet as two more quick explosions erupted fifty yards away. Crawling into the trees, a large shock wave from the last explosion rolled over them. Bryan put his arm around Liz and they buried their faces in the earth. Bryan knew what was happening and the reality hit him as hard as the shock waves from the bombs. The ground jerked underneath them and the blast from three more bombs rolled over Bryan and Liz. Acrid smoke swirled around them as fragments of dirt, trees and metal rained down.

Lee Cordner stared at the formation of B-17's from the mouth of the Vona River. In horror he watched the bombs falling into the jungle and heard the deep crump of the explosions. They're completely mad, he thought. The bleeding Yanks are trying to kill their own people. He watched as the big bombers completed their run and turned to the south.

"We're heading up the river," he yelled at Gravely. Ringing up full ahead on all engines, Lee turned the boat for the center of the narrow waterway.

Andy Harkins lay on his side, barely aware of the world around him. Small fires burned in the brush, an aftermath of the explosions. A large crater lay less than 40 yards south of the Lieutenant. He slowly got to his knees trying to focus his eyes and find Abner. Besides a loud ringing in his ears he only felt bruised, not seriously injured. Picking up his Sten, he staggered to his feet. Looking around he saw an arm extended from underneath a small tree. Bending down he moved a branch to one side. Abner lay face down with a deep wound in his right side. Harkins knelt down and felt for a pulse in the man's neck. Nothing. Getting back to his feet the Australian looked at his watch. It read 0555. He turned and moved north into the jungle.

As the wave of bomb impacts approached them, Leonard and Baurichter jumped up and sprinted toward a large banyan tree. Diving toward the base of the trunk they took shelter in the cavities made by the roots. Shrapnel from the explosions screamed past them, embedding itself in the tall trunk. The two huddled at the base of the tree for three minutes after the last explosion, then Tiny slowly climbed out of his refuge.

"Don, you okay?"

From behind a large fold of wood the young sailor's head rose slowly.

"Holy shit, what was that?" Baurichter reached down and retrieved his weapon.

Tiny slung the Thompson over his shoulder, "Come on."

The two returned to the observation spot and were shocked to see what remained of the compound. Not a single hut remained standing. Bodies littered the clearing and small fires burned throughout.

"Let's go," he said to Don.

"They might have killed the Skipper," the young sailor said.

Tiny didn't like to think about what might have just happened. "Let's worry about carrying out our own orders."

The two headed down the slope toward the rendezvous.

Bryan felt drunk. He fought hard to stand up and remain steady on his feet. Liz knelt in the dirt next to him. Looking around he saw they were five yards inside the jungle perimeter. No sign of the others. He turned to Liz, putting his hands on her shoulders.

"Okay?"

She nodded.

"Stay right here."

He moved back to the edge of the brush and saw the two Americans laying face down on the ground but no sign of Ted. Rogers groaned softly, the back of his shirt stained with blood. Collins raised his head and looked up at Bryan who now knelt next to Rogers.

"Come on, we gotta get going," he said to the young sailor. "Help me."

Collins got to his knees, wincing with pain.

"You hurt?" Bryan asked.

"Just my knee. Twisted it."

"Grab his arm."

The two lifted Rogers who began to come around.

"Let's go."

The three struggled into the jungle and met Liz in the small clearing.

"He's been hit," Bryan said. "Can you take a look at him? We need to get out of here. Just make sure he's not bleeding too badly."

They helped Rogers sit down. Liz checked his back quickly but gently.

Rogers grabbed the front of Bryan's shirt and pulled him close.

"Michaels," he said, his voice strained. "I can't be taken by the Japs."

Bryan saw the desperate look in the man's eyes.

"Don't worry, we'll get you back."

"I'm serious." The pressure increased as he pulled Bryan closer. "I've got classified information the Japs can't get. If we're going to be captured you have to kill me."

The look in the man's eyes told Bryan he was deadly serious.

"Let's hope it doesn't come to that."

Liz finished her exam.

"There's one puncture I need to keep pressure on. But he can move."

Two minutes later they moved out. Liz pressed a makeshift bandage from a piece of her blouse against Roger's back as the two men supported the wounded American.

After the hell of noise and fire the jungle was quiet. Only the occasional bird cry broke the silence. The dense underbrush combined with carrying Rogers made for slow progress. Bryan guessed it would take them at least thirty minutes to reach the rendezvous point.

A bush moved off to Bryan's right and he whispered,

"Freeze." Reaching down to his holster he pulled the .45 out and pointed it in the direction of the noise.

"It's me. Ted," a quiet voice said from jungle.

The islander slowly emerged from the green vegetation. His clothes were torn and blood ran from multiple cuts on his face. He carried Bryan's small pack. They all knelt down in the grass.

"I couldn't see you back at the hut," Bryan said.

The young man grinned. "I ran very fast when I saw what was happening. But that's not important. Just now I saw Japanese soldiers moving in this direction. We can't go this way."

Bryan tried to picture the chart of the island. If the Japs were moving northwest they might be paralleling the river. Maybe trying to get away from the destroyed camp, he thought. They had to stay away from those soldiers. He opened his small pack and pulled out the canteen. The escape and bombing had taken their minds off their thirst. Now they each took a few swallows of the tepid water.

"We'll have to cut due west and cross the big ridge that runs toward the beach," Bryan explained. "If we can get to the beach one of the boats should be there to pick us up."

"What boats?" Collins asked.

"We've got two patrol boats up here. They were told to come back at sunset if we missed the first rendezvous." Bryan turned to Ted. "I need you to scout out in front of us. I'll try to follow a course due west. That should keep us clear of the Japs as long as they don't push farther into the jungle." Bryan pulled a small hand compass from his rear pocket.

Ted nodded. He picked up his rifle and moved off through the vegetation.

Bryan turned to Liz who had been watching the exchange. Seeing the calm look on her face, he winked at her and she smiled.

"Okay, let's go."

PT 142 moved slowly up the river as the crew anxiously scanned the jungle on both sides of the narrow waterway, their guns loaded and ready. The shriek of birds and monkeys provided an exotic background. The engine's mufflers muted the exhaust to a quiet bubbling as the boat glided toward a tall pillar of smoke in the distance.

Approaching the first big bend in the river, Lee eased the wheel to the right. The boat responded slowly, remaining in the center of the river.

As they finished the turn, Lopez spotted a group of men on the river bank. He trained the .50 caliber mount to the right and called back, "Soldiers on the bank."

Several of the Japanese began to fire their rifles at the American boat while the remainder ran into the jungle.

"Open fire," Lee cried.

Lopez squeezed the triggers and a stream of fire laced across the water. The heavy slugs tore into the soldiers and shredded the bamboo trees behind them.

"Keep firing!"

The 37 millimeter opened up, the explosive rounds crashing into the jungle. The barrage lasted for thirty seconds until Cordner order a cease fire. On the bank, smoke and dust drifted away revealing a scene of complete destruction.

"Stay alert," Lee called. They were almost to the tall column of smoke and he knew the camp must be around the next bend.

Fighting his way up the rising terrain, Bryan struggled to maintain footing on the wet slippery ground. Rogers was losing his strength and after each fall it was harder for Bryan and Collins to get him back on his feet.

Liz did her best to help them as she kept pressure on Roger's wound.

Behind them Bryan recognized the rhythm of American .50 cals and the bark of a 37 millimeter. He knew it must be Lee but also knew they couldn't go in that direction without running into the Japs. He put it out of his mind and kept struggling up the slippery slope.

Seven members of the 362nd Infantry Regiment of the Imperial Japanese Army worked their way into the jungle and away from the American guns. Lieutenant Tamatso Ishida decided he had to find higher ground and take up defensive positions. This must be the first part of the anticipated American landings and he would be ready.

Tamatso Ishida had been in the Imperial Army for three years, including combat during the Philippine campaign. But Ishida was a junior officer and he had no orders from Captain Nobuki. He assumed the Captain had been killed in the attack on the camp. Ishida knew he must take charge and uphold the reputation of the regiment. Remembering reconnaissance patrols west of the river he thought of the high ridge where they would be able to see the ocean. He would go there and establish a defensive position he told himself. A professional course of action and Lieutenant Ishida prided himself on being a professional soldier.

Only Andy Harkins and Tully Graves made it back to link up with Joseph at the rally point. Harkins looked at his watch and knew they must move out to make the rendezvous time with Lundeen's boat. It went against his grain to leave anyone behind but the bombing raid might have killed everyone. He'd heard the exchange of gunfire and knew there might be Japanese in the area. Better to get to the boat, regroup and decide the next move.

"Let's head back to the beach," he said.

Joseph stood up, as did Tully Graves.

Harkins reached down to pick up his Sten and found himself on the ground, not knowing what had happened. He heard the sound of rifle shots and the whine of bullets through the leaves. Trying to roll over, he realized he couldn't. Looking over at Graves, Harkins saw his friend on his back with a bullet wound in the center of his chest. Joseph lay sprawled over a log. He lowered his head back on the damp earth to rest for a moment, pain beginning to grip his chest.

Bryan heard the distinctive crack of the Japanese Arisaka rifle behind them and turned to survey the jungle. He saw the exhaustion in the faces of Liz and Collins. They had to keep going and get to the top of the ridge he told himself. Then they would rest.

"Bryan, he needs to stop," Liz said.

"We can't stop."

"Two minutes. He can get some water and I can look at his back."

"Okay."

The two men lowered Rogers to the ground. Liz stepped back, her hands sticky with blood.

Pulling the canteen from his pack Bryan raised the Lieutenant's head and put it to his lips. He choked briefly then took two sips of water.

"Thanks." He looked Bryan in the eyes. "Don't forget what I said." Rogers sagged back to the ground.

Liz rolled him on his side and examined his back. She turned to Bryan with a worried look.

"That last group of shots came from Japanese rifles. We need to keep moving up to the ridge and then down to the beach." He looked at his watch. "The boats may not be there now but they'll come back at sunset. Come on, let's go," he said and leaned down to pick up Rogers.

Lee Cordner put the engines to idle and the boat's momentum continued to carry them toward the camp. Fires burned in several of the huts, the smoke continuing to rise vertically over the destruction. The pier looked to be intact. Bodies lay strewn among the remains of the compound.

"Petty Officer Gravely, stand by to go alongside the pier."

"Aye aye, sir."

The boat moved ahead slowly as Schulz ran forward to tend the bow line.

"Keep the .50's manned," Lee said, not taking eyes off the

pier."

"Aye aye, sir," Gravely replied.

"Also, I want a couple of men to go ashore with me." Lee put the engines to reverse then stop as the hull nudged against the pier. Smoke from the burning buildings drifted over the boat, the acrid smell bitter and harsh. Only the crackle of burning huts disturbed the silence around them.

"Petty Officer Gravely, be ready to move in case we get into trouble. I want to check the area to make sure our people aren't here. After that we're on our way."

"Yes, sir. Wilskie and Harris will go with you. They've got .45's, if that's all you need."

"That would be splendid," Cordner said. He walked to the port side and jumped down to the wooden pier. Schulz had secured the bow and stern lines and now stood on the pier. Harris and Wilskie jumped down to the pier and hurried to catch the Australian as he walked toward the camp.

"All right, gents. Stay alert. We're looking for our chaps. Follow me and keep an eye open for anything that moves. Some of the Japs may only be wounded, so be ready."

Both men pulled their pistols from the holsters and chambered a round.

"You want us to shoot the wounded, sir?" Wilskie asked.

"Do you have a problem with that?"

"No, sir. Not a bit. Just wanted to know how you felt."

"They'd certainly shoot us," Lee said as he stepped from the pier to the land.

Smoke drifted across the destroyed compound, the stench mixing with the smell of dead men. The three men spread out and walked toward the large group of bodies, noting they were all Japanese. Only one man moaned while the rest were motionless. Most were wounded multiple times by shrapnel, some missing extremities. Flies buzzed in large swarms around the corpses as Lee looked down at the wounded man. The Japanese soldier had a large wound in his belly and held his stomach with both hands, the blood oozing through his fingers, pooling on the ground. The man looked up at him with a mixture of fear and pain. Lee turned to check the other bodies.

In ten minutes they were able to cover the entire compound.

"Just looks like Japs," Wilskie said.

Lee nodded. There was still hope for Bryan.

'Well done, men. Now back to the boat, no reason to tarry here."

Wilskie and Harris trotted down to the pier and climbed aboard the boat. As they climbed aboard the boat a single shot rang out. They ran to the bow and saw Cordner briskly striding down the pier.

"Doesn't pull any punches," Harlon Wilskie said quietly to his companion.

"Nope."

Chapter Eighteen

Bloody Ridge

Roy Lundeen had seen the bombing attack and reached the same conclusion as Lee Cordner. His concern heightened when no one arrived at the beach for pickup. He continued to patrol off the beach until 0730 when he picked up the 142 boat approaching from the northeast. The two boats linked up off the beach and Lee reported on his search of the camp.

"We've got to be back at sunset for a pick up three miles south of the original landing spot," Lee called through his megaphone.

"I'm going to need fuel," Lundeen replied.

Lee needed fuel too. He had enough to make Tulagi but if they came back tonight he would run short.

"Let's try the *Monaghan*. Why don't you give the call? I don't want to draw attention to Bryan's absence at this point."

"Concur."

The two PT boats found the destroyer twenty miles west of Vona Vona.

Lundeen completed refueling and pulled abeam the destroyer. Lee took the 142 alongside, the fueling hose snaking down to the waiting crew. Twenty minutes into pumping Lee looked up to see the Commanding Officer of the *Monaghan* standing at the destroyer's deck edge looking down into the PT's cockpit.

"I'm Commander Long. Where's Lieutenant Michaels?"

Lee couldn't think of anything else to say but the truth. "He's on Vona Vona, Commander."

"And you're in command of that boat?"

"Ah yes, sir. Temporarily, of course

"And who are you?" The stocky Commander looked irritated.

"Lieutenant Commander Lee Cordner, Royal Australian Navy, sir."

Commander Long didn't say anything for a moment, then knelt down to get closer to Lee. "I think a quick brief would be in order."

Lee took ten minutes to fill in the situation including the attempt at the alternate rendezvous.

Long listened then said, "Our latest intelligence summary gives a high probability we'll have a run by the Tokyo Express tonight. The question is which course they'll take. If it's the westerly course you might be up to your ass in Jap tin cans tonight."

Lee knew the danger but he had to return to the island.

"Where will you be, sir?"

"I'm to head south to join with Destroyer Division Twelve. We'll attempt to intercept the Express."

"Sir, our intent is to make the rendezvous and pick up our people. If we can't do that we'll return south. There may still be Americans and Australians on that island and I've got to try and get them off."

"Good luck, Commander." Long turned and walked forward toward the bridge. "You're going to need it," he said under his breath.

A final desperate effort put the small group on the crest of a high ridge overlooking the ocean. They had used the last reserves of their strength and lay exhausted in the shade of several trees. Bryan searched the water west of the island but there were no vessels in sight. The PT's would have been gone for hours.

"Will they come back?"

He turned to see Liz looking out to sea also.

"They'll come back, don't worry. How're you holding up?"

She wiped the sweat from her forehead with the back of her hand. "Considering everything that's happened, I'm okay."

He put his arms around her. "Whatever happens I'm just thankful I was able to find you."

She held him close and said, "I love you."

Bryan kissed her lightly on the lips. "I thought I'd lost you."

Rear Admiral Michaels read the op immediate message again from the Commanding Officer of the *Monaghan*. He felt numb. "Lt Michaels of PT 142 led a landing party to Vona Vona Island. Following the morning air raid on the island none of the landing party arrived back at the pick up point. PT's 135 and 142 will attempt to contact any surviving members of the landing party at sunset tonight."

It took every ounce of self control for Michaels to remain calm. His fury at the situation could not overwhelm what he must do now. The Admiral knew there was very little that he could do to directly affect events on the island, but he had to try. He knew Pete Long on the *Monaghan*, a destroyer sailor with a solid reputation. He knew Long would do the right thing.

He called in his writer.

"Draft a message to the CO of the *Monaghan*. Tell him to use his discretion in support of PT's 135 and 142. Send it Op Immediate."

Forty five minutes later, Pete Long looked up from reading the decoded message and turned to his Officer of the Deck.

"Mr. Kelly, reverse course and set a direct course for a point ten miles west of Vona Vona."

"Aye aye, sir."

"And Mr. Kelly, let's expedite."

As the bow of the *Monaghan* turned north, her hull began to vibrate with her main engines accelerating to full speed.

When Tiny Leonard heard the volley of rifle fire he knew there were Japanese near.

He held his hand up to stop Don Baurichter and listened for any more fire.

"We need to go west toward the ocean," he said.

"Whatever you say, Boats."

"If something happens to me keep working your way toward the water. Try to stay away from the Japs at all costs. There are bound to be more of them than us."

Don looked at the big man. He felt confident that Tiny Leonard would get him out of this.

"Okay let's go."

The early morning sun provided enough direction to start their journey. They quickly realized the difficulty of breaking a trail through jungle without machetes. The long grasses and branches of the trees were almost impenetrable until they discovered how to burrow like an animal on their hands and knees. Soon they were covered in mud and filth from the damp jungle floor. The insects were at least partially deterred by the layer of mud encrusted on much of their exposed skin.

"Watch out," Tiny said quietly and he lowered his head to escape the long thorns on a reddish green vine. Their conversation had been confined to a minimum as they made their way west. Four hours of steady walking and crawling brought them to an upslope. "It shouldn't be more than two or three miles to the water. Let's take a break before we push over this ridge."

Don Baurichter saw a small tree and he gratefully sat down. Mud and sweat streaked his face. The adrenaline of the morning's events had worn off giving way to a deep exhaustion. Holding the Thompson between his legs he put his head back against the tree and closed his eyes. "If my folks could only see me now."

Leonard smiled. "Where're you from?"

Don opened his eyes. "Central City, Iowa. A little farm town about fifteen miles north of Cedar Rapids."

"What made you join the Navy?"

The young sailor laughed. "I'd never left Iowa and when I saw that recruiting poster about seeing the world it sounded pretty good."

"I felt the same way...." Tiny froze and held up his hand to indicate silence. Pointing to the south he rose slowly and knelt with the Thompson at the ready.

Rolling to his left Don lay on the ground pointing his sub machine gun in the same direction.

"Don't fire, I'm a friend." A voice came from the bush. "I'm coming forward."

Neither man said a word but kept their weapons pointed at the jungle. Bushes moved to their left and they saw the islander named Longol step into the small clearing. He looked to be in good shape and still carried his .303 rifle.

"Good morning, Gentlemen. I am relieved to find you."

Tiny and Don were stunned, the man's high British accent in stark contrast to his frizzy hair and bare torso. A pair of khaki shorts and a small knapsack slung over his shoulder were his only articles of clothing. He walked up and squatted next to them.

"Bit of a muck up back there. I made it back to the rendezvous and found the two Australians dead along with Joseph. The Japanese were moving west so I decided to do the same. Hoped there might be an opportunity to kill some of the buggers and then get to the beach by sunset."

"Where are the Japs?" Tiny asked, his voice quieter.

"Two hundred yards north of here, a little higher up the ridge."

Tiny felt tired. He hadn't relished the idea of climbing over the ridge, now they had Japs to deal with.

"How many did you see?"

"Small patrol, six men and one officer. No heavy weapons."

267

"Those odds are more to my liking," Tiny said.

"So we ambush the Japs?" Don asked.

"Precisely," Longol replied.

Bryan watched Ted work his way up the west side of the ridge returning from scouting to the west. The young man smiled as he caught his breath from the climb up the slope.

"All clear from here to the water. There's a grove of trees near the water we can shelter in while we wait for the boats. I found a stream about 300 meters down the slope, water's good."

Bryan knew they needed the water. But the breeze and ability to watch the ocean from heights told him they should stay on the ridge until an hour before the sun went down. He'd send Ted back to fill their two canteens and bring water back for Rogers.

Walking back to the shaded area he retrieved his canteen from Liz.

"Ted found water down the slope. He's gonna head back down there and fill both canteens. How's Rogers doing?"

Her face betrayed her concern and she spoke quietly. "He's lost a fair amount of blood and is going into shock. If we can't get him to some kind of medical facility soon I don't think he'll make it."

Bryan looked over to where the young man lay on his back in the shade, his face very pale. Collins sat next to him waving the flies away. He looked at Liz, captured by the Japs, losing her friend and now stuck in this miserable jungle but she remained calm and kept doing her job.

"If the pickup goes on schedule we'll have him in Tulagi late tonight or early tomorrow morning. It's the best we can do."

She nodded. "I know."

"It's 1330 now. We'll plan on starting down to the water at 1630. Will he be up to a move then?"

"I don't think he'll be able to walk, even with help. He may not be conscious by then."

268

The steep slope gave Bryan an idea. "What if we can make a litter to carry him?"

Her face brightened. "That will do it, I'm sure."

Bryan remembered a stand of long bamboo not more than a quarter of a mile back down the slope. "Ted and I will go cut some bamboo for a litter."

Ted assured Bryan that he knew how to fashion a litter with bamboo stalks and tough vines from several of the trees.

"We'll try to be back in an hour," he said to Liz. "Collins, you know how to use a .45?"

The sailor got up and nodded. "Yes, sir. We had to qualify in aircrew school."

Bryan handed him the pistol and the two extra clips of ammunition.

"Stay alert. Keep watching off shore for any boats."

"Aye aye, sir."

Bryan turned to Liz. She looked tired but smiled. "We'll be back as soon as we can."

"I'm counting on it, sailor. Don't keep a girl waiting too long." She stepped closer. "Bryan, be careful." She squeezed his arm.

"Don't worry. Just two Boy Scouts going out to work on a merit badge." He held her hand for a moment then released it. "Come on, Ted."

A twenty minute hike brought them to a stand of bamboo. Ted began to cut the tall stocks with his machete. Bryan could tell that the young islander had done this before as he deftly cut two equal diameter stalks six feet long. Next Ted turned to a large bush with multiple vines climbing a banyan tree. He began to chop the vines into six foot lengths, handing them to Bryan. Fifteen minutes later they had the bamboo stalks on the ground and were lacing the vines between the two to form a litter.

"This will work."

Without taking his eyes from the vines Ted said, "With all of us working we can get the Lieutenant down to the beach. No problem."

Sweat soaked Bryan's shirt as they wove the vines together and tied them off.

"That's good, let's get back up the ridge." Standing up he wiped his face with the back of his hand.

Two quick shots rang out in the distance. Both men turned toward the sound as several more shots from different weapons echoed off the trees.

"Shit." The first two shots sounded like a .45, but not the last. "Come on. Let's go."

Ted followed Bryan back up the slope toward their make-shift camp.

Fifty yards from the clearing, Bryan knelt down in the bush with Ted at his side. Breathing hard from the rapid climb up the ridge, sweat dripped off his face as he peered toward the large tree where they had left their comrades.

"I can't see anything, we've got to get closer," he whispered.

"You stay here." Ted handed Bryan his Enfield. Down on his hands and knees the young man began to move forward very carefully. In a moment he had disappeared into the underbrush.

Ted's Enfield resembled the Springfield '08 rifle he'd drilled with at the Naval Academy. If he remembered correctly a full magazine on an Enfield held ten rounds. This rifle was all they had.

Lieutenant Ishida looked down at the body of the American sailor sprawled on the ground. Blood oozed from two bullet wounds in his chest. The man's pistol lay on the ground next to his body. Ishida reached down and picked up the weapon. Something to take home to my father, he thought. His men had two Americans at bayonet point. They must have escaped during the bombing attack. The woman knelt next to a wounded man, her hand resting on the man's chest.

He walked over to the woman who looked up at him. He saw anger in her eyes. He wished he knew the importance of these prisoners. If they were being held for interrogation then he must also keep them under guard until relieved. But who would arrive first, the American invasion fleet or his own forces? Lieutenant Tamatso Ishida of the Imperial Japanese Army would set up a defensive position and hold until relieved. If the Americans arrived first he would kill the prisoners.

"Tie her hands and feet," he ordered Sergeant Tadashi.

"Yes, sir." The short stocky man found two straps in one of the men's small packs. He pushed Liz down and tied her ankles together. Rolling her over, he wrenched one arm behind her back and then the other. Taking the last strap he cinched both wrists together hard.

Ishida stared at the ocean and wondered when he might see the American fleet.

"I saw six Japanese soldiers and one officer," Ted said quietly. The two men stood behind a wide green and yellow leafed tree.

"What about our people?" Bryan asked.

Ted shook his head. "Hard to tell. They were on the ground next to Lieutenant Rogers."

Bryan's eyes asked the question which Ted quickly answered.

"I couldn't tell if they were dead or alive."

Outnumbered and outgunned, he thought. Two against six and they all have rifles. If we wait until dark we might be able to sneak in and take them one by one. By then any PT boats will have come and gone. *Shit.* An old aviation saying came to Bryan's mind 'out of airspeed and ideas.'

"Is there anyway to get close to our people?"

Ted shook his head. "No cover close to them. It looks like the officer has his men in a circle around the clearing."

Bryan wished he knew more about infantry tactics. Maybe a charge and take them by surprise. But with the Japs spread out we couldn't expect to get them all.

271

He reached down and touched the machete that Ted carried in a wooden scabbard on his belt. "Have you ever used that on a Jap?"

Ted looked surprised. "No."

Bryan turned his head and saw movement in the undergrowth twenty yards south of where they stood. He pulled Ted down beside him as he quickly fell to one knee.

"There's someone out there," he whispered to Ted.

The young islander slowly slid his machete from its sheath. Bryan slowly worked the bolt to chamber a round and raised it to his shoulder. He sighted along the barrel at the moving branches. He saw a dark torso and then recognized Longol moving into the open. Bryan quickly lowered the rifle when he saw Tiny Leonard follow the islander out of the jungle.

"Tiny, over here," he said in a low voice.

Longol and Leonard ducked at the sound of Bryan's voice but quickly stood up. The two, now joined by Don Baurichter, walked across the clearing to Bryan and Ted.

Tiny moved past Longol and extended his hand. "Damned aviators show up in the strangest places."

"It's about time you got here," Bryan said.

Leonard looked at his friend and saw the anger in his eyes. Changing his tone Tiny said, "I guess we know why they sent that recall order. What the hell's going on?"

"Tiny, I don't know. But if I get out of this you can bet I'll find out. And some son of a bitch is going to answer for it."

"Longol found Harkins, Graves and Joseph. The Japs got 'em."

Bryan shook his head, "I was afraid of that. I heard rifle fire right after the attack."

Tiny looked at his friend. "Did you find anyone in the camp?"

Bryan nodded. "They were all in the northern hut. We got them out during the attack."

"Where are they now?" Tiny asked.

"About a hundred yards up the slope. Along with a patrol of Jap infantry. Ted and I were down here building a litter for Rogers when the Japs jumped them. We don't know if they're alive or dead."

"But Liz was okay up until then?"

Bryan nodded, "Yeah. I should have never left her alone."

"Let's not worry about that right now," the big man said. "Tell us everything you know about the Japs."

Ted drew a crude map in the dirt and explained what he'd seen during his trip up the ridge. When he finished the group sat in silence looking at his diagram.

"We've got surprise on our side and two Thompsons," Tiny finally said.

Bryan knew they must do something now if they were going to have any chance of making the rendezvous with the boats.

"Can we get to them before they have a chance to hurt our people?"

Longol had been quiet since they arrived. Now he spoke up. "Perhaps I might even the odds if I can reach one or two of them before they know we're here."

Bryan's surprise at hearing a formal British accent from Longol was matched by the man's suggestion.

"Can you get near them during daylight?" Tiny asked.

Longol nodded. "I would expect so. I've done it before."

Bryan looked at the machete hanging from Longol's belt.

"Use that?"

The young man nodded again. "It's quiet and they don't make much noise if you can cut their throats."

Twenty minutes later the small group finalized their plan. Ted and Longol moved up the ridge. The three Americans were to follow in fifteen minutes. Bryan removed the clip from Tiny's .45 and checked that it was full.. Tiny and Don went over their Thompsons making sure they were ready to fire.

"I still can't believe our own planes bombed us," Tiny said when he finished checking his weapon.

"Apparently our Lieutenant Rogers is important enough that they'd kill him rather than let the Japs keep him."

"Christ," Leonard said.

"That's got to be it. I can't figure anything else that makes sense. If we get back I'm going to personally tell everyone who is willing to listen what happened." Bryan's adrenalin fueled his anger.

"Let's just get back first." Tiny looked tired.

Baurichter sat beside them without speaking. He waved his hand in front of his face to distract the small swarm of gnats that buzzed around him. Sweat covered his face and soaked his shirt.

"You alright?" Bryan asked the young sailor.

He nodded yes.

But Bryan saw the concern in the man's eyes.

"We can do this. Just stick to the plan and fire when we do."

"Yes, sir."

Tiny looked at his watch. "We need to be down on the beach in three hours. I wonder what Cordner and Lundeen did when they saw the bombers hit the island?"

"Hope they didn't decide to head for Tulagi."

"They'll be here and you know it," Tiny said, sensing Bryan's frustration.

Bryan knew he should be scared but he didn't care. The same fury he'd felt attacking the Japs before was returning as he squeezed the handle of the .45. This was personal.

"Come on, let's go."

Private Soichi Tatagumi sat underneath the shade of a large banyan tree twenty meters down the slope of the ridge east of the Lieutenant's position. He wanted to take a drink from his water bottle but the Sergeant had told them to save their water. Eighteen years old, Soichi had been in the army for thirteen months. He didn't like being a soldier but knew his duty to his country and his family. The young soldier remembered the cool weather of Sasebo this time of year. How he longed to return home. Hearing a noise he started to turn when a slashing movement severed his windpipe and opened his carotid artery. The young soldier slumped sideways against the tree trunk. His body convulsed twice and then he was still.

Longol listened and looked toward the clearing for any reaction from the other Japanese. He turned to see Ted providing cover with his rifle. Motioning with his free hand he pointed in the direction of a second Japanese sentry. Ted acknowledged and began to move across the slope.

"Sergeant, we need to prepare to make camp here for the night."

Kenji Tadashi looked at his Lieutenant and got to his feet. A veteran of ten years in the Imperial Army, he had seen his share of good officers and bad ones. A young officer, Ishida tried very hard to be a good officer. Tadashi hoped he would make the right decisions now that he had to act without the Captain.

"Yes, sir."

"Take two men and gather wood for cooking. We need to find a stream for water." He looked at the two Americans on the ground. "Before you go, have the men drag the body over and roll it down the slope."

The Sergeant barked an order and two of his men walked over to the body of the dead American. Each man grabbed a leg and they dragged him to the edge of the clearing.

Bryan knelt and watched two Japanese soldiers pull Collin's body across the low grass. Blood covered his upper torso and his head flopped from side to side as they dragged him. Liz and Jerry Rogers lay on the ground twenty yards away but he could see her moving. Checking his watch, he knew Tiny would commence his attack shortly. They'd split the camp into an imaginary clock face. Tiny would take out every Jap from nine o'clock clockwise to three o'clock. Don had the other half of the camp. Bryan would protect the Americans. Ted and Longol would take out as many sentries as possible then wait for the first shots from Tiny.

He slowly slid the action back on his .45 and put a round in the chamber. Two spare clips were in his back pocket and he still had his sheath knife on his belt. He felt sweat running down the small of his back, the afternoon heat becoming brutally oppressive. Bryan watched the two soldiers walk back to their sergeant. That man now pointed south and both soldiers barked a response. They picked up their rifles and began to walk south on the ridge.

The first burst from Tiny's sub machine gun hit the two soldiers in their chests, throwing them both violently backward. A second gun opened up and the remaining Japanese fell to the ground seeking cover. Several single shots rang out from the jungle. So far there had been no return fire from the Japanese. One of the Japs rose to his knees and lunged for cover behind a fallen tree trunk.

Two down for sure, Bryan thought as he broke cover and sprinted five yards and threw himself on the ground. Desperately he pushed to his feet and ran toward a small bush only ten yards from Liz. Sporadic rifle shots cracked from behind him. Stay low...keep moving...stay low...Bryan heard another shot rang out, the bullet's ricochet splitting bark off the large tree. He lunged to his right, hitting the ground and rolling as shots cracked across the clearing. He saw a man moving to his left. Planting his elbows on the ground he sighted on the man's chest and pulled the trigger twice. From fifteen yards the impact of the .45 spun the man around and sent his rifle flying into the air.

Bryan lunged forward as another burst from a Thompson ripped the air. He heard multiple shots from the Japanese Arisakas as he raised his head to see Liz still on the ground next to Rogers. She lay on her left side, her wrists and ankles bound with rope.

Bryan threw himself forward and slid to the ground alongside Liz. He put the .45 on the ground and pulled the sheath knife to cut her wrist restraints.

"Keep your head down," he said urgently. "Here." He reached with the knife and cut the ropes binding her ankles.

A burst of sub machine gun fire erupted from the jungle.

"How's Rogers?"

"I'm not sure, he's unconscious."

Bryan saw movement to his right and turned to see a Japanese soldier on his knees two yards away. The man had a long sword in both hands drawn back ready to hack down at Bryan. In a moment of horror he realized the .45 was out of reach as the man stepped forward and began to swing the blade downward. Blood and bits of flesh sprayed from the man's chest as a burst of submachine gun fire tore his upper torso apart. Bryan saw Don Baurichter running toward him, the Thompson at the ready.

Four shots rang out and Baurichter went down. Bryan turned to see a Japanese officer holding a pistol. The man pointed the gun at the two Americans on the ground.

"Get down," he yelled at Liz and pulled her back from Rogers and to the ground. One shot cracked from the officer's pistol. Bryan heard the bullet whine past them. He saw the man throw the pistol down and pull his long sword from its scabbard. Raising it high in the air he sprinted toward Bryan, yelling as he raised the steel blade high over his head..

Bryan lunged for the .45, barely grabbing it before rolling on his back.

The attacker began to swing the blade down, both hands on the hilt.

Bryan's bullet hit the officer squarely in the forehead. The back of the man's skull exploded in a crimson flash.

The Jap staggered then collapsed, his sword dropping harmlessly to the ground.

The silence was sudden and complete.

Quickly releasing the clip from his pistol, Bryan slammed another into the bottom of the .45 and chambered a round. Cautiously he rose. He didn't see any Japanese. Looking past one Jap body he saw Don Baurichter roll on his back and gasp with pain.

"Tiny, do you see any more Japs?" Bryan yelled.

From the brush he heard a muffled reply, "I think we got 'em."

"None over here," Longol called from the east side of the clearing.

Slowly he got to his knees and scanned in all directions. He saw Longol and Ted emerge from the trees.

"Be careful," he yelled and stood up slowly.

Bryan made his way over to Baurichter who lay on the ground holding his knee. Blood oozed from between his fingers. Bryan knelt down next to him.

"Let me take a look at that."

Baurichter didn't say anything, but released his grip over the wound. Blood flowed from a large tear that had opened up his knee from the kneecap up and out to the side of his thigh.

"I'll get our nurse. Keep pressure on it with the flat of your hand."

"Yes, sir." His voice strained as he fought the pain.

"I'll be right back."

Bryan ran back to see Liz standing over Rogers. She turned toward him and shook her head.

"He's gone."

"One of my guys is down with a knee wound. Take a look a him. I'll find Tiny."

Longol and Ted were moving to each of the dead Japanese checking their bodies.

"Have you seen Leonard?" Bryan asked.

Both shook their heads.

"We may have another problem," Longol said. "We've counted the bodies and one is missing."

"What do you mean?"

"I counted six soldiers and one officer, Ted said. "We can only find six bodies including the officer. One must have escaped."

"Shit. Check around and see if you can find any sign close by. But we need to start moving down to the beach. Petty Officer Baurichter may not be able to walk so we may need that litter."

"Right," Ted said as he and Longol walked toward the nearby brush.

Bryan turned toward the opposite side of the clearing. "Tiny, where the hell are you?"

"Over here." The reply came from a clump of heavy bushes.

He ran over and knelt down to see under the heavy leaves. Tiny Leonard lay on his back, the Thompson by his side. A dark red stain covered the front of his shirt. Crawling under the bush he knelt next to his friend.

Tiny looked up at him. "How's Liz?"

"She's okay. Baurichter got hit in the leg but he should be okay. Let me take a look at you."

"Bryan, don't bother."

"What do you mean?" Bryan cut Tiny's shirt open and saw a single bullet hole just left of his breastbone. The blood flow trickled slowly down his chest, a red stain growing on his khaki pants.

"I can't move my legs."

Bryan put his hand on his friends arm and their eyes met. They both knew.

"You need to get down to the beach and I need some sleep."

"Let me get Liz, she might be able to do something."

"I'd like to see her."

Emerging into the clearing, he saw Liz walking back from Don Baurichter who lay on his back with his leg propped up on a log.

"I put a quick tourniquet on his leg. If I had some bandages I could keep the wound clean but it'll have to do for now. He needs a hospital as soon as possible."

"Liz, Tiny's been hit. He's in the bushes up there." Bryan paused then said slowly, "He took a round in the chest....can't move his legs."

"Let's go."

Both of them crawled under the bushes and knelt on either side of their wounded friend. Sweat covered Tiny's ashen face and his breathing started to become labored.

"Hi, kid," Tiny said softly as he looked up at Liz.

279

"Mr. Leonard, we meet in the strangest places. I'm just going to take a look at you." She carefully moved his shirt and then used her fingers to move blood away from the entry wound. "Bryan said you were having trouble with your legs?"

"Can't move 'em."

Liz reached down and pinched his lower left leg. "Can you feel that?"

Leonard shook his head. His breathing had become more labored.

She looked at Bryan. Her eyes told him what she didn't have to say.

"I'll go get something to make a bandage," Liz said.

"A waste of time," Tiny said, his voice soft. "You need to get these people down to the beach. Now get going."

Bryan looked at his friend, the life slipping away. "We're not leaving you."

"Just get me out into the clearing where I can see the ocean. ..... I'd like to see one more sunset."

The two friends looked at each other.

"Okay. You're giving the orders."

Twenty minutes later the small group began to move down the path to the beach. The men had moved Tiny Leonard to a small knoll that overlooked the blue water of Gizo Straits. Propped against the trunk of a jackfruit tree, the large leaves provided shade from the late afternoon sun. Liz had put a bandage on his wound to slow the bleeding. A canteen lay at his side. Ted and Longol, carrying the litter with Don Baurichter, began to carefully work their way down the slope.

Liz and Bryan knelt next to their friend. She took Tiny's hand and squeezed it softly. "Thank you." The tears welled up in her eyes as she quickly leaned over to kiss his cheek. Liz got up and walked after the two litter bearers.

"Is there anything you want me to do for you?"

Tiny shook his head. "Leave the .45."

Bryan nodded. He pulled the pistol from his holster and pulled the clip out. Six brass bullet heads were aligned in the black clip. He slipped it back in the pistol and worked the action to chamber a round. With the hammer locked back and ready to fire Bryan laid the weapon next to Tiny's right hand.

"There is something you can do for me."

"Name it."

"I always wanted to be buried in Arlington. See if you can get me a marker there."

Bryan looked at his friend but the words wouldn't come. He nodded.

"Now get the hell out of here and leave a man in peace."

Bryan reached down and took his friend's hand for a last time. There were no more words to be said but the look between the two men carried an unspoken message, two shipmates would meet again someday.

With the U.S.S. *Monaghan* keeping a watchful eye for aircraft or the Tokyo Express, PT's 142 and 135 executed a rescue of the landing party at 1815 hours.

As the PT's closed on the big destroyer, a flashing light message blinked from the signal bridge.

"Skipper, it's a message from the CO of the *Monaghan*. He wants to know if you made it back aboard."

Bryan leaned against the bulkhead, enjoying the fresh air.

"Petty Officer Schultz, send back to him, 'affirmative, thank you'." He wanted to say more but it would have been unprofessional.

Chapter Nineteen

A Time of Reckoning

The setting sun slipped below the horizon as the small formation made its way south toward Tulagi. For the last hour, the formation had steamed south at top speed after rendezvousing off Vona Vona. Stationed on each quarter of the larger ship, the two PT's made wide wakes in the dark waters of the Slot.

Below deck, Liz watched over Don Baurichter. She'd told Bryan the young gunner could make the transit to Tulagi without too much danger and it would not make sense to transfer him to the *Monaghan*. For now they had to keep him quiet and monitor his vital signs.

Lee Cordner remained at the helm of the 142 but Bryan sat with him in the cockpit. After a corned beef sandwich and almost two quarts of water Bryan felt ready to take the helm if needed.

"We'll plan on spending a day in Tulagi, give the crew a chance to rest. We can press on to San Cristobal the next day."

"What do you plan on doing when we get back to your base?" Cordner asked.

"I plan on raising hell, that's what."

Lee turned to look at Bryan. "With whom?"

"I'll start with Rosenberg, then go up the chain." Bryan's voice flared with anger.

"A bit of professional suicide?"

"Damn it, how many died because they sent in a bombing raid. We could have pulled the prisoners out without a problem."

"They'll say that if you hadn't put people ashore they would be alive now."

Bryan knew Lee might be right but he didn't care. "And write off the three Americans?"

"One of which turns out to be your girlfriend."

"We left three Americans and two Australians on that island. I don't want the brass to forget that."

"You're right," Lee said. "We both lost good friends back there. But there are no absolutes in this war, mate. I just think you need to think about it before you throw yourself on the altar of righteousness."

Petty Officer Gravely came out of the darkened hatch that led below decks. "Skipper, Lieutenant Sommers would like to talk to you."

The below deck red lighting turned to white when he closed the door to the XO's stateroom. Liz sat in the one chair watching Don Baurichter, who lay on top of the grey Navy blanket. A clean bandage covered his elevated knee, now held steady by rolled up towels. They both looked up.

"How're you feeling?" he asked Don.

"Glad to be off that island, sir."

"Our patient holding up well, nurse?"

Liz smiled softly. "He's doing fine. I think he's starting to catch on that he's going to be spending some time mending and not riding around on PT boats."

"A little time being pampered doesn't sound bad, does it?"

"I'm getting used to the idea, Skipper."

"Liz, why don't you go up and get some fresh air?

She looked at him curiously then nodded. "Good idea."

When she left, Bryan sat down in the chair.

"If you hadn't taken out that Jap, neither she nor I would be here tonight. I want to thank you, Don. It wasn't just ballsy but you were a damned good shot. I'm going to recommend that you be decorated for bravery."

"Thanks, Skipper." Baurichter stared at the overhead. "I'm sorry about Mr. Leonard. He took good care of me out there. If it hadn't been for him I don't think I would have ever made it to the ridge."

"He took care of a lot of Navy men in his career. You and I are just two of many."

"Yes, sir," the young man said.

The early hour contributed to the general confusion during their arrival at Tulagi. Both boats eventually tied up alongside the long main pier. Within ten minutes men from the local PT boat squadron swung into action. It took half an hour to get an ambulance from the small hospital down to the boat. Liz supervised moving Petty Officer Baurichter off the boat and safely on his way.

"He's going to be fine, Bryan. Trust me."

They both watched the olive drab truck pull away and head into the trees. A jeep pulled up where the ambulance had been parked and a tall Lieutenant Commander got out.

"I'm looking for Lieutenant Michaels," he said.

"I'm Michaels."

"Welcome to lovely Tulagi. I'm Joe Addison, the squadron commander. We received a radio message for you from San Cristobal. They want you to refuel and proceed directly back to base." He handed Bryan a folded piece of paper.

"Sir, right now both these crews need some sleep and then a decent meal."

Addison nodded. "Okay, it's 0300. Let's plan on refueling at 1000 and we can get you on your way by noon. I'll make sure my storekeepers get some stores down here for your men."

"Thank you, sir. Any chance we can get a set of wheels to use while we're here?"

"We've got a duty driver who hangs out in that hut over

there. He can take you anywhere you need to go."

"Yes, sir. Thanks."

Addison got back in his jeep and headed up the road after the ambulance.

"We need to get you in to see a doctor too," Bryan said to Liz.

"I'm fine. What worries me more is trying to find my unit."

"After getting shot down, captured by the Japs and escaping I believe you're entitled to what's called survivor leave. Thirty days to rest and recuperate."

"Bryan, all I need or want is a hot shower, a good meal and sleep. Preferably in that order."

"Come on, you can bunk in my stateroom. I'll take Deke's. Let's get some rest and sort it out in the morning."

She took his hand in the darkness and they climbed down the ladder below deck.

"Damn it, Michaels. You ignored a recall order and because of it we lost five people. What the hell were you thinking?" Rosenberg's face was flushed, a sure sign of his nasty mood.

"I was there and knew what was going on...."

"Bullshit! That's the whole point. You didn't know what was going on and that's why I'm pissed and so is headquarters."

Bryan didn't expect to be welcomed with open arms but he didn't understand Rosenberg's anger.

"I had a better chance of getting Rogers back and that was my mission."

Rosenberg looked across the desk and shook his head, the anger spent. "Well the brass wants a piece of your ass and I can't do much to protect you. They're sending a transport to pick up you and Lee Cordner and take you back to Brisbane. And I get to go along to get my ass chewed too. MacArthur's staff is involved for some reason, so God help us all."

Walking down the pier he saw Lee Cordner talking to Roy Lundeen. The boats were tied up adjacent to each other after their arrival from Tulagi. The return trip had been uneventful and he felt better leaving Liz when they learned her unit had arrived on Tulagi waiting further transportation to Tualo.

"They're flying the two of us back to Brisbane. Seems like the rear echelon boys aren't happy with how things turned out."

"Bloody public execution would be my guess," Lee said.

"I'm gonna throw my stuff in a bag, maybe they'll let me keep it in prison." Bryan disappeared down the hatch to his cabin.

Five minutes later he heard a knock on his door.

"It's open," he yelled.

Slowly the door opened. Charlie Morrison stood in the doorway, his cap in his hand. The mechanic's white tee shirt showed random drops of oil and a smear of grease or two.

"Excuse me, Skipper," he said tentatively.

"Petty Officer Morrison, come in. I was just packing my gear. I get a trip to Australia to explain our last trip."

"Yes, sir. We heard a little scuttlebutt from the Admin Shop. You aren't in trouble are ya?"

Bryan stopped and looked up at Morrison. He saw a look of concern to go along with the tone of indignation in Morrison's voice.

"I'll be honest with you, I don't know. Guess I'll find out in Brisbane."

"Sir, that's bullshit. You did a great job out there and any of the guys will tell anyone who needs to know." The words tumbled out of Morrison's mouth as he wrung the white hat in his hands.

Bryan stood up and stepped over to the mechanic. He extended his hand to Morrison.

"Thanks, that means a lot."

"Yes, sir."

As he finished packing Bryan knew that regardless of what happened to him now, he didn't much care.

After the primitive conditions of the Solomons, the order and cleanliness of Brisbane were pleasant reminders of civilization.

Bryan's father met the aircraft in a staff car and they quickly got on the road to town. With Lee in the car, the conversation stayed light, the Admiral not touching on the recent events. Bryan had put his father in an embarrassing position and knew it.

They planned to drop Lee at the local Naval District Headquarters on their way to the Metropolitan Hotel where the Admiral was staying.

"I don't know where this is going, mate," Lee said as he got out of the car. "But you did the right thing and I'll tell anyone in your chain of command or mine the same thing."

The two shook hands.

"Thanks, Lee."

Twenty minutes later Bryan and Rosey sat behind closed doors in the Admiral's room. Chuck Michaels poured scotch in three glasses and handed one to Rosenberg. He turned to his son, handing him the second drink.

"Did you get the recall order?" his father asked the tone of his voice even.

"I did."

The older man looked at his son and his eyes narrowed slightly. "Well you better give it to me in detail. You have the distinction of being in the dog house with both the Army and Navy."

"I'd do it again."

"Damn it, Bryan, that's not going to help," Rosey said.

"Just tell me everything you can think of about what you knew and what you thought landing on that island might accomplish."

"I thought I could save some Americans, damn it."

"Bryan, back off. In case you haven't figured it out, I'm on your side," his father said and sat down opposite him at the small table. "There're going to be some hard questions asked and you need to be ready to answer them."

"All right."

The Admiral took notes for forty minutes as Bryan related every detail he remembered of the planning and execution of the landing on Vona Vona. He asked an occasional question but mostly let his son talk. Rosenberg added details that might help their case with MacArthur's staff.

"It's a different war, son."

"I don't have anything to compare it to but I can't imagine killing your own people was ever condoned." Bryan's anger had been simmering below the surface and now came out strong.

"The knowledge that Lieutenant Rogers possessed was more important than his own life. I suspect he knew that too."

Bryan remembered what Rogers had said to him if they were going to be captured. Now it made sense. The intel officer knew his death might be necessary to protect critical information.

"He did. I didn't realize that until just now. He told me to kill him if we were going to be captured by the Japs."

"That takes a special kind of courage."

Bryan sat in his father's room confused and unsure now if what he did really made sense. Did he use Rogers as his excuse to try and save Liz? If he did, what kind of officer did that make him? Five men died because of that decision.

"So what's going to happen to me?" Bryan asked, now feeling very much at the mercy of events.

"I'm not sure. When I talked with MacArthur's Chief of Staff, General Sutherland, it sounded like the Supreme Commander wanted to talk to you.

Bryan shuddered. He'd heard the tales of General MacArthur chewing up generals and spitting out the pieces. As a lowly Navy Lieutenant he had no chance.

"Now that you're here I have to let them know in the front office. Let's find you two rooms and then get some dinner. I'll talk to Sutherland first thing tomorrow.

General Douglas MacArthur's office was located on the fourth floor of a large sandstone building formerly the headquarters of the A.M.P Insurance Company. An Army MP checked Admiral Michael's identification card before he selected floor four on the elevator.

Room 409 had a heavy wooden door painted "General MacArthur." Inside were three desks manned by Army enlisted men.

"I have Lieutenant Michaels and Lieutenant Commander Rosenberg here to see the General." Chuck Michaels announced.

A Master Sergeant said, "Just a moment, sir." The man picked up a phone receiver and spoke briefly. He replaced the phone and stood. "Lieutenant, would you please follow me. Commander Rosenberg, General Sutherland would like to talk to you separately."

Bryan looked at his father who nodded slightly.

Rosey followed a Corporal out into the hallway thinking this is the way they interrogate prisoners.

General MacArthur sat at a large wooden desk reading papers. He wore an undress khaki uniform with no tie. Looking up he said, "Thank you, Sergeant. Lieutenant, please have a seat."

Bryan said, "Yes, sir."

"I've been reading a briefing from my staff on your career." MacArthur looked up without smiling. "You were an aviator."

"Yes, sir."

"And you flew in both the Battle of the Coral Sea and Midway."

"Yes, sir, dive bombers."

"It says here you were shot down and wounded at the Coral Sea."

"Yes, sir. We were rescued by an Australian patrol boat."

"But only a month later you flew at Midway."

"I was medically grounded but launched anyway."

"You have a penchant for doing things your way, Lieutenant. Bryan didn't answer.

"What do you think would happen if everyone in this war did what they wanted to?"

"We'd have problems, General."

"Quite so. But you took it upon yourself to ignore a recall

and executed the raid on Vona Vona." The General had stopped referring to the briefing paper and now sat back in his seat looking at Bryan with a hard stare.

"General, I was there and had the most current intelligence. I felt we had a good chance to rescue the Americans that were being held by the Japanese."

"During the First War I was constantly frustrated by the orders that came down from the staffs that were miles from the action. I will agree that most of the time the commander on scene does have an advantage over the chain of command."

"Yes, sir."

"Unfortunately this was not one of those times. Lieutenant Rogers possessed our most sensitive of cryptologic information. If the Japanese high command had been able to discern the extent of his knowledge, many Americans might have died. Those are the type of decisions that senior commanders have to make every day."

Bryan realized MacArthur just admitted that a decision had been made which resulted in the bombing raid on Vona Vona.

"Lieutenant, your decision to land on that island resulted in the loss of five men. Two of those men were Australians and that means we owe some answers to our allies."

Bryan felt the anger welling up inside. He remembered Tiny Leonard and the others. "Sir, I wasn't ready to let those people die without at least trying."

MacArthur's eyes narrowed. "That includes Nurse Lieutenant Sommers?"

What the hell, Bryan thought, they're going to throw the book at me so I might as well tell the old bastard what I think. "General, I can't deny that it had an effect on my decision. But I like to think I would have done the same thing regardless of her. I couldn't just write them off as easily as you did."

The look on the General's face could have frozen the sun. "Lieutenant, don't you ever think I take the life of any American serviceman lightly. I have to make decisions every day that I know will result in the loss of life. That is something I will carry with me forever. But we all accept that when we put on the uniform."

Bryan remembered Lieutenant Rogers telling him that he must not be captured. "I'm sorry, General. I shouldn't have said that."

The General stood up and walked over to the window and looked out. He crossed his arms in front of himself and turned to Bryan. "You may find this hard to believe Lieutenant Michaels but I probably would have done the same thing. We train our officers to make the best decisions on the information they have available. As a young officer I would have tried my utmost to rescue my countrymen."

Bryan felt confused. He expected to be court-martialed and now the Supreme Commander tells him he would have done the same thing.

The General continued, "The question now is what will you do the next time you're in a situation like Vona Vona? Will you follow orders or will you do what you think is best?"

Bryan hesitated for a moment. "Sir, I would still exercise my best judgment and do what I felt was needed to accomplish the mission."

MacArthur showed no surprise at Bryan's admission. "There are some who say that's the reason we will ultimately triumph over the Empire of Japan. The Japanese school their officers to follow orders to the letter and to the death if necessary. We are still a culture of cowboys. But I agree with that school of thought. Up to this point we have been overwhelmed by strength of numbers. As we bring our resources to bear on the enemy we will inevitably succeed."

"Admiral Nimitz said the same thing to me before the Coral Sea," Bryan said.

"He did?"

"Yes, sir, he said that it was up to the people in the battle now to hold the line until the men and equipment get out here."

MacArthur took his chair. "I have the greatest respect for the Admiral and agree completely. How did you meet Admiral

Nimitz?"

Nervously Bryan pushed the hair back from his forehead. "He intervened to get me back in a cockpit after I had a problem, sir."

Douglas MacArthur laughed and threw his head back. "Well I must say the Admiral and I have walked down the same road."

"Yes, sir." Bryan felt a little foolish.

Picking up his phone receiver the General said, "Sergeant, bring your pad in please."

The Sergeant who had shown Bryan in originally entered with a stenograph pad in his hand.

"Take a message. Personal for Admiral Nimitz from MacArthur. Subject: Lieutenant Bryan Michaels, U.S. Navy. 1. Michaels distinguished himself in combat during actions behind enemy lines in the Solomons. His knowledge of the operating area and established relations with Australians make him a superb candidate as the American representative on an upcoming critical mission in support of our next phase of operations. 2. Desire Lieutenant Michaels be attached on temporary duty to my staff. Officer has volunteered for this hazardous duty. Sign it warmest regards. Let's get that typed up and transmitted as soon as possible. Thank you, Sergeant."

Bryan watched the Sergeant exit, not sure he'd heard correctly what MacArthur had just said.

"I have no reason to believe that Admiral Nimitz will disapprove my request. And I'm sure you're ready to volunteer for whatever will help the war effort." MacArthur's tone changed slightly, a hardness in his words.

"Yes, sir." Bryan decided you don't tell a four star general 'no.'

One of the General's aides de camp told Admiral Michaels that Lieutenant Michaels would be busy during the afternoon but he might see his son later that night. Standing in the hallway of the A.M.P. Building with Rosey Rosenberg, a very confused Rear

Admiral watched his son walk away down the corridor.

"Admiral Michaels?"

He turned to see the General's writer standing by the door.

"General MacArthur asked if you would have a moment to talk?"

Captain Paul Farrell escorted Bryan down to the ground floor where they were met by an Army sedan driven by a Corporal.

"Hop in, it's just a short drive," Farrell said smiling at Bryan.

Bryan climbed in behind the driver. "Where exactly are we going?"

"A military compound on the outskirts of town." Farrell didn't elaborate.

"Right," Bryan said and sat back in the seat.

Thirty minutes later they pulled off the two lane road and continued on a winding gravel road that led back into the low hills. Cresting a ridge he saw a cluster of temporary buildings all painted a nondescript brown. They pulled up to a gate manned by an Australian sentry.

"Captain Farrell to see Commander Coyne." The aide pulled out his identity card.

"Just a moment, sir." The sentry handed the card to another soldier within the small guard house who looked at the card then dialed the phone.

"Proceed, sir. The Commander's office is in the second building on the right."

Bryan saw no indication of what service or unit resided in the small camp. Looking around he saw mostly Australian uniforms. The door to the building didn't offer any additional information.

"Lieutenant, I'll leave you here. They'll look after you. At some point this week you need to stop back at the staff and we can finish your transfer paperwork." Without another word Farrell closed the car door and drove off.

Nothing should surprise me anymore but this is damned strange, Bryan thought. What the hell, he said to himself and opened the door. At the end of a corridor, an open door showed a young sailor sitting at a desk.

"I'm looking for a Commander Coyne."

"This is his office, sir. Please come in. You must be Lieutenant Michaels." The sailor stood up at his desk. "I'm Yeoman Harris."

"That's right. Nice to meet you, Harris." Bryan walked to the window hoping to see something that might help solve the mystery of this camp. Only buildings much like this one were in sight and he turned back to the young man.

"The Commander asked me to have you wait in his office, sir. He should be back shortly."

Bryan followed the young man into the inner office and took a seat in one of the two wooden chairs by the small desk.

"Can I get you some tea, sir?"

Bryan shook his head. "No thanks." A wooden nameplate with "R. Emmet Coyne, CDR, RAN" sat on the single wooden desk. In addition to the desk, he saw one filing cabinet and a very large metal standup safe like the ones he'd seen in banks back in the states. Must be something worth locking up, he decided. *What the hell did I get myself into?*

He heard steps in the outer office and a stocky man in khakis walked into the room.

"Lieutenant Michaels, sorry to keep you waiting." The man removed his hat to reveal short cropped black hair. A ruddy complexion betrayed too much time in the sun, the lines around his eyes telling the same tale. He extended his hand. "You're the first Yank we've been assigned. Glad to have you. Please sit down. Corporal, would you ask Number One to step in for a moment?" Coyne removed a web belt and holster putting it on his desk. "I suspect you have a few questions. I though having my Executive Officer here might help answer them."

There were two knocks on the door frame and Bryan turned

to see Lee Cordner walk in the office. He grinned at Bryan.

"Welcome aboard, mate."

He smiled at the befuddled look from his American friend.

"I think I do have a lot of questions."

Lee sat down next to him.

Commander Coyne lit a cigarette and exhaled. "You've been attached to what is loosely known as the Allied Intelligence Bureau. We are a part of that group but we are also a very special group within the AIB. We go by the rather plain title of Unit 331. Most of the Bureau is Australian and Army to boot. That is due in large part to the inclusion of our commando types as part of the organization." He stopped to inhale from his cigarette then tapped it on an ash tray. "We're charged with the field intelligence operations for the entire theatre to include the dirty trick boys and the signals intelligence types. We're in charge of the naval portion of any behind the lines operations. Clear so far?"

Bryan said, "Yes, sir. I think so."

"As we push north at the Jappo's there's a need to be able to operate behind the lines and at sea. We gather intelligence, insert coast watchers, create a little havoc when necessary and uphold the honor of the senior service if you know what I mean."

"Bryan," Lee Cordner added. "More and more we're operating together with your Navy. As MacArthur moves on New Guinea it will only increase. We need someone with us who can speak the language and has a feel for what the war is like in this part of the world. As it turns out the trip to Vona Vona brought you to the Supreme Commander's attention. Our boss had been trying to get an American for us for almost three months. As soon as MacArthur decided not to court martial you, everyone's problem was solved."

"Okay," Bryan said tentatively.

Coyne stuffed out his cigarette. "Take a look around, talk to Lee and see what we do. If you don't think this is for you, I'm sure we can figure out something to keep the General happy."

Later that afternoon Bryan took a walk around the compound. A former ranch, there were walkways, open fields and several gardens in additional to the newly constructed rows of buildings. He enjoyed the pleasant afternoon weather after the terrible humidity of the Solomons. As he walked he reflected on the last year. So much had happened. Pearl Harbor, the Coral Sea, Midway and now the Battle for the Solomons. Tim Hutchins, Bill Nance and Tiny Leonard all close friends gone forever. And Liz, how much she meant to him and how close he'd come to losing her.

This was the biggest war mankind had ever seen and the lives and fortunes of men and countries would be changed forever. He knew he should just forget about the future. Worry about here and now. Don't think about what might happen or what the future holds. That would have been easy a year ago, before he met Liz. Now he couldn't avoid the truth, he wanted to survive and be with her. But something inside of him pushed him to stay in the action. What the hell is it? Thousands of men the world over would happily do anything to go home. He'd turned down the chance once and now Coyne was giving him a free pass if he wanted it.

The high ceiling of the dining room at the hotel reminded Bryan of the Hotel Grant in San Diego. For a brief moment he remembered a dinner long ago with his parents after he had learned of his appointment to the Naval Academy. He saw his father at a table by the tall windows overlooking the street.

His father looked up as Bryan approached. "I suspect you'll need a stiff drink?"

Sitting down, he smiled. "Let's start with one, but it's only a start."

A white coated waiter nodded wordlessly when the Admiral ordered two gin and bitters.

"Interesting day?" Chuck Michaels asked his son.

"Very interesting."

"I talked briefly with the General after you left. From what he told me there isn't much we can talk about in public. Oh by the way Rosenberg met a young Australian lady in the bar and sends his regrets."

Bryan laughed. "She doesn't know what she's in for."

The waiter arrived with their drinks.

He waited until the man had left. "Did the General mention what they want me to do?"

Chuck Michaels took a drink. "Nothing specific but he led me to believe it was dangerous."

"Hell, what isn't anymore? Oh yeah, Lee Cordner's in the outfit. They call it Unit 331."

"331, interesting. I guess that explains Lee showing up on that last trip."

Bryan nodded. "It wasn't just a coincidence."

"You have any idea what you'll be doing?"

Shaking his head Bryan said, "Not yet. In fact they've given me an out if I decide I'm not interested."

"Who told you that?"

"My new Commanding Officer, an Aussie Commander named Coyne."

The two sat in silence watching traffic outside the window.

Chuck Michaels finished his drink and motioned to the waiter. "Have you decided what you're going to do?"

"I'd like to talk it over with Liz. But I don't see anyway I can pull that off."

"Don't be too sure of that. She's arriving tomorrow afternoon by air. Two weeks survivor leave and she heard there might be a certain Navy Lieutenant in Brisbane."

Bryan's heart leaped. "Liz is gonna be here tomorrow?"

"If my office has their information correct and the transport doesn't break down." The father smiled at the look on his son's face.

Although they had seen each other only four days before, Liz flew into Bryan's arms at the military side of the civil aerodrome. The two held each other, oblivious of the glances from other

297

passengers.

Lee stood back at the edge of the tarmac waiting for the two lovers. "Welcome to Brisbane, Liz," he said at they approached him.

"Thanks." Liz smiled and kept her arm tight around Bryan's as they walked to the car.

"Hop in." Bryan said as he opened the door to the official sedan.

Commander Coyne had been briefed on Liz by Lee Cordner and immediately called several local contacts. "How was your trip?" Cordner asked as he pushed the starter.

"A lot better than my last airplane flight" she said.

Lee looked shocked, realizing what she meant. "I didn't mean…"

Bryan laughed and so did Liz.

"So where are we going?" Liz asked Bryan.

"You have to ask Lee. No one will tell me anything. We are the victims of a cruel Australian kidnapping plan."

"Too right," Lee said as he turned the car onto Pruitt Highway and headed north.

The Mountjoy Hotel nestled among a large grove of trees on the outskirts of the city. Built in the 1920s, it had been a favorite get away for the wealthier Brisbane tennis set. Eight grass courts were separated by gravel walkways and tall eucalyptus trees. Painted totally white, the two story main building reminded Bryan of a southern plantation complete with false columns at the entrance. Lee pulled around the circular driveway and brought the car to a halt next to tall wrought iron stanchion with metal rings on the side.

"Welcome to the Mountjoy. That's where they used to tie up their horses while they had a drink or played some tennis. Not many horses around anymore but still lots of tennis. Come on, let's get you two settled."

The double doors opened into a large lobby. At the reception desk a tall elderly man looked up from his ledger.

298

"Good afternoon. I'm Lieutenant Commander Cordner. My office should have called ahead with reservations for Lieutenant and Mrs. Michaels."

The man smiled. "Quite right, sir. We have it listed right here, the bridal suite reserved for two weeks."

Liz, who had her arm hooked around Bryan's, squeezed it hard.

"Welcome to the Mountjoy, sir," the clerk said. "Pleased to have you and the Mrs. with us. If I might ask you to sign the register?"

Bryan grinned and wrote his name in the guest book.

"You should find some incidentals in your room. If you need anything, contact Mr. Wheeler. He's the manager and knows Commander Coyne very well. And with that, I'm off."

"Do you have time for a beer?" Bryan looked at Liz.

"Yes, please do, Lee," she said. "It will give us time to wind down."

"Then I'd be pleased," Lee said, "But only one. Let's go out on the veranda, it's a grand view of the ocean."

"If you gentlemen would excuse me, I'll be right back." Liz turned toward a door that said "Ladies."

The two walked out a side door toward the wide wooden veranda that spanned the entire side of the hotel facing the water.

"The bridal suite? Nice touch."

"I thought you'd like it. Besides, by the end of the week you might very well be married. Right?"

Bryan laughed. "I don't think I'd go that far."

Despite everything they had been through in the last two weeks, Liz and Bryan were awkward as they explored their suite on the second floor. The incidentals Lee mentioned included swim suits for both of them and they jumped at the idea of a late afternoon swim.

The beach was nearly empty except for an elderly couple sitting on one of the wide benches that lined a wooden boardwalk in front of the hotel. They walked to the water and then down the beach letting the small waves wash over their legs.

Bryan reached down for Liz's hand. "Are you feeling all right?"

She nodded. "I'm okay. A couple days of sleep, some decent food and I'll be fine."

"It seems hard to believe where we were less than a week ago."

He turned to look at her and saw there were tears running down her face.

She looked at him, the tears continuing. "Bryan, I can't stop thinking about Nancy and Tiny….all the rest."

When he heard Tiny's name it brought back the memory of that last day. "I know."

"I guess I didn't understand this war until now. Even at Pearl Harbor, we took care of the wounded but never saw it for real."

Bryan didn't say anything for a moment, thinking about Tim and Bill and all of the others who had died.

"Liz, it's going to get a lot worse before it's over. You saw what they were like on that island. We have to take on the bastards all the way across the Pacific and then invade Japan itself. It's almost too hard to think about."

They walked on in silence, the waves softly washing the shore. Bryan put his arm around her.

Liz stopped. "Bryan, let's make a deal. We won't talk about the war, or the past or even the future. Let's forget about everything except us."

He smiled and kissed her. "I love you. And you're right. I'm ready to forget the war for now. God knows it's going to find us again before we're ready."

She took his hand and looked into his eyes. Raising her head she kissed him softly on the mouth.

For the next two weeks the reunited lovers immersed

themselves in the activities of peacetime. They rode two of the horses that were kept in a small stable just north of the hotel. Both of them dusted off their old tennis game and found they were equally matched as singles. The food proved to be wonderful and Bryan wondered what Lee had to do with the constant procession of beef and seafood the hotel would serve at their reserved table. The rest and relaxation had its desired effect on both of them. They slept soundly and rose refreshed. Physically they both felt themselves gaining lost strength each day.

Chuck Michaels came by the Mountjoy for dinner at the end of the first week and remarked how well they both looked. On one of his frequent trips to Brisbane, the Admiral wanted to see how they were recovering. He'd been working hard on coordinating the many elements which had to come together for the offensive north into New Guinea. Bryan saw the effect of the long hours and strain on his father.

Lee Cordner joined them for Sunday brunch at the end of the second week. There had been no contact with Lee since he'd dropped them off and now Bryan guessed this was a warning call that the war wanted them back.

"You look like a new man," the Australian said to Bryan while they waited for Liz to come down to the dining room.

"I'd forgotten what it was like to feel good," Bryan said. "I think I've fallen in love with Australia."

"No argument here to be sure. 'Course there are some parts that aren't as hospitable as Brisbane."

"Some day you'll have to show me." He picked up his cup and took a drink. "My God, I've even started to like tea."

"Then there is definitely hope for your ultimate redemption."

Both men laughed.

Lee turned serious. "I don't want to cast any shadows but are you going to be ready to jump back into it shortly?"

Bryan looked at his friend. "I've lost any bravado I ever had, Lee. Am I chomping at the bit? No. Am I ready to come back and give it a shot? Yeah, I guess. It's hard to get your mind back on the war after the two best weeks I've ever had."

They both looked up as Liz walked into the dining room. Lee tried to conceal his surprise at the change in her appearance. Liz radiated happiness, all signs of her capture gone forever.

"Please sit down," she said as they started to get up. Liz slipped into the chair next to Lee. "I can't tell you how much I appreciate everything you've done for us." She leaned over and kissed him on the cheek.

Cordner blushed. "It was nothing, really. But thanks very much."

"And please tell your Commander Coyne he has made a girl from Seattle very happy."

"I would be happy to pass it on. He acts a bit like a gruff old bastard but he's a good man."

They made small talk while they ate, no one daring to discuss the war and impending end of their leave. After saying good night to Liz, Lee asked Bryan to walk him out to the sedan.

They walked in silence across the driveway until Bryan asked, "Can you tell me anything on what's up?"

Lee stopped at the door to the car. "A bit of a reconnaissance at this point. Looking for some key information that might have a big impact on the move north. But we've plenty of time to cover all that when you're back. Enjoy these last two days. I'll call for you Tuesday morning. We've set up transport for Liz and we'll see her off."

The two men shook hands. "Don't be too early on Tuesday," Bryan said.

That night they lay side by side, both awake but silent. While they'd had a wonderful day, the weight of their impending good bye was beginning to show.

"Did you talk with Lee about the unit?" Liz asked softly.

"I thought we made a pact not to talk about the outside world," he replied.

She rolled over, her head on the pillow facing him. "We both know it's not that simple. It's been wonderful but now I have to talk about the future. We don't know what's going to happen and I'm having trouble with that."

"Liz, we're like the other millions of people in this war. No guarantees, no idea if they'll survive, only hope. I know I love you more than I ever thought possible. All I can do is hope we're both here when it's all over. I don't know anything else to do."

"And why am I guessing whatever you're doing now is just as dangerous as before."

"I don't know if it is or not, honestly." He hesitated, then said, "The CO said they would let me off the hook if I asked them."

"What does that mean?"

"They'll find some way to get me out of this assignment, no questions asked."

"Is this job important?" Liz asked.

"I guess if MacArthur is personally involved, it must be."

She lay back on the pillow. "I feel like Dorothy, caught in the tornado."

"Well this sure as hell ain't Kansas," he said, leaning over to kiss her.

"So what are you going to do?"

"Same thing you are. Do my job and not worry about the future. I don't think there's anything else we can do."

"My God, what a story to tell our kids."

He kissed her bare shoulder. "Let's not tell them everything."

She reached over and pulled him toward her. "Good idea."

Chapter Twenty

Go for broke...

On arrival back at the unit, Lee took Bryan directly to Commander Coyne's office.

"Ah, there you are, Michaels. Good to see you. Come in and have a seat." Coyne's ruddy complexion shone with enthusiasm. "A good leave I hope?"

"Yes, sir. Thank you. They took very good care of us at the Mountjoy." Bryan had been surprised at the small bill he received from the hotel on checkout.

"Lee, remind me to ring the manager and let him know we appreciate their efforts."

Cordner nodded. "Right, sir."

"Now, ready to jump into the fray as it were?" The tone of Coyne's voice left no doubt the pleasantries were over.

"Ready to go, sir."

"Then let's go down to the intelligence shop. There's some charts I want you to see."

Bryan followed the Commander and Lee through a door marked "Entry Restricted." They walked between large charts of the Pacific theater mounted on wheeled platforms. On the walls were several cork boards with enemy force recognition panels. In the center of the room six desks were manned by men intently pouring over charts and message boards.

"Over here," Coyne said and walked to the far side of the room stopping at a large wheeled chart board. "Here we go. Petty Officer Andrews would you please move this into the briefing room."

A tall sailor walked over and maneuvered the board through a door into an inner briefing room. He turned on the lights as he passed the threshold.

Two rows of chairs faced several chalk boards on the front wall.

"Right there is fine. Thank you, Andrews. Close the door on your way out. Please sit down, gentlemen." Coyne flipped the front chart back exposing a larger scale chart labeled "Ulithi Atoll."

"Bryan, the classification of this is *Top Secret.* To take that a step farther it is considered *Level Two.* You are now cleared for this level. Please remember the critical nature of everything you will hear in the future. Understood?"

"Yes, sir," Bryan replied.

Coyne continued, "A little background first. You are aware both sides use code in communicating with their forces."

Bryan nodded. "Not much more than that, sir."

"No, of course not. And there's a reason for that. The world of codes is very tightly controlled. Both sides try to break the other's codes. The Japanese, to the best of our knowledge, have not broken our current codes. What they don't know is that we have indeed broken the main operational code used by the Imperial Navy."

"It was critical to your success at Midway," Lee offered. "Keeping the other side in the dark about code breaking is one of the most critical aspects of the world of intelligence. The reason we went after your Lieutenant Rogers is that he knew of our breaking the JN25 code. We couldn't risk the Japs finding out what he knew."

Instantly Bryan realized what General MacArthur had meant

about Roger's sensitive cryptologic information.

"So you knew all along?" Bryan asked.

Cordner nodded. "Couldn't tell you. You weren't cleared for it."

"But now you are and it's critical for our next op," Coyne said and turned back to the chart. "This is Ulithi Atoll, a series of islands and islets that surround a large deep water lagoon. We suspect the Japanese might want to use it as a fall back area if Truk becomes untenable. But for now they only have a small caretaker force. The largest island has the improbable name of Mogmog. There are by our estimate about twenty Japanese personnel on the island. They are manning a communication relay station. Under certain weather conditions, the relay station at Ulithi is critical in their ability to contact forces operating north of New Guinea. We are privy to information that they are in the process of distributing the next version of their naval code, designated JN29. Once this code goes into operation our ability to beat them to the punch will be severely degraded."

Coyne walked over and grabbed a chair from the row, pulled it out and sat down facing the two junior officers. "That's where you and Lee come in. We want you to take a team to Mogmog and take a look at the new code books. And we have to make sure the Japs don't know you've seen them. Bit of a challenge, wouldn't you say?"

These guys are crazy, Bryan thought.

"I've been working on this the last several weeks and I think we've got some good ideas." Lee looked serious.

"Why don't I leave you two to discuss the specifics? I'll be in my office when you're done."

When the Commander closed the door Bryan turned to Lee. "This has got to be good."

Lee laughed. "I haven't taken leave of my senses."

"Really?"

"I didn't say it was going to be a walk in the daisies. But I do think we can give it a good run."

"Okay, I'll listen. If nothing else it should be entertaining." Bryan saw Lee cut his eyes at him. "Hey, I'm just pulling your leg."

"Right." Lee stood up. "First thing there's someone I want you to meet. Let's head over to the Armory. I suspect that's where we'll find him."

A one story brick building surrounded by its own small barbed wire enclosure served as the unit's arms and ammunition storage facility. Lee produced a key to open the heavy wooden gate. Inside the building a faint smell of gun cleaning solution filled the air. Behind the counter a tall corporal was reading a ledger.

"Good morning, Perkins. Is the Sergeant Major in?"

Corporal Perkins turned toward a closed door. "I'll tell him you're here, sir."

A minute later a man wearing the uniform of an Australian Army Sergeant Major walked out the door of the office. He strode directly around the counter and came to a smooth position of attention.

"Good morning, sir."

"Sergeant Major Tobin, I'd like to introduce Lieutenant Michaels, United States Navy."

Bryan offered his hand which the Sergeant Major accepted. He sensed Tobin was quickly evaluating him.

"Glad to meet you, sir," he said.

"Do you have time to cover a few items now, Sergeant Major?" Lee asked.

"No problem, sir. Perkins, make sure we're not interrupted. Gentlemen, let's use my office."

While both officers outranked Tobin, Bryan sensed Lee greatly respected Tobin.

"I read a report on your operation on Vona, Lieutenant. Quite interesting, actually," Tobin said.

Bryan couldn't tell if the Sergeant Major meant his comment as a compliment or criticism. "We did what we had to."

Tobin's expression didn't change, but his voice softened.

"You did very well in a tough situation. This time we'll have a chance to organize a proper mission."

Lee interrupted, "The Sergeant Major is a member of the team. He's spent a great deal of time behind Jap lines and has the skills we need to get in and out again."

"How big is the team?" Bryan asked.

"Right now we're thinking four, five at the most. Besides the three of us, we'll probably bring an experienced commando type who could double as our radioman."

"I think Corporal Louis would be the best man for the job," Tobin added.

"What's the general idea? It looks like you guys have already put in a lot of planning." Bryan said.

"Pretty straight forward actually. We take an amphibian aircraft, land in the Ulithi lagoon and paddle ashore. After we reconnoiter the area and determine where the code books are most likely kept, we put together a plan to slip in and photograph them. Then we rendezvous with our aircraft and head south."

Bryan watched Tobin and saw no reaction to what struck him as an incredibly crazy mission.

Lee continued, "We'll train together for the next several weeks and then lock in a date for execution."

The term execution gave Bryan a strange feeling.

The next three weeks were the most intense training Bryan had ever seen or endured. Hand to hand combat, weapons training and sheer physical conditioning put him in bed each night exhausted. Sergeant Major Jock Tobin lived up to his reputation as a perfectionist in every sense of the word. He drove Lee and Bryan through their paces regardless of their seniority.

Corporal Alistair Louis trained with them each step of the way despite his current proficiency in every facet of commando operations. Recently completing a crash course on Japanese the young radio operator had now been on active service for two years.

Lee Cordner had also studied Japanese at university prior to the war. Lee described himself as moderately proficient in Japanese and Dutch, both learned in preparation for a career in the shipping business in the South Pacific.

Since graduation from the Naval Academy Bryan had not paid much attention to physical training other than recreational tennis on occasion. His day now included five mile runs, calisthenics, swimming and lifting weights. Muscles that hadn't been used for years were reawakened and put through their paces. Most of their swimming took place in the ocean and included training with an inflatable four man raft. Despite being the oldest member of the team at thirty six, Jock Tobin participated in every event and made it abundantly clear that he was capable of outperforming the three younger team members handily in any activity.

"You'd best not be running out of steam like that on Mogmog, there might be a Jap right behind you," he yelled at the three of them as they completed a five mile run at sunrise. Tobin ran backwards with apparent ease as he berated them.

The three younger men were breathing hard as they worked hard to keep up with Tobin

"As a special reward for rather mediocre performance, we will continue on to the firing range. There you will demonstrate your ability to field strip your Stens and then fire for qualification."

Bryan looked over at Lee in the growing light.

The Australian grinned at him. "Splendid idea, Sergeant Major. Just what we were hoping for," Lee called to Tobin who had now jogged ahead of the three heading for the firing range.

"The man's a machine," Bryan said, his breathing labored.

"But he's our machine, sir," Alistair Louis chimed in. The young soldier had blended in well with a group of seniors. He'd been consistent in his ability to handle every task and with surprising good nature.

Thirty minutes later the sound of rapid fire echoed off the

309

armory buildings as the team fired clips of nine millimeter ammunition from their recently reassembled Sten submachine guns. The choice of British commando forces, the compact weapon had also been selected for the Allied Intelligence Bureau.

After a session with the Stens, Tobin passed out their side arms, the American .45 caliber pistol. Sergeant Major Tobin liked the stopping power of the big semi automatic.

"Hit one of the little bastards anywhere in the upper torso and he won't get back up again. Can't say that for the Webley. And if one of them is coming at you with one of those bloody big swords you better stop him the first time."

Bryan enjoyed shooting the heavy weapon. The recoil confirmed its ability to stop an opponent with one round.

After cleaning their weapons the three team members left the armory for breakfast.

"We confirmed with the meteorologist that the week of the 19th will be the right time for moon illumination at the atoll. Initial liaison with your chaps has them sending a PBY from New Caledonia one week prior for some familiarization training. I believe they'll be coming from your Patrol Squadron Twelve."

Bryan remembered the PBY that went down with Liz aboard. "What kind of guidance did we give them on the experience level of the crew?"

"I don't think we did, actually. Rather assumed they would send us their top pilots. That's certainly what we'd do." Lee looked surprised.

"Every outfit's different. Some commanding officers would do just that. But there are also those who will use a mission like this to get rid of a problem crew."

"Point taken. I'll talk to Commander Coyne."

Alistair Louis stepped up to the dining facility door and opened it for them.

"Let me," Bryan said. "I'm sure there's something I can do to help."

One week later a single PBY-5 Catalina arrived in Brisbane from Patrol Squadron Twelve. Bryan and Lee met the aircraft at the Naval Base. The amphibian aircraft moored to one of the Navy's buoys normally occupied by Royal Australian Navy destroyers. The two men watched as the motor launch ran out to pick up the crew and their baggage.

Standing in the open boat were six aircrew, two wearing khaki uniforms and four in dungarees. Several canvas sea bags lay in the bottom of the boat. Australian line handlers quickly secured the boat to the pier and the American crew climbed out.

Bryan walked down the pier toward the Americans. A Lieutenant detached himself from the small group unloading their baggage from the boat.

"I'm Gene Porter. Are you Michaels?" The Lieutenant was thin as a rail with jet black hair.

"Bryan. Welcome." Bryan shook hands with him. "This is Lieutenant Commander Cordner."

"Welcome to Brisbane, Lieutenant. We have transport for you and your crew. They have you at the transient facility downtown. Not a bad place. You're welcome to come out to our compound, but there's not much for your men to do out there."

The rest of the crew had walked up behind Porter. "Thanks. We've been living in tents on New Caledonia and we're looking forward to a little civilization."

Lee looked over the crew. "If you mean beer and women, we have them both."

The crew laughed. "You got that right, sir," one of the dungaree clad flyers said.

"Come on, let's go."

Later at transient billeting Bryan told Lieutenant Porter they would collect him at 0730 the next morning. Until then they were free to enjoy the local liberty.

"The distance is gonna be tight. A round trip to Ulithi from Darwin is right at our max distance. We're not gonna be carrying

311

any ordnance, right?" Gene Porter stood looking at a large area map in the unit intelligence spaces.

"No need," answered Bryan.

"And just four of you?"

Cordner got up from his chair. "That's our plan for now. Not set in stone but probably only four."

"How long do you plan on being on the island?" Porter sat back on the top of a desk and crossed his arms. The rest of his crew had remained at billeting, sleeping off a hard night on liberty.

"We hope no more than four days. That will give us time to observe the Nips and figure out their routine. Once we've completed our mission you come pull us out." Bryan tried to sound nonchalant. Since they began the planning all of them made assumptions which were optimistic at best. "We'll have a radio to let you know when to be there and a timed backup if the radio craps out."

"How close do you think we can taxi to the island?"

Bryan's confidence in the Catalina's crew increased as Porter kept asking the right questions. The Commanding Officer of Patrol Squadron Twelve must have decided to send his best on this mission. "It'll be dark and you'll be at idle," Bryan answered. "We think you can take it in to a mile safely. The less distance we have to paddle the raft the better for us."

"I hope you've been practicing," Porter said. "Open ocean in one of those rafts is a bitch. You should be protected from big swells inside the lagoon, but the wind and surf might be a problem."

Bryan nodded. "We've been in the raft almost every day since we started training."

Step by step they went over every aspect of the insertion and rescue. By the end of the first day Lee and Bryan felt the mission was in good hands with Gene Porter.

Later that night the team from 331 and the PBY crew conducted what they called a 'reconnaissance in force' to a number of the local pubs in Brisbane.

The American crew carried only six of their normal nine crewmembers. This would allow carrying the team, their gear and extra fuel on the long flight to Ulithi. Gene Porter's co pilot was a wise-cracking Lieutenant (junior grade) named Steve Richmond. Apparently a superbly talented pilot, Richmond had no use for the restricting regulations of the U.S. Navy. Mark Mendillo, a First Class Radioman, would handle all communications and the newly installed surface search radar during both the insertion and extraction flights. A good looking kid from Los Angeles, he turned out to be the lady killer of the crew. Porter told Bryan that Mendillo had girl friends in every port within twenty four hours of landing. Brisbane had been no different and the young man already had an invitation to a local young lady's apartment later that night.

The quiet member of the crew was the flight engineer, Chief Petty Officer Ted Loftus. Responsible for all aircraft systems, routine maintenance and handling any in-flight problems Loftus had acquired the nickname "Pops." Doug McSwain and Larry Roberts were the two waist gunners. They would man the forward and aft .30 caliber guns in addition to their waist-mounted .50 calibers. They were the youngest members of the crew, both only 18.

Lee secured the use of two large sedans and after picking up the Yanks they drove to Murray's, a watering hole located not far from the main naval facility on the river. Sergeant Major Tobin sat in the front seat of the lead sedan. While he still maintained his professional demeanor Bryan had noticed a subtle change. He began to assume his duties as team member and relinquish his role as team trainer.

An awkward silence while waiting for the first round of beers rapidly transitioned to a lively discussion on the best beer in the world when the waitress put a large Australian lager in front of each of them. In short order the group's opinions were split exactly along national lines. The eventual desertion from the Pabst Blue Ribbon group by Bryan threw the evening into a chorus of good

313

natured taunts back and forth.

"Lieutenant, what did they do to you down here?" Steve Richmond asked.

Before Bryan could answer, Sergeant Major Tobin said in his best parade ground voice, "We polished off the rough edges if you must know, sir."

"Sergeant Major, I can defend myself," Bryan said. "I spent some time exploring the local culture and came to the conclusion that if God made anything better than Australia he kept it for himself."

"Well said, Lieutenant." Tobin raised a glass of scotch in a single toast.

Lee Cordner watched both groups getting to know each other. They all talked about their hometowns and exchanged stories of life in their own services. Both groups displayed a pride that did not detract from the other. They all understood how important it was for them all to do their jobs well. Australians also spent time answering many questions about their country and Queensland in particular.

At the Brighton Arms the rounds of drinks were accompanied with a specialty of the house, meat pies. The Americans had been subsisting on canned and dried food since their arrival in the Solomons and the fresh vegetables and meat in the pies were welcomed with very vocal approval.

By the time they arrived at Dutton's Bar, the rather drunk group began to offer toasts in praise of Australia, the food of Australia, and particularly the women of the nation. From the Australian group came recognition of the effort by the United States to defend Australia. The ships and crews from the Battle of the Coral Sea were toasted and when they discovered Bryan had been in the pivotal battle, more toasts were made.

Bryan leaned over to Sergeant Major Tobin. "I think we should head back."

The older man nodded.

"Think we can do this?"

314

Tobin turned, his expression suddenly serious. "If I didn't think so, I wouldn't be sitting here right now."

Not sure if Tobin was angry or drunk Bryan decided to drop the subject.

"Are you having second thoughts, Lieutenant?"

Am I? Bryan asked himself.

"I'm not sure what odds a bookie might give us, but I'm guessing strong money would be on the Japs."

Tobin finished his scotch and placed the glass on the table with deliberate care. "You may be right. But we won't know unless we give it a go, right?"

Bryan thought about the Sergeant Major's brutally simple test for their survival and laughed. "Right, Sergeant Major, absolutely right."

Chapter Twenty One

The mighty ocean...

The landing of Japanese forces on islands across the Pacific completed a strategic plan devised shortly after the conclusion of the First World War. The many claims to territory from colonization and treaties resulted in the United States and Japan becoming the two main competitors for the scattered atolls, archipelagos and islands which covered the millions of square miles of ocean. Japan knew if they were to expand their empire they must acquire a protective ring of territories to protect their eastern frontier.

Ulithi Atoll provided a large deep water protected anchorage for fleet staging and support. In the early stages of landings across the Pacific the Japanese Navy landed men on both Mogmog and Falalop to provide the initial support for follow on force build up. Shortly after Pearl Harbor a communication detachment joined the naval infantry ashore at Mogmog. A series of large antennae were constructed by Naval Engineers and the communication relay station became operational in March of 1942.

Commander Masuyo Kazuki commanded the Japanese forces on Mogmog which consisted of 5 members of the Naval Infantry, 17 communications specialists and 8 support personnel. While they were constantly in contact electronically with Fleet Headquarters, physical contact consisted of a monthly logistics run from Manila. Several small machine guns protected the communications antennae and transmitter station. Barbed wire barriers set up on the main southern beach comprised the island's only physical defenses. Occasional foot patrols were conducted by the infantry as a matter of form rather than substance. No one expected an attack this far from any American shore base. Boredom proved to be the biggest threat to Kazuki's men on Mogmog.

Lieutenant Commander Kuro Hideki served as Kazuki's second in command and Communication Officer. A career communications specialist, Hideki viewed this assignment as critical to his future. He must assure the equipment stayed in top condition and that all messages were relayed quickly and error free to Japanese Naval Units throughout the Pacific. He took that duty very seriously.

"Petty Officer Uchida, is this all of the morning messages?"

Uchida stood up and nodded. "Yes, sir. They came in on the morning watch."

Hideki flipped through the flimsy carbon copies. He stopped when he saw the message addressed to all operating commands in the Pacific. It directed the shift to JN-29 as the primary naval code at 0000 Tokyo time on December 1, 1942. The young officer had been eagerly awaiting this decision. Correctly transitioning to this new code without errors might make the difference between success and failure against the Americans. He thought of the code books that had been delivered on the last transport. Currently locked in the large safe in the transmitter room, he would have to break them out and begin training his petty officers on the many changes to this new code. At least the training would provide some distraction from the every day routine.

The final week of training in Brisbane had gone by quickly. Two days of launch and recovery training with the PBY off one of the local islands proved very beneficial. Bryan enjoyed the short flights in the PBY and sat behind Porter watching him put the big Catalina through her paces. The short amount of distance the PBY needed to land surprised Bryan. Conversely the takeoff run took forever. During the training flights the PBY carried only 40% fuel and Gene told him that a fully loaded Catalina would take much longer to get airborne. Two days prior to departure from Brisbane for Darwin the maintenance crew put the PBY into its periodic check cycle. This gave the team an unexpected break in their tight training schedule.

Bryan was relaxing on the veranda of the bungalow he and Lee shared at the southern edge of the compound. He saw Lee coming down the path which lay next to the line of small cottages. His friend carried a paper bag.

Lee climbed the steps and sat down in the chair next to Bryan.

"You look like you've been up to no good," he said to Lee.

Without saying a word Lee reached into the bag and withdrew a bottle of Glenfiddich Scotch. He grinned at Bryan.

"My gosh, where'd you get that?"

"It still pays to be a native, my good man." He went inside and returned with two glasses.

Bryan sat quietly while Lee poured their drinks.

Handing a glass to Bryan he raised his own. "Cheers, mate."

"Thanks," Bryan said as he touched glasses with his friend. They sat there for a minute then Bryan asked, "What do you really think about this little trip we're about to go on?"

"It's sure to be a bit dicey. I guess all we can do is give it a go and see how things work out." Cordner took a long drink.

Bryan knew the last few weeks of training had made an enormous impact on their small group. They were in shape and certainly had mastered the skills they would need on the island. But he found it difficult to imagine breaking into a Jap compound and getting away with the codes. He remembered the wonderful two weeks with Liz and how he looked forward to their future. Now he might jeopardize all of it on a Pacific Island. Cordner took all of this in stride, what let him do that? Lee didn't have a wife or girlfriend but still he didn't have a death wish either. The others on the team were certainly gung ho but they were also pretty level headed types. Are we all caught up in a drama we can't stop?

318

"I think my Dad's back in town. Mind if I try to see him for dinner tonight?" The two of them had planned to go to one of Lee's favorite restaurants.

"Of course not. If my father was in Brisbane tonight I surely wouldn't be spending my night with you." Lee laughed and poured another drink.

Bryan took a chance and had the duty driver drop him off at his father's hotel. He checked at the front desk and the clerk told him he had seen the Admiral go into the cocktail lounge not more than twenty minutes previously.

Taking a moment for his eyes to adjust to the dim light in the bar, Bryan saw his father sitting at a table with a very attractive woman. As he walked across the room he heard them laughing, obviously enjoying each other's company.

Chuck Michaels looked up and frowned momentarily as if he hadn't expected to see Bryan. His face broke into a welcoming smile and he stood up offering his hand.

"Bryan, I didn't know if you were in town. Please sit down."

The lady smiled at Bryan as he passed behind her chair and pulled out another.

"Linda, this is my son Bryan. This is Linda Sims. She's on MacArthur's staff."

Linda turned to Bryan and smiled. She had chestnut brown hair and deep blue eyes. Probably ten years younger than his father, she had an air of quiet confidence about her.

"I've heard a lot about you, Bryan. It's nice to finally meet you."

His father sat down and motioned for the waiter.

"I figured you'd be tied up with your unit," he said.

"Uh, bit of a stand down. I wanted to try and catch you.

"That's great. Why don't you join us for dinner?"

Bryan felt like he had crashed his father's party. He never thought of his father with anyone except his mother.

"Actually, Chuck, I have to get back to the office. Why

don't you and Bryan spend some time together?"

Bryan looked at Linda. They had obviously intended to have dinner together.

She put her hand on his sleeve. "Spend some time with your father. I really do have to get back."

The two men stood as she did.

"Bryan, it was delightful to meet you. Chuck, let's try to get together for dinner tomorrow."

When she had gone the two men sat down.

"I wasn't trying to be a third wheel," Bryan said.

"Linda and I met when I first got out here. We hit it off and enjoy each other's company. She's a great lady."

"Dad, I'm glad. She seems terrific. I hope I get the chance to know her."

Something in Bryan's tone alerted Chuck Michaels.

"Is something up?"

Nodding he said, "Yeah."

"Can you tell me anything?"

"Not really." Bryan felt like a ten year old trying to confess he'd broken a window. "I'm just.....well this one could get a little ugly."

Michaels looked at his son. "After what you've seen in this war it must be something pretty bad for you to say that."

"I just wanted to see you before we shoved off. And I wanted you to hold this letter for me." Bryan took an envelope from his inner coat pocket and laid it on the table. There was one word on the front: "Liz."

The Admiral looked hard at his son, seeing the concern in Bryan's eyes. He picked up the envelope and put it in his jacket. "I'll give this back to you the next time we meet."

"Thanks, Dad." Bryan took a long drink.

Chuck Michaels had spent his entire life in uniform. He knew the rules and expectations. The profession of arms demanded accepting the risk of death or injury. When the worst happened you simply moved on to the next job, not forgetting those who had been lost, but not flinching from your duty. Now his son sat before him, perhaps for the last time and he found it hard to accept. Thirty five years of doing your duty did not make it any easier.

Bryan sat back in the high backed wood chair and tried to concentrate on Gene Porter's brief, but his thoughts kept returning to his father and Liz...... "the flight will take a little over eleven hours"....was this how his life would play out?..... "touchdown inside the atoll will be just after sunset"......How many letters like mine were being written every day across the Pacific? ..... "our route will be across the Arafura Sea, south of New Guinea and overwater to Ulithi" ..... What are you supposed to say in a letter like that? ...... "remember much of the flight we are in range of land based Jap fighters" ..... the words were so ordinary..... "there's a large frontal system that should provide us some cover during the second part of the flight" ....But I tried to tell her what she means to me, that's all you can do, right?

Bryan checked his watch, estimating they were half way to Ulithi. Their world had turned into a steady drone of engines, the team finding comfortable places to curl up while the flight crew went about their business. He turned to Lee Cordner who sat reading a newspaper. "I'm going up to the cockpit." He'd been up front for all of the takeoffs and landings during the training and since their departure from Brisbane. As a single engine carrier aviator he found the world of seaplanes strange and interesting. The two Catalina pilots enjoyed sharing their knowledge and it helped pass the time.

Bryan noticed they were in and out of a ragged cloud layer and the altimeter indicated 10,800 feet. Gene had his hands on the yoke but the precisely trimmed aircraft required only the smallest corrections.

"When do you guys start serving the steaks?" Bryan joked.

Richmond turned and saw their passenger. "Not until after

we finish cocktails and that isn't for another hour."

"How's it going?" Leaning down he peered forward into the billowy clouds seeing a break of blue sky here and there.

"Good fuel figures at this point, estimating we have a quartering tailwind, so that helps." Porter reached up and adjusted the compass indicator.

"Still in the weather I see."

Gene nodded. "We're definitely out of range of any land based Zeros. The only threat might be someone like a long range patrol bomber. If the intel guys were right there's no Jap carrier within a thousand miles so we're good there. I think this is turning into the proverbial milk run."

"Let's hope so," Bryan agreed.

"Your guys doing okay back there?" Steve asked. He lit a cigarette and blew the smoke down toward the floorboards.

"No complaints so far. The army can sleep anywhere so they've been sacked out most of the time. Cordner's like me, if it's moving we have to be awake."

"Well I'm beat," Richmond said. "Why don't you hop in the seat? I'll go grab a quick nap."

"Happy to," Bryan said and moved to one side so Steve could exit the co-pilot's seat.

Slipping in behind the yoke Bryan felt comfortable. He'd never flown a multi-engine aircraft or any aircraft with a yoke but this didn't feel strange to him. Instinctively he started going over the cockpit instruments and switches as if he might take over the controls. Asking Gene questions about flying the Catalina kept his mind off their destination. Richmond's one hour nap stretched to two.

The weather had been clearing and the last view Bryan had before he climbed out of the co-pilots seat on Steve's return was a vast ocean stretching from horizon to horizon. He'd seen that sight before in his flying career, but this time he truly appreciated the vastness of the Pacific.

Petty Officer Mendillo gave the first indication their navigation plan had been successful.

"I think I have it," he called to the cockpit. Hunched over the small radar scope, he adjusted the controls.

Bryan turned to check out the scope. On the dark screen a tell-tale bright spot that signified the radar return of a piece of land blinked at them. Returns from other islands on the atoll rim began to glow on the scope, confirming they were near their destination. That was their target island, he thought, watching the bright spot fade then intensify as the radar antenna rotated.

"Okay, gents, it's that time," Gene Porter said and pulled power on the engines to begin the slow letdown toward the sheltered water inside the atoll.

"Gene, how long?" Bryan asked.

"Be ready to set her down in about ten minutes."

Walking aft he felt nervous but ready to get on with it.

"Everyone strapped in?" Chief Loftus stood in the aisle making one last walkthrough.

Lee Cordner nodded as did the rest of the team.

The Chief sat down against the bulkhead and cinched a lap belt to secure himself right before the Catalina touched down with a roar.

As they taxied north, the water beat on the forward hull adding a sense of urgency as the team broke out their gear. The warmer temperature at the surface and the humidity created condensation inside the fuselage and moisture covered the thin skin of the Catalina.

The uninflated raft sat under the starboard observation blister they would be using as an exit. Next to the raft were waterproof parcels which contained their mission essentials. Each man would carry his Sten bandolier style with their .45s in shoulder holsters.

Lee Cordner knelt between the two pilots as they reduced

their taxi speed to dead slow. He looked forward with a set of binoculars and saw two points of light. Intelligence had figured there would be some type of lighting on the single pier that ran south from the beach. The Japs used the pier for unloading ships that delivered supplies to the island. Bryan stood behind Lee watching the Catalina's progress.

"I'm guessing we're inside two miles. How much further do you want to go?" Porter asked.

"Far enough gents, time for us to earn our pay. Come on Bryan." Cordner turned to go aft then stopped. "Thanks for the ride."

"Hey," Richmond called after Bryan. "You watch yourself out there."

"Just don't forget to come back and get us," Bryan said.

The starboard engine idled smoothly as Pops Loftus opened the large blister. He reached down and attached a boarding ladder to two brackets at the edge of the opening, the ladder extending down to water. Lee and Corporal Louis manhandled the raft out the hatch. Once it was clear of the fuselage, Lee pulled a long lanyard which activated the CO_2 bottles.

In one minute the raft inflated fully and Alistair Louis climbed down to stow the parcels being handed to him.

"Sergeant Major, in you go." Lee Cordner stood next to the boarding ladder. "Watch your step. We don't need you swimming tonight."

"Not to worry, sir. I can do this in my sleep."

Cordner turned to Bryan. "You ready?"

"Sure." The dark water didn't look inviting but there was no turning back from here.

The Australian followed Bryan down the ladder. Loftus held the raft's manila bow line and Lee looked around one last time.

"Ready to cast off?" Loftus asked.

"Okay, Chief. All right, give way together," Lee said, "Let's get clear."

After thirty seconds of stroking the rhythm from hours of

324

practice kicked in and they began to move steadily toward the dark island.

"Steady….steady," Lee said urgently. The raft was riding roughly on the swells.

"Come on gents," the Sergeant Major cracked, "The best cure for seasickness is hard work."

They all grinned and continued to pull hard for the beach

Forty minutes of steady paddling began to take its toll on their strength as they closed in on the island. They could see the white sand of a beach with breaking waves.

"Keep her steady," the Sergeant Major said harshly as he used his paddle to hold the nose of the raft toward the shore. The force of the waves began to take control, accelerating the raft toward the white water.

"Watch it," Lee yelled as the wave picked up the raft and slewed it sideways.

"Pull….Pull," Tobin called desperately as the right side of the raft began to rise off the water

"Oh shit!"

Bodies were hurled forward as the raft rolled over, throwing men and equipment into the tumbling water.

Already out of breath from paddling, Bryan's body screamed for air. Tumbling in the dark water he was slammed hard into the sandy bottom. Pushing up, his head broke the surface. Gasping for air, another wave knocked him violently back down into the sandy bottom. Flailing with his arms Bryan came to the surface coughing hard. His hand touched the bottom and he pushed hard trying to regain his footing. He half swam and half crawled onto the wet sand. *Shit!* He lay in the sand trying to catch his breath as the spent waves washed over his legs.

Ten yards down the beach, Lee Cordner struggled to his feet.

Between Lee and Bryan a figure knelt next to the overturned raft.

Bryan got to his feet and ran to the raft, seeing Lee coming from the other direction.

Corporal Louis had already grabbed the bow line. The three men dragged the raft up on the beach.

Lee looked up and down the beach. "Where's Tobin?"

"Over here," a voice said.

They turned to see the Sergeant Major pushing through the receding water from the last wave.

"Let's get this bloody thing right side up," Cordner said and without a word the men manhandled the raft over.

Numerous parcels remained in the raft where the team had tied them during the trip ashore. The largest waterproof container containing the radio rested in the bottom of the raft. Several loose packages were scattered in the shallow water.

"Doesn't look too bad," Lee said. "We'll need an inventory first thing. Right now we need to grab the loose parcels and find the paddles." Cordner turned to Bryan. "Work your way up the beach. Louis, you look the other way. Be quick about it and stay low. We'll move the raft up to the tree line."

"Right," Bryan said. Louis turned and walked down the beach.

Twenty minutes later they all knelt next to the now deflated raft. Four wooden paddles lay on the sand.

"We're only missing one parcel. Unfortunately it's the one with the cameras and film in it," Cordner's voice remained steady but they all knew what it meant to lose the cameras. Without the cameras to photograph the code books there was no way to get the info from the Japs without letting them know someone had been on the island.

The irony hit Bryan. They were a thousand miles behind the Jap lines with nothing to do. There's got to be something we can figure out, he thought.

"Nothing to be done now, best clear off this beach," Sergeant Major Tobin said.

After making sure they had covered the raft well, the four men headed north into the jungle. The heavy undergrowth made for slow progress. The adrenaline from the landing had worn off and now four tired men struggled to find a secure spot for their camp.

"Sergeant Major, check out that thicket of gum trees."

Tobin moved forward, returning in two minutes. "Looks like it was made for us."

"Let's get the gear out of sight. I'll take the first watch. Get some rest while you can. Any questions?"

Bryan felt bone weary as he lay down on a thin tarpaulin. The occasional bird or monkey call would echo off the trees. He closed his eyes wondering what the dawn would bring.

In the main communication hut Lieutenant Commander Hideki stubbed out a cigarette and sat back at his desk. He'd been reviewing the new code books all evening. *A code that is much more complex than JN-25*, he thought. *Just as well, we've been using Code 25 for too long.* The Americans and British both have talented code breakers and everyone who understood code knew breaking any code simply took time and manpower.

Hideki looked at his watch, 2235, a little over 48 hours before the shift to the new code. The training program by his senior enlisted specialist had been in full swing for over a week to ensure there would be no problems with the transition. Picking up the two books, Procedures and Codes, he walked to the large steel container and put them both inside. Closing the door he locked the heavy padlock. The small man placed the lanyard with the key around his neck and inside his shirt. *It's late, I must get some sleep.*

Alistair Louis stood up and stretched when the first rays of sunlight flicked across the dark green foliage. Somewhere in the distance a lone bird began chattering. The shrill call made his job of waking everyone easier.

Taking turns on watch, all of them had slept fitfully. Sand had worked its way into their damp clothes, shoes and hair.

Lee Cordner rubbed his eyes and said quietly, "Anything?"

Louis shook his head.

"Good," Bryan said. He looked at Lee and saw the left knee of his trousers torn. Blood stained the torn cloth. "What happened to you?"

"I hit something on the bottom when I came out of the raft. Hurts like the devil but I'll clean it up. Should be fine."

Tobin stood up and looked around. "First order of business is to pinpoint the Japs and see if they're doing any patrolling on this side of the island."

"We'll camouflage the camp then split up into two teams."

Ten minutes later they all knelt around a chart of the island.

Lee put his finger on the chart.

"We're about here. Our intel has the Jap camp here just north of the main southern beach. Bryan, you and the Sergeant Major work your way northwest and try to check out the far side of the island. I'll work due west and try to confirm the Jap location and layout. Remember, guns as a last resort. Any firing would be heard across the island. There are probably 20 or 30 Japs. If they realize we're here it's not going to be pretty. Use your knives if you have a choice."

Covered predominantly with thick trees and undergrowth, Mogmog stretched 6 miles from east to west. Bryan and Tobin made slow progress as they worked their way northwest. Thick undergrowth covered the hilly terrain. Traveling light, they chose to take only their pistols and short machetes to help get through the brush. Bryan found it hard to believe there were 30 enemy soldiers on the island. For two hours they worked their way quietly through the jungle seeing no sign of human habitation. Small animal trails crisscrossed their path, the only sign of any living creature on Mogmog. When they reached the northwest tip of the island they saw the beach line extending south out of sight.

Bryan sat down on a large boulder. He took his canteen out of the canvas sleeve which attached to his web belt. They'd found several small streams and filled their canteens. The water purification tablets gave the water a faintly medicinal odor.

"We can work our way further south on the way back.

Unless the Japs are holed up near that pier we might find out how far north they are."

Tobin nodded. He wiped his forehead but left his canteen alone. A light breeze blew onshore and after the humidity in the jungle it felt good. "Ready when you are."

Bryan looked at Tobin. In his mid-thirties, the Sergeant Major was career Army. Never married, he had worked his way up in the peacetime Army eventually finding himself and his battalion fighting in the doomed defense of Singapore. Overrun on the Malay Peninsula he led a small resistance group behind the Japanese lines. Eventually they made their way to the coast, finding a fishing boat which they used to escape south. Since that time he'd been on several raiding parties as the Army developed their own commando forces and doctrine. His experience and reputation had resulted in his assignment to Unit 331.

"Let's push off then. I understand we'll be having cracked crab on a bed of ice for lunch."

Tobin turned with a quizzical look on his face then smiled and said quietly to himself, "Damned Yanks."

Cordner and Louis were already back at the camp when they returned. The four sat down and shared tinned corned beef and a can of kidney beans while squatting around a crude hand drawn map.

"The compound is just over two miles due west. We found a good observation spot near the comm antennas. Didn't see perimeter wire of any kind but there was a barbed wire enclosure at the northern end of this open area. Couldn't see any posted guards or guard posts. Course they might have something after dark." Lee used his commando knife to spear a piece of beef which he removed from the knife and popped in his mouth. He continued using the knife as a pointer. "There're six buildings. These two look like barracks. There's a small mess hall here and this hut appears to be an officer's billet or mess. There's also an admin hut here next to what must be the communication building. There were cables running out to the antenna here and right next to the building is a generator. The only unusual thing is a large lay down area covered with construction material. It looks like they aren't finished building the camp."

Tobin asked, "Any sign of activity outside the central area?"

Louis shook his head. "The only people to leave all morning were in a small working party. They headed out with shovels and might have been heading for the pier. Never did see them come back."

Lee sat back against a tree. He winced as he flexed his knee. "I'll draw a better diagram of the place and then we'll set up a rotating schedule to observe the routine. That will give us some time to figure out our options. Corporal Louis, now that it looks like we'll stay in this spot, why don't you check out the radio?"

"Let's check out your knee first," Sergeant Major Tobin said.

The Sergeant Major's inspection revealed a deep gash on the left side of Lee's knee. The joint and surrounding leg had begun to swell.

"Some kind of infection. These damned tropics are a breeding ground for bad things. I'll clean it out the best I can and then put some sulfa powder on it. Try to keep it clean."

Lee nodded as Tobin began to work on his knee.

Over the next two days, the team split their time between observing the Japanese comm station, standing watch at their own camp and sleeping. The Japanese camp's day started with reveille at 0600, morning meal and a formation in front of the Admin Building. For the rest of the day the enemy occupied themselves with simple maintenance and upkeep. There were always two guards under arms in the compound. One patrolled the west perimeter and the other the east. The guards changed out at two hour intervals and never sat down or retired to a fixed guard post. Naval personnel, probably the technicians, visited the communication building frequently.

The monsoon cycle brought more rain and the team realized

how lucky they were to have clear weather when they had arrived. Thunderstorms struck the island at night sending bright flashes of lightening and thunder across the jungle.

It became a challenge to stay dry and by the end of the third day they had resigned themselves to being wet. The temperature remained very warm which at least made the damp tolerable.

Laying under two ponchos stretched over a bamboo limb, Lee and Bryan shared a tin of fruit cocktail and compared notes on the compound.

"The comm techs change shifts every four hours and the section is made up of two men." Lee read from a small notebook.

"The two officers we've seen around the comm building come and go but with no set schedule." Bryan lay on his stomach facing Lee while he ate the fruit cocktail with a metal spoon.

"We've got to get in closer to see the layout of the building," Lee said.

Bryan stopped eating. "You're forgetting our little problem, no cameras."

"I'm not forgetting anything," Lee snapped. "I think if we get more information we might come up with another plan."

"Okay, you might be right. But how do we get more info?"

"Tonight during the middle of one of their duty shifts we work our way into the compound and find out what we can see through the windows."

The idea of getting that close to the Japs sent a chill through Bryan but he knew they had no choice and it made sense for him to go and not Lee. The infection in Cordner's knee had started to affect his ability to walk.

"All right. I'll take Louis and we'll check it out tonight," Bryan said.

"Good. Louis can check out the radio set up and you can get an idea of the layout." Lee grimaced as he rolled over. "This damned knee. Something we didn't need."

A steady rain assaulted the island and rumbles of thunder

331

echoed in the darkness. Bryan's watch read 0036. The last shift of guards had been on watch since midnight. By now they would be soaked and thinking only of getting off duty. The sailors of the comm detachment should be completing their turnover and settling down for a long boring watch. There were two outside lights on the closest side of the building. They were sheltered by metal covers which directed the light downward covering thirty foot circles. Between the two illuminated areas he could see a dark corridor 10-15 feet wide.

"We'll go in between those two lights."

"All right."

The two men knelt in the underbrush, the rain making a steady patter on the leaves. Bryan shivered despite the warm temperature. Cold or nerves he wondered? As he stared at the building the reality of what they were going to try to do hit him like a bullet. Just like flying, he thought, press on and do what's expected of you whether or not you think you can.

"You ready?" he asked Louis quietly.

"Ready as I'm gonna be I'd say."

Bryan liked the young commando. The Corporal had never tried to show any false bravado

"Let's go," Bryan whispered, although they were over 70 yards from the camp and the noise of the rain constant.

Following the contour of a small ridge they moved down toward the two circles of light. Bryan held up his hand and they stopped.

Where's the sentry? Looking left and right in the pouring rain he saw no sign of movement. Forcing himself to move forward he maintained a crouch. Approaching the building he stepped very slowly and carefully.

Suddenly Louis poked him in the back. Bryan froze and peered into the sheets of rain. The eastern sentry was walking in their direction not more than twenty feet away. The man had his head down, the rain running off the flat brim of his cap. A poncho wrapped around his shoulders covered the barrel of a rifle poking up behind the man's cap.

There was no way they could turn around without being seen. Bryan knelt as the man slowly approached knowing it was just a matter of time. Don't panic....he doesn't see us yet....you have the advantage of surprise. Bryan reached down and slowly pulled the knife from its sheath. Up hard below the ribs and into the heart before he can cry out. He knew he was about to take the man's life but there was no option. Three more steps and he would move. Gritting his teeth he tensed his arm, ready to thrust up into the man. Suddenly the sentry turned and walked toward the building.

The Japanese soldier stepped up on the raised porch of the comm building and removed his cap, shaking the water off. Replacing his hat the man reached under his poncho. In a moment, the spark of a match told them he had lit a cigarette.

Bryan slowly exhaled, his body relaxing. The sentry stood under the small overhang and finished his cigarette while they remained motionless in the rain. If the man stepped off the closest edge of the porch he would be heading directly for them again. Bryan squeezed the knife handle to reassure himself as he watched the man take a last drag on the cigarette.

The rain will muffle any cry he told himself but kill him with one thrust....one thrust. The sentry tossed the still lit butt on the ground then turned away from Bryan and walked down the porch, stepping off the far end. Both men remained motionless as the soldier walked away into the darkness.

"Jesus," Bryan whispered, the tension suddenly gone.

"Yeah."

"Come on."

The rain beat a steady cadence on a large fuel tank. Next to the tank a generator ran steadily, the exhaust streaming into the night. They moved past the closest circle of light and next to the long side of the structure. Three equally spaced windows showed light coming from within the building.

A flash of lightening froze them in place. Bryan's heart jumped at the unexpected brightness. Back in darkness he took a deep breath.

"Bloody hell," Louis said quietly.

"Yeah."

They moved down to the middle window. During their observation periods there had never been any type of curtain or blind on any of the windows. Rising up carefully, Bryan removed his forage cap and moved his head slowly to look into the room. One Japanese sailor sat at a desk facing sideways from the window reading from a manual. File cabinets lined the wall and next to the last file cabinet stood a heavy duty storage locker that looked to be made of steel. A large padlock secured the thick metal band that spanned the door. *Code storage I bet.* Slowly lowering his head he examined the window. Two panels held the glass within wooden frames and it looked like they rotated outward to open. Looking up he saw what looked like a locking latch holding the two panels closed.

Bryan crouched down and joined Louis who had been watching the area.

"What can you tell on the radio set up?"

Alistair Louis pointed to a heavy cable that ran across the sandy ground to the side of the building. "The main power comes in through the cable running off the generator. You can see the transmission cable running from that small pole by the edge of the building out to the antennas. If you didn't see any radio equipment in that last room it must be in here." Soft light came from the window closest to the front and Louis gestured toward it.

"Let's see what's there," Bryan said quietly and stepped around Louis toward the light. He again removed his cap and looked carefully around the window sill. Two men sat in front of electronic cabinets. A bench ran the length of the cabinets upon which a typewriter and two teletype machines sat. The two sailors were casually watching the instruments.

Bryan knelt down next to Louis. "On target, lots of radio equipment and two operators. You need to see any more?"

Louis shook his head.

"Let's go back and have a beer."

"So all we need now are our cameras," Lee said. The disgusted tone of his voice added to their low spirits from the constant rain.

"I think we should send a message and have the Catalina bring out another set of cameras," Bryan said.

No one said anything. The idea of another flight by the PBY, while not desirable, made sense.

"Besides that leg of yours isn't getting any better," Tobin added.

Cordner knew the Sergeant Major was right. The infection had spread and the team didn't need an invalid.

"If we send a message now they should be able to be here tomorrow night. We make our try as soon after that and get the hell off the island." Lee knew it was the right decision.

"If they send someone to take your place we would have a back up in case of problems," Bryan said.

Cordner nodded. "I'll leave that up to Coyne. Until then we keep watching the Japs and take care of ourselves. Louis, crank up the radio."

Commander R. Emmett Coyne, Royal Australian Navy, surprised his yeoman when he read the top secret operational message from the team on Mogmog.

"They must be out of their bloody minds," he exclaimed. Called in to the office by the duty officer, he wore civilian clothes and hadn't shaved. The clock on the wall read 0457.

Yeoman Harris had not often heard the quiet officer lose his composure.

"Do you have a reply, sir," he said as diplomatically as possible.

"I do but I'd be court-martialed if I sent it." As he calmed down, Coyne considered the options and realized he had none. He knew another flight would increase the possibility of detection and hazard the mission. But if they didn't have their cameras the mission had no chance of success. "Arrange priority air transport to Darwin, two passengers, leaving as soon as possible. Also contact Senior Naval Officer, Darwin via secret message and have him put the American PBY crew on standby. Finally get Major Mabry down here as quick as you can."

"Aye aye, sir."

Major Phillip Mabry, DSO, walked smartly down the corridor and turned into Commander Coyne's office. Despite the early hour he was impeccably attired. Fit and tanned, his dark hair was combed straight back, a small thin mustache highlighting a plain face. The only physical attribute that everyone noticed immediately about Mabry was his eyes. A pale blue, they had been described as lifeless.

Entering the office he stared at Yeoman Harris but said nothing.

The young Yeoman stood quickly and said, "Please go in, sir."

The Major knocked twice on the door as he swung it open.

"Mabry, please come in and have a seat."

Assigned as a liaison officer to British General Headquarters, Mabry had seen extensive combat in France and Norway before being recalled to help stand up Australian commando operations. Currently he had the lead on an operation planned into Burma later in the year.

"We've got an op in progress on one of the islands north of Palau. Lee Cordner is leading the team and they've had a bit of bad luck. On the landing they lost some critical equipment and Lee managed to get hurt. They've requested re-supply and I'd like someone to fill in for Lee."

Mabry showed no emotion. "That someone sounds like me."

"I know it's short notice but I don't have many options."

"No problem, sir. The Army's always happy to rescue the Navy." There was no humor in his voice.

"Quite right this time I'm afraid. Now let me give you the details. We need to be on a flight to Darwin in three hours."

Steve Richmond lay face down in his darkened hotel room. The PBY crew had several rooms in Darwin's Exeter Hotel while they waited for their next flight. The crew took the opportunity to enjoy the food and drink they found in town, remembering their imminent return to the Solomons.

"Hey, wake up. I just got a call that we're flying tonight." Gene Porter stood at the door. He flipped on the overhead light. "Come on, let's get cracking."

The prone figure rolled over slowly and raised his arm to protect his eyes from the glare. "What time is it?" Richmond said sleepily.

"Almost noon. We're supposed to meet Commander Coyne down at the Naval Admin Building as quickly as we can get the crew together. So get moving."

"I had plans for a steak dinner tonight."

"Your dinner's gonna be a baloney sandwich in a box lunch. I'll find the rest of the guys. Grab a shower and meet me in the lobby in fifteen minutes."

"Whatever you say, mon capitan." Richmond swung his legs over the edge of the bed. "But I was really looking forward to that steak dinner," he said to himself as the door closed.

"Gentlemen, I appreciate your quick reaction." Commander Coyne sat on the edge of a desk as he addressed the PBY crew. "The team on Mogmog lost some critical equipment when they went ashore. In addition Commander Cordner has been injured. This necessitates a flight to deliver the equipment and replace the Commander. Time is of the essence. The longer the team is on the island the greater the odds they might be discovered. For that reason we need you to leave as soon as possible for Ulithi."

Lieutenant Porter leaned against the back wall, his arms folded on his chest. "With an eleven hour flight up there, and if we can get airborne within two hours that would have us landing about 03 or 0400. We might be bumping up against dawn by the time the team gets the raft back to the island."

"That's a chance we've got to take. You'll be taking Major Mabry along with the replacement equipment." Two packages had been put together by Coyne's armorer prior to departure from Brisbane. There were two sets of cameras with extra film and replacement CO_2 bottles for the raft.

Mabry stood up. "Good afternoon, gentlemen. If we have time I'd like to sit down with you briefly to go over your plan. I assume you'll follow the routine of the previous flight." His steady voice sounded very matter of fact.

Porter paused then said, "The tough part is connecting with them in the open ocean. We'll taxi in directly south of the island to a mile and a half. The original plan was to use one blue flashlight from the aircraft pointing at the island and they would show a white light to seaward. They did have a Very pistol for emergency signaling but that would tip off the Japs."

"I see no reason to deviate from the original plan," Coyne said. "I'll send them a message when you get airborne to set the rendezvous time. Please monitor our HF frequency as before in case there are any changes."

"Yes, sir."

"All right. Time to get moving. I've asked the meteorologist to get the latest info and meet us here shortly." Coyne stood up. "Good luck."

"Lieutenant." Phillip Mabry walked behind Porter and Richmond as they left the Admin Building.

Porter stopped and faced the Australian.

"I received the distinct impression that the weather briefing did not suit your taste." Mabry stood very erect, no emotion showing on his face

"No, sir. It wasn't the weather I'd hoped for."

"They said the route was clear of clouds and the sea state at the destination was within acceptable limits. What other issues are there?"

"No clouds to hide in, Major," Steve said.

"I don't understand."

Gene said, "During the flight we're within range of several of the Jap air bases. If we can use weather to hide there's less chance the random Zero will use us for target practice?"

"I see. And we don't expect to have much cover during the flight."

"A few clouds here and there but no big fronts where we can stay in the goo for hours," Richmond added.

"Then we shall just hope for the best, right?"

"Right," Steve said with a touch of sarcasm. "What's the worst that can happen?"

"I suppose we all die, wouldn't you say?" Mabry turned and walked away.

"Shit," Porter said with the Major out of ear shot. "Where did they get that guy?"

After twenty minutes of paddling, Bryan realized how their time on the island had sapped his energy. The surf had been light and thankfully they pulled through the small breakers without incident. Now they had to maintain some semblance of a navigation picture as they paddled south from the island. A southerly wind helped to keep them from veering too far east or west while they peered into the darkness for the PBY's signal light. The four men paddled in silence, each listening for what they hoped would be idling aircraft engines.

Lee sat on the starboard side aft with his leg stretched out as much as possible. The leg felt on fire and every move became more painful. As they paddled he knew that if they didn't find the PBY he would rapidly become a problem for the rest of the team. He pulled hard at the dark water trying to ignore the pain from his leg.

The light chop reverberated against the PBY's metal hull. In the starboard blister Doug McSwain swept the horizon with a set of binoculars. Larry Roberts did the same from the port side. They all knew that finding the raft might mean the difference between success and failure for the mission. In the worst case it might mean the difference between life and death for the four team members if they were swept out past the outer edge of the atoll into the Pacific.

"Where the hell are they?" Richmond's frustration showing. The flight had been long but thankfully uneventful with the only other airborne sighting being sea birds. A radar altimeter made the night water landing a little easier but no one ever took night landings lightly. Now the crew had to find the team floating in a small black raft on the dark night sea.

"We've gotta be getting close to a mile and a half from the beach, I'm gonna turn back seaward," Porter said.

Mabry knelt behind the two pilots watching the activity but saying nothing as the aircraft swung to the left.

"Let's head south for a mile and then reverse back toward the island."

"Listen!" Tobin said and quit paddling.

The others stopped their efforts as the raft bobbed in a wave trough.

"I hear it too," Bryan said. He pulled the flashlight from inside his shirt and looked expectantly as the raft rose on a swell. Bryan saw the glint of metal across the waves. "There they are!" He switched on the flashlight pointing it desperately at what he realized was the PBY heading away from them.

"Christ almighty, they're leaving," Tobin spat out.

"Paddle, damn it," Cordner said harshly.

The four men began to paddle furiously. Bryan kept the flashlight in his upper hand trying to paddle and keep the light pointed at the PBY. It became readily apparent that their efforts were not having any effect. The big seaplane slowly receded into the darkness. Five minutes of hard paddling left them alone again as they all stopped paddling, their breath labored.

"Shit," Louis said, his first comment since they left the beach.

"That, Corporal, is my exact feeling." Cordner sat back, his leg aching. He knew they were now in serious trouble. While they'd been chasing their PBY the wind had increased and now pushed them farther away from Mogmog. Lee turned to see Bryan looking back toward the island.

"It's gonna be a long pull back to the beach," he said. "We've still got the Very pistol as a last resort."

The men sat in the bobbing raft soaked through and weighing their options.

"I'm not ready to scrap the mission just yet. Let's head back to the beach now. If we don't start we won't make it by the time the sun starts to come up." Cordner knew what this meant but he didn't have any other options. "Come on lads, let's go." He began to steer the raft around toward the north.

All four began to pull hard with their paddles as if the fury of their efforts would let them forget the failure to rendezvous with the PBY. Water splashed over the front of the raft as the wind began to increase in their faces. Deep inside each man, the discipline and drive they each had learned in their own ways began to show.

"Good to have that breeze," Sergeant Major Tobin said. "Don't want to get over heated. It's not good for you."

They all smiled as Bryan said, "My sentiments exactly, Sergeant Major."

Ten minutes later they had established a rhythm and were steadily moving toward Mogmog when Bryan stopped paddling.

"Wait a minute!"

The men stopped their efforts, the respite welcomed regardless of the reason.

Behind them the faint sound of engines drifted across the sea.

"Son of a bitch," Bryan said and pulled the flashlight from his shirt. Twisting around he held it up as far as possible and twisted the light to cover the area south of them.

Silently Lee Cordner prayed they would be seen, the last few minutes had made him realize he had no strength left.

"There's a light twenty degrees starboard," Petty Officer Mendillo yelled.

"Tally ho," Porter said. "Stand by to recover the raft, port side." He knew it would be tricky to bring the aircraft too close to the men in the water without risking problems. He normally would have shut down the engine on the side they would recover the raft but 1000 miles behind enemy lines he didn't want to risk not getting it started again. "I'll take it in as close as I can then turn hard starboard. Get back there and supervise getting a line out to them."

"Rog," Richmond said climbing out of his seat and heading aft.

As the seaplane swung to the right the port sponson just cleared the men in the raft. A weighted line thrown by McSwain landed across the raft and in a minute the rubber boat bobbed alongside the PBY.

Lee Cordner climbed over the edge of the PBY blister hatch. The faint light illuminated several men around the entry way.

"Cordner, how are you old man?"

"Mabry, is that you?"

"In the flesh. Coyne felt it was time to let the Army have a crack at this."

The two men shook hands.

"Good to see you. Afraid I'm a bit done in. Let's get the rest up here and sorted out.

A quick transfer of gear while the PBY taxied closer to the island enabled the team to return to Mogmog as the first rays of the sun glinted across the eastern beach.

Chapter Twenty Two

The final test

"So you think the code books are stored in the room at the back of the building and accessible through that center window?" Phil Mabry lay on his stomach next to Bryan at their observation position. The Major had allowed the team one hour of sleep after they returned to their camp before setting out to see the Japanese compound.

"That's our best guess from looking through the windows. They had two operators in the front room working the equipment. There was one Nip in the back in what looked like an office. What I'm thinking is the decoder would be in the back working on messages the operators have received up front."

The tall Australian nodded but didn't say anything. With the binoculars resting on a horizontal piece of wood he continued to observe the compound.

"And you saw one sentry who moved in east to west and stood under the roof overhang?"

"Yes, sir. It was raining pretty hard and he stopped for a smoke."

"Have you ever seen more than two sentries in the compound?"

Bryan shook his head. "Two is all we've ever seen."

Suddenly the air was pierced by a loud whistle coming from south of the compound. Bryan noticed Mabry didn't flinch.

"Have you heard that before?" he calmly asked.

"Never."

Mabry put the glasses down. He kept watching the area as he slowly got to his knees.

"Sounds like a ship's whistle. They do have a regular supply run but it's not due for another ten days or so. Curious. Is there somewhere we can see the dock without going back to the beach?"

Bryan pointed to a gulley that ran south from their position.

"If we move down that ravine, it takes us to a hill that overlooks the dock and the road up to the compound."

Twenty minutes of slow progress through the underbrush and a quick climb up a low hill brought the two men to a concealed position overlooking the crude road running north to the Japanese camp. Two hundred yards south at the wooden pier they saw a tramp coastal freighter.

At one time the lower hull might have been a solid black but now rust had replaced most of the paint. The upper works were grey lightly streaked with rust. A nameplate on the starboard side of the bridge read, *Salang*. On the stern, the red rising sun centered in a plain white field, a Japanese merchant flag hung limply.

"Looks like some kind of supply run," Mabry said. He raised the glasses as surveyed the area. "Cripes," he exclaimed softly.

Bryan looked down and saw there were two rows of men lined up on the pier. He raised his own binoculars and estimated there were twenty or so men wearing remnants of khaki uniforms. The group turned and began to shuffle up the pier toward the camp. Neither man said a word as the two rows approached their position, only twenty five yards from the road. Four Japanese Army guards moved on each side of the prisoners who walked slowly in the increasing heat. The men were emaciated, most all with beards and uncut hair. Their uniforms consisted of tattered shorts and some type of shirt, in some cases sleeveless. Only two of the men wore caps and both of them walked at the head of the column. It took fifteen minutes until the men disappeared around a bend heading to the camp.

Mabry spoke with an underlying fury. "Our men. Probably captured at Singapore. We know the Japs are using them for slave labor on the Burma railway. This is the first time I'm aware they've sent them out of Malaysia. The poor bastards."

"That might explain all the construction material that's piled in the compound. They must be using these men to finish building the station." Bryan wondered how anyone could expect these pathetic creatures to build anything.

"No doubt. If what we're hearing from Burma holds true, they work them until they're dead. Don't have to worry about feeding them or providing any medical care." Mabry sat up and put his glasses back in their case. "The Germans are a nasty lot. Fight like there's no tomorrow and kill you with their last bullet. But when the fighting's over they observe the rules. The Japs play by a different set of rules. They'll regret that someday." Mabry's voice was chilling. "Let's get back."

Commander Kazuki stood on the porch and watched the Australian prisoners walk into the compound. An Army Sergeant detached from the column and marched over to the Commander.

Saluting smartly, the man said, "Sir, I am Sergeant Soichi. I have twenty three prisoners for construction labor."

Kazuki noted the Sergeant needed a shave and his uniform was soiled.

"I was told there would be thirty men."

"Sir, we were given twenty seven prisoners in Singapore and four died during the transit."

Kazuki knew it would do no good to complain to headquarters. They would expect him to complete the second phase of construction on time.

"Very well, Sergeant." Turning to a Chief Petty Officer

behind him he said, "Take over," and went inside the building.

"Put the men into the stockade," the Chief barked at the Sergeant. "You can draw rice from the cook hut and water from the storage tank. There is canvas for cover. Your men will billet in the far hut."

"Yes, Chief," the Sergeant barked and did an about face. Marching up to the column he ordered his men to direct the prisoners into the area surrounded with a barbed wire fence.

One of the prisoners turned to the men as they filed into the open area.

"Stand easy, men." The man walked to the edge of the wire and bowed slightly to the Jap guard. "Sergeant, my men need water." He made a drinking motion with his hand.

The soldier stared back at him coldly. "Hei."

Captain Robbie Anderson did not trust Japanese non-commissioned officers. They had consistently been the most brutal of all ranks encountered during their captivity.

During the trip from Singapore his men had been given only a minimal amount of water and thin rice gruel on the six day voyage. On the ship the heat, lack of water, and no food had contributed to the deaths of four men. The nightmare which began almost a year ago with the fall of Singapore continued to get worse.

He had no illusions of their fate now that they were on an island far from any neutral observers. He would try to make his men comfortable and give as little aid to the Japs as possible. The result would be the same, he thought bitterly.

Two of their guards brought over two buckets of water with a single scoop.

"Sergeant Sims, take charge and ration the water. Lieutenant Waters and I will wait until later." Anderson looked at the two meager buckets and wondered if there could really be a God to let this happen? He turned to look at his second in command. Steve Waters, five years younger than Anderson, suffered from malaria and dysentery. His white complexion and sunken eyes told the story of the disease's terrible toll. He'll never see Australia again,

Anderson thought, none of us will.

"Come on, men," Sergeant Sims said to the men waiting for their water. "The buggers gave us some canvas. Let's get busy and see if we can rig some protection from that sun."

"Diggers? On this little piddling island?" Sergeant Major Tobin sounded skeptical as Major Mabry described their morning reconnaissance.

"They look in none too good a shape either," Mabry added.

"That may explain the construction material we saw at the northern end of the compound. This may be the labor to finish the station," Bryan said.

Tobin nodded. "Makes sense. There aren't many Japs and most of those are radiomen. With no native labor available you use prisoners."

"It certainly throws a pitch into our plans," Mabry said. "More guards and more activity in the compound."

"Our plans? This has got to change our plans, Major," Tobin said.

"I'm sorry, Sergeant Major. But we can't let this get in the way of our mission. If we try something with the prisoners we hazard ourselves and them also. To say nothing of losing any covert chance to get away with the code. And that's the reason we're here in the first place."

Tobin started to say something then turned and walked away.

Mabry turned to Bryan. "We need to see if the arrival of the prisoners changes the guard's patrols. In particular we need to decide if you can still use your original route to the building."

"Corporal Louis, would you see what the Sergeant Major is doing?" Bryan said.

"Yes, sir." The young man walked after Tobin who had disappeared in the thick brush.

"Let's get this straight," Bryan said. "You intend to still get

347

the code and then fly off to Australia leaving those men on this stinking island."

Mabry's eyes narrowed, he wasn't used to being questioned by subordinates. "Lieutenant, might I remind you that those men are Australians? No one is more aware of the situation than I am. However we must complete our primary mission. The lives of many more men will be saved if we can get that code back to Australia. We'll certainly make the chain of command aware of their presence on the island. At some point they may be able to mount a rescue mission."

"And what if it's too late by then, Major? A reasonable sacrifice for King and country? I saw this same bullshit in the Solomons."

The Major stepped toward Bryan, his fists clenched. "Don't you ever lecture me, Michaels. I was fighting the Germans when your country was still trying to hide behind the Atlantic. I watched our soldiers die in France, Belgium and Norway while you Americans played bloody games. Lieutenant, we will complete our mission and nothing else. Is that clear?" His anger spent, Mabry turned and walked out of the camp leaving Bryan standing by himself.

"Not on my watch you pompous son of a bitch," he said quietly.

Captain Anderson stood at attention in front of Commander Kazuki's desk.

"You and your men will be working to build two buildings," Lieutenant Commander Hideki interpreted. "My men will provide direction. I expect the work to be rapid and of high quality. Failure to meet my schedule or standards will be punished. Do you understand?"

The Australian stood listening to the translation then replied, "Commander, my men are sick and starved. If you expect them to work I must have food and medicine. My second in command is very ill and needs a doctor." Anderson looked at Kazuki while his

348

translator spoke.

Showing no reaction, Commander Kazuki stood up and walked to the window. "If I see superior effort and immediate results I may increase your food allowance. It is up to you, Captain. Work well or die, it is your choice."

Anderson walked back across the hot sand to the stockade. Sergeant Sims waited inside the moveable barbed wire gate.

"Any luck, sir?"

Anderson shook his head. "A vague promise if we do a good job they might reward us."

"Bloody hell. But I guess we shouldn't have expected any different from the bastards. I'm worried about the Lieutenant. He's having trouble getting around." Sims fell in step alongside Anderson as they walked over to one of the makeshift canvas shelters.

Inside they found Steve Waters laying on a piece of canvas, his breathing shallow and labored. Sweat beads covered his deathly white face.

Robbie Anderson knelt down next to his friend. "How do you feel?"

"Bit punk today. Just need a little rest." Water's voice was almost a whisper.

"I talked to the Jap Commander. They have us constructing two buildings for them. We'll get the lads busy first thing tomorrow. It will do them good to stay busy. Right, Sergeant?"

"Yes, sir." Sims answered the Captain but kept his eyes on Waters. Both of the men stared at the young Lieutenant who now lay with his eyes closed.

Anderson turned quietly and left the tent. The Sergeant followed a moment later.

"Keep an eye on him, Sergeant," Anderson said quietly. He looked at Sims, seeing the fatigue on the man's face. "I'll go check on the men." He walked away toward a small group of men across the stockade.

Sims watched his Captain walk away. "Yes, sir."

Sergeant Major Tobin moved forward on his hands and knees to the observation post. Reaching the covered position he lay down next to Bryan. In front of them the compound broiled under the late afternoon sun.

"What's happening?"

"All quiet down there. The prisoners have been in and out of their tents most of the afternoon. It appears there's one permanent sentry who watches the prisoners all the time. We need to see if they keep their two roving guards at night and if they keep the same routes." He handed the binoculars to Tobin.

"All right, easy enough to che...." Tobin froze in mid sentence, the glasses to his eyes.

Bryan looked down at the camp but saw nothing out of the ordinary. "What's wrong?"

"Mother of God, it's Captain Anderson and Larry Sims." Tobin lowered the glasses to the sand. "My old outfit. I got separated from them south of Teligalong when the Japs overran our positions. I made my way to the coast with a group of diggers and we were able to steal a boat. That was almost a year ago." He raised the glasses back to his eyes. "They're skin and bones," his voice trailed off.

It had been hard for Bryan to watch the Australians in the compound. Now they had names and he felt Tobin's anger.

"And we're supposed to walk away and leave them to the Japs?" Tobin said bitterly.

Bryan began to agree then stopped. No need to inflame an already bad situation, but there had to be something they could do.

When Robbie Anderson saw the plans for the two temporary buildings he felt relieved. The structures rested their main support beams directly on flat earth foundations. He knew his men would never have the strength to dig real foundations in their condition.

The sun had already driven the temperature over 80 degrees. Some of the men had fashioned crude headgear from pieces of oil paper they found wrapped around the lumber planking. According to the Japanese Commander, the two structures were to be completely finished in four weeks. Robbie knew it would be difficult to meet that schedule even if his men stayed healthy and he knew the odds against that.

A Japanese Army guard sat under the shade of a small tree and watched the men work. On the ship his men had nicknamed the man "Mole Face" because of a large purple birthmark on his left jaw. Mole Face looked totally uninterested in their activity and his eyes would occasionally close as he nodded off in the heat.

A single Japanese Chief Petty Officer stood to one side directing the Australians. The man knew some English but most of his directions came from pointing and gesturing. He constantly referred to a diagram using a measuring stick to verify the work conformed to the plan.

"We should be done with the prep work by the end of today," Anderson said.

Sergeant Sims wiped his forehead with the sleeve of his shirt. "Yes, sir. It's going a lot easier than I expected."

"Thank God for that. Keep an eye on things. I'm going to see if the Japs plan to feed them at mid day."

"It doesn't make any difference, Sergeant Major." Major Mabry took a drink from his canteen. "I know it's hard to see your mates down there. But there's nothing we can do. The sooner you realize that, the better. Do I make myself clear?"

Tobin stared Mabry in the eye. "Very clear, sir. Very clear." He turned and walked away.

Bryan watched Tobin as he disappeared into the jungle.

"Tough situation," he said to Mabry.

The Australian snapped, "I don't need you to tell me that, damn it. Those are diggers down there."

"So why don't we figure out how to get them out of there?"

"It would compromise the mission."

"How about I figure out how we can do both?"

Mabry raised an eyebrow. "You're welcome to try," he said sarcastically.

Halfway through his mid morning watch Bryan lay in the concealed observation position watching the Australians smooth two patches of ground. A slight little breeze off the ocean did little to counter the blazing sun. They must be miserable, he thought, watching the ragged group rake and shovel earth under the cloudless sky. He'd gone over the options many times with no answer to the question of how to save the Australians. The team wasn't large enough to mount a direct assault on the Japs. Any attack could result in Australian casualties caught in a cross fire. They could try something at night but there were almost a dozen Japanese soldiers who would be hard to pinpoint in the dark. And how did they get twenty five men back across a thousand miles of hostile ocean? *Shit!* Picking up the glasses he saw the two Japanese officers walking from the Admin Building to the work site.

The Japanese Chief Petty Officer turned and saw Commander Suzuki walking with his second in command.

"Good morning, sir," the Chief Petty Officer said.

Mole Face quickly got to his feet, standing at attention fifteen yards away.

"Chief, how is the work progressing?" Suzuki watched the prisoners go about their work.

"It is going well, Commander. We have almost all of them working and should be ready to start building the foundations tomorrow." The Chief remained at attention while he spoke.

Suzuki turned to look at the Chief, his voice questioning. "What do you mean almost all?"

"Two of the prisoners are ill. I told their officer they did not have to work."

"Everyone will work! I don't care if they are dying. This project must be finished on time." Suzuki saw Anderson standing next to Sims at the first work site. He turned to Hideki. "Get their officer over here."

"Captain, come here," Hideki said in heavily accented English.

"Good luck," Sims said as Anderson walked away.

Suzuki and Hideki returned the Australian's salute.

"The Commander has ordered all men to work. There will be no excuses for not working," Hideki's voice was very steady and emotionless.

Anderson's anger flared. "I have two men who will die if they're put to work."

Hideki translated for the Commander.

"They will work or they will be executed. The Imperial Japanese Navy does not tolerate shirking."

"You bastard," Anderson said angrily. "Civilized people don't treat humans like this."

Hideki translated and Suzuki's eyes flared, his face flushing with anger. With surprising speed the Commander lashed out catching the Australian's face with the backside of his fist. A large ring on Suzuki's finger ripped a gash in Anderson's cheek as he staggered from the blow. Mole Face ran toward the group, his rifle at the ready.

Robbie Anderson swayed on his feet trying to regain his balance. The Japanese officers shouted orders and he heard the soldier behind him. A blow from the soldier's rifle stunned him and he pitched forward, collapsing in the sand.

Bryan watched the encounter through the glasses and the fury welled up within him. He watched the Jap soldiers reach down and roughly pull the Australian to his knees. One Japanese Officer stood five feet from the small group with the second officer directly behind him. The taller officer had pulled his sword from the scabbard and faced the kneeling Australian.

Robbie Anderson's arms were pulled back behind him by the two guards, forcing his head forward. When he saw the sword held by Suzuki he realized with horror what was about to happen. His thoughts were a jumble as he listened to Hideki translating Suzuki's words.

"You have insulted me and the Japanese people. For that you will die. Someday your country will understand that Japan rules this ocean and pay us the proper respect. Until then we will show our enemies no quarter." Suzuki held the heavy blade in both hands as he slowly walked up to Anderson's left side.

Staring down at the sand, he gasped for breath. Things were happening too fast. This can't be. If only he had time, his mind screamed, I need time to think. He heard the sand compress under Suzuki's boots. Steady…be steady…he repeated…his heart pounded as he waited for the blade, anger and terror consuming him.

Suzuki slowly raised the sword as the two men pulled harder on Anderson's arms.

Sergeant Larry Sims watched in horror as the blade rose above Anderson's head. Behind him the men had stopped work and were standing silently.

As the blade began its downward stroke, the burst of a Sten submachine gun shattered the silence.

Sims saw the Japanese Commander jerk backwards, dropping the sword over his head as he fell to the sand.

The two guards released Anderson and turned to look for their attackers.

Sims saw a single man running across the sand. Fifteen yards from Mole Face the man fired a short burst that caught both Japanese guards in the chest. They fell in the sand next to Anderson.

The second Japanese Officer turned and ran toward the Admin Building.

The Australians hesitated for only a moment then ran toward their Captain who was being helped to his feet by the stranger.

Totally confused, Robbie Anderson tried to ask, "Who…"

"Never mind. Grab the rifle and that son of a bitch's sword," the stranger said harshly.

Sims ran to the two men.

"What's happening?" the Sergeant yelled.

"Get your men into the jungle," Bryan said. "We'll hold them off as long as we can."

Bryan and the two Australians ran to the piles of lumber and tar paper on the edge of the jungle. The remainder of the Australians continued on toward the tree line, some still carrying shovels. Several Japanese appeared at the doors of the other buildings and on seeing their dead comrades they ducked back inside.

"Where'd you come from?" Anderson asked, still breathing heavily.

"Long story," Bryan said as he watched the buildings and tried to grasp what had just happened.

"You're a Yank," Sims said. "Where are the rest of your men?"

"Right now, I'm it. Here," he said and handed his .45 to Anderson. "You know how to use one of these?"

Robbie nodded.

"Make each shot count. I'm not sure if we'll get any help. There are three more of us back in the jungle. I'm hoping they heard the shots."

Two Japanese carrying rifles ran from the back of one of the barracks and disappeared behind the Admin Building.

"Surprise is on our side for now. They don't know what they're facing."

"Two of my lads are still back there," Sims said.

"Shit," Bryan said.

"Sergeant, go after the men and try to get them together." Anderson turned to Bryan, "Where are your troops?"

"Actually the other three are Aussies. In fact one of them knows you. Sergeant Major Tobin."

"Jock Tobin!" Sims exclaimed. "We thought the Nips got

him."

"Escaped and made his way south. He recognized you yesterday." Bryan kept his eyes on the compound. "Our camp is about two miles due east of here."

Anderson grabbed Sims' arm. "Then off with you, Sergeant. And take that damned sword. I'd prefer not to see it again."

"Right, sir." Sims stopped for a moment and put his hand on Anderson's shoulder. "Good luck." He turned and ran in a crouch for twenty yards to the jungle.

The two men silently watched the Japanese camp.

"I can't leave those two men back there."

Bryan nodded. "I know."

Phillip Mabry pushed his way through the brush toward the observation point. Tobin and Louis trailed five yards behind him, spread out to either side. The firing in the distance had sounded like a Sten meaning their mission must have been compromised. Mabry hoped the firing didn't involve the American but he knew that unlikely. Ahead Mabry saw movement. Dropping down on one knee he held up his hand and heard both his men stop also. A man wearing khaki stepped from behind a small tree and Mabry raised his Sten. Instinct told him to hold up. Then he saw the man's face. Mabry stood up and the man stumbled as he tried to stop his headlong flight.

"Easy, mate. We're Aussies."

The man stood swaying, his chest heaving from exertion. Behind him another man emerged from the high grass and froze for a moment, then slowly approached.

It took two minutes to determine what had happened, the two men blurting out their story.

"Sergeant Major, it looks like we have a bit of a problem." He looked at the first man who knelt on the ground trying to catch his breath. "What's your name, soldier?"

"Bailey, sir. Corporal Bailey."

"Well, Corporal Bailey, the three of us will head to the

camp. Try and round up your men and remain in this area.

"Yes, sir," Bailey said as two more men came out of the bushes. He suddenly focused on Sergeant Major Tobin, his expression curious. "Tobin? Sergeant Tobin?"

"Yes, Corporal Bailey, it's me. Now go round up the lads."

Mabry motioned with his hand. "Let's go." The three commandos began jogging toward the camp.

Larry Sims froze when he heard men moving toward him. Slowly he stood up, raising both hands.

Tobin recognized his friend instantly.

"Good to see you, mate."

"Jock, I'm glad I found you," he said quickly. "The American and Captain Anderson are still back there. Lieutenant Waters and Private Duggin are still in the stockade."

Mabry stepped forward. "Come on, you can show us."

Eight Japanese soldiers broke out of the two buildings and ran toward the construction pile. The enemy had taken fifteen minutes to mount a frontal charge.

Bryan handed Anderson the extra clip for the pistol. "That's it for spare ammo."

"It's enough."

They watched the Japanese soldiers split into two groups running up each side of the clearing. Bryan fired two quick bursts at the group on the left and three of the men went down. The last man charged forward, yelling as he ran. Anderson leveled the .45 and put a round in the man's chest knocking him backwards.

"They're trying to get behind us." Anderson kept the pistol pointed toward the Japanese moving behind the lumber but didn't have a clear shot.

Bryan knew they could run for the bush but they would lose their advantage. Here they knew where all the Japs were.

Two men ran to their right and rifle bullets impacted the lumber piled in front of them. More shots were now coming from the other men on the right, driving Bryan and Anderson down behind the wood for cover.

"I don't think I thanked you for saving my life," Robbie Anderson said as they both crouched down. "I don't even know your name."

Bryan surprised himself by laughing. He turned to his companion. "Michaels, Bryan Michaels."

The Captain grinned back, "Robbie Anderson."

The shots stopped. Both men rose carefully. Ten yards in front of them, four Jap soldiers ran at them with fixed bayonets.

"Shit." Bryan fired a burst from the Sten hitting one soldier in the stomach. The man stumbled once and sprawled in the white sand.

Anderson dropped one man with his last round. He reached down and grabbed a shovel, raising it in desperation as a second Japanese soldier lunged with his bayonet. Deflecting the bayonet thrust, Anderson drove the Jap's rifle down. Quickly he reversed with the shovel and hit the soldier in the back of the head with all his strength. The man crumpled to the ground.

Another soldier ran forward and Bryan side stepped the bayonet, smashing the Sten hard into the man's helmet. The Japanese soldier stumbled forward dropping his rifle. Bryan dove on top of the man and swung his empty weapon hard against the man's head. Clawing with his free hand the enemy soldier grabbed Bryan's shirt and brought his fist up into Bryan's stomach. The Jap rolled over on top of Bryan smashing his fist into the American's face. As they struggled, the Japanese pulled Bryan's commando knife from its sheath. The soldier wrenched free from Bryan's grasp and held the knife ready to strike.

Bryan painfully tried to regain his breath. He saw the knife in the soldier's hand as it came down for the killing blow and desperately grabbed for the man's arm. From the corner of his eye he saw a blur as Anderson swung the shovel and knocked the knife from the soldier's hand. With a second blow he knocked the soldier on his back. Anderson raised the shovel and brought the blade down hard on the man's neck almost severing his head.

Bryan rolled on his side gasping and coughing as he regained his breath. Robbie Anderson released the shovel and fell back against the lumber pile, his chest heaving.

They both heard the yells coming from the camp and pulled themselves up to look over the piled wood planks. The Japanese officer ran toward them, his long sword held high in the air. A mixed group of sailors and soldiers ran behind him, all carried rifles with fixed bayonets.

Bryan realized with no weapons or ammunition they had little hope of surviving the charging men.

"Let's go," he yelled and pulled Anderson's arm.

"Right."

The two men began to run toward the tree line.

Lieutenant Commander Hideki ran ten yards behind the two men who were now twenty yards from the trees. He knew his men would make swift work of the two enemy soldiers as he raised his sword in anticipation of hacking the Australian from behind.

"Michaels, get down!"

Bryan recognized Mabry's voice and turned to tackle Anderson, the two men landing hard and rolling on the ground.

Sustained automatic fire erupted from the trees, cutting the charging Japanese down like a scythe through grass. The officer's hat flew off as he dropped his sword and collapsed only feet from Bryan, blood stains spreading out from three holes in his back.

Mabry came out of the woods and ran toward the Japanese who were now in confusion. Firing methodically he killed two men, changed his magazine and resumed firing at the remaining soldiers who ran back toward the buildings. Tobin and Louis were on his heels also firing sporadically at the retreating enemy.

Bryan lay on the ground, Robbie Anderson next to him. He felt suddenly exhausted, his heart pounding in his chest. Lowering his head to the ground he closed his eyes and tried to regain his breath. In the distance he heard an Australian voice yelling, "Over here. It's the Captain."

Chapter Twenty Three

A Homecoming

The only Japanese alive after the last charge were six enlisted men found hiding in the mess hall and three soldiers who had been injured in the fighting. Mabry directed they all be securely tied and then locked in a storage room in the building. Once the Japanese were secured he took Bryan aside.

"I don't fault you for what you did. It was either damned brave or incredibly stupid. I haven't made up my mind yet. But it doesn't matter now, what's done is done. Our immediate problem is to figure how to take care of these men and get them home. The mission is busted but I'm sure Coyne will understand."

"We've gotta go by air. They'll just have to send enough PBY's to handle everyone," Bryan said.

"Get Louis and we'll put together a signal. I would love to see Coyne's face when he sees this one."

Captain Anderson equipped his men with Japanese weapons and established sentries in the compound. He also detailed one man to watch the pier in the event of any unexpected arrivals by water. The two ill Australians were treated by Alistair Louis using medicine from both the team's equipment and Japanese material found in the Admin Building. Two of Anderson's men got busy preparing food for the men and within two hours had prepared a

361

meal of boiled rice, canned crabmeat and oysters.

Bryan walked through the now deserted Communication Building looking at the radio transmitting equipment. Crossing the room he looked out at the still running generator. How soon before the Japs would realize this station wasn't operational? And how long would it take them to get units here to check it out? Moving around the desks he went into the back room where he found the code area. On the far side of the room sat the large metal storage locker he had seen before. *Funny, the new code books are probably locked in there and now it doesn't make any difference.* He reached down and lifted the heavy padlock that secured the door. An idea began to form in his mind. Why not stick to the original plan? If they could get the books, photograph them and leave them undisturbed the Japs might not realize they'd been compromised. In any case if they did feel the codes were compromised they'd have to stay with the current code for some time before they were able to provide the entire fleet with new code books. In the interim we'd still be able to read their communications. "It's worth a try," he said to himself.

Mabry stood watching Louis set up the radio on the porch of the Admin Building.

Bryan stepped up to the Major and said, "We can still do this."

The tall Australian turned, his expression showing skepticism. "I'm listening."

For the next five minutes Bryan covered his plan trying to address any objections before Mabry would bring them up.

Crossing his arms across his chest, Mabry walked to the end of the porch thinking about what he had heard.

"It might work. Surely no reason not to give it a go. Corporal, keep working on the radio. I'll be back shortly."

Fifteen minutes later Bryan called to the Major, "I found it."

Around the second Jap officer's neck hung a lanyard with a large multi-tooth key. The two men headed back to the Comm Building.

Even before trying the key in the large padlock, Bryan knew it would work. One turn and the hasp eased out of the lock body. The heavy steel door moved easily on lubricated hinges. Inside they found the two Japanese code books.

Using two cameras Bryan and Mabry took duplicate photos of each page of both books. The film was then sealed tight in waterproof pouches and put in two separate bags for the return to Australia. Returning the books to their original position, Bryan locked the door and walked back to the officer's body and replaced the lanyard and key. Would it work?

Robbie Anderson sat on a stool next to Lieutenant Water's cot. The young officer looked better after taking food and water.

"You missed all the excitement," Anderson said.

Waters smiled. "Tell me."

"There's plenty of time for that. The important thing is they're sending six seaplanes to take us home. We should be in Darwin by this time tomorrow."

Waters stared up at him. Tears welled up in his eyes which he tried to wipe away in embarrassment.

"That's right, Steve. We're going home. And I feel the same way."

Six PBY's from Patrol Squadron Twelve launched at fifteen minute intervals from Darwin bound for Ulithi. Arriving just after sunrise they were each loaded at the end of the long wooden pier. The ill and injured were the first off the island. An Australian Army physician flew on the first aircraft and provided medical care to the diggers on the long flight home. One by one the big planes taxied in, loaded the homebound Aussies and left for Darwin. They put one bag of film on the first aircraft with Corporal Louis, the second bag to go with Mabry, Michaels and Tobin on the last aircraft.

The Japanese truck jerked to a stop at the head of the pier.

Robbie Anderson watched the single PBY at the end of the wooden jetty. The three team members got out and walked across the sand.

To the north, heavy black smoke rose in the morning sky above the compound. Diesel fuel from the generator tank had been liberally spread throughout the wooden structures and then set afire. Only the building holding the Japanese had been spared. Mabry left them locked in the storeroom. His comment, "They're not my problem."

"Robbie, ready to go home?" Bryan put his arm on Anderson's shoulder.

"Wouldn't be going anywhere if it wasn't for you, Bryan."

"It's the least I could do for a man who was going to save my life ten minutes later." The two men walked down the long pier toward the PBY.

Gene Porter and Steve Richmond were going through their pre-takeoff checks as the PBY taxied south from the pier.

"I figured it would be you two," Bryan said as he knelt down between their seats.

"And we knew you'd be the last to leave. What did you do to your face?" Porter asked as he saw Bryan's face in the light.

"Had a bit of a run in with a Jap soldier." The left side of Bryan's face was now swollen and heavily bruised from the blow by the Japanese.

Porter leaned forward and scanned the horizon. "Then we better get you back to Australia. I hear tell they have medicinal alcohol."

"Best idea I've heard since we left Brisbane."

"Nice job getting the pier ready for us," Steve said. He offered his hand to Bryan.

"We took a vote and decided we didn't want to row that damned rubber boat again," Bryan said as the two men shook hands.

"Glad to have you back. The only crummy deal is now they'll send us back to the Solomons. I've gotten real used to sheets on my bed and running water."

"And the beer," Porter said as he turned the PBY left lining up with the surface winds. Going to full power he began his takeoff run.

"And the beer."

"Here we go."

In a moment Porter had the PBY clear of the blue water and climbing at a steady 400 feet per minute.

"How's the weather?" Bryan asked.

"We'll be in and out all the way," Richmond said as he turned off the boost pumps. "The Japs have been pretty quiet the last couple of days."

"I think I'm gonna go catch up on a little sleep. Give me a wakeup call at Darwin."

Moving aft he surveyed the team. Mabry sat with his head back against the bulkhead, his eyes closed. Bryan didn't know if he would ever warm up to the man. But in a fight he'd like the Major with him.

Sergeant Major Jock Tobin lay asleep against the aft life raft. The iron man looked very tired in the subdued light. But he'd trained a team to complete a mission and that's exactly what they'd done. In some ways Tobin reminded him of Tiny Leonard, the professional backbones of every military. He missed his friend and knew that would never change. But just as he was proud of Tiny, he felt the same way about Tobin.

Robbie Anderson lay with his eyes open staring at the overhead. What's he thinking Bryan wondered? About his wife, the friends he'd lost or his future? Hard to say, but he's a good officer and we need every one of them we can get.

Curling up on the floor he closed his eyes allowing himself a moment to think about Liz.

Larry Roberts yelling at the top of his lungs jolted Bryan out of a sound sleep. Sitting upright he felt the aircraft yaw left then begin to turn as the port wing rose. As he struggled to his feet the sharp whine of bullets passing through the fuselage made him duck.

365

The engines screamed at full power, as the big Catalina's nose dropped. Bryan lunged forward two steps and was thrown to the floorboards as the PBY's nose came up hard then pitched forward again. Fighting his way forward on hands and knees he felt a rush of air coming back from the cockpit. He saw Porter struggling with the yoke, a spreading red stain on the back of his khaki shirt.

"What happened?" Bryan yelled. He saw Steve lying against the control yoke. Porter was fighting to hold the nose up.

"Grab him," Gene said, fighting to get the words out as he struggled with the yoke.

Steve's head flopped to one side as Bryan pulled him back in the seat. He looked down and saw the young pilot's face cruelly torn apart by the bullet's impact. "Chief Loftus, get up here," he yelled, still holding Steve's body away from the controls.

Gene leveled the aircraft and turned to see his friend and co-pilot. His look of horror masked with a quick, "Christ."

Chief Loftus put his hand on Bryan's shoulder. "Yes, sir."

"Give me a hand, Chief. Hold his shoulders back while I undo his lap belt." Slimy with blood, the metal release buckle took two tries before the catch would release. The two men struggled to pull Steve's body from the seat and back into the aisle.

Once clear, Bryan grabbed the Chief's arm. "Get something to cover him up. I'm staying up here. Porter's been hit. Get the first aid kit." He turned and climbed into the co-pilot's seat automatically checking the airspeed and altitude. They were level at 9,400 feet above the ocean indicating 115 knots.

"There's blood on your back. Are you hit anywhere else?" he asked Porter.

"Just my right side. Doesn't hurt too bad but I'll tell ya, I've felt better."

Bryan saw a stain of blood soaking the pilot's shirt and running down on the seat cushion."

"Fucking Jap Betty. Came up from behind and hit us before we knew they were there. I ducked into the soup and haven't seen them since."

"Where are we?"

"About four hours from Darwin. We just passed over the New Guinea coast heading south. Shit."

"Gene, I'll take the aircraft. You've got to get a bandage on that to stop the blood flow.

"Okay, I'll be back in a minute. Steering 208 degrees magnetic." Gene watched Bryan take the yoke and then let go of his controls. Slowly he raised himself up and turned to get out of the seat.

Bryan saw four bullet holes in the aluminum skin on the right side of the cockpit. One of them must have hit Steve. There were exit holes on the left side of the cockpit. We were lucky none of the bullets hit the instrument panel, he thought. Automatically he rechecked that the wings were level and they were steady on course. It had been a long time since he'd flown on instruments and knew he had to use all of his experience to keep the aircraft under control. The adrenaline from the last few minutes was beginning to wear off and he felt bone tired. Checking the engine instruments he relaxed a little when he saw that oil pressure and cylinder head temps were normal. The fuel tanks were about one third full which should be plenty to make Darwin.

Over the noise of the wind he heard someone making their way to the cockpit.

Major Phillip Mabry knelt at Bryan's left shoulder. Leaning toward Bryan he said, "The pilot's lost a great deal of blood. We have a tight bandage on him and it looks like we stopped the loss of blood. But he simply can't come back up here in his condition. At best he'd pass out. He could bleed to death."

The reality of their situation hit Bryan. Flying an aircraft he had only watched others fly, he would have to navigate to Darwin and then land the PBY without killing them all. At least he had some time to think about what he'd have to do. But first he'd have to navigate across 200 miles of open water and find Darwin.

"In that case, Major, you were just promoted to co-pilot. I'll need help with navigation and watching the gauges. We'll need the crew chief up here too."

Mabry looked at Bryan who kept his eyes on the instrument panel. "Right. I'll get him up here."

Slowly Bryan got the feel of the aircraft. The nose was heavy and not responsive like the Dauntless. Surprisingly the ailerons were light, almost like a trainer. He knew the engines were radials just like the Dauntless but the two motors were pulling a much larger aircraft. He remembered the two PBY pilots talking about the slow response when you added power but when you took power off, the PBY tended to float like a glider.

He continued to scan the instruments checking his wings level with the artificial horizon and his course steady on 208 degrees on the magnetic compass. Something wasn't right but he couldn't put his finger on it. Perhaps it's sitting in this strange cockpit. What was it? Looking left at the oil pressure gauges he suddenly realized he could see without turning his head, the pain was gone. Slowly he looked from right to left without moving his head. For the first time since the Coral Sea he moved his eye without pain.

"Sir, I made the Lieutenant comfortable. He's sort of drifting in and out." Pops Loftus knelt behind him.

"Chief, I'm gonna need your help along with the Major's to get us home. Have the crew check over the aircraft for any more damage. I don't want to find out about a frayed control cable when it's too late. We've got about four hours to go for Darwin so tell them to take their time and make it thorough. I think we have all the charts we need up here but if you have any more in back bring 'em up."

"Can do, Lieutenant." Loftus sounded positive but Steve Richmond's death had shaken the tight knit crew. He turned and moved aft.

"Major, slide in the seat and we'll have a little cockpit check out."

Wordlessly Phillip Mabry sat down behind the yoke with both hands in his lap.

Over the next thirty minutes, Bryan showed Mabry the key switches and controls they would need for the descent and landing. Mabry's questions gave Bryan a feeling of confidence that the Aussie understood what he had to do and when he had to do it.

The engines droned in synch as the two men sat watching the instrument panel. Occasionally a brief patch of blue sky told Bryan they were flying at the top of a cloud layer and he might find clear air if he climbed. He decided to remain in the clouds for as long as possible to ensure there'd be no more surprises from the Japanese Air Force.

"Michaels, if you don't mind me asking, what is a U.S. Navy pilot doing on assignment to Unit 331?" For the first time since meeting Mabry the Major's tone was friendly rather than professional.

"Managed to get shot down at the Coral Sea and lost my medical clearance. I was assigned to PT boats in the Solomons and got involved in a rescue on one of the islands. Wound up talking to MacArthur and next thing I knew I met Commander Coyne."

"You've been busy."

"That's one way to put it," Bryan said.

They flew along in silence for a few minutes.

"Can you get this thing down in one piece?" Mabry asked. His voice didn't show concern, only curiosity.

"I think so. Let's hope we have light winds and the sea's flat. All we should have to do is trim the aircraft for a stable approach and touch down. As long as we don't dig in a wing tip or bury the nose we should be fine."

"That's good," Mabry said slowly with a hint of skepticism.

"I'm going to be counting on you to watch the airspeed and keep reading it off during the final approach. We don't have flaps, so it's critical to get our approach speed under control and make sure we don't get slow at the end."

"I don't understand."

"With a stable approach speed, in our case 75 knots, we'll be coming down at a manageable rate of descent of 100 feet per minute. We hold that until right before touching down and then pull the nose up just a bit and land. If we get too slow then pull the nose up we can stall and the aircraft stops flying. Not a good thing."

"I think I understand. Although I might have been more comfortable in ignorant bliss."

Mabry's dead pan tone made Bryan laugh.

"I've got it, sir." Pops Loftus had been tuning the direction finder to locate the Darwin radio beacon.

Bryan watched the needle waver for a moment then steady up just left of the nose. Estimating 45 minutes to Darwin he pulled the power back slightly setting up a 100 foot per minute rate of descent. They were still okay on fuel and they would burn less in the descent.

Jock Tobin squeezed up the aisle.

"If you can establish radio contact we need a doctor as soon as possible. Lieutenant Porter must be bleeding internally. I think he's gone into shock."

"Keep him warm and we'll see what we can do. Chief, dial in the frequency for Darwin Military Radio"

Bryan gave him a moment to rotate the selector knobs.

"Darwin Radio, Darwin Radio, this is Navy 12643, over."

They all waited expectantly.

"Navy 643, this is Darwin, go ahead."

"Darwin, 643 is thirty minutes out, declaring an emergency. I have wounded aboard. Need medical service immediately on landing."

A new voice came up on the net.

"643, this is Navy 12545. We just landed. Can we provide any assistance?"

Bryan realized it must be the PBY that departed Mogmog in front of them. Why hadn't he thought about that?

Keying the radio he said, "That's affirmative, 545. We could use your help to get this thing on deck. Both pilots are out of action. A talk down would be greatly appreciated."

"Say again, 643. Who's flying the aircraft?"

"A broken down Dauntless pilot and an Aussie ground pounder."

There was a long pause.

"Do you want me to get airborne and rendezvous with you?"

"Don't want to waste the gas and Porter needs a doctor."

Another pause.

"Okay. I'll taxi out to the landing area and talk you through the approach. The winds are currently light and variable so I'd recommend landing to the south. Let me know when you have Point Barlow in sight."

"Wilco, 545."

Chapter Twenty Four

Full circle

Commander R. Emmet Coyne arrived in Darwin the next afternoon. He found Bryan nursing a hangover in the dining room of the Officer's Mess.

"There you are. Major Mabry thought I might find you here." Coyne strode across the deserted room between dining tables.

Bryan turned and began to get up.

"Please don't get up. I understand you're moving a bit slow this morning." Coyne stopped at the table and motioned to the single attendant at the back of the room. "Might I get a cup of tea? Thank you."

Coyne sat down, placing his hat on a table behind them.

"We were making a bit merry last night," Bryan said sheepishly. For the first time he could remember Coyne actually smiled.

"As well you should have." The Australian's eyes narrowed slightly. "My goodness, your face looks dreadful. Did you have anyone take a look at it?"

Bryan nodded. "After we got Lieutenant Porter to the medics I talked to one of the Docs."

"No permanent damage I hope."

"Actually it may have done some good," Bryan said. His eye had continued to move without pain.

"Really? That's a rather odd comment." The attendant placed a mug of steaming tea on the table in front of Coyne.

"I'll tell you about it some time."

The Australian sipped his tea. "I'm not sure it was a good idea to kidnap Cordner. But I understand he's none the worse for wear."

"Yes, sir. It seemed like a wonderful idea at the time."

"I'm sure it did." Coyne put his cup down. "I discussed events on the island with Captain Anderson. He told a rather remarkable tale."

"Yes, sir." Here it comes, Bryan thought.

"I suppose some people would call your actions foolhardy. A single handed assault on a Japanese camp, to say nothing of the risk to the primary mission." Coyne's expression remained impassive as he sipped at his tea.

"I guess I couldn't watch Anderson die without trying to do something about it."

"No, of course not." Coyne took another sip of tea. "By the way, Major Mabry fully supports your conduct and is recommending that your actions be officially noted. We shall have to see if your deception worked on the Japanese. I expect the next month will confirm that one way or the other."

"Yes, sir."

"Michaels, I'm proud of you and the entire team. To be perfectly honest I gave the mission a one in five chance of success."

Bryan turned in his chair to face Coyne. "You didn't think we'd pull it off?"

"It was a very ambitious mission."

"What chances did you put on us getting back in one piece?" Bryan's voice had taken on a hard tone.

Coyne put down his mug. "This is a nasty business, Bryan. You've been around long enough to know we often challenge the odds. It's called unrestricted warfare. We do what we have to do in order to win. If you think about it that is exactly what you've done since this war started."

Bryan started to question what he had just said when Coyne continued.

"Once you were proposed to us we thoroughly vetted your entire career. From day one."

"Everything?"

"The reason we accepted you for 331 and this mission was because of your entire record, not in spite of it. Despite your rough edges, you consistently demonstrated initiative and disregard for rote obedience. We happen to think those are some of the key traits found in exceptional officers."

Bryan didn't know what to say in response.

"Well, I better be off. Many details to wrap up before we head back to Brisbane. By the way, if you're free I'd like to get together for drinks and dinner later. Say 1800 hours?"

"Commander, I look forward to it."

Three days after the team arrived in Brisbane, Bryan received a note from Chuck Michael's aide telling him that his father had arrived in town. The Admiral was free for dinner if Bryan could break away.

After visiting Lee Cordner in the local naval hospital, Bryan found a taxi out to meet his father at Finnegan's. The public bar had a small dining room known for its grilled steaks. Opening the main door he walked into the bar. From the back of the dining room he saw a hand motioning him to the table.

Chuck Michaels stood up and grasped his son's hand with both of his. The older man said nothing for a moment as they held the clasp.

"Sit down, Bryan. I ordered a scotch for you."

"Thanks."

Chuck looked at Bryan's face in the subdued light which still showed severe bruising on his cheek.

"You lose an argument?"

Bryan took a drink of the scotch. "Actually I won it. As they say, you should have seen the other guy."

"I was called in to see General MacArthur this morning. He told me that you were just back from a very critical mission. After telling me that he wasn't at liberty to divulge the exact details he said that you distinguished yourself with an act of personal bravery that will most certainly merit award of the Distinguished Service Cross." Chuck Michaels looked at Bryan quizzically.

"I feel good about what we did and I think it was important. Just can't talk about it. The funny thing is my eye seems to be better now."

The Admiral leaned forward. "What do you mean?"

Bryan said, "The pain's gone. I was hoping to get hooked up with a flight surgeon and have it looked at."

"Let me work on that. Our senior medical officer has some pretty good connections out here. You think you might be able to fly again?"

"I don't know. But if there's a chance I've got to try."

A waiter walked up to take their orders.

"They have great steaks here," Chuck said.

"I'd like a steak and another scotch, please."

Over a leisurely dinner the two men talked about the war, the future and finally Liz.

"When did you last hear from her?"

"One letter last week. She didn't tell me where she was or much of anything else. She was tired but her spirits were good. I can't wait to see her."

"That will depend on whether you stay here or go back to your squadron on San Cristobal. Any idea what choice you have?"

Bryan rotated his glass. "I'm on orders from MacArthur. I suppose I'll stay here until someone on his staff decides they don't want or need me anymore."

"So patrol boats are probably not in your future."

"I think that's a safe bet."

"We each serve where they tell us to. It's no different for

admirals."

"I think I finally understand that."

During the drive back to the unit Chuck Michaels told his son he would try to line up a flight physical as quickly as possible.

Colonel Nathan Grigsby was the senior Royal Australian Air Force Medical Officer in the area. Chuck Michaels told Bryan that the Fleet Surgeon from the Seventh Fleet assured him any exam by Dr. Grigsby would be as thorough and stringent as required by the Navy's Bureau of Aeronautics. If Bryan received a "medical up" by Grigsby, Bryan's request for return to flight duty would be forwarded to the Commander in Chief, Pacific.

After thirty minutes in a darkened room, the Doctor turned on the overhead lights.

"Remarkable. Lieutenant, I can see no reason why you should not be classified fully qualified for aviation duties. You have passed our Air Force's induction exam with flying colors. I can clearly see where there had been injury but functionality appears unaffected. You have full range of motion and acuity that is actually better than we require."

A flood of relief swept over Bryan coupled with questions on his future.

"Doctor, I'm trying to get back on flying status. A report on this exam is the first step if you would be willing to write a letter for me."

The tall man sat down at a wooden desk and smiled at Bryan. "The Australian Forces are not as massive as our American Allies. There is an active and effective communication network that keeps everyone in touch with what's happening to our boys. I'm aware of the return of our men from that Pacific island and your part in the action. It would be my honor to forward a report to whomever you feel needs the information. That would include Franklin Roosevelt if you like. And if they won't put you back in a cockpit, please come back, we would love to have you."

Cdr Coyne dropped the single page on his desk. "Our presence is requested at General MacArthur's headquarters tomorrow morning at 0930."

Bryan asked, "Any idea what it's about?"

"Don't know. Just put on your best bib and tucker and be here at 0800. We'll go in my car. I've never met the General before. I'm not sure what to expect."

"I've only met him once and there's no doubt he's the Supreme Commander. It's not the trappings of the office either. There's a sense that he's carrying the whole war on his back. It was the same thing I sensed when I met Nimitz. They *are* really larger than life."

A beautiful day made the drive from 331 into town pleasant. Coyne remained quiet and Bryan didn't try to make conversation. He'd heard nothing of his request which he signed the day after seeing Doctor Grigsby. Better to take it one day at a time he cautioned himself.

Rather than going to MacArthur's office on the fourth floor, an Army Captain escorted them to the third floor. As they entered a conference room Bryan saw his father standing by the window talking to a Navy Commander. Looking around he was surprised to see Gene Porter and the rest of the PBY crew. Lee Cordner sat in a chair next to Gene. Jock Tobin, Alistair Louis and Phillip Mabry stood to one side, all in their best service uniforms. He walked over and knelt down in front of Porter.

"You're looking a lot better than the last time I saw you."

Porter smiled. "They tell me you did a passable fair job of landing that beast. Wish I could have seen it."

"Gentlemen, General Sutherland," another Army Captain called to the room as MacArthur's Chief of Staff entered the room.

"Please stand easy, gentlemen. We're waiting for the General, who will be here in a moment. He has a visitor who just arrived and he wanted a few minutes of privacy."

Sutherland walked across the room to Bryan. He extended his hand.

"Lieutenant, glad to meet you."

"Thank you, General. Can you tell me what's going on?"

Sutherland grinned at him.

"This is an awards ceremony, Lieutenant. And you are the star player. So smile and be gracious."

"Yes, sir." He saw that General Sutherland was enjoying his confusion. Looking over at his father he saw a twinkle in Chuck Michael's eye.

"Gentlemen, the Supreme Commander."

Douglas MacArthur walked into the room and all eyes turned. The General smiled and turned to his left to allow Liz Summers to step into the room.

"Good morning, gentlemen. Thank you all for being here this morning."

Bryan's eyes met hers and she beamed. He didn't know what to do.

"Lieutenant Michaels, front and center," the Army Captain called.

Tentatively walking to the center of the room, he watched MacArthur move to meet him. They shook hands.

"Good morning, Lieutenant."

"Good morning, General."

The General put his hands at his sides and looked straight ahead as his aide began to read.

"Pursuant to Bureau of Naval Personnel letter of 15 November, 1942. Lieutenant Bryan A. Michaels, United States Navy, serial number 98074, is promoted to Lieutenant Commander with date of rank from 1 December, 1942."

From the side, two aides removed his Lieutenant bars and while MacArthur pinned on one gold oak leaf, Liz stepped up and pinned on the other. She leaned over and kissed him as the audience laughed.

MacArthur smiled at the crowd. "Although popular with our French Allies, I will forego the kiss." Laughter broke the quiet solemnity of the ceremony.

Liz stepped back near the door.

The aide began to read, "The President of the United States takes pleasure in awarding the Silver Star Medal for services as set forth in the following citation….."

Bryan listened as the events on Vona Vona returned to his thoughts. As the aide read the citation, Bryan remembered Tiny Leonard and their last moments together.

"…his actions demonstrated great courage and were in keeping with the highest traditions of the United States Naval Service. For the President, Douglas MacArthur, General, United States Army."

The aide removed the medal, handing it to MacArthur who pinned it on Bryan's shirt.

Bryan felt very self conscious. Seeing Liz, having all the people here with him and being decorated by Douglas MacArthur.

"The President of the United States takes great pleasure in awarding the Navy Cross for services as set forth in the following citation…."

Bryan heard "classified location….at great personal risk….personally attacked…..against superior enemy troops….."

General Sutherland handed a second box to MacArthur who removed the blue ribbon which supported a pewter cross. Pinning it next to the Silver Star he said, "I am very proud of you, Commander."

In April of 1943, Lieutenant Commander Bryan Michaels, United States Navy, reported to Torpedo Squadron 95 as the Executive Officer. Stationed at the Naval Air Station, Alameda California, the squadron would fly the new TBF-1C Avenger. Following a six month work up period, the unit would deploy aboard one of the new Essex class carriers coming out of the Hunter's Point Naval Shipyard.

Two more years of war lay ahead for Bryan Michaels and the Navy's fast carrier task forces as they fought across the wide expanse of the Pacific to the home waters of Japan. However the tide had turned. From Pearl Harbor to Midway to the Solomon Islands, the first to fight had stopped the Japanese advance and allowed America to mobilize. The desperate battles of 1942 were fought and won by young Americans, Australians, New Zealanders and the native populations of the Pacific. It was a time when the destiny of men and nations was decided in the vast Pacific Ocean.

Epilogue

The U.S.S. *Enterprise* sliced through the Pacific Ocean one thousand miles east of the Philippine Islands. Two miles astern, the nuclear guided missile frigate *Bainbridge* maintained assigned station on the carrier which served as the flagship of Carrier Group Seven. The two ships were on transit for the Gulf of Tonkin via a port visit in Subic Bay, Republic of the Philippines. Aboard the huge carrier, the aircrews of Carrier Air Wing Fourteen prepared for combat operations in Viet Nam. Today the ship would conduct proficiency flying to maintain combat readiness honed over the last six months of training off California. An air of expectancy hung over those aviators who had not gone in harm's way before. A portion of the air wing pilots had made the last combat cruise and now provided the backbone of experience for the rookies.

In a time honored ballet the carrier began to turn into the wind in preparation for the first launch of the morning. The roar of jet engines was muffled for those on deck by the use of protective ear cups. Each man also wore a colored jersey and float coat indicating his specialty or job. Everyone had goggles in place to protect their eyes from the jet blast and debris whipped up as the jets taxied to the catapults. Steam wisped up from each of the long catapults that would hurl the jets airborne after only two hundred feet of travel.

Just forward of the carrier's island, an A6A Intruder, side number NK 500 inched forward in response to the taxi director's signal.

"Okay, here we go," the pilot said to his bombardier as he pushed the parking brake in and inched the throttles up slightly to get the aircraft moving. With the nose wheel steering button selected the pilot gently steered the large jet to the right, watching each movement of the director. With only inches of clearance from the other aircraft, the trip to the catapult was an exercise in precision and patience.

The bombardier navigator in the right seat began to recite the challenge and reply takeoff checklist:

"Trim?"

"Zero, zero and six units nose up."

"Aux brakes?"

"Fifteen cycles."

"Hook?"

"Checked Up."

Above the deck, the ship's Commanding Officer professionally surveyed the entire deck as aircraft made their way to the catapults. Although ultimately responsible for everything that happened on the deck, he seldom intervened unless safety was at stake. Today he paid a little more attention to 500 knowing the Admiral was in the pilot's seat.

In Primary Flight Control the carrier's Air Boss also watched 500 carefully. The Admiral was very familiar with the deck having flown with the Air Wing during work ups and also during the last cruise. The Boss wasn't worried about the Admiral. He was concerned one of his young directors might make a mistake.

As the jet blast deflector lowered on catapult number two Rear Admiral Bryan Michaels taxied forward slowly.

"Wings coming down," Lieutenant Fred House said. The hydraulically operated wings spread slowly until they were fully down. House locked them in place with a small electrical switch. "Locked."

"Flaps and slats coming down," Bryan said as he moved the flap lever to the takeoff position. "All indicating down and out."

Slowly he moved the control stick counter clockwise to

ensure the controls were free.

A young sailor ran up to the bombardier's side with a mechanical weight board that said, "49.0" indicating the weight of the aircraft in thousands of pounds. House gave him a thumb up.

"Forty nine point oh."

"Roger," Bryan responded.

The aircraft jerked as the catapult went into final tension. The catapult officer's signals told Bryan to take his feet off the brakes and push the throttles full forward. The two J52 engines were now at a deafening roar as the aircraft strained at the holdback fitting. Crouched around the big jet the squadron's final checkers watched intently for any sign of trouble, ready to raise their arms in the abort launch signal.

Bryan watched the engine gauges stabilize. One last cycle of the controls and he said, "Engine instruments are good. Ready to go?"

"Yes, sir."

Bryan saluted the catapult officer and put his head back against the ejection seat head rest.

As the catapult fired, the Intruder's nose dipped and the bomber accelerated toward the end of the deck. The force of the catapult shot pressed each man back hard against the seat. Both sets of eyes scanned the instruments for any sign of a problem. Off the end of the deck they both noted the airspeed already at 150 knots and increasing.

"Good shot," Bryan said calmly and raised the landing gear handle.

God I love this, he thought. Leveling the jet at 500 feet he accelerated to 400 knots and departed the carrier's airspace. Bryan knew his flying days were numbered. Sometime during this cruise he would receive orders sending him back to Washington, D.C. and a desk. Pulling the nose up, he saw the airspeed indicator reading 410 knots and did a roll to the left. The sheer exuberance of flight off the ship.

"Okay, let's head out to the coordinates I gave you."

House reached down and cycled the navigation system to provide steering to geographic coordinates the Admiral had provided in the brief. "Steering looks good, sir."

"Thanks, Fred."

Turning the jet he aligned the steering symbol and leveled the wings. He noted the distance to the point read 124 nautical miles. Twenty minutes he figured to himself.

A razor sharp horizon cut the flat sea, separating the light blue of the clear sky and dark shade of the ocean. *Funny, I've been flying over this damned ocean for thirty years and it never changes. I could be back in an Avenger right now and it would have looked just like it did in '43.* He remembered his old squadron for a moment. Thrust into command when the Skipper had been shot down off the Marshall Islands, he led the squadron for over ten months in combat. *They're all retired now. I'm the only one still in uniform.* Then he thought of Bill Nance. The pang of loss came back as if it were yesterday, memories of two young men, flying above this same ocean and fighting to stop the Japanese Navy. He remembered Tim Hutchins, a great young officer who died on the first day of that terrible war trying to save his men. Every time the ship sailed into Pearl Harbor he took time to visit the rusting hull of the *Utah* and Tim's grave at the Punchbowl National Cemetery. During this trip to the Philippines he would make one last visit to the large cemetery south of Manila to touch Tiny's white cross, one of 17,000 stone markers marking the ultimate sacrifice of Americans from the Pacific War. Years before Bryan had fulfilled his promise to his friend and placed a duplicate cross in Arlington National Cemetery.

"I'm getting a radar return at that point, Admiral."

"It's a small island. Thought we could go take a look."

"Yes, sir," House said, not sure what the Admiral really meant.

"I was there a long time ago."

He remembered all of the islands, San Cristobal, Tulagi, Vona Vona and the island on the nose at sixty miles, Mogmog.

Although the island later served as a U.S. Navy recreation site when the fleet used Ulithi Atoll as an anchorage, he never went ashore. For some reason he didn't want to see the change. He didn't want to drink beer and play softball on the same spot where he had killed men. It was hard to understand and his squadron never did. But the Navy left years ago and Mogmog had returned to the same condition he had found it in 1942. Now he wanted to see it for what would probably be the last time.

"There it is," he said quietly on the ICS.

A small dot on the horizon grew larger as Bryan descended to 100 feet over the ocean and increased their airspeed to 400 knots. He saw the beach where they came ashore and on the left the remnants of the old pier. Screaming over the beach he rolled the aircraft to the right and looked north over the island, now mostly trees. Pulling hard he turned right and began to climb away from the water.

"Let's head back. I've seen what I came for."

Over the small island the roar of jet engines slowly faded, leaving the quiet sound of waves breaking on a deserted beach.

Glossary

20 mm: Small-caliber automatic gun used primarily
                   for anti-aircraft defense.

AAA: Anti-Aircraft Artillery - general term for
                   any weapon used for defense from air
                   attack.

Azimuth: Angle measured against north.

Bofors: Swedish designed 40mm automatic weapon
                   used for both AAA and light attack.

BOQ: Bachelor Office Quarters - billeting for
                   unmarried officers ashore.

CINCPACFLT: Commander In Chief, U.S. Pacific Fleet.

CAP   Combat Air Patrol.

Corpsman: Enlisted medical technician, U.S. Navy.

CWO: Chief Warrant Officer - senior to all
                   enlisted, junior to commissioned officers.

Dauntless: SBD-2/3 USN dive bomber manufactured
                   by Douglas.

Enterprise: US aircraft carrier, hull number CV-6.

Flat hatting:	Unauthorized acrobatic, daredevil flying.
Hornet:	US aircraft carrier, hull number CV-8.
JAG:	Judge Advocate General Corp, legal arm of the Navy.
Khakis:	General term for all uniforms which were light brown.
Lexington:	US aircraft carrier, hull number CV-2.
Mae West:	Inflatable life preserver worn by aircrew.
Mayday:	Term broadcast by any aircraft in distress.
Number One:	Second in command of an Australian ship.
Oerlikon:	Swiss-designed 20 mm autocannon.
OOD:	Officer of the Deck - senior watch officer aboard ship underway or in port.
Quonset Hut:	Temporary building formed by semi circle of corrugated steel.
Sitrep:	Situation report, sent during and after all major combat action.
Skivvy(ies):	Navy term for underwear.
Wildcat:	Grumman F-4F fighter.
XO:	Executive Officer.

HISTORICAL NOVELS BY THIS AUTHOR INCLUDE

DESTINY IN THE PACIFIC

THE FLAMES OF DELIVERANCE

WINDS OF BATTLE
The Journey of James Addington

The Jack Stewart Trilogy

THE KING'S COMMANDER

JOURNEY OF HONOR

THE FALKENBERG RIDDLE

The author welcomes your comments via email and/or
FACEBOOK.
Facebook : "John Schork Novels"
Email: John@johnschork.com

Author Note: Thank you for purchasing this novel. I
hope you enjoyed reading it as much as I enjoyed the writing of it. I
would enjoy hearing from you.

www.ingramcontent.com/pod-product-compliance
Lightning Source LLC
Chambersburg PA
CBHW071223250626
47163CB00001B/82